A Bloody London Sunset

Book #2 in the Sunset Vampire Series

Jaz Primo

RUTHERFORD LITERARY GROUP

www.rutherfordliterary.com

Novels by Jaz Primo

The Sunset Vampire Series
Sunrise at Sunset: Revamped
A Bloody London Sunset
Summit at Sunset
Wicked Sunset
Sunset Rising
Sunset Burning **

** Additional Titles Forthcoming

* * *

The Logan Bringer Urban Fantasy Series
Bringer of Fire
Bringer Unleashed
Bringer's Law *

* Additional Titles Forthcoming

* * *

Gwen Reaper
(A Young Adult Paranormal Romance)
**Winner of the Paranormal Romance Guild's Reviewer's
Choice Award for Best Young Adult Novel of 2012!**

* * *

All titles published by Rutherford Literary Group

Published by:
Rutherford Literary Group
1205 S. Air Depot, PMB #135
Midwest City, OK 73110-4807

Cover art by Albert Slark
Edited by Edit911

Library of Congress Control Number: 2011903363

ISBN 098286132X
ISBN-13 978-0982861325

DEDICATION

For all those who hope that love can overcome and endure through most hurdles. One only has to believe and then commit to make it happen...

CONTENTS

JAZ PRIMO

ACKNOWLEDGMENTS

This novel is dedicated to loved ones lost far too soon, lessons learned both early and late, and the music-fueled muses who continue to inspire me.

All my love and appreciation to Lori, who continues to support, promote, and encourage my passion for writing. Sincere, heartfelt thanks to my family and friends, who continue to cheer me on and assuage my anxieties throughout the creative process. Special shout-outs to my mother, Phyllis, and my mother-in-law, Joyce, who turned out to be quite the Sunset vampire fans.

A huge thank you to Al Slark, who is arguably one of the most talented, gifted, and impressive cover artists in the publishing industry. Thanks to Lauren, Scott, and Kalli for bringing the striking figures of Katrina, Caleb, and Paige to life for the world to see. My appreciation to Brandon for the supplemental assistance and creativity regarding all things "webby and fonty." Special thanks to my amazing editor, Julia, for her suggestions and meticulous ministrations in preparing my manuscript for the light of day.

As always, thank you to my dear friends Jimmy, Jessica, Teresa, Crystal, Victoria, Amie, Lisa, Shannon, and Nancy for their invaluable proofreading, input, support, and encouragement. The piers of my self-confidence are grounded in the bedrock of wonderful people who care about me.

A Bloody London Sunset

JAZ PRIMO

PROLOGUE

Caleb

Caleb Taylor's heartbeat thundered in his ears as he raced down the hallway.

Have to help Katrina!

Speeding through the living area into the dining room and wielding the polished sword over his head with both hands, he closed on the unprotected back of the hideous-faced vampire, Chimalma, who was battling the woman he loved. Katrina's eyes widened for an instant, enough for the disfigured female vampire to notice. Chimalma's bared fangs and blazing hazel eyes targeted Caleb. She jerked her hand away from Katrina's grip, throwing a dagger at Caleb as he charged.

The dagger hammered into Caleb's upper chest with a force that caused him to topple backwards from the impact. Intense pain cascaded through his chest and shoulder, and the sword slipped from his hands and skittered across the floor towards Katrina. The red-haired vampire managed to grab the hilt as it nearly slid past her and whipped the blade upwards, plunging the sword into Chimalma's heart. With a twist, she broke the sword tip off in the vampire's chest. Chimalma sharply gasped and grabbed at one of the arrow bolts stuck in Katrina's chest with her free hand, pressing it

1

into her further, causing Katrina to scream in pain.

With one swift sweep of Katrina's right arm, the broken blade swooshed upwards, neatly separating the vampire's head from her shoulders. As Caleb lay on the floor in horror, Chimalma's head rolled across the floor, spraying a mist of cascading blood in its path. The body slumped to the tiled floor with a squishy *thud*, and Chimalma's head came to a stop against the far wall, shock reflected in her face.

Caleb gasped as he lurched into a sitting position in the darkness, covered in sweat. Katrina appeared at his bedside and placed her soft, warm palm against his face.

"Another nightmare, my love?" she asked softly with glowing green eyes.

He nodded.

That's the problem with vampires, he thought sourly. Even when you kill them, they still manage to haunt you.

CHAPTER 1

Domestic Life

It was a late-January Monday afternoon at Robert Fulton Community College in downtown Atlanta. Caleb gazed into the mirror mounted on his office door at a tired-looking face with pale blue eyes and sandy brown hair. He had lost a lot of sleep recently from recurring nightmares, though he was happy that the events of the previous month were behind him.

Stretching his legs in the chair behind his modest desk, he smirked at how his lean, muscular frame fit comfortably in the small pocket office. Only twenty-six years old, he was happy to be the newest history professor in the Social Sciences division. It was his second semester of employment, but he still felt like he had won the lottery at being freshly hired out of graduate school. Given the poor state of economy, perhaps in a manner of speaking he had.

Glass formed one side of his first-floor office, revealing the winter grounds of the campus. While the wind was cold and brisk outside, at least the sunny blue skies made the winter feel somewhat less depressing. Caleb had always enjoyed sunny days, but more and more he longed for night when the ultraviolet radiation was no longer a threat to those about whom he cared dearly.

His life partner, though the official title was "mate," was a tall, red-haired vampire named Katrina Rawlings. At least, that was her name until the time again came to change identities and localities, yet another of the many issues with which eternal beings had to contend. Katrina, whom he had affectionately nicknamed Kat, was the love of his life. A rush of warmth and pride flowed through him merely at the thought of her and of all she meant to him.

He smiled appreciatively, pulling a silver chain from beneath his pressed blue dress shirt, and gazed at the sterling silver heart-shaped pendant engraved with the inscription, *Caleb belongs to Kat*. He warmly recalled how Katrina had given it to him as a Christmas gift. She had a matching pendant, though inscribed differently.

When he had first viewed Katrina's pendant, he had been shocked to see that hers was inscribed with *Caleb is mine*, which had caused him to gape incredulously as he re-read his pendant's inscription to note the seemingly singular theme of the set.

She had laughed while flipping her pendant over, revealing the additional inscription, *Kat belongs to Caleb*. He chuckled, recalling how much she had appreciated his initial shocked reaction to her little joke. However, he was relieved the pendulum swung both ways.

A knock sounded outside his open office door, and he turned to see a young, dark-haired student. He could not recall the young man's name, but recognized his face as one of his morning history students. Slipping the pendant back inside his shirt, Caleb greeted his visitor with a welcoming smile. He recalled the recent memo from the campus president, Dr. Patrick Beaumont, emphasizing that improved student retention began with a positive, welcoming demeanor from all faculty and staff. While only the second week of the spring semester, the battle had already begun to advise students not to drop out from classes. And the faculty was charged with encouraging their students to that end. The economic conditions in Georgia were especially poor, and the state's colleges were fighting for improved enrollment numbers to justify funding increases.

The student, Tim Dominguez, wanted some advice on how to handle some schedule change requests that involved moving from his morning section to one of Caleb's two evening sections. Caleb momentarily thanked fate that he was teaching both of his evening classes on Tuesday and Thursday night, giving him ample evenings each week to enjoy activities with Katrina. After advising Tim, he leaned forwards in his chair to sort his notes for the next day's classes. He failed to notice the light fading outside as the winter's early sunset approached.

Setting his notes aside, he raised his arms over his head to stretch and yawn. Then his cell phone rang. The caller was a stately mannered, English vampire named Alton Rutherford, who was both a close friend of Katrina's and her former mentor. Alton was not yet someone whom Caleb considered a close friend, but the vampire had earned his respect, admiration, and appreciation for all he had done for them in recent months. Additionally, he was advising Caleb on how to help Katrina through a tough emotional experience following her battle with Chimalma. He felt particularly fortunate to have survived that dangerous adventure in mid-December, just days prior to the Christmas holidays. Alton had been instrumental in helping with that challenge as well.

"Hi, Alton."

"Hello, Caleb. I hope I haven't called at an inopportune time," the vampire countered in his crisp English accent, sounding entirely like a titled nobleman.

Caleb knew virtually nothing about Alton's past, including how old the vampire might be. Alton had never actually indicated he was from royalty or noble birth, though it was not a stretch to think he might be. When they had first met, Caleb had referred to him as Sir Alton, to which the vampire corrected, "Just Alton."

"Caleb?" Alton asked.

5

Caleb broke from his reverie. "Not at all, Alton," he stammered. "It's always a pleasure to hear from you."

The vampire chuckled. "Very kind of you to say. I'm calling to find out how your recovery is coming along.

Caleb frowned. "I've been doing much better, actually. It's just…"

"Yes?"

"Well, we've been getting along fine. It's just that she's stopped feeding from me for some reason."

Silence.

"Really?"

"After the night she accidently attacked me, she stopped," Caleb explained. His thoughts drifted back to when Katrina had been immersed in a series of aggressive and violent endeavors following the unexpected appearance of Chimalma in their lives last December. He shivered while recalling how he had been savagely bitten by Katrina as she experienced a disturbing nightmare. The resulting pain had been physical and emotional for both of them.

"And sex?" Alton asked.

"Well, that part's okay, actually," Caleb replied with a grin.

"I see. Well, bear in mind that your near-death experience prior to Christmas interrupted our original plans to curtail Katrina's renewed desire for violent activities," Alton explained.

"I've been thinking about that lately," Caleb absently noted as his thoughts drifted to a past conversation. Alton had told him that Katrina previously spent large portions of her life pursuing violent activities, and the desire had been rekindled during their recent trials to stop Chimalma. He had explained that Katrina was an alpha vampire who was innately drawn to participate in violent, aggressive activities, marking her as one of her kind's most dangerous predators. Having seen Katrina's aggressions firsthand, he could only agree wholeheartedly with Alton's assessment.

"Do you recall what I recommended?" the vampire

asked.

"Of course," Caleb replied. Alton had devised a two-phase process for him to help Katrina adjust to her violent feelings in a more positive manner. Phase one had been easy for him. It involved encouraging Katrina with less aggressive activities, such as more displays of affection, appreciation, and intimacy. He avoided arguments and confrontations with her and told her how much he needed and appreciated her. That had worked fabulously and was perfectly suited behavior for his peaceable, easy-going personality.

Phase two involved more physically challenging pursuits, and Alton had asked him to adopt an exercise regimen to improve both his muscular and cardio-vascular conditions. However, he had been partially debilitated during his recovery from nearly dying of injuries sustained in the final battle with Chimalma.

"Phase one worked well," Caleb said as he shut the door to his office, preventing his voice from carrying out into the hallway. "In fact, my increased physical workouts haven't raised Katrina's suspicions at all. She associates it with my recovery from last December."

"Excellent," Alton remarked. "Are you ready to begin phase two?"

While Caleb understood that he was expected to engage in hunting-styled activities that Katrina might enjoy as much as the dangerous pursuits from her past, Alton had been rather vague regarding the details.

"Sure, I'm in pretty good shape, actually," he replied, thinking of the improved diet and stamina-building activities that had increased his muscle tone and endurance.

Alton fell silent, but somehow Caleb imagined him smiling at that moment.

"Excellent. Shall we proceed?" Alton baited.

"Um, sure," Caleb replied. "What exactly does that involve again?"

"Think of it as an aggressive form of hide and seek," Alton suggested. "Approach it like a playful form of escape and evade."

Caleb silently nodded his head. "Okay, I can do that. Any suggestions?"

"Certainly," Alton continued. "Find terrain that poses a challenge for her. Preferably somewhere outdoors, such as a forest or national park. After some practice, you can vary the location and setting. Just try to avoid public places where the use of her vampire abilities might be noticed."

Caleb considered that for a moment. "But wouldn't a public place restrict her abilities and make it more challenging for her?"

"Hm," Alton considered. "You have a point."

Then Caleb frowned. "I don't stand a chance without getting a head start," he ventured. "But I could pre-stage somewhere and call her on the phone. I should also give her a time limit because, once her gaze falls upon on me, I'm as good as bagged."

"Also excellent points," Alton agreed. "You're actually better at envisioning this than I gave you credit for, young man."

Caleb beamed at the rare compliment. "Honestly, though, I don't think humans stand much of a chance against pursuing vampires."

"Caleb," Alton mildly chastised, "it's not as if anyone's trying to harm you. This is all for Katrina's amusement. Besides, you may learn to enjoy it over time. And she's bound to be grateful for your efforts. There could be rewards forthcoming you haven't even considered yet."

Caleb slyly smirked at the suggestion. "That's always nice."

"Let me leave you with some final advice," Alton interjected. "Remember that Katrina can see much further than you and in the dark. And since you'll have to do this at night, you'll be at a disadvantage. Most of all, don't try to hide from her; keep moving. She can hear your heartbeat when she's near you. She also has your scent imprinted, so she would locate you immediately if you tried bunkering. As your mate, Katrina has finely tuned and honed her senses to your body's signature."

After momentarily considering those final pieces of advice, he replied, "Thanks so much, Alton. I appreciate the helpful advice, and I'll let you know how it goes."

"Good luck," Alton offered. "Oh, and by the way, I extended an invitation to Katrina for the two of you to come visit me in London during your spring break. I hope you'll decide to take me up on that offer."

"How could I possibly refuse? I'd be honored," Caleb said. "I've never been out of the country before, and I've always wanted to see Europe."

"Excellent," Alton confirmed in a strangely satisfied tone. "I believe you'll find it an interesting experience. Well, I must be going for now. Again, good luck on your new hunting venture. And do call me if you have questions or concerns."

"Thanks, Alton," Caleb said before hanging up. "Nice talking to you."

He leaned back in his chair to mull over ideas regarding his hunting venture with Katrina.

Hide and Seek with a vampire?

The minutes passed as he lost track of time, and then lurched suddenly in his chair upon realizing it was getting late.

Katrina will be wondering about me.

The drive home to Katrina's estate in Mableton, just outside of Atlanta, took less time than Caleb expected. He grinned while pulling through the regal-looking front security gate to the exclusive Pine Valley addition in his older model Honda.

Who would've thought I'd ever live someplace like this?

He proceeded down the central dark road that wound through the remote, heavily wooded area. Each property was at least five or more acres in area, and most of the homes were veritable mansions. Each estate was a reflection of an owner's taste, resulting in diverse styles of architecture.

However, most estates sat so far from the street that few

were visible without entering the private driveways leading onto each property. In the case of Katrina's estate, which had become his residence in December, a private wrought-iron gate blocked the entrance to the driveway.

After he activated a button on his remote control, the gate swung open, and Caleb proceeded up the lengthy driveway to the four-car garage. He still marveled at how expansive the six thousand square foot manor looked from the driveway. It was a beautiful place to live, sporting all of the modern technological conveniences, including a state-of-the-art security system.

As he pulled into the garage, he glanced to the right to see Katrina's black Audi sports car parked inside. He longed to see her again after a long day at the college. Despite the months that had passed, he remained in awe at having been chosen as her mate.

She could have picked any man in the world, but she chose me.

Caleb glanced down for only an instant to place the car in park, but when he looked up again he saw Katrina already standing next to his car. She observed him with an endeared expression as he exited the vehicle, and he smiled brightly at her. He stopped while reaching into the back seat to retrieve his book bag to take in the magnificent vision of his mate.

My vampire.

Katrina wore designer jeans and a crew neck sweater. Her long red hair cascaded across her shoulders like a mantle, and the gaze from her deep green eyes seemed to penetrate directly into him.

She's ravishing for someone who's over five hundred years old, he mused as he took a moment to appreciate her nearly six-foot, lean physique, and the way her skin looked almost milky in the light.

Though pale skin was a telltale indicator of a vampire, it didn't imply that she was a corpse. Vampires were definitely alive, breathing beings with blood flowing through their veins. Their inhuman characteristics set them aside: the ability to regenerate from wounds, retractable fangs, vast strength, amazing speed, and heightened senses of sight, smell, hearing, and touch.

They're amazing, breathtaking, and terrible all at the same time, nature's perfect predator, although their favorite prey is humans.

She gazed at him with a curious expression. "Welcome home, my love. It's getting late, and I was growing concerned that something might have happened to you. Is everything okay?"

"Sorry, Kat. I got distracted doing things at the office. I would've called if something happened."

During the weeks of recovery from his December injuries, she had behaved more protectively around him. However, in recent days, he sensed an added sense of attentiveness from her.

Not that I'm complaining, of course. Who wouldn't want to be the center of attention to a loving vampire mate?

He walked around the car to her and glanced down to realize that, despite the cold concrete floor, she was barefoot. "Let's get those cold feet back inside."

She giggled in a charming fashion. "Silly boy, I'm nearly immune to extreme temperatures."

"My vampire superhero," he quipped. Being a couple inches shorter than she, he tilted his head up to kiss her soft lips warmly.

"Are you hungry?" she asked as they made their way through the garage and into the house.

He noted a sly smile on her face. "Actually, yeah," he replied as the scent of fresh-cooked food wafted from the kitchen. It smelled like sausage, eggs, and hash browns.

That's strange, he thought. *I'm the only person in the house who eats food.*

Not that vampires couldn't consume human food, of course. They merely didn't need anything except blood for sustenance to survive. As he walked into the kitchen from the small hallway leading from the garage, he saw those very items on the stovetop.

"You cooked those?" he asked as Katrina appeared at

the stove in a blur and began serving up everything onto a large plate.

She pulled a tray of biscuits from the oven, slipped two onto the plate, and placed the food on the kitchen counter before one of the barstools.

"Guess what?" she asked in a giddy manner that was completely out of character for her. "I've been watching some cable cooking shows over and over on the DVR, and I think I've managed to make breakfast!"

He dropped his book bag to the floor with a thump and alternated stares between the plate and Katrina in amazement as she retrieved a glass of ice water for him and placed it next to his plate.

Katrina cooking, he mused. *Is this the Twilight Zone or the apocalypse?*

"Wow," he said.

She continued smiling and ushered him to the counter to sit down. "Go ahead," she urged excitedly. "Give it a try and tell me what you think. I know it's evening and supper time, but I couldn't wait for you to try everything."

As he picked up the fork lying next to the plate, he glanced up at her with a smirk and teased, "What have you done with my normally somber vampire?"

Her smile faded, and she adopted a predatory expression. "Eat, my love, while you still can," she offered grimly.

His smirk transformed into an evil grin. "Now that's my lethal lover."

Caleb tried each of the items and was astounded by the taste.

Truth be told, she nailed these perfectly.

"These are terrific, Kat. Honestly, this is wonderful. I appreciate it, and not just because I'm hungry."

Her former smile returned, and she propped her chin on one hand while leaning on the counter next to him. "Thank you," she cheerfully replied. "I wanted to do something nice for you. Cooking is a little offering of myself that I can give to you. I haven't cooked in centuries."

His eyebrows rose. "You never tried cooking for your previous mates?"

"Nope. You're the first since my human husband, Samuel," she replied with an endeared expression.

Caleb beamed with pride at that, given how important Samuel had been in her life.

She hasn't cooked since the early 1500s then, he realized.

Out of the corner of his eye, he noticed an overly stuffed large plastic trash bag sitting on the floor. He frowned, recalling that he had taken the trash out that morning before heading to work.

"So," he carefully ventured, "did you have to practice much?"

Katrina's eyes darted to the trash bag still sitting nearby and innocently looked back at him. "Not so much, I suppose," she said. "Although I might have made a couple of orders to the grocery store on more than one occasion."

Thanks to online grocers, he mused.

Last December when she had sequestered him in the house to protect him from Chimalma, she had located an Atlanta-based grocery chain that offered online ordering and delivery.

"I see," he said with a smirk as he continued eating.

"I'm just going to take the trash out, and I'll be back," she said.

"I thought I took the trash out this morning?" he asked after swallowing a forkful of eggs.

"Oh, hush," she mildly chastised as she walked out to the garage.

He smiled while continuing to eat.

She returned in seconds and washed her hands at the kitchen sink. "Alton called today," she mentioned as she dried her hands on a towel. "He invited us to London when you go on spring break in March."

"Yeah, he called me earlier about that, as well," Caleb admitted. "It sounds like fun."

Her eyes narrowed. "Really? Did he mention anything

else?"

"Not so much," he replied elusively. "Except to ask how I was recovering. He wanted to make sure I'd been rehabbing well from my injuries."

She nodded, though her gaze was penetrating as she observed his reply.

Caleb knew why. Vampires had an uncanny ability to sense lying and deception in the human condition by monitoring heartbeat, pulse, eye reaction, and muscle tension. They were amazing lie detectors in an eerie way. Fortunately, everything he said was true.

I wouldn't try to lie overtly about anything important.

Trust was vital in a relationship, more so when your mate was a powerful vampire.

"You've been exercising quite a bit recently," she observed. "Your dedication is impressive, and your muscle tone is better now than before your injuries."

His eyebrows rose slightly as he realized very little got past her. "You noticed?"

She confirmed in a seductive manner, "You're always a subject of focused study for me, my love."

He shivered slightly, and his eyes darted fleetingly to her as he chewed his food. Katrina had a way of unnerving him slightly when she wanted to, but always in a manner that he found both mysterious and pleasurable.

It's a remarkable quality, he conceded.

She walked behind him to caress her fingernails playfully down the back of his neck. A tingling sensation rippled across his skin, and she kissed him softly on the back of the neck. Then she silently exited the kitchen and walked deeper into the house.

"I'll be in the sublevel room, my love," she said. "I'll start making our travel arrangements for the trip to England."

"You mean you're going to the lair?" he teased.

He had playfully coined the phrase to describe the large room that was at one time an oversized basement, but had since been converted into a mini-apartment. There were no windows, and Katrina had added a full bathroom and walk-in closet. Other additions included a wet bar, a wall-mounted LCD television with a surround sound system set before a large couch, two desks, a king-sized bed, and other bedroom furnishings.

The centerpiece arrangement was an oversized computer hutch containing her vast array of computer equipment and the controller for the estate's security system. If Katrina had been a superhero, the sublevel room would be her secret hideout. It did have an obscure entrance in the form of a hidden panel door leading from the main hallway, appearing as nothing more than a section of the wood paneling lining the hall.

Katrina stopped in the hallway and turned to stare at him. "Maybe we should start calling it our chamber," she suggested with an edge to her voice.

"That works, if you prefer," he said agreeably before lifting a forkful of food to his mouth. For reasons beyond his understanding, she didn't care for the nickname he had selected.

"When you're finished, please change into something casual," she advised. "We're going out tonight."

"Will do," he acknowledged.

After he finished eating, he cleaned up the kitchen and washed the few dirty dishes and pans. He proceeded to their chamber and changed into a pair of khakis, but kept his blue dress shirt on.

He appreciated how gracious Katrina had been to allocate space in a chest of drawers and the walk-in closet for his clothes and belongings when he had moved in with her. Fortunately, his former apartment had been small, so there were relatively few clothes and belongings he needed to move into her estate. And though he still had trouble considering it his home, he enjoyed living there with her.

Maybe if she'd let me pay part of the bills, I'd feel better about it, he mused while brushing his teeth.

Katrina appeared behind him, which startled him, much

to her amusement. He shook his head and rolled his eyes to the ceiling as he finished brushing.

"Surprise," she offered with a smirk.

He admired her reflection in the mirror. She had changed into black slacks and a turquoise turtleneck cashmere sweater. Her hair was tied back in a single ponytail, accented with a sterling silver clasp.

"You look great," he observed after rinsing.

She grinned appreciatively. "Thank you. About ready?"

They made their way to the garage, and Katrina pulled the keys to the Audi from her small purse.

"May I drive?" he asked tentatively. "Please?" he added with a hopeful smile.

She cast an amused glance at him, knowing that he loved driving her car. Happy to indulge him, she tossed the keys to him. Ever the gentleman, he held the door for her and smirked on his way around to the driver's side.

He drove contentedly to the nearby highway, but then realized that he didn't know where they were going. Katrina interpreted his frown and curious sidelong glance.

"The chauffeur can proceed to the High Museum of Art, midtown just off of Peachtree Street," she offered with a smirk.

He nodded and replied in his best mock-English accent, "Thank you, miss. We're on our way."

After a short time on the highway, something occurred to him.

"Hey, isn't the museum normally closed on Mondays?"

She smiled. "Not tonight. They're promoting a new exhibit that started last week. It's a special traveling gallery of select eighteenth century artwork."

He arched one eyebrow. "Sounds intriguing."

After locating a downtown parking garage, they held hands on the walk to the museum. The High Museum of Art was actually a grouping of three primary buildings. As one of the premiere museums in the country, it was a key hub for special exhibits. There were over three hundred thousand square feet of space in the multi-storied buildings.

Each was styled in an appealing mixture of angles and curves, while making excellent use of glass panes along portions of the exterior for a thoroughly twenty-first century appearance.

After they made their way into the main building, Caleb scanned the interior while paying for their entrance fees. The museum seemed well attended, but not overly crowded, for which he was thankful so as not to feel rushed while viewing the exhibits.

The museum's interior was bright and open, sporting multiple tiers of curved walkways bridging each floor.

They made their way leisurely to the newest exhibit area and browsed the collection. They stopped at a particularly striking landscape painting called "Gainsborough's Forest," also titled "Cornard Wood." It was labeled circa 1748 and credited to the English landscape painter Thomas Gainsborough.

It depicted people performing daily activities among a hilly and tree-strewn terrain accented by a nearby stream and pond. One worker gathered branches into a bundle, while two others appeared to be working beside a dirt road as another man observed them.

Caleb stared at the painting at length and then looked at Katrina, who was appreciating another work hanging a few feet away. He contemplated that she had been a vampire at the time of the painting, which seemed utterly surreal to him.

Ever since the past December when she had revealed that her human birth was in 1506, he had struggled to wrap his mind around the idea that she had experienced over five hundred years of human history.

It's astonishing, he mused while staring at her.

Her eyes darted to look at him and noted his penetrating gaze. She smirked, moved to stand beside him, and snaked her left arm loosely around his waist. "You're staring at me with that look again," she whispered in his ear with amusement.

"What look?" he whispered, once again staring at the painting.

"You know what look," she challenged while tightening her grip around his waist. "That faraway, doe-eyed expression that says, 'I can't believe she's that old.'"

He blushed over how well she had been able to read his expression. He had marveled at that alarmingly accurate ability since their initial courtship the past fall. "Well, maybe a little," he conceded. "It's just amazing, that's all."

She sighed and confessed, "I realize it's a lot for a human mind to comprehend, given your limited life span."

"Was it really like that in the 1700s?" he asked while staring at the painting.

She considered the painting silently. "Well, yes, actually. Everyday life for the average person was rather mundane, mixed with toil and struggle and interspersed with occasional moments of celebration or some personal noteworthy accomplishment."

"Do you ever miss anything about those times?" he asked, looking around to ensure that nobody was close enough to overhear their conversation.

She considered his question at length. Finally, she replied, "For the most part, no. Technology makes things so much easier for vampires. However, I miss the formal gowns and dresses, as well as some of the lavish balls and parties. Everyone is so casual in this day and age. People rarely dress formally anymore."

He nodded as she gently steered him towards another painting.

She whispered in his ear, "Of course, during those days I would've been preoccupied with my next hunting experiences, so I attended very few formal events. Blood banks didn't exist yet, and I spent a lot of time planning to secure my meals clandestinely. I had to be discreet at formal events because people grew suspicious if someone abruptly disappeared from the party. As is much the case today, the poor and working class took the brunt of the average vampire's focus."

Caleb contemplated that and asked, "Did you normally kill your prey?"

Katrina pulled him close to her and bent down slightly to place her lips against his ear. "I killed animals and humans alike. But often I tried to get a person plied with enough liquor so they would pass out. Then I could have my meal, leaving them with nothing more than a sense of lightheadedness after they woke. That was particularly useful if I selected someone from the formal events we just spoke of. It could all be attributed to their overindulgence of spirits. Then perhaps I could revisit a previous target for future consumption. By rotating around to various people, my meal sources lasted longer. And using my saliva to heal fang wounds made the feeding process inconspicuous as well."

Though being a firsthand beneficiary of such ability, Caleb nevertheless shivered upon considering the leechlike behavior that vampires engaged in while feeding. However, given the tender manner with which Katrina always treated him during feedings, it wasn't as if he was complaining.

Of course, that's before she stopped feeding on me altogether, he reflected morosely.

She frowned after noticing his sudden physical tremor and glanced down at him. She placed her lips to his check and kissed him for a moment longer than a simple kiss would have lasted.

He appreciated the comforting feeling of her soft lips and turned to press his own against hers before she pulled away from him.

She used her arm, still wound around his waist, to lead him towards a small secluded alcove nearby. He thought she was guiding him to another painting, but when he glanced up at her, he noted her gaze was focused upon him fully.

In the alcove, she turned her body away from the main gallery and pulled his body close to hers. Her lips pressed against his, and he gratefully and passionately kissed her in response. As her left arm encircled his waist, her right hand cupped the back of his neck, and she kissed him in a slow, deep manner.

He felt completely mesmerized as his pulse increased dramatically. It was a feeling he never tired of and one he greedily wished would never end. But in a matter of moments, she withdrew her lips from his.

He elevated himself up on the balls of his feet to pursue her, but she tightened the grip on the back of his neck to hold him in place, though without causing him any pain or discomfort.

"I want to kiss you some more," he whispered in an almost pleading fashion, causing him to blush slightly from the admission.

She smiled slyly and promised, "Oh, I realize that, and I'll accommodate your wish very soon, my love. But first, we need to take advantage of this rare artistic opportunity."

"Sorry, Kat," he apologized.

Her emerald eyes locked onto his pale blue ones with sudden intensity, and she reassured him, "You never have to apologize for that. It makes my heart soar that you feel that way."

"I love you so much," he whispered fervently, "More than anyone or anything."

The insistence in his voice spoke volumes, which pleased her. "And I you, my love."

She cast a quick glance over her shoulder to scan the area and turned back to him to bend down and kiss him warmly on the lips for a few brief seconds. At the last moment, she drew her breath in sharply as their lips sealed against one another, and he felt a momentary dizziness wash over him as his breath was abruptly pulled from his lungs.

I just love doing that to him.

Their lips parted, and she held his waist firmly to steady his balance. She slowly led them from the alcove, noting a dapper museum aide walking towards their location. Seeing them departing, the aide stopped and diverted to another direction once they began moving towards other paintings.

Attentive staff, Katrina mused with a smirk.

They enjoyed browsing through the remaining exhibits and periodically paused to discuss appealing aspects of various pieces. As the mood struck him, Caleb took the opportunity to ask additional historical information related to the eighteenth century and was intrigued how Katrina seamlessly elaborated upon or validated a painting's depictions as historically accurate. It seemed as if he were accompanied by his own historical accuracy meter. In turn, she reveled in both his pronounced interest and rapt attention, and they both thoroughly enjoyed the evening.

The crowds thinned to the point that the gallery seemed nearly deserted by the time they left the museum. They held hands during the brief walk from the museum grounds to the parking garage.

Once again, Katrina permitted him the satisfaction of driving them home in the Audi. Halfway home, he smiled while recalling the occasion when he had asked why she typically wanted to drive.

"It's not a reflection on my confidence in your driving skills," she had assured him. "It's merely that vampires have quicker reaction times, which is safer for both of us."

He had wisely conceded the logic of her argument. However, it didn't stop him from asking for the keys from time to time.

Upon arriving at the estate, they had no sooner exited the car and walked into the house, when Katrina tugged on Caleb's left arm from behind. She spun him around to face her and noted that his eyes had widened with surprise. As she adopted a sly smile, a wave of passion crashed over her, and she sought his lips aggressively.

She pressed her body to his, forcing him backwards into the dark hallway behind him. Her hand quickly cupped the base of his head to prevent it from smacking the wall, and she kissed him with passion. His arms reached out to encircle her waist as she wrapped her free arm around the small of his back.

He responded eagerly to her passionate kisses and felt her silky tongue press its way into his mouth. Their tongues met as they continued to kiss deeply. A longing grew in each of them, though hers was torn between both the desire for sex and the craving for his blood.

It had been weeks since she had taken his blood, an episode she recalled ruefully and all too well. It had been the second night following her and Alton's return from battling Chimalma. Her reunion with Caleb went seamlessly, and she had felt as if their lives were returning to normal again. However, while sleeping beside him, she had a horrible nightmare in which she had been attacked by assailants. Then one assailant transformed into the visage of Chimalma. In her dream, Katrina attacked Chimalma by sinking her fangs into her.

But the real nightmare began when she tasted Caleb's blood in her mouth and awoke to hear him screaming in the darkness next to her. She had unconsciously bitten into his upper shoulder, and blood had streamed from the gouges formed as he had tried to dislodge her fangs by lurching away from her. One of the gouges had been so severe that he still retained a small, faint mark on his upper left shoulder, despite the healing power of her saliva.

Since that horrible, fateful night, Katrina vowed not to take blood from him. Instead, she had shared and displayed her love and intimacy with him in the traditional human manner of sexual coupling. In fact, she had not slept beside him until just a couple of weeks ago, though she had often lain awake in bed beside him to share at least in the intimacy of being next to him while he slumbered.

Her sleep was attended to via naps taken during the day and always when he wasn't beside her merely to avoid any accidental recurrences of nightmare-induced attacks.

However, that evening, sleep was the last thing on Caleb's mind. His desire grew rapidly as they kissed lustfully in the hallway. His breathing and pulse were both elevated significantly, a fact not unnoticed by his red-haired mate.

She used a proportional amount of strength with her arm around the small of his back to press him in the direction of the mostly dark living room, where the only available light emanated from the glow of the exterior eaves' lights through the sheer curtains.

He eagerly complied as they kissed, not paying attention to the path they took, but instead concentrating on the amorous application of his lips to hers.

Katrina giggled, interjecting a pause in their kissing, and Caleb felt a faint smile form on her lips. The moment they were sharing felt comfortably familiar to her. She instantly recalled the first time she had kissed him in the front entry room, not far from where she had herded him through the kitchen.

"What?" he whispered with confusion.

"The first night we made love," she prompted. "Remember?"

He rolled his eyes and smirked, easily recollecting that night. He had been so nervous, having deliberated for days following the abrupt revelation to him of her true vampire nature.

He recalled that night, marking his first experience when she drank his blood. It had been both exhilarating and terrifying at the same time. But in the end, he had felt bonded to her in a far more special manner than he had with any other person. Most of all, it had made him feel special and desired.

How could I forget?

"I remember," he recalled. "The first time we made love. And the first time you drank from me."

"I knew then you were the one for me," she whispered before kissing him warmly.

Caleb's smirk faded as the realization resurfaced that his lover had not taken blood from him in over a month. It was something he had been hesitant to bring up, not sure how sensitive a topic it was for her. He was already aware of how guilty she felt following the accidental attack on him that

December evening. He had long since forgiven her, particularly after Alton had helped him understand the difficult truth about her aggressive nature, the unfortunate catalyst for the attack. Still, he was encouraged that she was once again sleeping beside him, and there had been no recurring accidental attacks thus far.

With sudden resolve, he withdrew his arms from around her waist. Katrina looked down at him quizzically as he unbuttoned his shirt. She took her arms from around his body as she watched him in the dim light of the room. He removed his shirt and t-shirt, revealing his toned, muscular chest adorned only by his sterling silver pendant and chain.

He reached down and pulled his shoes and socks from his feet, never breaking his penetrating gaze into her eyes, which were glowing like miniature beacons. He hesitated, recognizing that her glowing eyes likely indicated either lust for sex, hunger for blood, or a combination.

His slacks dropped to the floor, and he stepped from them wearing only underwear. Reaching up to his chest, he took the heart-shaped sterling silver pendant between his thumb and forefinger and lifted the pendant up towards her.

"What does this say?" he asked boldly.

She arched one eyebrow, not needing to look at the pendant to recall its inscription. She had carefully crafted both their pendants' inscriptions.

"Caleb belongs to Katrina," she stated possessively.

He stood, suspending the pendant proudly before her. "What does that mean?"

She smirked and answered in a firm, passionate tone, "It signifies our mutual commitment. You belong to me. You're my mate. You are mine."

He beamed with satisfaction even as a slight tremor ran through his body from the possessive tone in her voice. It excited him and made him feel very wanted and loved. It was an aspect to her assertive nature that never failed to captivate him.

"What specifically belongs to you?" he insisted.

"Your love."

"And?"

"Your body," she added.

"And?" he pressed.

"Your blood," she stated emphatically.

He nodded his head slowly and demanded, "Then take it. Take my blood, Kat."

Her eyes flashed brightly for a moment as the desire for his blood soared. Her ever-present thirst wanted to unleash itself, but she constantly strove to control it, bending it to her will. As an alpha vampire, control was one of her requisite skills.

But the memory of her nightmare-induced attack on him replayed in her mind, and she frowned.

I can't risk hurting him again.

He noted her consternation and anticipated the nature of her thoughts. "Don't you want my blood?" he asked.

"Of course I do," she reassured him, and she bent towards him, seeking a kiss.

But he backed away from her, dropping the pendant against his bare chest, and challenged, "Are you going to drink from me?"

"Caleb, please," she murmured while reaching out to him.

"There's a special bond we share when you take my blood," he continued. "Now it's missing, and I want it back for both of us."

She regarded him with a frown while contemplating his earnest appeal. She had never wanted to make him feel undesired, unloved, or unwanted. And she certainly felt the desire for his blood at that moment, despite having consumed a packet of blood from the basement refrigerator that afternoon.

"You're the love of my life, Kat," he explained affectionately. "But I won't demand that you take what you no longer want."

He turned away from her as she stared down upon the

man she loved even more than her own life. She swallowed hard and came to an immediate decision. While stepping behind him, she wrapped her left arm around his lean waist.

Her grip tightened around him as she reached up from behind with her right hand and firmly grasped his chin between her fingers. Using gentle but deliberate pressure, she tilted his head up and firmly placed her lips against the supple skin of his neck.

Caleb breathed in sharply as his pulse increased, and she smiled into his neck while slowly, passionately kissing near his jugular vein. His hands grasped her arm tentatively as it tightened around his waist. His body was guided backwards as she pulled him against her, his head lolling back against her left shoulder. Her body's warmth felt soothing against his bare skin.

As she continued to kiss his neck, she intermittently nipped his skin with her teeth in a teasing fashion, appreciating the sharp intake of breath that it evoked from him. She pressed her tongue against his neck as her lips sealed against his skin, waiting for the effect of her saliva to take full effect.

He felt her silky tongue press against his neck, followed by the progressively soothing, numbing sensation that spread around the area where her tongue and mouth concentrated. He reveled in the sensation, decrying its absence, and momentarily wondered if she intended to drink from him while standing, which would be a first.

Caleb recalled the fleeting, distant feeling that assailed him as she fed, and his muscles tightened as he wondered if he'd be able to stand ably enough.

As if reading his thoughts, though more accurately sensing his body language, Katrina drew him towards the nearby couch as her mouth remained sealed over his neck.

Relaxing his body in her grip, he allowed her to lay him down onto the couch cushions. He stared into the fabric of her sweater as she knelt beside his prone form. The numbing sensation increased until he scarcely felt her tongue against his skin.

She parted her lips long enough to whisper, "Freeze."

It was the signal, and he remained perfectly still. He felt a slight pinprick against his neck as her fangs pierced his skin. Her mouth sealed against his neck, and he heard the telltale, subdued slurping sounds as she drew his blood.

He closed his eyes and let his mind and body drift across a sea of soothing darkness, accented only by the sounds of his breathing and the faint noises she generated from her consumption. A warm feeling of serenity and compassion flowed through him as she took communion of his blood.

Her left hand lay flat against his bare chest, pressing his pendant between her hand and his skin. The fingertips of her right hand gently massaged his scalp as she ran her fingers through his hair. He grinned, reveling in the waves of ecstasy and pleasure as they washed over him.

Finally, he thought.

Time held little meaning to him as he lay with his lover's body draped across him. The darkened room merely added to the lofty sensation of peacefully hovering in nothingness.

After a time, she ceased drinking and pressed her tongue against his skin to heal the punctures in his neck. The renewed numbness signaled the end of his soothing journey, and he almost regretted its passing.

However, he knew that if it never ended, it was only a matter of time before his body's functioning ceased from blood loss. He wasn't ready to depart the world so long as Katrina was still part of it.

Then, as if on cue, she kissed his neck affectionately and moved to kiss his lips in similar fashion.

"My love, who so willingly submits himself to me," she whispered with ardor.

Images from the past December replayed in her mind. Caleb had slit his own throat to enable his blood to save her as she lay dying on the dining room floor. The truly selfless nature of sacrificing his life for hers touched her in a beautiful and profound manner, which shook her to the very core of her being.

No human had voluntarily surrendered such a thing to her. And quite frankly, she had doubted such a selfless human even existed until then. His near-fatal sacrifice eliminated any doubts of his devotion and commitment to her.

And if not for Paige, I'd not have him today, she mused. Paige Turner, her best friend and former pupil, had used her vampire blood to save Caleb's life.

Yet another debt I can never fully repay.

Her head rested against Caleb's chest, and she kissed him. Her taste buds savored the lingering flavor of his sweet blood as she listened to his strong heartbeat, as well as the rush of blood flowing through his veins. It was the music of his body and a beautiful symphony to her ears.

"I'm a lucky woman," she whispered, caressing his chest with her fingernails. He was the only being who had such a hold on her heart and soul. For all of her strength, determination, aggression, and power, she was like a fragile rose before his needs and desires. It was a vulnerable feeling and one that as an alpha vampire she wasn't accustomed to.

And yet she embraced it deeply within herself and held onto it as if it were the very source of her life force. However, she knew such feelings needed to be tempered properly and revealed to him only in appropriate apportionment.

After all, it's in an alpha vampire's nature, she mused as she once more kissed his chest. *My nature*, she added.

"Did I taste different given last month's blood transfusion?" he asked.

She didn't want to dwell on that line of thought at such an enjoyable moment and instead offered in a satisfied voice, "Oh, no. You tasted as sweet as always, my love."

He made a contented sound and whispered, "I'm glad."

After a few minutes, she felt his hand creep underneath her sweater. His fingertips softly massaged her bra-covered breast, and she giggled.

She rose up slightly and slipped her sweater off. Her pale skin shimmered in an unearthly manner in the dimly lit room as his eyes played across her body.

"My loving vampire," he whispered possessively as he reached out to pull her hand to his lips. He kissed her open palm reverently.

Katrina smiled at the endearing reference and at the tone in which he made it. "Always, my love," she replied.

His hand traced her shoulders then slipped back to her breasts.

She gazed down at him, sensing his new yearning. As she slipped from her bra, her breasts gently suspended before him. "Do you want me here?" she asked.

His eyes were intense as he gazed into her eyes. "Yes," he whispered.

"As you wish," she agreed, moving in an almost feline fashion while removing her boots and the remainder of her clothing. Her attentions returned to him as she deftly slid his briefs down the length of his muscular legs. She gazed appreciatively at his nude, masculine form with approval while pulling him from the couch and onto the floor with her. Then time stood still.

* * *

Tuesday passed quickly for Caleb despite the fact that Tuesdays and Thursdays were his extended days that semester, having both daytime and evening classes, as well as office hours during the late afternoon. Nevertheless, he was grateful when Wednesday arrived. He had special evening plans in store for Katrina. It was time for phase two of his and Alton's plan to spring into action.

Caleb had stowed a pair of faded blue jeans, a sweatshirt, and hiking boots in his car's trunk that morning before Katrina noticed what he was doing. That afternoon, while still at the college, he changed clothes and prepared for a new challenge that he intended to call Find Caleb.

He was filled with anticipation as he cleaned off his desk and snapped the lid of his briefcase shut. Thankful for his thick sweatshirt, he hurried out to his car as evening approached. It was cloudy, windy, and somewhat cold that day, but fortunately wasn't raining.

He returned to the estate just as darkness fell, but instead of entering the garage, he parked his car in the driveway. After reconsidering the weather, he left his leather jacket in the car, but slipped on a pair of leather gloves.

Just in case Katrina viewed the house's surveillance system, he walked back down the driveway and out the main gate before heading into a large wooded area adjacent to the estate. The undeveloped area was native forest slated for future development among the large acreage of the addition. He smirked while reflecting upon how perfect the grounds were for his new game.

The night was dark with no moon, and he was pleased he'd brought a flashlight. However, he quickly realized that once he called Katrina, the light would immediately alert her keen vision to his location. He sighed, conceding there were so many considerations that had eluded him as he prepared for the event.

Well, I suppose with practice comes proficiency.

The forest was eerily quiet, save for the sounds of tree branches clacking against one another and the rustling of dry leaves. After negotiating to the middle of the forest, he selected a couple of possible routes of egress in the event…no, rather, for when Katrina located his position. He wondered how much time he should give her to find him and frowned as he tried to gauge how far and fast she could move.

"Easy. Just time a lightning strike," he muttered.

He made a mental calculation and removed a glove so he could retrieve his cell phone. He auto-dialed Katrina; the phone rang merely twice before she picked up.

"Caleb?" she asked guardedly. "Where are you? I noticed your car is already in the driveway."

He hadn't meant to concern her and quickly replied, "Sorry, Kat. I was preparing a special event for you and didn't want to spoil the surprise."

There was a silent pause at the other end before she asked warily, "What kind of surprise, my love?"

He knew that she wasn't keen on surprises; a key aspect of alpha vampires was that they liked to be in control. He rolled his eyes heavenward at the gross understatement of that particular thought and hoped she would be pleased in the end once she understood what he had planned.

"How would you like to play a game with me tonight?" he asked playfully.

Another pause.

"Game? What kind of game?"

"It's called Find Caleb," he replied with a smirk. "It's simple. All you have to do is find me, and catch me, before the timer on my watch goes off."

Another pause.

"You'd better not be doing something dangerous, or I'm going to be upset."

He winced at her admonishment and sensed her protective nature kicking into high gear. Upsetting her was the last thing he wanted, because vampires weren't particularly pleasant to be around when they were angry.

"No, really. I thought this out already, and it's perfectly safe," he reassured her. "This is just playtime for adults, that's all."

Silence.

"Perhaps," she hedged in a milder tone. "Tell me more, I suppose."

"Okay. I'm somewhere outside, not far from the estate. You just need to come looking for me. But you have to tag me before the time limit expires."

"Hm," she replied. "Sounds intriguing. What do I win if I beat the time limit?"

He was perplexed, not having anticipated the need for prizes. But then inspiration struck, and he smiled. "Tonight, the prize is a foot massage," he declared proudly.

"Both feet?" she teased.

He adopted a bland expression and replied flatly, "Yes, both feet."

"Ankles too?" she pressed as she resumed typing on her computer keyboard.

She sure enjoys spending time on her computer.

He sighed and agreed, "Okay, ankles too."

He shook his head over the bargaining required just to get a vampire to chase him around the woods.

Just wait until I tell Alton about this.

"Okay," she agreed. "When does this start, and how much time do I get?"

"Let's say a ten minute time limit, which starts as soon as I hang up the phone," he ventured.

He heard her chuckle.

"I'll be seeing you very soon, my love."

The line went dead, and he realized with a smirk that she had been the one to hang up the phone to initiate the game.

That whole alpha control thing, he mused.

He also found her overt sense of confidence somewhat unnerving and wondered just what kind of game Alton had signed him up for.

Caleb put his phone away and slipped his glove back on. He waited, listening to the sound of the wind rustling through the trees around him. The dry branches clicked against one another in a cacophony, and he strained to listen for the sound of crunching leaves that might indicate she was nearby.

* * *

Katrina hung up the phone, clicked the mouse to close her browser, and replaced her slippers with running shoes. She considered her jeans and long-sleeved knit shirt in the mirror, ultimately deciding they were perfectly fine for her endeavor.

She grabbed her house key and hurried to the front door. After setting the alarm, she pulled the door closed behind her and took a moment to take in the cold, crisp night air.

It's a beautiful night.

She walked to Caleb's car and paused beside it while smelling the night air, categorizing its scents. Cocking her head to one side, she listened for telltale noises. She walked to the side gate serving as her property's access to the adjacent neighborhood park and paused while smelling near the gate handle, but failed to detect Caleb's scent.

Frowning, she considered other avenues of egress. The only other reasonable place was the driveway gate, and she raced over to it. Instead of using the gate code, she effortlessly leapt over the wrought iron structure. After landing on the other side with catlike reflexes, she sniffed the air for his scent.

However, given the blowing wind and the intelligence of her mate, she anticipated he would be somewhere downwind of her. She listened again for any sounds that might give him away and darted around the area in the fast-moving pace of which only vampires were capable. However, she was careful to be wary of approaching cars or other humans that might be nearby.

She spent almost six minutes moving in a circular pattern hoping for a quick hit on his location before appreciating how challenging her mate's impromptu game was proving to be. Then she paused in the woods, not far from the neighborhood park, and caught a whiff of Caleb's scent. Listening to the rhythm of nature's sounds, she separated them out individually.

Her hearing filtered out the wind, the tree branches hitting against each other, the rustling of leaves, and the flap of an owl's wings as it flew overhead. Abruptly, she picked out the unusual sound of other movement nearby. Something or someone was rustling leaves while moving among the trees less than fifty yards from her.

She heard the sound of a man's voice quietly chuckling and knew immediately it was Caleb. She glanced at her watch to note how much time she had left and stealthily moved towards her target.

* * *

Caleb stood amidst the trees, feeling relatively confident that Katrina was going to run out of time. He quietly and deliberately moved through the woods to ensure he didn't bunker down in one location as Alton had cautioned. Yet he tried to keep noise to a minimum, as well as to stay downwind from the estate to keep his scent from carrying on the breeze.

Glancing down at his watch while activating the glow button, he registered that Katrina had only two more minutes left to locate him. He quietly chuckled, pleased that the first occasion of his new game with her was going so well. He started to relocate to a new position when he heard a strange clicking noise, much like the sound of a clock ticking. He tilted his head to one side and tried to listen closer, but the sound stopped.

"Found you," Katrina's voice cooed in a lilting, teasing tone.

A shiver went up his spine, and he glanced over his shoulder to look behind him with a wide-eyed expression. She stood not thirty feet away with her hands on her hips, staring at him with a sly expression. She opened her mouth slightly and clicked her tongue against her teeth to generate the noise that sounded like a ticking clock.

He bolted away from her as fast as his legs could carry him, not daring to take the time to glance at his watch, and instead concentrated on navigating through the dense trees in as speedy a fashion as possible. If only he could expend just a little more time, maybe the timer would go off before she tagged him.

He hadn't run more than fifty feet before he felt two arms wrap around him like a steel vice, pinning his arms down to his sides.

"Got you!" Katrina exclaimed.

A second later, Caleb's watch emitted a beeping alarm

indicating that time had expired.

She stood with him in her arms, effortlessly lifting him above the ground a few inches, and began walking away with him. His legs swayed back and forth slightly as if she were carrying away an over-sized ragdoll.

"What are you doing?" he demanded with exasperation.

"I'm taking my foot massage trophy home now," she said with an uncustomary giggle.

"Oh, brother," he moaned.

She kissed him on the cheek. "That was fun. I like playing Find Caleb."

He sighed as she hauled him before her, muttering, "Just great."

She giggled and kissed him on the cheek again for good measure.

* * *

On Thursday afternoon, Caleb sat in his office chatting on the phone with Alton to fill him in on the results of his first Find Caleb experience. The vampire was particularly amused, occasionally chuckling as Caleb recounted the event. Alton conceded that Katrina had already spoken with him earlier in the day, but said that he appreciated hearing an alternate perspective of the experience.

"You were very successful, dear boy," he said. "Katrina was quite complimentary regarding your performance, and it seemed to provide her with an enjoyable diversion. We appear to have found a viable outlet for her hunting need. Now simply vary the venue, as well as the prospective rewards."

Caleb blushed. "Heard about the reward, eh? I hadn't anticipated the need for one, actually."

Alton chuckled again. "Well, it seems you have an alternate career option as a masseur."

Caleb groaned.

Then the stately vampire's tone turned serious. "But

really, Caleb, please continue with that regimen, and I believe we can consider the matter successful."

"Thanks for your help, Alton. Oh, and I intend to up the stakes a little by moving my next attempt to someplace more scenic, and hopefully more challenging, for her."

"That sounds fine, young man. Somehow, I anticipated that you might take to this easier than you first expected."

Caleb paused, thinking he heard operatic music in the background.

"Are you at a concert?"

"Actually, the opera," Alton replied. "It's Paisiello's *Fedra*. The intermission's just ending."

Caleb promised to keep Alton informed of his success, and they exchanged hasty goodbyes. Flipping the lid of his cell phone shut, he momentarily marveled at how natural his communications with the English vampire had become.

Barely a year ago he would have considered the very notion of the existence of vampires to be outlandish. However, he had come to embrace not only their existence, but their social importance in his life. He had a vampire mate, a vampire guardian and best friend, and a vampire cultural advisor.

A light knock sounded at his door, breaking his reverie, and he opened it to reveal a friendly acquaintance. Dr. Tanisha Browning was a Professor of Women's History at the college and was just two offices down. She was a petite African American in her early thirties, renowned as one of the most dapperly dressed professors in the Social Sciences Department.

Caleb had formed an immediate respect for the impressive lady. She was intelligent, insightful, and very successful in both her academic and personal endeavors. Dr. Browning was also a keen judge of character, helpfully steering Caleb away from a couple of potential troublemakers in the division.

Tanisha flashed a disarming smile at him and teased, "Hiding from the students again, Caleb?"

He grinned. "Me, hide? Well, now that you're here, I guess it's safe to open my door again."

The hazel-eyed professor had a reputation among her students of being a fair, but challenging instructor. And it was well-known that she didn't accept excuses for poor performance. However, she had earned a great deal of respect from both her students and her peers over the years. Caleb envied how her former students were among her biggest fans.

Dr. Browning adopted a suspicious expression as her eyes darted around her, and she mocked, "Hey, don't say that too loudly, or they'll come looking for me too."

He chuckled.

"Actually, your arrival is perfect timing. I was planning to stop by your office this afternoon because I have a small favor to ask," he said. "And it's no problem if you say no, because I know it's short notice."

"Which is just as it should be," she replied. "Ask away, Caleb."

"I'm planning a surprise for Katrina tomorrow night at the Arabia Mountain Heritage Preserve, and I want to know if you'll drop me off there?" he asked. "I know this sounds odd, but I was hoping for Katrina and me to make the journey back home together, which wouldn't be possible if I also drove there."

He had selected the Arabia Mountain Heritage Preserve because it was quite scenic and located within a twenty-minute drive of Atlanta near the town of Lithonia. The two thousand-acre site sported wetlands, pine and oak forests, two scenic mountain tops, streams, and a lake, all of which seemed an ideally challenging environment for Katrina.

"Is there a reason you're not going together?" she asked.

"Uh, well, I wanted to scope out camping locations for us ahead of time," he said.

Tanisha considered him for a moment. "Or if you prefer, I could drop Katrina off for you while you made your way there in your car. Then she wouldn't have to drive."

He smirked. "True. But I think Katrina's going to want

to drive herself."

A knowing smile formed on her lips. "Ah, yes. Katrina certainly seems to enjoy the driver's seat."

He nodded, noting her innuendo. "Katrina's more comfortable being in control."

Her expression turned curious. "You seem pretty easy-going, Caleb, but does it ever bother you that Katrina's the way she is?"

His eyebrows rose as he stared into her eyes. "To tell you the truth, Tanisha, I'm okay with it most of the time."

She smirked. "William and I were talking about you two just the other night. You and Katrina seem to have a very caring dynamic, and I'd venture you're both in love, but I get the impression you two have a somewhat unconventional relationship."

Caleb considered it was a pretty good read on Tanisha's part. He and Katrina had attended both a movie premiere and a jazz concert with Tanisha and her husband during the past two weeks and he was gratified to find that all four of them seemed to get along quite well.

"Conventional is an antiquated term, don't you think?" he countered. "There's usually more to a couple's relationship than what's presented to the outside world. There is always something that's only known between just those two people. What's important is that a couple arrives at mutually agreeable terms for the structure of their relationship."

"So true," she readily agreed, but frowned. "However, I'm usually pretty good at reading people, and I think Katrina has more than just a protective nature about you."

Caleb tensed slightly as he considered the direction in which the conversation was going.

"It's subtle, but I noticed a couple of times that her eyes follow you when you're across the room from her. It's like she always has you on her radar. Take the other night at the movie theater, for example. Katrina and I were chatting near the refreshments area waiting for you and William to return from the restroom, when three rough-looking young men walked into the lobby. You exited the restroom just as those guys walked past you. Well, one of them bumped your shoulder as he passed, and I noticed Katrina's eyes narrow. The way the light caught them, I thought for just a second her eyes were almost glowing."

Caleb's expression turned serious, and he listened closely to what Tanisha was telling him. It was something Katrina hadn't mentioned from that night.

She continued, "It was just an effect of the lobby lights, I'm sure. But her expression made me think, just for an instant, mind you, that she was ready to plow through a lobby full of people just to get to you. It was like she was a canon ready to fire, you know? Frankly, she looked dangerous."

He nodded and tried to appear only casually interested in what she was telling him. But inside, his mind was racing as he easily imagined the event. Although it wasn't as if he had never seen Katrina with a dangerous look about her, either. He reflected on how intimidating and feral she could appear when provoked or angry.

But then, that's an alpha vampire for you.

Tanisha laughed. "Well, I was thinking I would hate to be the person who tried to hurt you. Katrina suddenly seemed to be wired as tightly as an attack dog."

He grinned, "Well, it's true that her martial arts knowledge would come in handy in a dark alley."

Her expression turned more serious and introspective, and she asked, "Caleb, was Katrina ever in the military or law enforcement?"

"No, not that I know of. Why do you ask?"

She shrugged. "No reason. I have a younger brother, Richard, who's an Army Ranger, and he gets that same look in his eyes sometimes. He's seen some heavy combat duty in Afghanistan and Iraq, and once in a while he can almost appear scary to me. I thought that a couple of Katrina's expressions reminded me of Richard's."

Caleb reassured her, "Nope, no combat zones for Katrina. She's the most loving, gentle, and kindest woman

I've ever known. But I suppose that, much like any of us, Kat probably has a dark side."

His thoughts mulled over what Tanisha said, and he confessed that Katrina intimidated him on rare occasions as well. Yet, he loved her more than life itself. Moreover, he had to be on guard that his conversations with Tanisha stayed well away from any hint of his mate's vampire nature. Rule number one of his oath to Katrina was to ensure he never revealed her true identity to anyone.

However, it wasn't as if the other six rules were any less important to him. He was ready to reveal to Katrina any knowledge or suspicion of anyone who might have determined her true existence or nature. He would never willingly give or submit himself to another vampire. And he certainly would only partake in Katrina's blood when she offered it to him.

That's handy, he thought, recalling how her blood had saved him from possibly dying of a horrible case of the 'flu.

As for the fifth rule, he was not to accept blood from another vampire. The only problem he found with that rule was that Katrina had allowed Paige to give her blood to him to save his life after he had given too much of his own blood to heal Katrina's injuries.

Obviously, exceptions exist.

The last two rules seemed ominous to him. Rule six: he must never ask to become a vampire. That effectively prevented him from joining Katrina for eternity. It was painful to think that he had to endure a vulnerable, finite lifespan that would ultimately set her free from their mate-bond. The very thought was nearly painful to contemplate. Finally, rule seven: he must never lie to Katrina in matters concerning any of the aforementioned rules.

And that was it in a nutshell: the seven rules he was bound to and had sworn an oath to Katrina to uphold. He sighed and realized Tanisha was staring at him intently.

"Caleb? Are you okay?"

He blinked. "What?" he asked. "Sorry, I was distracted

by something you said about your brother. That must be tough being stuck in a warzone twenty-four hours a day, seven days a week until you're given permission to rotate out."

Tanisha nodded with a curious expression. "Listen Caleb, I'll be happy to drop you off at Arabia Mountain if you'll just answer one question for me."

He raised an eyebrow suspiciously. "Okay."

She stared directly into his eyes and drew out each word carefully, "Are you in a happy and healthy relationship with Katrina?"

He was taken aback by the nature of her question, and he blinked once as her question fully registered in his mind.

What an odd question.

He wasn't exactly sure what constituted healthy, but he was happier than he had ever been with someone his entire life.

Healthy? Katrina makes me feel loved, protected, and encouraged. She's someone who's willing to accept me just as I am without condition. And I feel desired and needed by her.

A sincere smile formed on his lips as he looked back at her with a determined expression. "Tanisha, I can answer you with a resounding yes to both qualifiers. My relationship with Katrina is the best thing that's ever happened to me, and I'm completely in love with her."

The sage-looking professor merely sighed. "Okay, Caleb. You've secured your ride for tomorrow. And I'm happy for you regarding Katrina. But if you come to work with two black eyes someday, I'm calling the cops on your behalf."

His smile faded somewhat, and he wondered how to respond as his pulse increased slightly.

But before he could speak, she winked at him with a grin. "I'm just having fun at your expense, Caleb."

Relief surged through him, and his grin quickly returned in earnest. After providing Tanisha with the details for Friday, he taught his two evening classes and headed home.

During the drive to the estate, he kept thinking about the

conversation he had had with Tanisha. The woman had a knack for keen observation, and he sighed with the realization that he would have to be careful regarding both what and how he spoke with her regarding Katrina. He began to realize the full impact and weight of Katrina's rules and how difficult befriending other humans could become. Since meeting his mate, he had only maintained sparse contact with his old friends, all of whom had either moved away or returned to other parts of the country following college.

Tanisha was the first human he had formed a close contact with since college, and he already felt wary and pensive about it. His closest relationships since meeting Katrina had been formed exclusively with vampires, although that didn't bother him in the slightest.

When he walked into the house from the garage, he heard Katrina's voice coming from the kitchen. She was talking on the phone while sitting at the kitchen counter, looking cute in her cotton sweats and thick, fuzzy socks. She smiled at him and quickly kissed him on the lips while listening to the phone.

Caleb continued through the kitchen and casually mentioned, "I had a nice chat with Tanisha Browning this evening. She said if I come to work with black eyes, she's calling the police on you."

"Excuse me?" Katrina demanded abruptly.

"I'm going to take a shower," he muttered as he walked down the hallway wearing a mischievous grin, knowing full well he would have to explain himself later, but wanting to have some fun first.

He heard Katrina ask irritably, "Just what the hell's so funny, Paige?"

Later that evening, Caleb slipped beneath the cool sheets of their king-sized bed and turned out the lamp on his nightstand. The lamp on Katrina's nightstand cast only a dim glow in the sublevel room. He lay with his eyes closed for a short time before hearing the pocket door at the top of the stairs open and close again.

He waited and felt someone sit beside him on the edge of the bed. The soothing scent of cherry blossoms, Katrina's favorite, permeated the air.

"I know you're not asleep yet, my love," she whispered.

He smirked and slowly opened his eyes to stare into her lovely emerald irises. Her tight-lipped expression spoke volumes regarding her concern.

"I love you," he offered earnestly. "No matter how unconventional our relationship is."

Katrina frowned, and he recounted the conversation he had with Tanisha. When he finished, her expression appeared more relaxed.

"I'll also need to be more careful around her in the future," she noted.

"Tanisha means well," he said. "And I think we're becoming fast friends."

"Hm. Be cautious, as you should with all other humans."

"I will."

Her expression turned thoughtful. "Caleb, are you truly happy being with me?"

His heart skipped a beat, and his pulse increased anxiously. "Of course, I am," he stammered while raising himself up on his elbows. "Why would you even ask me that?"

She smiled at him adoringly and gently caressed her fingertips against the side of his face.

Because I want you to be happy.

"Just checking," she said simply.

He frowned and lay back on the bed while absently grasping the pendant he wore around his neck. His lack of self-confidence bothered him at that moment.

She noted his gesture and reached out to take his hand in hers as he fingered the pendant. "I'm yours forever, my love," she stated resolutely. "You never have to question that."

Caleb nodded as he lay back against the soft pillow behind him. She leaned down and kissed him affectionately, which he returned in kind.

"And?" he teased as he flicked his pendant between his fingers. "Anything else?"

She adopted an aggressive expression, and her hand firmly cupped the base of his neck. She placed her lips against his and stated, "You're mine, Caleb Taylor. And don't you ever forget it."

A rush of excitement coursed through him, and he only had a second to smile before she kissed him passionately.

Unconventional suits me just fine, he mused.

CHAPTER 2

Unwanted Notoriety

"Daytime again," Katrina lamented while sitting at her computer in the sublevel room, or rather, her chamber. She finished putting her long red hair in a ponytail and stared at the computer screen while toying absently with the sterling pendant around her neck that commemorated her commitment to Caleb.

As she finished reviewing a list of books she was interested in ordering from an online bookseller, her thoughts drifted to her sandy-haired young mate.

Caleb was so kind, gentle, and caring towards her, like her late husband, Samuel, who had died over five hundred years ago when she was just a human herself. To Katrina, Caleb was the complete package as a mate, and she loved him dearly. As she narrowed her book selections, she fondly smiled at how happy he made her.

So much like Samuel, and yet, so different. But in a good way.

She refocused her attentions on the online order before her. The first book was a biography on the life of Theodore Roosevelt, which she could discuss at length with Caleb. She enjoyed their history-related conversations, being an amateur historian herself.

Face it, survive five hundred years, and by natural selection, you're a historian.

She fondly recalled taking Caleb's introductory history class the previous fall semester and the subsequent attraction she had felt towards him from that first day. Frankly, she had been caught off guard by that initial spark of desire for him.

The other book she ordered was a romance novel set in the late eighteenth century. She had been a vampire since the 1530s, so it was a period she recalled vividly, though without many of the glamorized trappings presented in historical romance fiction. Still, she had a soft spot for the genre and smiled at how Caleb would likely tease her over that.

Alpha vampire and romance reader.

Yet I'm a woman. I deserve occasional romance, right?

She had tried to demonstrate that to Caleb regularly and openly, mainly so he wouldn't be intimidated by her.

However, being a woman doesn't mean being a pushover.

Fortunately for her, Caleb wasn't someone who challenged her for the alpha role. And while she wanted to claim that her commanding nature was important in order to protect him better, she admitted that she enjoyed being in control.

Thankfully, he doesn't seem to mind that either, she thought with a smirk. *He even seemed to enjoy it at times.*

Yes, he's so unlike my previous relationships.

She moved quickly from browsing the Internet, which was undoubtedly one of her favorite pastimes, to reading new emails. She read some jokes that Paige passed along, including viewing a humorous video of someone falling off of a ladder in a buffoonish manner while painting his house.

There was another series of emails similar in tone to others she had been receiving for weeks. Most were from vampires with whom she hadn't previously corresponded. Each congratulated her on killing Chimalma or asked for further details of her exploits in doing so. Frankly, she was happy to leave the entire affair in her past, as those horrific events had nearly brought about her demise, and more importantly, Caleb's.

Still, she went through the process of responding to each message, as she had nothing more pressing on her agenda. She was merely passing time until Caleb called to inform her about the mysterious plans he had for them that evening.

Lately, he had been very creative about their time together, and she approved of his most recent game, Find Caleb. Despite having only played once, she was already looking forward to future activities in that same vein.

* * *

As agreed the day before, Tanisha waited a little longer at her office than planned that Friday afternoon in order to transport Caleb to the Arabia Mountain Heritage Area.

He removed a medium-sized backpack, heavy brown winter coat, and rolled-up sleeping bag from the trunk of his Honda Civic and transferred it into the back of Tanisha's light brown Cadillac Escalade.

"That's all you're bringing?" she asked.

"Yep," he replied. He glanced overhead at the sunny sky, appreciating the favorable weather conditions.

Once inside, he took a moment to appreciate the regal interior of the vehicle and the comfortable seating. It made his older-model Civic seem like a horse-drawn carriage. He smirked at how odd Katrina's garage looked with his car parked next to her sleek Audi.

Maybe with the money I've been saving from sharing expenses with her, I'll be able to trade in my car on a new one in the next year or so.

"Nice ride," he said.

She smirked as the Escalade's engine purred to life. "Thanks. William teased me when he bought it, saying his African Queen had to travel in style."

Caleb grinned, recalling that he had called Katrina a "Queen of the Vampires" not so long ago.

"Not that I'm complaining, mind you," Tanisha added with a sober expression. "A little respectful attention is a proper way to treat a woman."

"Ah, so William calls you his queen, then?" he teased.

She grinned slyly as they pulled out of the parking lot. "Mm-hm. He's a caring and loving man, my Will. He still courts me even after ten years of marriage. But it probably isn't like with you and Katrina. We're a little more…"

"Conventional?" he interrupted with a grin.

"Hey, I'm not judging anybody."

He shook his head as they made their way to the highway for the short trip to Lithonia.

It was late afternoon when Tanisha pulled up at the side of Klondike Road, adjacent to the preserve. Caleb thanked her and reassured her that Katrina would be joining him very soon. After he removed his sleeping bag and backpack from the Escalade, he waved goodbye and watched her turn around and drive away. He briefly considered how well things were going with him and Tanisha and how he was thoroughly enjoying getting to know her.

He turned and headed towards an area where the forest was growing thicker. His plan was to transfer his scent to a number of surfaces, including large rocks and trees, so he could confuse Katrina from going directly to his location once she arrived.

There weren't many people around on that cold, late January afternoon, which suited him just fine as he was enjoying the peace and quiet. As he trudged amidst the lush pine trees, he realized it was time to call Katrina to reveal the location of their evening plans.

He was thankful to see he still had two bars of signal strength on his cell phone.

Didn't think about that beforehand.

He made a mental note to verify cell phone availability in future Find Caleb locations. Safety was a condition Katrina insisted upon, and he didn't want to cause her undue worry by overlooking something essential.

The phone only rang once before she picked up, and he smiled.

That was fast.

"Caleb?" she asked.

"Hi, Kat," he greeted. "Tonight, it's time for another exciting episode of Find Caleb. I hope you're feeling up to it."

He thought he heard a brief, uncharacteristic giggle at the other end. "I'm always ready to find Caleb. Where's the location, and what are we playing for tonight?"

He was pleased to hear the anticipation in her voice, and he realized he was as excited to take part as she seemed to be.

Alton was correct, after all.

"Tonight's hunt takes place at the Arabia Mountain Heritage Park and Nature Preserve. It's less than half an hour's drive via highway from the estate, and even during the winter, it's a beautiful location. The game starts as soon as you arrive, and tonight we're playing for an all-over body massage!"

She snickered. "Okay. Time limit?"

"You have until daybreak," he said smugly.

"Daybreak?" she asked with surprise.

Just where the heck is this place?

He heard her typing furiously on her keyboard, followed by rapid mouse clicking sounds. Initially, he had been surprised that Katrina was so very tech-savvy, because he had always envisioned vampires as Old-World beings. He quickly learned that vampires utilized technology to the best of their advantage. They had to keep up with human society in all areas if they were expected to survive and maintain their anonymity.

"Caleb!" she exclaimed, "There's nearly two thousand acres for me to search!"

That's a hell of a leap from the woods near our house, she fumed.

"It should be a challenge," he conceded. "But you have all night, and I've seen you move, or more pointedly, not seen you move. You're fast and can cover a lot of ground in a short time."

She sighed, though he wasn't sure if it were with resignation or disapproval, and he frowned. He wanted her to have both an enjoyable and challenging experience.

"It's supposed to be cold tonight, Caleb," she warned. "Are you sure you're prepared?"

"Oh, yes," he assured her. "I brought water, some snacks, a sleeping bag, and even some of those chemical warmers for camping. I also have some pepper spray in case I run into any unfriendly wild animals."

Silence.

"Pepper spray, huh? Hm. Well, okay. But if I haven't located you by 4 AM, or if anything feels dangerous, you'd better be signaling me somehow."

"I can agree to that," he replied.

"It wasn't a negotiable request, my love," she stated emphatically.

Your safety is paramount to me, silly man, she thought while shaking her head.

He swallowed and amended his statement with, "Understood."

"Much better," she said in a more upbeat tone of voice. "I'll be there just after sundown. Be careful. Love you."

He smirked as the line went dead and tucked his cell phone into his belt holder. Then he went about covering as much territory as possible, spreading his scent around by brushing against trees and other surfaces.

By the time evening fell, it had turned very dark in the preserve. His scent-spreading efforts tired him out, so he stopped in a densely wooded area to eat some trail mix and drink some water. He was thankful he had packed a few bottles of water in his backpack.

The nighttime air had a definite chill to it, and while activating a chemical hand warmer to place inside his winter coat, he mentally congratulated himself on bringing them. Fortunately, the cotton-lined leather gloves that he wore were doing an excellent job of keeping his hands warm.

He decided to trudge around a little more in order to stay warm and proceeded out of the trees and down a nearby hiking trail that led towards a high peak on the east side of the preserve. Despite the cool conditions, he thoroughly enjoyed the outdoors and was pleased he had selected the venue for their latest challenge.

As time passed, he contemplated the relationship he had formed with Katrina. It was so different from any he had experienced with other women. He was unused to being the focus of her attentions, and despite her tendency to be overly protective and somewhat commanding at times, he nevertheless loved her for it.

There seemed to be nothing he wouldn't try to make her happy, including trudging around in cold, remote areas of Georgia during wintertime.

He glanced at his watch with a yawn, realizing nearly two hours had passed since he had last spoken with Katrina.

Surely she's at the preserve by now.

He felt a surge of adrenaline reinvigorate his system and tried to listen more closely to the sounds around him. He considered that he needed to keep more to the trees so she wouldn't easily see him and focused on trying to move more stealthily.

Still, there's a lot of territory for her to cover, and she may be miles away from me right now.

After no more than half an hour of quietly maneuvering between pine trees and listening for unusual noises, Caleb settled down a few feet into the trees from a nearby hiking trail and laid out his sleeping bag to try to rest up a little.

The cool winter air penetrated his jacket, and he activated another hand warmer, slipping the spent one he replaced into his pack. He absently placed his backpack against the trunk of a large pine tree. He unwound his sleeping bag, slipped into it, and sat up with his back against the same tree.

Zipping the sleeping bag closed, he was able to hide most of his face inside the enclosure for warmth.

As he listened closely to the natural sounds around him, he failed to notice when he was lulled asleep.

"Well, what have we here?" a deep voice resonated as he lurched awake.

Caleb squinted into the darkness to see a large man towering above him. His heart rate soared instantly, as he was completely surprised that anyone else besides him or Katrina might be trudging around the preserve in the middle of a cold January night.

Maybe a park ranger, he wondered.

"I didn't expect campers out here during winter," the baritone voice observed. "But then, I haven't been hunting around here for very long, either."

A hunter then, Caleb mused.

"You startled me," he said as he unzipped his sleeping bag. "I was just resting, but I'll be on my way now."

The tall man chuckled. "No need to leave on my account."

Caleb tried to focus on the man before him. Although it was dark, he distinguished blue jeans and a dark-colored sweater, though he wasn't wearing a winter coat or gloves. He appeared to be sturdy-framed, broad-shouldered, and African-American by his dark skin tone. A final quality sent a shiver through Caleb's body: the man had glowing violet eyes.

A vampire, he gasped with realization. *What are the odds?*

The vampire emitted another deep chuckle, and a scowl showed on his face as he perched his large hands atop his hips, glowering at Caleb from above.

"You're a vampire," Caleb muttered with as much reassurance in his voice as he could muster, fully realizing his revelation wasn't a positive one.

The vampire's scowl faded abruptly, and his arms went out to his sides in an aggressive posture as he demanded, "How so?"

"Your eyes," Caleb said as he slipped his hands from his gloves and grasped a small can of pepper spray in his jacket pocket. "The glowing eyes are a dead giveaway."

"Just how do you know so much about vampires?" the figure demanded.

Caleb turned on a small flashlight with his left hand and saw that the vampire's expression appeared unsettled. "I'm a vampire's mate," he announced boldly.

"Oh, really?" he asked with a white-toothed smile, revealing pronounced fangs. "And just who might that be?"

"Katrina Rawlings," he stated calmly despite his turbulent emotions.

The tall figure frowned, and his violet eyes narrowed slightly. "Seems like I've heard that name somewhere," he growled.

"My name's Caleb. Caleb Taylor."

The vampire squatted down to look him in the eye. "Devon Archibald, although it's not really going to matter much in a few more minutes."

Caleb's eyes widened, and he pressed, "Wait! I already told you I'm a vampire's mate."

Devon smirked and made an elaborate gesture of looking to his left and then to his right. "Well, where is she? I don't see, or sense, any other vampires besides me," he challenged. "I've been here since just after sundown looking for wild game and haven't seen anyone else but you."

"She's here somewhere," Caleb promised. "We're just playing a hunting game."

Devon grinned. "It looks like I won. Well, small game is better than no game."

Caleb's heart nearly stopped, and he immediately made an effort to glance past the man's shoulder as if recognizing someone. The hulking vampire frowned and glanced over his shoulder for just a second, giving him the time he needed to withdraw the pepper spray from his pocket. As Devon turned back to him with a frown, Caleb activated the dispenser, spraying the vampire's face.

Devon growled angrily, and his hands went to his eyes as Caleb launched himself up from the sleeping bag and lurched onto the hiking trail, using his flashlight to light the path before him.

"Ka-trin-a! KAT!!" Caleb shouted desperately from the top of his lungs as his heart pounded away in his chest. "Need help, Kat!!"

As he ran, horrific fear raced through his mind that perhaps she wasn't nearby, or worse, not even at the preserve.

But she has to be, or she would've called me by now!

His thoughts quickly returned to his current situation and his desperation to be as far from the hulking vampire as possible. He gripped the pepper spray tightly in his right hand as he ran frantically along the hiking path. He considered glancing over his shoulder behind him, but decided to keep running instead.

"Ka—" he started to yell before being knocked to the ground from behind.

The pepper spray flew from his hand, but he managed to hold onto the flashlight as he hit the hard, uneven ground before him with a thud. His body no sooner hit the ground before he felt a huge hand wrap around the back of his neck, hauling him upright as he struggled to get his footing so his weight wasn't being suspended from his neck alone.

His right hand darted to the vampire's grip on his neck as he clawed futilely to pry his attacker's hand loose.

"That was stupid!" Devon barked. "And now we end this."

Caleb was frantic, and his mind was a flurry of thoughts. His right hand slipped into his front jeans pocket, and he managed to extract his small pocket knife. The small blade was only a couple of inches long, but was easy to use because it had a thumb release on it.

"You better not!" he yelled, stalling for precious time as he stealthily opened the pocket knife. "Katrina's an alpha!"

"What?" Devon demanded.

Caleb tried kicking at the vampire's knees from behind, but he couldn't get a proper angle to be effective. He felt Devon's hot breath at the back of his neck, and he tensed his body, bracing himself for the painful tearing of his flesh that he recalled from Katrina's involuntary attack.

In a last-ditch effort for freedom, he swept the knife blade backwards and slammed it into the vampire's upper right thigh, burying the short blade to the hilt. The dark, towering figure howled with pain as he abruptly released Caleb's neck.

Caleb immediately darted up the trail with speed born of a fear-induced adrenaline rush, yelling, "KAT!"

His feet seemed barely to touch the earth as he darted across the uneven ground and around the abrupt turns in the trail. The light from his flashlight bounced frantically in front of him, but he hoped it would provide an additional indicator to Katrina of his changing location. Given that vampires could see in the dark, it was a moot point to avoid using the flashlight to elude his pursuer. Besides, he needed the benefit of seeing the path before him as clearly as possible.

Caleb's heart pounded as he ran through the night, and for a brief moment he thought he could get free. He wasn't certain how far or for how long he had been running. Time seemed suspended as the cold winter breeze chilled the skin on his face, and his lungs felt as if they were on fire.

He thought he heard a rustling in the night to his right and glanced in that direction for only a second, though he saw nothing. His body shook to an abrupt halt as it felt like a tree limb fell across his chest. He had only a vague sensation of falling backwards as his body plummeted downwards, and the breath was knocked from his lungs.

His back impacted with the cold, hard ground with a bone-jarring thud, and he thought he heard a gruff chuckle. He realized he was lying in darkness, uncertain as to what happened to the small flashlight. He felt his left leg being hauled upwards, and his body was being dragged across the ground.

He managed to force air back into his lungs, although the effort sent pain coursing through his chest. As the back of his head bounced across the hard turf, he reared back with his right leg and savagely kicked at the figure pulling on his other leg.

The heel of his boot impacted with something solid, and a growl emitted from above him. But instead of his left leg being released, his body was lifted into the air and abruptly slammed painfully back onto the ground, again knocking the breath from his lungs.

Pain coursed through his body, and he felt a wave of nausea roll through his stomach. A hard set of fingers grabbed his hair from behind and drew him face-up from the ground, sending a fresh wave of pain through his neck and shoulders. He managed to use his aching arms to push himself up from the ground, while at the same time he felt a knee press into his lower back. His body was spent, and all that he wanted was for the pain to stop. Mercifully, he began to feel himself losing consciousness.

"I love you, Kat," he whispered desperately as he willed his final thoughts to be of the woman he loved.

His body was dropped face-forward back onto the ground following the sound of a speeding truck impacting a meaty wall. He managed to keep his face from impacting the cold earth as he heard intense hissing and snarling and what sounded like breaking tree branches.

He reached behind him to rub at the back of his head with his right hand as he tried to focus on the commotion going on in the darkness around him.

He managed to spot his flashlight on the ground nearby and painfully crawled over to it. Grasping it tightly in his hand, he shined it in the direction of the hissing and growling.

Caleb watched as the burly vampire rushed at Katrina only to crash into the trunk of a large pine tree as she darted to the side. She raked some sort of blade across his upper shoulder and darted just out of arm's reach. Devon roared with rage and rushed her.

It appeared that, while very fast compared to a human, the large-framed vampire's dexterity was much slower and more sluggish than hers. The advantage was clearly in Katrina's favor, and she used each opportunity either to slash or stab her blade into her opponent.

To Caleb's confusion, each cut or stab she used seemed intended upon progressively disabling her opponent without actually making a fatal killing strike.

A loud snapping sound startled him as he propped himself up with difficulty. He heard a whooshing noise followed by the sound of another tree trunk's breaking. With a sudden burst of speed, Katrina appeared less than twenty feet from Caleb in some sort of combat stance, wielding a large military-style knife in her hand.

He spotted Devon standing beyond her as he brandished part of a tree limb in his right hand. The huge vampire was dripping blood from multiple locations on his body, including a steady stream oozing down his dangling left arm and dripping off of the fingers of his hand.

"This was a mistake!" the hulking vampire barked as his violet eyes burned brightly in the darkness. "He was easy prey, that's all!"

"Did he tell you he was a vampire's mate?" she demanded savagely.

"Maybe he said something about that," Devon countered. "But I didn't believe he was telling the truth at the time."

Her eyes blazed bright green as she decreed in a cruel, flat voice, "Your last mistake."

"Whoa, whoa!" Devon insisted as he held the tree limb out to his side in a less aggressive stance. "Let's just calm down. This was all a horrible misunderstanding!"

Caleb issued a dry-throated cough and rasped, "You shouldn't threaten her with a tree branch, idiot."

His mind flashed to the time Katrina had revealed her vampire nature to him, and he had fearfully brandished a tree branch at her. She had neatly disarmed him, although at the time she had meant him no harm, unlike with the vampire before her.

"Huh?" the large vampire asked with barely a glance at Caleb.

Devon tossed the branch down beside him and held his hands up in a more peaceable gesture towards Katrina, who seemed to be selecting the optimum moment to attack. "Please, just for a moment, let's just stop," he entreated.

"You didn't grant Caleb that benefit a moment ago," she noted in a flat, lethal voice. Her focus swtiched to dispatching the opposing vampire and seeing to Caleb's injuries as soon as possible.

The vampire's eyes momentarily flashed with surprise, and he apologized, "No, you're right. That was a bad mistake, and I'm sorry. This doesn't need to get ugly for either of us. Really."

"You don't know ugly yet," she seethed through fury-lit eyes as she maneuvered closer to the hulking vampire. She had selected the preferred entry point under his guard and was ready to initiate a killing blow.

"I told you she was an alpha," Caleb spat with satisfaction, though his mind felt hazy and dazed. He managed to sit upright on the ground, despite the ribs on his right side's aching terribly. Pain coursed through his body.

Devon nodded and chuckled nervously. "Yeah, I'm seeing that now. But this is all wrong. I'm willing to make good on this and let bygones be bygones."

Katrina's mouth upturned in a cruel fashion as she maintained her combat stance and expertly brandished her knife in her right hand. Another minute, and she could focus all of her attentions on helping Caleb. "Goodbye," she whispered under her breath as she darted forward.

Devon saw Katrina's body in action and barked, "Please! Listen!"

Katrina scowled cruelly and lunged at the vampire as she shouted, "Too late!"

She darted around to Devon's left side, and her knife thrust underneath his injured left arm and upwards to his exposed throat. The huge vampire's eyes widened and pleaded to her as his arms went up over his head in surrender.

Just as Katrina's knife blade touched Devon's neck, she hesitated and stopped her intended killing strike. There was something about his eyes that made her pause, though she was on guard for any trickery. She felt confident that in his injured stated he would be of little challenge if she changed her mind. Her eyes darted to Caleb to make sure that he seemed stable.

Devon soberly regarded his opponent as he gauged the dangerous and feral nature of the red-haired vampire before him.

"My name is Devon Archibald, just as I introduced myself to your mate over there. I've just recently relocated to the Marietta area from Richmond, Virginia, and I had no idea this was your territory. I don't want to start any trouble with regional vampires."

Katrina regarded him dubiously.

"Please. I'll abide by any territorial claims you make, and I can even be helpful enforcing your interests, if necessary," Devon offered in a gruff voice.

"My primary interest is that man over there, my mate," she seethed, gesturing towards Caleb.

Caleb tried to stand and managed to stagger to his feet. Excruciating pain shot through his back, ribs, and chest, and he was forced to drop back to his knees onto the cold, hard ground. Both vampires regarded him for only a moment, though Katrina's gaze lingered for a second longer before returning to Devon.

"I offer my sincerest apologies for the misunderstanding. I promise it'll never happen again," he insisted before turning his attention to Caleb. "Besides, he looks hurt, and I can't afford for him to die on me now."

Caleb noticed Katrina's blazing eyes focusing on him again, and he thought he saw a worried expression wash across her features. Unfortunately, he felt like he was starting to black out, and he pressed his palms to the cool earth beneath him while lowering his head.

Katrina shot a dark look at Devon and carefully moved to where Caleb was on all fours. Her right hand brandished the combat knife while her left hand reached down to press softly on his shoulder.

"Lie down on the ground and try not to move until I can look at your injuries, my love."

He nodded, slowly lying on his side, and then curled up in his coat while hugging his ribs. He felt numb all over, and his head was throbbing as a mix of dull aches and sharp pains coursed through his chest, back, and ribs.

Katrina's attention returned to Devon, where the large-framed vampire was still standing statue-still. His face appeared calm but haggard, and he leaned heavily to his right to favor his injured left leg.

She worried about Caleb's condition, and she berated herself for not having killed Devon already. But for some reason, she felt like she could turn this situation to both hers and Caleb's advantage.

"I concede the fight," he declared. "And I'll honor terms to you, if you'll just agree to a truce."

She frowned and momentarily reconsidered the merits of arriving at some agreement. Her more immediate concern was to aid Caleb, and any further issues with Devon could be handled at a later time, if necessary. "Very well," she agreed warily. "We will finalize matters later. Expect to hear from me soon, Devon Archibald."

Devon's eyes darted to Caleb where he was lying on the ground nearby and back to Katrina. "Understood," he agreed. "And once again, I apologize for the misunderstanding. I invite you to Marietta, where you must grant me the opportunity to solidify an agreement and reintroduce myself in a proper fashion."

Katrina nodded curtly, and Devon turned to depart into the thick pine trees next to the trail. But then he stopped and looked at Katrina with eyes that no longer glowed. "My word is honorable," he insisted. "What was your name again? Your mate mentioned it, but I don't recall."

"Katrina Rawlings of the Atlanta area."

Devon's eyes widened. "Wait, the one that killed the Aztec who was murdering other vampires?"

Katrina's face turned stony, but she nodded. "That's me."

Devon sighed, shook his head, and muttered, "Yeah, just

my luck." He turned to look at Caleb and offered, "My respects to him. I've never encountered a human who fought so hard before. He's a tough little bastard, and he gave almost as good as he got."

Katrina scowled. "I'm sure he's happy to hear that."

"Thanks, asshole," was all Caleb managed to rasp in response as he glared at the vampire from where he lay on the ground.

Devon frowned deeply, turned away from them, and disappeared quietly into the forest. Caleb blinked, and when his eyes opened again the hulking vampire was nowhere to be seen. A fresh wave of pain shot through his ribs as he tried to take a deep breath, and his head felt woozy and ached.

Katrina moved in a blur as she both sheathed her knife and sped to Caleb's side. She knelt beside her prone mate with a concerned expression, removed the leather jacket she'd been wearing, and laid it over his prone form.

"Everything will be okay, my love," she tried to reassure him.

I'm taking care of you.

He murmured something unintelligible and escaped the continued pain by welcoming the darkness as it finally overcame him.

* * *

Caleb heard Katrina's voice talking when he regained consciousness, though he couldn't immediately understand what was being said. He shifted his body slightly, resulting in pain, and realized he was lying in a bed. He slowly opened his eyes to discover the room was dimly lit, and he recognized the estate's sublevel room.

He moaned while lifting his hand to his head as dull aching persisted behind his eyes, which he closed tightly.

"I have to go, Alton. He's finally awake," Katrina urged in a near whisper. "I'll call you soon."

Caleb felt the edge of the bed shift next to him, and he

opened his eyes to see Katrina sitting beside him in a pair of cotton lounge pants and a t-shirt. Her gentle fingers caressed the skin on the side of his face, and her warm smile soothed him.

"Welcome back, my love," she offered.

I'm relieved he's finally regained consciousness.

She was confident his body was healing, but worried he might have a mild concussion.

He felt disoriented and somewhat confused as he tried recalling anything beyond blacking out on the hard ground in the forest, but nothing came to mind.

"What happened?" he asked. "How long have I been out?"

"Twelve hours or more," she replied. "How do you feel?"

He tried to swallow and noticed his throat felt raw. "Like hell, but better than back at the forest."

She retrieved a glass of ice water from the nightstand, and he noticed a blood-tinged syringe lying nearby. His eyes met hers with a curious expression.

"How bad was I?" he asked before drinking greedily. He realized from the syringe that she must have injected him with some of her blood.

"Bad enough, my love. You had a couple of broken ribs, likely a mild concussion, and I'm fairly sure from the sounds in your chest that you had fluid in one lung," she replied grimly.

"Holy crap," he muttered. He had no idea his body had endured that level of punishment.

"I should have killed him," she half-lamented.

"You didn't?" he asked with a frown. "I only remember lying on the ground and blacking out."

She explained how she agreed to a truce and Devon's promise to establish an agreement for restitution with her. What concerned her was that he had no recollection of any of that dialogue, although he had seemed semi-conscious at the time.

"You took a lot more punishment than I thought," she said. "What do you remember?"

A pang of guilt flowed through her as she wished she had been faster in tracking him down when she heard him shouting her name in the distance.

He described his encounter with the hulking vampire, including as much of the dialogue as he could recall. He told her how he initially used pepper spray against Devon, followed by his pocket knife to stab him in the leg, and finally his attempt to kick him in the knee or groin to try temporarily disabling him.

She adopted a look of approval, admiring his tenacity and fortitude, though surprised he had engaged in so many melees with Devon. "So that's why you're a 'tough little bastard,' then," she surmised. "I'm proud of you, my love. It probably saved your life until I was able to find you."

He grimaced. "Great. I got my ass kicked by another vampire. Real valiant, that was."

She smirked at the level of aggravation evident in his tone and kissed him on the forehead. "Archibald said he never saw a human fight as hard as you did."

"Sure. Then again, maybe he hasn't attacked many people before."

She considered that line of thought. "I did get the impression he wasn't particularly skilled in combat, but rather more of a brawler. Or perhaps he isn't that old a vampire," she speculated. "But he was a brute-sized fellow. He probably hasn't encountered many people capable of putting up a fight. Obviously, you were a surprise of sorts."

"Obviously you were too," he added, recalling brief images of how handily she had engaged Devon in combat.

She bent down and lightly kissed his lips. "My previous years of combat experience came in handy. But more importantly, I think you're getting better at fighting vampires. If he'd been a human instead of a vampire, I'm pretty sure he would have fared very poorly. You seem to have thought quickly on your feet with the resources you had available.

We'll continue adding to your fighting skills in the future."

"Yeah, well, thanks for playing Find Caleb again," he said with a scowl. "Given the added challenges, I suppose you get to pick the prize."

"I already picked him."

And hopefully I'll do a better job of protecting him when he needs it.

He nodded, exchanged a warm kiss with her, and reached out to stroke her affectionately on the thigh. He was relieved she had arrived in time to help him, although he wouldn't mind being able to take care of himself better in a fight.

He resolved to learn how to put some serious hurt on a vampire for any future repeat performances. And with the way his luck typically went, he had the feeling he needed all the help he could get. Then his thoughts turned to the unlikely nature of his encounter.

"Just what are the odds of my running into him out there like that?" Caleb asked. "I'm either the unluckiest guy in the world, or there's a hell of a lot more vampires out there than you've implied. Either way, I'm not encouraged."

"I'm way ahead of you," she agreed grimly.

"Of course you are. But then, you've been conscious for the past twelve hours too," he pointed out.

She rolled her eyes at him. "Devon said he was hunting for wild game, which makes sense on a wildlife preserve, so it's likely you were merely a target of opportunity. For all we know, he's been visiting the location regularly."

Caleb considered that and recalled, "I think he said something about not seeing anyone out there on a winter's night before."

She frowned. "I'm curious about how many vampires are wandering around Georgia. I've never taken much interest in other vampires, but now I have a mate with an apparent sense of adventure, so I have incentive to be curious. This business with Devon has made me consider declaring a territory."

Caleb frowned. "So, what do you mean by that exactly?"

She sighed. "Well, in vampire terms, I would be announcing my location and declaring a specific area as my personal interest. That has the added detriment of garnering unwanted attention by the vampire community, but it means there should be more communication from the socially active of my kind who might travel through here or relocate nearby."

"I'm really kind of surprised to hear you say that, Kat," he ventured quietly.

"It was Alton's idea, actually. I prefer as much anonymity as possible, but our recent exploits with Chimalma have unexpectedly launched us into the spotlight."

He frowned. "What do you mean?"

"I've been receiving emails the past couple of weeks from vampires I didn't even know existed. Apparently, about half of the emails are congratulating me, and the other half just want more details regarding what happened."

Caleb's surprised expression spoke volumes. "So, you're a celebrity now?"

Katrina shrugged. "Not me. Us. A number of emails have pointed out that you're one of the few humans to survive a vampire attack from Chimalma."

He grimaced and added bitterly, "And an attack from the Incredible Vampire Hulk, Devon."

She smirked at him and shook her head slightly. Always the comedian.

He moved gingerly to the other side of the bed, and she frowned.

"Where are you crawling off to?" she asked.

He managed to make it across the bed and swung his legs over the edge with an effort. His body felt like it had been pummeled, but at least it seemed functional.

"Bathroom," he replied with a groan as he fought the soreness in his body and tried to acquire his balance.

She sped around to him in a blur and wrapped her arm around his torso to steady him. "Oh, of course."

After helping him into the bathroom, she closed the door to give him some privacy. Her cell phone buzzed on the computer hutch, and she sped over to check it.

A text message from Paige was waiting for her: How's our boy?

Her speedy fingers typed: *Ok. Just woke up.*

Healed?

Katrina responded: *Yes. Better now.*

My best 2 you both. Hug N kiss kiddo 4 me.

Katrina smirked as she heard Caleb opening the bathroom door. She helped him back into bed and bent down to tuck him under the sheets.

He felt exhausted merely from the journey to the bathroom and back and sighed. He was genuinely happy to be back in bed.

"Paige texted me just now," Katrina offered while caressing her fingers lightly through his hair.

He smiled. "What's my babysitter up to?"

"Asking about you, of course," she replied with a grin. She bent down, held his body against hers gently and pressed her lips to his cheek to pop a quick peck against his skin just as Paige frequently did.

He chuckled. "From Paige?"

She smiled and nodded and kissed him warmly on the lips. His lips responded greedily despite his exhaustion, and he felt her hand supportively wrap around the back of his head. Her soft lips nipped at his skin lightly as she kissed hm.

"And that was from me," she murmured softly, curling next to him on the bed with her arms around him as he settled down to rest again.

You're amazing, Kat, he thought with satisfaction as he drifted off to sleep.

* * *

Caleb awoke with a yawn and a sense of confusion. His perception of time was distorted during his body's recovery, and the situation hadn't been helped being in the windowless sublevel. He scanned the dimly lit room, but didn't see Katrina anywhere. Raising his arm to glance at his watch, he felt an ache permeate his shoulder and back.

It was already midday Sunday, which meant he had slept for another twelve hours or more. He stretched, realizing he only had part of the weekend left before he was expected back at work. At that moment, his stomach growled with hunger. He reached over to the nightstand and emptied a glass of water in a matter of seconds, his thirst nearly as urgent as his hunger.

He returned the glass to the nightstand and perched his body up on one arm. The sliding pocket door into the room opened quietly, and he glanced over to see Katrina peering inside with a grin. In a blur of motion, she suddenly appeared at his bedside. He smirked, amazed again by how quickly vampires could move when they wanted to.

"Welcome back to the world of the conscious, sleepy head," she teased. "You're looking much better, my love."

He nodded. "I feel better, too."

"Do you feel up to a shower? I'll make you something to eat while you freshen up."

It was then he noticed her attire. She was dressed in a fashionable pair of blue jeans, black turtleneck sweater, and stylish black leather boots.

"Yeah, that sounds fine, thanks," he replied absently. "Going out?"

She gently stroked the side of his face with her fingertips and explained, "Yes, once the sun goes down, of course. I plan to meet with Devon Archibald in Marietta tonight. It's important we finalize details on our new arrangement with him while the iron's still hot."

He considered that for a moment and felt nothing but animosity for the hulking vampire. He tried to look past his own personal feelings, but found that his recent experiences were just too fresh in his mind to move beyond them.

He's not happy about that, she noted. *But then, I can't say that*

I blame him.

"I guess I don't need to ask you to be careful," he said with resignation as he reached out to grasp her hand. "I don't trust him."

Katrina reassured him, "I'll be just fine. And I hope you don't mind my not asking if you wanted to go."

"Uh, no. Not on my to-do list," he replied tersely.

She nodded and pulled his hand up to her face to rub the back of his hand against her cheek, which elicited a brief smile. She hoped she was making the right decision regarding the mysterious Devon Archibald.

After she went back upstairs, Caleb showered, shaved, and changed into a pair of jeans and a sweatshirt. He went upstairs to the kitchen where Katrina had just finished preparing his food. She laid out a plateful of turkey bacon, wheat biscuits, and a tasty-looking cheese omelet.

There was also a jar of black raspberry jam and a steaming mug of Darjeeling tea, a blend she had introduced to him that had become one of his favorites.

He wrinkled his nose at the turkey bacon as he sat before the kitchen counter and sniffed at a piece before nibbling tentatively on one end.

Katrina rolled her eyes. "It's healthier than pork with fewer calories and less fat, but supposedly just as tasty as regular bacon."

He shrugged and adopted a playful smirk as he offered a slice of the bacon to her. "Oh, really? Care to try some?"

She grimaced and stated emphatically, "Not on your life. I just cook it. The grocer was the one who said it was as good as pork. It's all just stinky dead meat to me."

"Thought so," he replied knowingly and tried a bite of the omelet. "That's really good, Kat," he offered. "You're getting pretty good at cooking breakfast."

She smiled and watched him eat for a few minutes before glancing at her watch.

"I need to call Alton before I go, and there are some emails I need to respond to," she explained before hastily kissing him on the cheek.

He frowned. "Still getting fan mail?"

She sighed. "Yes. Like you, I'm starting to wonder just how many other vampires there are in the world. And we're apparently a lot more social than I gave us credit for."

"Why are they interested in you all of a sudden?" he asked while taking a bite out of a jam-slathered biscuit.

She paused to contemplate his question. "Well, this is the first time in decades that a vampire has gone on a killing spree of their own kind like this. The last time was, of course, also by Chimalma. She was viewed in the same way that humans would a serial killer."

"Oh," he replied while thoughtfully considering her comparison.

Her eyes sparkled as she added, "But some of the vampires are intrigued about you, as well. It seems word got around about my mate contributing significantly to Chimalma's demise, as well as sacrificing his life to save me."

His eyes rose to stare at her intently, and his fork remained suspended in midair on its journey to his mouth. "And just how is word getting out about that?" he inquired suspiciously.

Great, that's all I need, more vampire attention.

Katrina shrugged. "I mentioned it to only a couple of vampires in confidence. One must have spread the details to others."

He frowned and set his fork back down on the plate. "That's not the kind of attention I'm excited about, Kat."

She patted him on the back. "No offense, my love," she began gently, "But I suspect most of my kind aren't specifically interested in you for the most part. Many probably view you as 'that devoted human of hers.' Everyone thinks that I was the one who issued the killing blow and rid our community of a scourge of sorts. However, I'm happy to set others straight on your important role in that fight. If you'd chosen not to pick up my late husband's sword and come running to aid me..."

She let her voice trail off as she contemplated the horrible consequences of losing to Chimalma.

Likely, she would have hunted Caleb down and tortured him just for spite. But then, perhaps Alton and Paige would have been able to hide him away.

She was happy things turned out the way they did. No, she was ecstatic.

Caleb nodded and noted her distant expression. He tried to refocus his anxious feelings by picking up his fork and continuing to eat.

Katrina broke from her reverie and watched him in silence, wondering what he was thinking. "You know, a few of my kind are jealous by the level of sacrifice and commitment you showed to me," she said proudly.

I'm a very lucky vampire, she thought with satisfaction while playfully running her fingers through his hair.

"I'd do the same again," he replied proudly. He finished swallowing a mouthful of food and changed the subject. "So, just how many vampires do you think there might be roaming around in the world?"

"Many," she temporized, "Probably hundreds. Maybe more."

His eyes widened as he contemplated hundreds of vampires roaming the world partaking in blood: some by voluntary donors and others through involuntary means. The thought sent a shiver down his spine, and he felt the world shrink a little bit in that moment. He was suddenly very appreciative for how compassionately and kindly Katrina treated him as her mate.

Katrina left to attend to emails and phone calls, leaving Caleb alone in the kitchen to clean up. As he washed dishes, he wondered what kind of events would unfold once she announced her desire to claim territorial boundaries. His thoughts darkened somewhat as the image of Devon Archibald's face formed in his mind. Another thought inspired him to call Paige.

* * *

Katrina sat at her computer hutch in the sublevel room sorting through emails, noting three more inquiries from vampires regarding her exploits with Chimalma. One was from Selesta in Brazil, another from Medyev in the Ukraine, and a third from Vince in Juneau, Alaska. She marveled at the continued stream of inquiries from around the world. Vampires were everywhere, it seemed. All the messages seemed innocent enough, but there appeared to be an undercurrent to each of them, almost as if some of the senders were subtly reaching out to her for acknowledgement, as if trying to get to know her better.

She picked up the phone handset next to her and dialed. Alton picked up by the second ring.

"Hello? Katrina?" he asked tentatively.

She wondered what he would say if it were Caleb instead of her calling. Then she frowned, wondering if he wouldn't be as surprised as she imagined.

"Hi, Alton."

"How are matters progressing?" he asked in his crisp English accent.

"Oh, I'm Miss Popularity in the world right now."

"Still?" he asked, although his tone failed to convey surprise.

What more do you know, Alton?

"Three more messages," she said. "Although I'll have to answer them later. I have business with Devon Archibald in Marietta tonight."

There was a pause before he inquired, "You've decided on a pact with him?"

"Perhaps. We'll see how things go when I get there."

"So, you still might kill him?"

"Again, I'll see how things go," she repeated, although part of her was still surprised she hadn't killed Archibald. Caleb had been injured severely and might have died had she been even seconds later than she was. A pang of guilt shot through her at the thought.

Maybe I should have killed him, she thought yet again.

She had lost count of how many times she contemplated that in the past twenty-four hours.

"A pact could be helpful to you, you know," suggested Alton. "There may be times when Devon could prove useful, particularly if you needed another set of eyes to watch over Caleb."

She conceded such a benefit. Paige had been enjoying her life in southern California, so she wasn't exactly handy to assist Caleb in a pinch. Still, her mate would need to build a rapport with the vampire, which might be unrealistic given their most recent encounter.

There are so many variables to consider.

"Why do I get the impression there's more to this than you're telling me?" she asked pointedly.

After a pause, he replied smoothly, "There seems to be a rift forming in the undercurrent of vampire politics as of late. I'm not yet certain regarding the specifics, but perhaps I'll know more by the time you get to London in March."

She frowned, pondering his revelation. "Do you think all the recent attention I'm getting has something to do with such a rift?"

"Perhaps, but as you've pointed out, we'll have to see how things go," he hedged. "Anything more on the subject would be unhelpful speculation on my part."

She had known Alton long enough to realize he wouldn't speak on a subject until he was ready, so there was no reason to waste time pressing him further. However, she resigned herself to keeping an open mind for the time being. It annoyed her that somehow the upcoming meeting with Devon was quickly taking on more significant connotations.

She sighed heavily. *Why does everything have to be so damned complicated?*

"Fine. I'll let you know how the meeting turns out when I return later tonight."

"Good luck," he offered. "And please give my best to

Caleb."

"Will do," she replied and hung up.

The drive to Marietta was uneventful and gave Katrina quiet time to consider what Alton said, as well as to strategize how to proceed with Devon Archibald.

Her thoughts drifted to Caleb, who had been less than happy that she was meeting with his attacker. Before leaving, he told her how he felt as if an aggressor's hostile actions were being ignored in favor of a summit. She had chuckled at his political analogy and wondered if he had been watching too much cable network news lately. Still, she couldn't blame him for the way he felt. She still harbored doubts regarding her own resolve that night.

Upon entering Marietta, she paid closer attention to her car's GPS regarding the proper route to Devon's home. That part of town was one of the older neighborhoods located on the outskirts of the downtown area. She pulled into the narrow, cracked driveway in front of the house, her eyes sweeping the structure before her. The two-story, square brick home was an example of utilitarian architecture from the late 1950s or early 1960s. A series of narrow windows spanned the front of the house, each with closed blinds.

There was no garage, and only a single car was parked in the driveway. As she exited her car, she briefly noted the older model Pontiac sedan, which had a faded paint job. She paused in the chilly night air to glance up and down the length of the neighborhood, noting surprisingly little traffic at such an early hour. Many of the surrounding homes emanated the glow of interior lights, and most driveways were occupied by at least one vehicle.

She approached the front porch with its halo of light around the lamp fixture next to the front door. She chuckled at the wholly unnecessary waste of electricity given her kind's night vision and wondered why Devon had bothered with the gesture. She rang the doorbell and waited patiently. She heard a figure approach the door from inside before the deadbolt made a sound.

The door opened slowly, and the tall, broad-shouldered figure of Devon Archibald appeared before her. He was dressed in gray slacks and a white dress shirt with the sleeves rolled partway up his arms. The surface of his smooth scalp appeared to shine slightly, as if just recently shaved and rubbed with lotion.

He appeared mostly relaxed, though slightly wary. However, he smiled invitingly as he stood before her. The notion of his unease struck her as humorous considering that he towered over her like a giant.

"Welcome, Katrina Rawlings," he offered in a deep voice. "Please come in."

Katrina glided past him and into a small entryway with polished wooden stairs on her left leading up to the second floor. To the right was a short hallway that passed the kitchen and led to a dining room. Devon gestured towards the living room directly before her.

The room was simple-looking. Katrina noted a small bookcase along the wall to the right as she entered, populated by older volumes of classic literature. A flat-panel TV sat atop a faux wood stand to the left of the entrance, and the remainder of the living room's furniture consisted of a sofa with matching end tables, a worn leather recliner with a small table along the left wall, and a central glass-topped coffee table set before the couch.

The walls were painted flat white, and there were only three pictures hanging in the room, each of pastoral wildlife scenes.

"I welcome you to my home, such as it is," Devon said. "Won't you please sit down? May I offer you a glass of water or perhaps some wine? I apologize for having no blood on hand, as might be more fitting."

Katrina absently perched on the edge of one end of the couch, distracted by the revelation that the vampire had no blood supply at his home. "No, thank you," she declined politely. "Pardon me for asking, but did I hear you correctly that you have no blood stock?"

He took a seat in the recliner near the couch. "I regret I don't. For one, I prefer fresh blood over stored. And for another, the expense is cumbersome on my limited budget."

Katrina frowned. His statement bothered her in that Devon apparently hunted his blood from fresh sources, a fact that portended potential complications with his living in proximity to Atlanta.

"So, you don't subscribe to a blood delivery service?"

"Alas, no," he responded. "I hunt when my hunger is most pressing."

"But doesn't that tend to make your stay around humans particularly tenuous? You are a vampire of large stature, and your blood need is likely beyond the regular capacity of live donors on a frequent basis," she ventured.

Devon inclined his head in deference. "That's correct. However, I make it a point to reside in locations with easy accessibility to populations of wildlife, such as deer."

"So humans—"

"—are usually prey of opportunity, which is less common, unfortunately. I primarily sustain myself on larger animals. Humans are very much the occasional prized steak in a regular diet of chicken."

The edges of her mouth upturned with amusement at his analogy. Despite her misgivings, there was something she liked about him. "And my mate…"

"—was what I thought to be an opportune steak, though I was actually stalking a wild boar the night I ran across him," he supplied.

"So pork was on the menu instead of chicken that night," she offered wryly.

Devon grinned, displaying a set of large white teeth. "Exactly."

Katrina nodded thoughtfully.

"How's your mate?" he asked.

Her expression turned serious. "Caleb's feeling much better, thank you. But his injuries were worse than I expected once I got him home."

"My apologies, of course," he offered. "I'll do my best to extend my apologies in person when, that is if, I see him again."

I think he appreciates the gravity of my visit, she considered. That easily explains the undercurrent of tension when he answered the door.

"Tell me a little about yourself, Devon," she encouraged, sitting back in a more relaxed fashion. Her assessment wouldn't be complete without a better understanding of his background.

Devon settled back in his chair, steepling his fingers before him. "I was born Thadeous Devon Stevens in 1928 near Thomasville, Alabama. My family was part of the working poor, and of course, being African American meant that life was even harder because the jobs were scarce for people of color. My father worked on a road construction crew, and my mother was a seamstress and laundry worker. While in my twenties, I worked odd jobs just about anywhere I could find them. I eventually made my way to Chattanooga by age thirty, where I met a woman while walking down the back alleys on my way back from some late night entertainment.

"Her name was Nadida Kendrick, and after only a brief conversation, she offered me employment as a general laborer at her estate. Her property was vast, one of the largest spreads I'd ever seen at the time. I started as a kind of groundskeeper, but within a matter of months I progressed to helping coordinate the remainder of the staff she employed. I discovered from one of the maids that the previous estate coordinator disappeared abruptly from her employ with no indication why he would've left."

Devon paused, as if collecting his thoughts.

"Ms. Kendrick, as we called her, never came out at daytime, and instead seemed somewhat reclusive, except for occasional socializing a few evenings each week. And though somewhat standoffish to the general public, she was always pleasant around me and the other staff. After about a year of employment, she revealed herself as a vampire to me. I awoke one summer night in 1958 to the sound of shouting coming from the large barn she stabled the horses in. When I went to investigate, I saw a well-dressed man trying to attack her with a pitchfork, so I intervened. Little did I know the lady really hadn't needed my help, but she seemed touched by my sense of chivalry. It was then I found out what she was," he said.

He paused and looked at Katrina with a curious expression.

"Please, continue," she encouraged.

"I was scared at first, of course. But she assured me that she meant me no harm, and I began to appreciate how being different was as much a threat to her in a human world as being African American was to me in a predominately Caucasian world. Over a year or more, we grew closer as she observed my trustworthiness and continued loyalty. Eventually, we became lovers. In retrospect, I suppose it wasn't really true love, per se, but rather an intimate partnership that included the offering of my blood. She encouraged my appreciation for classic literature and helped educate me in some of the finer knowledge of the world. Everything seemed fine until 1963 when that part of the country erupted with the early civil rights uprisings. You see, Nadida was wealthy in her own right, but she was a mulatto. At that time, anybody resembling a black was targeted for retribution by whites who opposed civil rights. She said she needed to relocate to another part of the world because she'd stayed in the area far too long. She sensed that her increased visibility was starting to raise additional suspicions. As for me, I didn't want to leave the country, but she promised she wouldn't force me to. Instead, she offered me immortality as a reward for my service and companionship before she left. She stayed only a matter of months after I was turned, just long enough to provide me with the basics regarding my new vampire life. Then she sold the estate and left the country. I've only heard from her on two occasions since then, but we haven't seen each other since she left me in early 1964."

Devon stared across the room in a contemplative

fashion, as if recalling some private thoughts.

He looked up with a hopeful expression and continued, "Since then, I've moved around the country and adopted the name Devon Archibald. I take odd jobs performing evening shift work in either manual labor or security. Naturally, given my size, I've managed to work as a bouncer from time to time. Right now, I'm a security guard for a tire manufacturing plant here in town and still do work as a bouncer at clubs on weekends when I need some quick cash."

Katrina considered everything she had heard, including Devon's rather humble and secluded lifestyle. His sincerity and forthrightness seemed genuine, and a part of her sympathized with his circumstances despite her intention to remain as neutral as possible to their meeting. Still, she couldn't allow her emotions to enter into her decision as to whether he would live or die that night. But she felt a small pang of guilt over that, as well.

Why shouldn't I kill him for attacking, and nearly killing, Caleb?

Devon regarded Katrina curiously as the silence grew and prompted, "Is there anything else you want to know?"

She broke from her thoughts and noticed an old copy of Dickens' A Tale of Two Cities sitting on the end table next to his chair. A place marker was stuffed between the pages approximately three quarters of the way to the end. Looks like he's still reading the classics.

"Do a lot of reading?" she asked.

He glanced absently to the book at his left and replied with satisfaction, "Yes, actually. I'm a varied reader for the most part, but I still reread the classics. It reminds me of my time with Nadida."

"I like the classics too," she agreed before falling silent. "So, do you have any questions about who I am?"

"I admit that I've already made some discreet inquiries to learn more about you," he conceded cautiously.

"Understandable."

This should be interesting.

"I discovered you've earned quite a reputation among

some in the vampire community," he began warily. "I had no idea how popular your recent experience with killing that Aztec vampire has become. I don't stay in regular contact with our kind, you see."

"Really?" she prompted.

"I generally don't have much in common with other vampires. I prefer human blood, but try to keep a low profile in my own community. For that reason, I spend more time outdoors hunting animals than I do being around others. What few human contacts I maintain are shallow because I haven't found anyone I trust enough to reveal my secret to."

I'm so fortunate to have Caleb, she affirmed.

"My prior experiences with women have often led to poor partings or having to dispose of a body and relocate to another part of the country," he continued. "And as for vampires, I see that with some of our kind, even honest misunderstandings might prove fatal. Although I'm interested to hear if reasonable restitution might be possible in my case."

She nodded imperceptibly and sat forward on the edge of the couch, allowing herself easy access to the combat knife hidden at the small of her back beneath her leather jacket. The time had come to make a decision.

"Devon, I appreciate your taking the time to tell me a little about yourself," she acknowledged politely. "And I can honestly say you have an intriguing and compelling life story."

He tensed slightly and quipped, "At least I was able to recite it out loud one last time, if nothing else."

The corners of her mouth upturned slightly in amusement. "There may be an opportunity to recite it again to others, if we can reach an agreement."

His eyebrows rose slightly. "What did you have in mind, exactly?"

"You seem to be well versed in security, so your skills might be helpful to me from time to time," she suggested tentatively. "I may need for you to check into concerns within the pockets of territories that I plan to claim. There may also be times when Caleb might need some additional assistance in the area of personal security."

He adopted a slightly amused expression. "Somehow, I think your mate may not be pleased to hear that right now."

"Very true, I'm afraid," she admitted. "But I preside over matters concerning his security, either with or without his acceptance. And not everything has to be done so overtly or even within his spectrum of awareness."

The large-framed vampire seemed intrigued by that statement. "Would I need to take orders from Caleb?"

Katrina's eyes narrowed. "Within reason, of course, though never when they countermand my explicit instructions. But no matter the instructions, one rule is paramount: he must be protected or defended at the expense of any other objectives."

"Your mate means a great deal to you," he observed respectfully.

"He's everything to me," she stated flatly. "Above all other concerns, goals, or interests."

Devon nodded with comprehension, but frowned with some confusion. "I think I get the picture. Now, pardon me if what I'm about to ask seems odd. But if that's true, and if he likely hates me right now for attacking him, why am I not dead already? Though, not that I'm complaining or anything, you understand."

Katrina fell silent as she considered his pertinent question. "You might be surprised to learn I don't have a precise answer for you on that right now. However, rest assured that I'm prepared to reconcile any incongruities in my logic as I deem necessary," she stipulated.

The broad-shouldered vampire appeared slightly unnerved by her statement and arched an eyebrow in surprise.

"Suffice to say that, in all honesty, I thought there was something about you that merited further investigation," she continued. "And yet, your continued longevity strongly depends upon your sense of personal integrity and in not proving me to be mistaken in my leniency."

His eyes widened. "Just before you arrived tonight, I checked my email, and I had received a message from another vampire who explained she had been seeking me out to perform a background check on your behalf. I believed her only because of the warning in her message."

"Warning?" Katrina asked with an arched eyebrow.

Devon nodded. "Yes. I thought it rather strange, because her message emphasized you were an alpha. She suggested you're quite experienced at killing both humans and vampires. She recommended I accept any reasonable offer made to me and stated that if I weren't on my best behavior for our meeting, I probably wouldn't live through the night," he recalled warily. "She also had a nickname for you," he added with a hint of amusement.

Katrina's lips tightened into a thin line. "Oh, really?"

Just who the hell is meddling in my business now?

"She said you were 'a red-haired bitch' when you get angry," he replied soberly.

Her expression turned steely. "And just what was this vampire's name, precisely?"

"Ah, yes. It was Paige," he replied.

She froze in place, though nearly wincing from the revelation, and slowly shook her head.

I'm so going to strangle you, my little blonde-haired friend.

Devon still seemed wary. "Is this Paige legitimate?"

She returned a half-smile and confirmed, "Oh, she's legitimate all right."

Legitimate pain in the ass sometimes. But one of the dearest, best friends I've ever had.

"So, as to an agreement between us, then?" he pressed.

Katrina's expression turned serious again. "Only if you agree to my terms: defend and protect Caleb, address any concerns within my declared territories, and maintain loyalty to our agreement for the agreed duration."

"What duration did you have in mind?" he asked

carefully.

She wondered what was both fair and reasonable for nearly killing her mate. Just the thought sent a wave of nausea through her, and she cursed herself for trying to assign a value against Caleb's life. "What do you think is reasonable?" she countered.

He seemed surprised to be asked and frowned as he fell deep in thought. Finally, he shrugged slightly and offered, "Ten years?"

Katrina realized how youthful in both mindset and lifespan the vampire sitting before her really was. Ten years was like the blink of an eye to most vampires. But he had barely been turned for forty years, so he was still thinking in finite human terms. It would have seemed amusing had the issue not related to someone so dear to her or for consequences she deemed so dire.

But perhaps ten years will be enough time, after all. Caleb will be thirty-six by then and in the prime of adulthood as a human, or quite possibly in his infancy as a vampire, she thought with anticipation.

She soberly regarded Devon and agreed, "Ten years it shall be."

Devon stood and reached out with his right hand to shake, and Katrina rose to return the gesture. Their hands met and gripped each other's tightly in a single motion.

"I'm an honorable person, Katrina Rawlings," he insisted. "And I keep to my bargains, oaths, and obligations."

She raised an eyebrow and agreed, "Good. As do I."

They released hands, and she withdrew a business card from an interior jacket pocket. She handed the card to him and instructed, "This has my home and cell phone numbers, email address, and home address written on it. Never share it with anyone unless I stipulate otherwise. I will contact you in the near future to confirm my territorial declaration before I announce it. Feel free to contact me if you have questions, concerns, or information you think would be helpful."

Devon nodded.

"Any questions for me?" she asked.

"Just two, really. First, how would you prefer to be addressed? And second, what do I need to know about your associate, Paige?"

She admired his quick thinking.

"You may call me Katrina," she offered. "I take it you prefer Devon?"

"Yes, please," he replied in his deep, baritone voice.

"And as for Paige, she's Caleb's surrogate guardian and protector. You should defer to her orders so long as they aren't in conflict with my own. I'll introduce you to her at the earliest opportunity," she explained, moving towards his entryway to depart. She wanted to return home to Caleb as soon as possible.

"I understand," he replied.

"Oh, and one more thing," she offered while glancing back over her shoulder. "Feel free to call Paige by her nickname."

Devon raised his eyebrows. "What's that?"

"Goldilocks," she slyly replied as she walked towards her car.

Right back at you, my little friend, she thought with a mischievous smirk.

He watched her depart, and then slowly walked back inside his house.

When Katrina returned to the estate, she found Caleb lounging on the couch watching television in her chamber, but his body language seemed tense.

"I'm back," she offered encouragingly. "I'm glad that's out of the way."

But he failed to look up at her as she leaned over the back of the couch to gaze down at him.

"You didn't kill him, did you?" he asked in a dark tone.

Her lighter mood turned subdued. "No, but we came to what I believe was a very suitable arrangement."

He made a derisive sound. "It figures," he noted with displeasure.

"Caleb," she placated, "please try to understand. Devon didn't target you maliciously, though he did fail to observe the courtesy of taking you at your word that you were a vampire's mate until proving otherwise. I spared his life, and he'll repay his debt to us by assisting us for a period of time."

"Well, that's just great, Kat," he spat. "So, I nearly die, and he gets community service. How nice that you made a new friend in the end."

She resisted the inclination to sigh and instead fluidly moved around to the front of the couch, perching next to where he was half-sprawled across one end.

"My love," she urged patiently, "he's not a friend. And this arrangement will be of mutual benefit to you, as well. He will serve as a protector to you as needed."

He turned to her with a stoic expression and answered flatly, "I already have Paige as an additional protector. I don't want his assistance. I want him dead."

She was taken aback by her mate's vehemence and frowned. It was so unlike the peaceable, good-natured young man she had known thus far. She reflected upon his recent exposure to violence, including the near-fatal attack of Chimalma the past December and considered that perhaps he wasn't coping well.

How is an innocent, gentle person supposed to react to such violence in his life? More to the point, what to do now?

Patience above all else.

"My love, it's true that Paige is your assigned alternate guardian, but she's in California," she explained. "You need someone besides me who's also local."

His jaw tightened noticeably, and he glared sidelong at her. "Look, I can't make you kill him. Hell, I'm completely powerless to do anything about it, in fact. But I'll be damned if I'm going to accept anything from him whatsoever."

"Caleb, please try to—" she urged.

But he interrupted her. "Look. Pardon me if I take it personally when someone tries to kill me. And I don't care about the justifications, or the vampire politics, or whatever the hell's going on here. I just hate him. Okay?"

She realized further discussion on the matter would be futile and resigned herself to taking the issue one day at a time. Still, she felt her decision was a reasonable one and hoped he might see the potential benefits once his temper over the topic had abated. However, she feared it would be more of a long-term process.

"I'm going to take a shower," she announced. "Perhaps someone would like to join me?"

"Thanks, no," he replied. "I took my shower while you were gone."

She returned a slightly dejected expression and sighed. "I see," she replied and rose to make her way across the room to her dresser. She picked out something comfy to change into following her shower.

Apparently, it's going to be a less than amorous evening for both of us. It appears I'll have time to call Alton with an update, after all.

CHAPTER 3

Photographic Memories

For days, Caleb silently fumed over Katrina's pact with Devon Archibald. It felt as if she had chosen the huge vampire over him. And while admittedly sanguinary, he wanted nothing less than revenge for having narrowly avoided death at the hands of his unexpected adversary. Seeking sympathy, he called Paige.

While she had listened patiently, his brief conversation with her had been useless; she had all but openly agreed with Katrina's decision. He came close to hanging up on her and decided to avoid talking to her for a while for spite.

His friend and teaching mentor, Tanisha, had been very curious on Monday morning as to how his camping event had gone that previous Friday evening. Unfortunately, he could scarcely tell her what actually happened. His reflection on their conversation had only raised his ire, accompanied by a sense of betrayal by his mate.

Still, he followed the rules he had promised to uphold and lied to his friend. He told Tanisha that he and Katrina had a nice enough time, but he didn't care to revisit the location anytime soon. Fortunately, his outward wounds had healed well enough that she didn't see any evidence of his physical injuries, though his body still felt very sore and achy in places.

However, his perceptive friend did detect something was bothering him, so he admitted that he and Katrina had argued Sunday night, and he was still somewhat upset over the event.

Tanisha advised him, "You know, Caleb. Part of loving someone is admitting to yourself you may not always be happy with your partner, but remembering that you love them. Sometimes you have to let go of festering resentment, or it will eat you alive inside and prove detrimental to the overall health of the relationship. In the case of arguments, it's hard to look beyond pride or ego on both people's parts and instead be brave enough to make amends for the benefit of the relationship."

He conceded the logic of her advice, but countered, "So, what do you do when William makes you angry by making a decision you believe is short-sighted, particularly where he didn't take your feelings fully into account?"

She paused to consider Caleb carefully. "Well, first, I'd ask him if he thought my feelings were important enough to him to consider more seriously."

"And then?"

"Then," she continued with a smirk, "if I thought he was sincere, I'd let him know how disappointed in him I was. And if he weren't sincere, he'd spend a few nights thinking it over while sleeping on the couch."

He smiled as she giggled and silently considered her solution might not work quite that well with Katrina. His alpha-vampire mate was cut from a little different cloth than the average person, even for a vampire. Instead, he merely sighed and thanked her for her advice. He half-considered calling Alton, but quickly discarded the idea because the stately vampire apparently agreed with Katrina on her decision. Of course, he was still boycotting Paige, as well.

By Tuesday afternoon, he was still vexed over the entire affair, though he realized he needed to work through his feelings somehow. However, Wednesday passed with no resolution.

By Thursday evening, he had two evening classes left to

teach and needed to refocus his attentions on the upcoming lectures. He went to the student union to eat dinner and was happy when Tanisha unexpectedly joined him. Apparently, she was teaching a section of Early American History on Tuesday and Thursday evenings for an adjunct professor who had just had surgery and couldn't teach for the remainder of the semester.

After a quick meal, his first evening class went well. But as his second section started, something odd occurred. He finished roll call and was bringing up the PowerPoint presentation for his lecture when he spied a quick blur of movement outside of his open classroom door. A pale-skinned, muscular man appearing to be in his early thirties and sporting a crew cut stood in the hallway curiously staring back at him.

Another shorter man of Native American heritage in his twenties appeared beside him. He also stared at Caleb while whispering something to his taller associate. A chill went down Caleb's spine as he realized their odd mannerisms and piercing eyes suggested they were likely to be vampires. It was when the taller one smiled and revealed two slightly extended fangs that Caleb finally had his answer.

He immediately looked down at the computer screen at the instructor station before him and tried to remain calm as he navigated through Windows. He announced, "Just a little delay getting my PowerPoint to come up, everyone. Go ahead and open up your books to chapter eight and review the questions at the back of the section for discussion. You might want to jot down some quick answers in case I call on you, as well."

He casually slipped his phone from its belt carrier and opened the facing to scroll to Katrina's number. He glanced up discreetly and noticed both of the men had disappeared, and he paused to consider what to do next.

If he dialed Katrina, she might send that monster Devon, exactly the guy with whom he didn't want to contend. But she would be angry if he didn't call her. Then again, neither of the men, or rather vampires, looked particularly threatening. Certainly, while unnerving, it hadn't caused the same feelings of fear he had felt that night in the wildlife preserve.

He sighed, finally deciding a text message might be the better part of valor. But instead of texting Katrina, he texted his friend and protector, Paige. Granted, she was in California, but she could at least advise him before he made a rash decision. And his class was just beginning, so he had a little over an hour on his hands to consider other options.

He hastily sent the message: *2x fangs outside class. Not scary right now. Plez advise. C.*

He set his phone aside and pulled up the PowerPoint for his class. A quick glance through the room indicated his students were still reading or preparing answers to the textbook questions. His cell vibrated, and he read Paige's reply: *Don't panic, kiddo. Stall for time. P.*

His reply was, *Wish U were here. Thx.*

He started his PowerPoint slideshow and glanced down to read another reply from Paige: *Me 2. B careful. Luv U.*

Sighing, he slipped his cell phone back into its pouch and anticipated that Paige was likely already on the phone to Katrina. So he did the only thing he knew he could do: he began lecturing, despite the anxiety forming in his stomach. But he was becoming a much better actor over time and barely skipped a step as he played his role as an engaging professor of history.

* * *

Katrina sat at the desk in her study going over some financial paperwork she had requested from one of her overseas bank accounts and an elite credit card company she used regularly.

She sighed, lamenting that her mate was very put out with her as of late, and wondered how much longer it would take before they either had another disagreement or managed to resolve his most recent conflicted feelings. Either way, she dreaded the thought of further arguments with him.

Gotta love those lose-lose scenarios.

The cordless phone on her desk rang, and she snatched the handset out of its charger station before the second ring. One quick dart of her eye at the caller ID revealed it was Paige.

"What's up, shorty?" she quipped.

But instead of a snappy comeback, she heard Paige's tense voice at the other end. "Red, our boy's in a little trouble tonight."

"What kind of trouble?" she demanded.

"He's at the college teaching a class, and apparently two vampires have shown up outside his classroom. He texted me to say he's not scared, but wanted advice. I told him to stall for time and stay calm, but I think you better haul ass up there."

"Thanks. I'm on my way," Katrina snapped as she slapped the phone onto the desktop and sped out of the room.

Dammit, Caleb, why the hell didn't you call me first? she fumed while grabbing her cell phone, keys, and combat knife.

* * *

After Caleb finished his brief lecture, he selected individual students to answer each of the questions at the back of the chapter. He realized only about half an hour had passed, but it was more than enough time for Katrina to arrive. There was no doubt in his mind Paige would have immediately called her following his text messages.

Maybe Kat's searching the campus for the vampires while I'm teaching.

He thought it odd that she hadn't appeared to indicate her arrival, but at least there had been no reappearance of the two vampires in his doorway, either.

The question and answer session with his students was completed in record time. Failing to have a plausible reason to detain them further, he adjourned his students approximately fifteen minutes early, wishing them a good evening and cautioning them to prepare for a possible quiz next Tuesday.

The students cleared the room before he even had time to shut down the instructor computer fully, and he found himself going downstairs to his office in near silence. As he unlocked his office door, he considered whether he should try calling or texting Katrina. He postponed making a decision in lieu of loading his briefcase with items he wanted to take home with him.

Unfortunately, the briefcase was too small, so he transferred everything into a backpack he kept in his office for such an occasion. An eerie feeling crept up his spine as he wondered where Katrina was.

He finished preparing his backpack for the journey home and decided to open his office blinds just enough to see what might be going on outside. Fortunately, most of the park-like surroundings outside the campus buildings were well lit by lamp poles scattered throughout the grounds, so he had a reasonable view of the immediate vicinity.

Suddenly, he noticed his two unexpected visitors standing beside a large pine tree approximately thirty feet away from the building. He had almost overlooked them because they wore dark clothing and were both standing on the shaded side of the tree sheltering them from the ambient light.

His heart leapt in his throat as he noticed one of his history class students stop near the men as they engaged her in conversation. Beth Wilkins must have lingered after class and appeared to be heading across the grounds to the parking lot on the opposite side of campus.

He wasn't sure what the vampires intended for him, but he knew Beth was in a particularly vulnerable situation and would have no idea of the potential danger posed to her.

He made an instant decision and grabbed his leather jacket before pulling his office door closed behind him. His heartbeat increased anxiously, but he deliberately walked out into the cold night air towards the trio. He adopted a stern expression and stopped perhaps twenty feet from the two vampires, who noted his approach with curious expressions.

Beth noticed the distracted attention of the two figures, and her head slowly turned to gaze at Caleb with an almost relieved expression as she clutched her book bag tightly to her chest. Apparently, even she had begun to grow wary of the two men, even though not realizing the true extent of their danger to her.

"Beth, it's getting pretty late," he observed. "Do you need someone to escort you to your car?"

Beth swallowed and replied appreciatively, "No thanks, Professor Taylor. I'm parked fairly close, but I better get going."

"Okay, see you next Tuesday," he replied with as casual a voice as he could muster.

I hope I'm around to see you on Tuesday, he thought anxiously.

She turned and walked away with hurried steps, glancing back over her shoulder twice before disappearing around the corner of the science building. Caleb's gaze settled on the two vampires, who appeared mutually amused by him.

"Caleb Taylor, I presume?" asked the tall vampire with the crew-cut. "Your student spoke very highly of your skills for a professor that's so young."

"I found my niche early, I suppose," he quipped, although his false bravado was shaken by the growing feeling of vulnerability forming from not seeing anyone else in the vicinity.

The shorter Native American-looking vampire smirked. "I can see why Pete wanted to stop and see if you were the real deal. You're gutsy for a human."

Caleb gathered the taller vampire was named Pete, and he frowned, wondering what they wanted with him exactly.

"Oh, he's the real deal, all right," came Katrina's level, steel-edged voice from somewhere behind him.

He started to glance behind him, but quickly decided it was more prudent not to take his eyes off the two vampires before him. He was glad for that, because he would have missed the priceless expressions of surprise and dismay as they looked past him to where Katrina must have been standing. But Caleb was startled noticeably as Katrina's body suddenly appeared before him and to the left, slightly blocking his vision. His eyes caught sight of the handle of a combat knife protruding from underneath the back of her leather jacket.

"Who are you, and what do you want with my mate?" she coldly demanded.

The two vampires stepped back slightly and held their arms out to their sides as if expecting to engage in combat at any moment. There was a palpable increase in the tension growing in the air around Caleb, and he flexed his muscles with anticipation.

"Wait," the taller vampire insisted with his hand held up. "We're not here to cause trouble. I'm Pete Crenshaw, and my friend is Eric Holata. We're from North Carolina and were just passing through town on our way to the Rockies."

The shorter vampire spoke up. "Yeah, we heard about how you and your mate killed that South American vampire. We just wanted to know if everything we heard was true."

"Why did you approach him? Why not me instead?" Katrina demanded.

The two vampires fell silent. Then Pete replied, "We, uh, heard about how you were an alpha—"

Eric interrupted, "We thought it would be easier to talk to your mate. There was no need to disturb you over something so trivial."

So, word's getting around about either Katrina's stern attitude or temper. Or maybe both, Caleb mused. He felt more at ease about the situation with each passing moment.

"You should've approached me first," she corrected Eric. "You both seem fairly inexperienced, so let me offer you a little tip. It's traditionally better protocol to approach a vampire first, rather than their human mate."

These two must be really new vampires, she mused. She

wondered who their creator was and why they hadn't been mentored better.

"I see that," Pete replied. "Thanks."

The shorter vampire cast a quick glance at his friend and offered, "We'll be going now, if you don't mind. Sorry to have disturbed you and your mate."

The two slowly backed away, but Caleb stepped out from behind Katrina. "Wait."

Both stopped and quickly cast glances at each other before focusing on him as he reached inside his leather jacket and pulled out a business card.

"Here, take this. Email me, and I'll answer any questions you might have about what happened to us," he offered as he extended the card in his outstretched hand.

Pete moved forwards slowly and took the card from Caleb, glancing momentarily at his college business card.

"Thanks," the vampire said. "I'll do that when we reach our new destination."

Both vampires nodded to Katrina deferentially and turned to depart in a blur. Caleb squinted into the darkness beyond the farther campus buildings, but could no longer discern their location. Katrina's hand firmly fell upon his right shoulder, and she rotated his body to face her.

"Why did you do that?" she demanded.

"Do what?"

"Your offer to answer their questions basically circumvented my directive to have them coordinate through me," she explained.

He looked away and matter-of-factly answered, "I was just being polite."

"I thought you didn't like menacing vampires showing up unannounced," she countered with an arched eyebrow.

He gazed up into her eyes. "Just the ones trying to kill me."

Her right hand darted out to grasp his chin between her thumb and forefinger, and she tilted his face upwards to meet hers.

"First, that was dangerous and reckless confronting them yourself, particularly with you being defenseless, no less," she chastised. "And second, I can probably guess why you contacted Paige instead of me. But if she's not in the immediate area, you call me first when trouble arises. Understood?"

She had anticipated he chose to call Paige first to make the point he was upset with her. It also occurred to her that he might have called Paige knowing she would call her, causing her to respond to the threat instead of asking Devon to assist.

Yeah, as if I would ever defer my responsibilities to him when I had the ability to respond in person, she thought.

Either way, she wasn't pleased with his decisions that night.

"My student appeared to be in danger, and I'm not going to just sacrifice her to the wolves without intervening," he retorted. However, he silently conceded she was correct about his being defenseless. It felt as if he would have had little chance against those vampires, even under armed and better prepared circumstances.

She continued to hold his chin firmly. "And as for calling me first when Paige isn't around, are we clear on that?"

You don't get a pass on that stipulation, my love.

"Clear," he replied flatly, after which Katrina released his chin. His eyes strayed back towards the social sciences building, and he saw Tanisha watching from her office window with a wary expression.

Damn. He had forgotten she was teaching a night class. He was one of the few full-time faculty teaching a class that late, so the offices were usually deserted by the time of his evening classes. He wondered what she might have seen from her office window.

Katrina noted her mate's distracted gaze and turned her head to look in the direction his eyes were staring. She fleetingly glimpsed Tanisha before the blinds were turned up. Her mind raced with the possibilities of what Caleb's friend may have seen.

Perhaps she didn't see anything vampire-specific, unless she noticed how quickly the two vampires departed. If so, she may have to be dealt with.

Caleb didn't like the look in Katrina's eyes, and his body tensed. "Oh, no. You can't," he challenged, anticipating something grim.

Katrina turned to head in the direction of the building.

"Hold on! You can't— No, wait," he stammered excitedly as his hand darted out to grasp her arm.

She glanced down at his hand, and then stared intently into his pale blue eyes. They had a pleading look, and she sensed the tension in his body and facial expression. However, the rules were quite clear on humans who risked her safety by discovering her true nature.

"Please. Let me find out what she saw first," he pleaded. "Just give me until tomorrow."

She drew in a deep breath and released it slowly while considering his request.

Perhaps one day's time will be reasonable to ensure I make an informed decision.

"Tomorrow. No later," she stipulated firmly.

He nodded. "Fine. Thank you," he replied with relief.

She bobbed her head curtly and directed him, "It's time to go home."

He acknowledged her, feeling very weary suddenly, and walked back to the building with Katrina following closely behind him.

She was happy she had arrived in time and that the vampires apparently meant him no harm. However, she was concerned about his continued angst towards her from sparing Devon Archibald's life. Maybe she had spoken with Alton far too much lately, but for some reason she was beginning to see the potential benefits to an additional vampire's being available, if even for a limited period of contracted assistance.

Katrina's thoughts quickly returned to Caleb, and a yearning, both physical and emotional, rose within her. She lamented how it had been over a week since they had last been intimate together. She took a moment to appreciate his masculine form as he stalked back into the building to retrieve his belongings and lock up his office.

She reflected on his recent efforts at working out more, of which she appreciated the results. Not that she hadn't found him attractive to begin with.

Nice butt, she observed with amusement.

Her body craved a sudden desire to take him home and make love to him. But her hopes were dashed quickly when he exited the building a few minutes later with a tight-lipped expression. His footsteps were heavy as he walked towards her, and he stopped a couple of feet away from where she stood.

"Thanks for coming to help me out tonight," he offered half-heartedly. "I guess I'll see you at home."

"Maybe a little kiss for my efforts here?" she suggested.

He stepped forward and bent his face up meet hers. But instead of bending down to meet him halfway, she made him step up on his toes to reach her lips. Although rather than a nice, passionate kiss, he merely popped his lips against hers in a brief peck.

"Thanks," she muttered darkly.

Of course, he's likely still upset with me over Devon. And I did just suggest I might have to kill one of the few human friends he's made recently.

She sighed and followed him to his car to make sure he was safe.

Why the hell does it seem like I'm always ending up the bad guy lately?

She was definitely starting to feel somewhat underappreciated.

* * *

Friday morning arrived quicker than Caleb wanted, as it had been rather late when he and Katrina had arrived home on Thursday evening. He had had trouble sleeping the night before. His mind had been preoccupied with thoughts of what he would ask Tanisha to ascertain what she had seen.

He certainly didn't want to lose his friend, but even more importantly, Tanisha had a family, and he didn't think he could live with himself if he deprived them of a wife and mother. Tanisha was a good, sincere person and didn't deserve to have her life cut short by something that should not have happened on campus. In fact, if anything, he felt as if the fault were partly his for bringing such threats to the campus by his very presence.

His eventual conversation with Tanisha took place later that morning while neither was teaching. They had the same schedule that day for open office hours. He entered her office and closed the door behind him. Then he plopped down into the empty guest chair next to her desk.

Tanisha barely looked up from grading essays before her and prompted, "Good morning, Caleb. I can bet I know why you're here. It's about last night, isn't it?"

"Yeah, last night," he replied quietly, though his pulse was already racing.

She pursed her lips and glanced over at him with a serious expression. "I saw you step outside to check on that student," she offered. "Was she one of yours?"

He nodded. "Yeah. Her name is Beth."

Tanisha's eyes narrowed. "Did you know who those two guys were?"

This time he shook his head. "Nope. Still don't, really."

"Yeah, I kind of got that impression just from watching your and Katrina's reactions towards them," she ventured as she stared at her desk like she was recalling past events.

He let the silence grow between them for a few moments and asked, "Did you happen to see them leave?"

She frowned. "No. I picked up the phone to call security, but stopped for some reason and glanced back to see what was happening. But they were already gone. I was surprised how quickly they left, because I only turned my head away for a few seconds."

A surge of relief flowed through him, and he had to force himself not to chuckle out loud.

Oh thank God, he thought.

"Yeah, they took off pretty fast," he agreed.

She arched her eyebrows and admitted, "It's true that Katrina can seem intimidating at times, but I can see where that could be handy on occasions such as last night."

Caleb was delighted, though more from relief than from what Tanisha had said. "Oh, she can be intimidating, all right."

Tanisha's hazel eyes stared directly into Caleb's. "Was Katrina angry with you last night? It looked like she was reading you the riot act right after those guys left."

He took a deep breath and let it out slowly to stall for time while considering a response. "She thought what I did was too risky."

She nodded. "It was. But that also doesn't mean it wasn't the right thing to do for your student. We're not just educators. Our students expect for us to look after them while they're here. This is our domain, and you were well within you're right to challenge those men."

"Thanks," Caleb replied with a pleased smile.

"Although a call to security might have been smarter before you walked out there," she added.

He rolled his eyes. "Oh, not you too! It's bad enough to have Katrina preaching to me."

She grinned. "Hey, just because Katrina can be gruff doesn't mean she doesn't have your best interests at heart, too."

He frowned as he considered that and conceded that his mate did indeed care very deeply for him. He loved her for that. And while he still felt miffed with Katrina over her Devon decision, it didn't mean he didn't love her. He shook his head and decided he was simply happy not to be forced to lose a good friend.

Later that evening, he told Katrina about his conversation

with Tanisha. She listened intently, observing his body language and staring into his eyes as if probing him like some sort of lie detector. Finally, she agreed no harm had probably been done. For that, he was thankful.

However, the entire affair impressed upon him how important discretion was when it came to vampire-related matters. The ordinary world was a much more difficult place to live in than he had thought just a few months ago.

By Saturday, Caleb had had time to reflect upon matters further. He acknowledged that even if he resented receiving assistance from Devon, he was wrong not to have called Katrina when those two vampires stopped by the campus. Even worse, his decision might have risked his own life and emotionally devastated the love of his life.

It was for that reason he decided to look past his own aggravation and seek to do something enjoyable with Katrina. One of their recent enjoyable endeavors had certainly been his Find Caleb exploits, so it seemed a natural choice. At least he hoped she might view it as extending an olive branch.

However, he was determined to make his third installment safer than the last, which meant selecting a site more familiar to him. It also meant he had to be more diligent regarding preparations.

He targeted a nearby abandoned construction site located off the highway outside of Mableton. The largely concrete and steel beam structure was just a few years old and had been abandoned when the original owner, a small recreational vehicle and boat dealership, had been unable to fund the remaining construction.

They had intended it to be a three-story structure, but only the concrete and steel framing had been completed, as well as a reinforced concrete stairwell in one corner of the building. The property was secured by a chain link fence, but his brief inspection revealed easy access underneath a section of the fence where the soil had been washed out by frequent rains.

Caleb decided to survey the area from atop the unfinished building during the daytime to become familiar with the surroundings, but he needed a pair of binoculars. Fortunately, he had previously purchased a nice set some years ago and had packed them away in one of the boxes stored in the garage. With Katrina in town that evening, it seemed the perfect time to scrounge for his binoculars.

After grabbing his iPod and queuing up Gram Rabbit's "Devil's Playground," he started pulling boxes from the shelf onto the floor. He rummaged through hordes of stuff, including old music CDs, books, tax forms, college expenditure records, and miscellaneous collectibles. As he removed the last box from the top shelf, it slipped off and fell onto the floor. The lid popped off, scattering a series of photographs across the floor.

"Damn!" he cursed while squatting down to sift carefully through the pictures so as not to bend or crease any of them. Most were photos from his college years, but a number of them were from childhood that his mother had collected.

He smiled while picking up a photo of himself at age four sitting on his front porch holding an old stuffed dog his parents had won for him at the county fair.

Another picture was his mother standing with him next to a sparsely decorated Christmas tree, which had been their first Christmas together the year his abusive father had disappeared from their lives when he was eight. He stared at the picture, noting that he and his mother both had forced smiles. It had been a strange year, his father disappearing one evening after work from their home and not even taking the family car with him.

Less than a year after the photo had been taken, his mother had secured their new home in the suburbs of Columbus, Ohio.

He slipped the picture back into the box and reached down absently to stack the scattered photos into a pile.

I can look at old photos some other time, he resolved.

His past, particularly his youth, wasn't necessarily something he wanted to reminisce about at length. As he grabbed at three remaining pictures on the floor, one slipped from between the other two and floated just out of reach.

After placing the other two in the container, he reached for the lone one. He quickly scanned the photograph, but something triggered in the periphery of his mind, causing him to scrutinize it at length.

The picture was of his mother and a number of her coworkers at Columbus Mortgage at the banquet where they had won a company raffle for their children's college scholarships. Caleb had no memory of the event because the children had not been present that evening, but his mind screamed with alarm when he saw not one, but two, familiar-looking faces in the photograph.

First was his mother, of course, but the second was a young brunette woman standing to the left of the winners. The caption read, *Columbus Mortgage Award Recipients with Company Owner, Amber Simmons.*

Though Amber's hair color was different, there was no mistaking her telltale green eyes and guarded smile. Her face resembled Katrina.

His ears rang with a piercing intensity that blocked out the music from his ear buds. Searing images flared within his mind like a series of vivid flashbacks, nearly blocking out his vision and causing him to lurch where he squatted on the garage floor. He saw brightly glowing emerald vampire eyes appear like giant orbs before him.

A split-second later came the image of his father bearing an evil grimace and brandishing a leather belt in his hand. That vision sent a rush of sheer terror though his body. He felt a sudden pain in his left arm, followed by the image of blood running down it.

A loud cracking sound like a branch breaking erupted in his ears, and he thought he saw the blurry image of his father falling to the floor. Then he was vaguely aware of sitting on the cold garage floor with the photograph lying on the floor next to him. He realized that the music on his iPod was still playing as if nothing had happened.

"Crap," he muttered breathlessly while trying to

understand what had just occurred.

The visions he experienced were all new to him, save for the flashback of Katrina's glowing green eyes. He'd seen them last fall on the night she revealed her vampire nature to him, the night he fled from her in panic after receiving a similar flashback.

His heartbeat raced, and a surge of adrenaline rushed through his body as the implications of both the flashbacks and the picture impacted him like a hammer to an anvil. His attention returned to the old photograph as he picked it up from beside him and tried to divine its meaning. Katrina knew, or at least had met his mother and was apparently the former owner of Columbus Mortgage, the company his mother spent years working for until her death just a couple of years ago. A host of questions buzzed through his head simultaneously.

When did she cease being Amber to become Katrina? How well did she know my mother? Did she know me as well? Was her enrollment in my history class last fall more than just a coincidence? Was that why Katrina seemed so familiar to me last fall when we first met?

"And why the hell didn't Kat tell me about this already?!" Caleb growled.

Since meeting him as a student in his history class last fall, she had never mentioned ever knowing him or his mother. In fact, during numerous evenings of getting to know each other, well before Katrina revealed she was a vampire, she had asked questions of him implying she knew nothing about him or his past.

She lied to me?

Caleb held the picture in one hand as he massaged his temples with the other, wondering if looking at the photo would cause additional flashbacks. He went into the house to the kitchen where he tossed the picture onto the countertop. After retrieving a bottle of beer from the refrigerator and twisting the cap off, he took a few swigs.

The cold liquid burned slightly as it coursed down his dry throat. Finally, he plopped onto a barstool with a heavy sigh and stared down at the picture before him.

"What the hell?" he demanded, his mind clawing for answers and meaning to the abrupt revelations.

Radiohead's "Reckoner" was an ominous soundtrack from his iPod as he ruminated over the picture and started on a second bottle of beer. He felt shock, anger, and a sense of betrayal at Katrina for having kept such important information from him. By the time he opened a third beer, he was unsure how long he had been sitting at the counter staring down at the picture. He was only half-finished with his beer when he heard the garage door open.

It's about time, he thought angrily as he heard the familiar purr of the Audi's engine.

* * *

As soon as Katrina exited the Audi, she noticed an open box lying on the garage floor next to the storage shelves. On her way into the house, she glanced casually at the box, noting that it contained some photographs.

When she walked into the kitchen, she noticed Caleb sitting at the counter listening to his iPod. She immediately smelled beer and saw two empty bottles and one that was half full. She frowned as she observed the dark, almost angry, expression on his face. It was a mix of pain and anger, but laced with confusion.

"Caleb?" she asked tentatively as she sat her purse on the counter. "Is everything all right, my love?"

He remained silent as he stared levelly at her and took another swig of beer. He swallowed the mouthful of beer in one gulp and firmly banged the bottle back down onto the countertop. She blinked from the harsh, clanking noise it made against the marble.

"No, not all right," he stated coldly, flicking the photograph in her direction with a swift motion of his hand.

She slapped her hand over the picture before it floated off the edge of the counter, and her keen eyes focused instantly on it with a mix of surprise and growing horror.

Her past had finally come back full circle to haunt her, and a secret she long wanted to reveal in her own time had been released prematurely. Suddenly, Pandora's Box was open, and it was too late to slam the lid shut.

Oh shit, she thought with a combination of shock and weariness.

"Please, Caleb," she pleaded. "Let me explain."

He jerked the ear buds from his ears, lifted his beer bottle to take a quick swig, and held it up to her. There was only a third of the contents remaining.

"You have about that long," he answered flatly.

She had never seen him act this way before, and it worried her. But she tried to concentrate on how best to approach the topic of the photo, desperately wishing she had more time. Yet time was no longer a luxury at her disposal, and her mind raced for something to say. "I owned Columbus Mortgage, the company your mother worked for. The picture was from an awards banquet for college scholarships—"

"I know that already! I'm not completely stupid," he snapped, causing her to wince at his tone. "I can deduct all that from the picture. Tell me something I don't know, such as why you never told me about this. When we first met, you made me think you didn't know my mother or my past. Why did you lie to me?"

He's so angry.

She took a deep breath and released it slowly. "I never lied to you, Caleb. I listened intently to everything you told me about your past, but I never actually declared that I didn't know you."

He wasn't amused and deliberately lifted the beer bottle to his lips to swallow a larger-than-normal mouthful. Then he placed the bottle down before him resolutely. Only a quarter of the contents remained, she noted distinctly.

Something else happened. He never drinks like that.

"Caleb, my love, you have to understand that I never wanted to hurt you. And I've done everything in my power to protect you from harm," she blurted.

But he ignored her last comment, demanding, "How long did you know my mother?"

She blinked. "I only spoke to her directly on one occasion, the evening of the banquet. Even after I arranged for Wanda to receive an offer for a position at the company soon after your father disappeared, I maintained my distance from her."

He frowned at length as he processed that information. "Wait. You arranged for her to be hired? Why did you do that? Who was my mother to you that you would do that?"

Here we go.

A cascade of memories flooded through her mind at once. She silently recalled how Caleb, then an innocent young boy, had helped her by calling for an emergency blood delivery as she had lain in a painful, burned condition beneath his father's car in their ramshackle garage. She remembered how bravely he had delivered the blood supply to her and later returned to check on her.

Later that night, Caleb's inebriated father had discovered him in the garage and been enraged, having assumed the child had been playing in the garage against his wishes. In the child's defense, she had killed Ted Taylor in that garage, though regrettably within Caleb's view. She had tried using a hypnosis technique, typically only useful for training animals, to try erasing Caleb's memory of the event.

Of course, she wasn't sure it was prudent to blurt all of that out to him in his current state and instead chose a simpler response.

"Wanda was a single parent to a wonderful young boy, and she needed help at a critical time in her life," Katrina answered, momentarily recalling the adorable image of him at age eight.

"But how did you know that?" he demanded irritably. "And why would you have cared? You've told me before you try to stay out of the lives of humans because they're a threat to you."

She frowned at his rather base opinion of her motivations,

but she accepted it in the interest of trying to placate his temper. Instead, she concentrated on how to answer best the more direct question.

"Because I cared about you, Caleb," she explained softly. "You saved my life when you were a child, and I couldn't help but try to repay your kindness in some way."

His eyes widened with shock as his gaze shifted to meet her eyes. His mind raced as he challenged, "What the hell are you talking about? I didn't even meet you until last fall in my history class." He once again recalled the sense of familiarity he had felt upon first meeting her, and yet had no idea why. There were no specific memories tied to that feeling, and it confused him.

Katrina saw the look of bewilderment on his face and moved towards him to try to comfort him. But he jerked his hand up with his palm held outwards to her.

"No," he insisted. "Just stay right there."

She stopped abruptly, folding her arms across her chest as she frowned at his curious reaction towards her.

What's gotten into you?

"I helped you to forget me, Caleb," she began with a sigh. "It was a technique that normally only works on animals, but somehow as a child you were susceptible to it."

"Why would you do that to me?"

She paused, wondering how he would react following her next revelation to him. "You were just eight years old," she explained quietly. "And you saw something no eight-year-old should see."

His heartbeat raced, and then the flashbacks from earlier in the garage flickered in his mind. Something bad happened that he was having trouble remembering. He had memories of an abusive father, but somehow felt there was something even darker, something critical that he simply couldn't remember.

She heard his heart racing and wondered even at that late moment if she were doing the right thing.

Please don't freak out on me, my loving angel.

"What?" he insisted in a raspy voice. "What shouldn't I have seen?"

A nervous, tense knot formed in her stomach as she stared directly into his eyes. "Your father was abusing you in your garage after you helped me," she began.

His jaw tightened, and his hand strangled the beer bottle as he listened and waited.

"And I killed him."

Caleb's jaw dropped open in shock, and he nearly slipped off of the barstool. "What?!"

Holy crap! Kat killed my father?

He shook his head. "No. I don't remember that. That can't be true. He disappeared, but—"

A flashback hit him like a lightning strike. A loud snapping sound rang in his ears, and he saw a horrifying vision of his father's face as he stared back at him through hollow, empty eyes. Then his father's body plummeted limply to the floor. Caleb lurched from the barstool as his hands went to his ears, and his eyes widened with distress.

Katrina was shaken as she watched his reaction, sensing that something had jarred both his mind and body.

A flashback?

She had seen that powerful a reaction from him only once before, last fall when they had walked in the park together. She had revealed herself as a vampire to him, and he had endured a flashback after viewing her glowing eyes. He had fled through the woods from her in terror and nearly fallen into a steep ravine. Fortunately, she had been able to grab his leg at the last minute to prevent him from falling.

"Oh God," he gasped once the flashback faded.

She moved towards him in a flash and wrapped her arms around him protectively, willing the pain from his body with her strength. But she felt him struggle in her arms.

"No," he growled. "Let go of me!"

He twisted his body in her grasp before she finally relented and released him. She was very worried about his reaction and wondered what thoughts were going through his mind at that moment.

Caleb backed away from her and shook his head resolutely. "This is too much. It isn't making any sense," he insisted as he backed further away from her. "What did you mean earlier when you said that I helped you? Exactly how did I help you?"

She slowly waved her hands in a calming fashion and urged, "Please Caleb, calm down. I promise to explain everything. Let's sit down."

Other thoughts played through his frayed mind, and he muttered, "Wait a minute. If that's true, all those years, all that time, Mom and I thought my father was still out there somewhere, but he was already dead. My mother wasted all those years preparing to defend us in case he tried to return, and it was for nothing!"

I never thought of that, she realized.

The room felt too small for him, and he had a hard time trying to catch his breath.

Gotta get some air, clear my head.

He turned and dashed through the house towards the front door.

She was at his heels immediately. "Caleb, where are you going?" she insisted with concern.

No, my love. Not another dangerous flight reaction.

"Outside," he mumbled.

"Wait! Your coat," she interjected, but he was already halfway out the door and onto the front porch.

She hastily grabbed his leather jacket from the coat closet and followed him outside, pulling the door closed behind her. He was already halfway to the end of the house, heading towards the neighborhood park area, before she managed to catch up with him using her vampire speed.

He's wound too tightly.

Caleb maintained a brisk walk in the cold winter air while staring at the ground before him. "What could I have done to help you as a child?" he asked with a frown.

He abruptly stopped, leaving Katrina a step ahead before

she stopped and turned to look at him. His eyes widened with realization as he stared up at her.

"Hold on. Did you drink my blood as a child?" he demanded.

It was her turn to be shocked, and she snapped, "No! Never children or pregnant women. Never them. I merely healed a wound on your left arm. Although your blood tasted so sweet, just as it still does."

He recalled the flashback of his left arm bleeding. He frowned and opened the gate at the side of her property facing the park. It felt like he had to keep walking, keep moving, to match the pace of his mind. He inhaled cold air into his lungs, trying to clear his head. "How exactly did I help you, then?" he asked.

She kept stride beside him. "You called a blood delivery service for me. Then you brought the cooler of blood to me so I could feed and heal."

His frown deepened. *I don't remember any of that. Is it even true?*

He had no way of knowing, so he was forced to trust her for the time being.

"Heal from what?" he pressed as they reached the concrete path winding throughout the park.

"I met the morning sun," she explained sadly. "I wanted to end my life."

Caleb stopped, completely caught off guard by her answer, and stared at her incredulously. She regarded him soberly, matching him stare for stare in the light of a nearby light pole.

"Suicide?" he asked with upraised eyebrows. "You?"

She shrugged, unhappy to dwell on that time in her life. "Life grew tedious, and boring, and pointless."

His mind tried putting the pieces together, although he still had no tangible memories to draw upon. "You changed your mind?"

She smiled thoughtfully and nodded. "Yeah," she replied. "The sunlight hurt like hell, and I lost my nerve."

He nodded. "Why me?"

She adopted a smirk, suddenly appreciating the simple coincidences in life. "Your family's detached garage was the closest building within my running path, the closest shelter from the sunlight. A completely unplanned coincidence, really."

He frowned and considered the oddity of her statement. He had never given the idea of fate or predestination much thought before. Thought it wasn't as if he thought divine intervention had much to do with vampires, or if there really were such a thing. Absently rubbing at his eyes, he turned to walk further down the pathway.

She patiently observed him as they walked. *At least he seems less agitated. And he hasn't made a run for any cliffs.*

"What made you want to keep living?" he asked, finding the change of subject soothing for some reason.

"You," she whispered.

He stopped and stared into her eyes as if trying to divine the honesty in her statement. "What?"

"No human had ever helped me like that before, much less a child," she explained with a distant expression, smiling. "You were—are so very special, so unlike anyone I've ever met."

He didn't know what to say and tried to force his mind to recall anything at all about what she was saying. But nothing came.

Her expression changed to something much darker, and she continued, "It was evening, and you came out to check on me again. I had healed a great deal after drinking the blood, and you were so curious to look underneath that old tarp-covered car to try and look at me. But then your father came into the garage, drunk and feeling mean. And you were his target."

Caleb balled his hands into fists at his side, and his stare became vacant as he recalled the man who was his father. He recalled the frequent beatings, sometimes for little or no reason, and the smell of booze on his breath.

Then he remembered his mother crying and the black eyes

she sometimes received from his father's abrupt temper.

Katrina watched his reaction intently and listened to his elevated pulse. "He whipped your left arm with his belt and drew blood. I was so angry, and I repelled his attack on you. I put you outside so you wouldn't see anything further, but you came back into the garage as I confronted him again. And this time, I snapped his neck, letting his dead body drop to the floor. But you saw the entire thing, and it almost broke my heart."

He recalled the snapping sound in his flashbacks and the vacant look on his father's face. "I hope the bastard rots in hell," he muttered angrily.

She waited a moment for his attention to return to her.

"I wanted to erase that memory and try to help you lead a normal life without someone abusing you," she offered gently. "I helped your mother to find employment at my company. Although her continued success was hers alone."

"Except the college fund," he interjected.

Katrina nodded. "Yes, the college fund."

"Wait," he said. He abruptly turned and walked down the concrete path again at a brisk pace.

She walked silently a couple of steps behind him, watching him intently. *He's doing better, I think. Thank goodness.*

He stopped next to a park bench and perched on the front edge of it. "So, then you deprogrammed me," he muttered absently.

She sat in the middle of the bench next to him and reached out with her left arm across the short distance between them. Her fingers were nearly at his shoulder when he stood up abruptly, stepping away from the bench while rubbing his eyes wearily.

Almost, she thought with a grimace. She wanted to touch him, soothe him somehow.

Maybe if I could just hold him. She sighed. "I hypnotized you somewhat, yes."

A thought occurred to him, and he turned to face her as she sat on the edge of the bench. "You enrolled in my history class last fall," he prompted almost as an accusation. "That was no coincidence, was it?"

She frowned, and then sighed with resignation. "No, it wasn't," she replied. "I wanted to see how you had turned out as an adult. I had no further contact with you after you had helped me, you see. Oh, I read some newspaper clippings about how you were doing on your school baseball teams, but nothing really substantive. And while I was traveling for years throughout Europe visiting with other vampires and seeing the world, I heard from a contact at the company that your mother had passed away. I knew then that I had to check on you. So I came to Atlanta, and here we are."

Caleb felt the chill from the evening breeze begin to penetrate his sweater, and he folded his arms in front of him as he stood steadfastly before her. "So," he ventured carefully, "you didn't program me to fall in love with you, then?"

He wanted his feelings for her to be real. *Hell, I want anything to be real right now.*

Katrina looked at him sharply, only to find him staring back at her intently. She leapt up from the bench in a blur and wrapped her arms around him snugly. It caught him off guard, and he spun in an almost complete circle from her impact. But she held him upright firmly and pulled him against her body.

"We genuinely fell in love, Caleb," she assured him. "It's all real. Just us. No programming, no hypnosis. In fact, I never actually thought I would see you again once I left my Amber identity behind to become Katrina."

He appreciated the warmth from her and stood in her arms for a moment as he contemplated her response. He suddenly felt so tired and tried to move towards the nearby bench, but she was like a statue bolted to the ground, and her embrace was like a steel cable wound around his body.

She frowned down at him, suspecting the nature of his effort. Instead of releasing him, she moved in a blur, pulling him onto the bench beside her, happy to maintain her embrace around him once she had him next to her. However, she did momentarily free one arm to pick up his leather jacket beside her and drape it across his shoulders.

He appreciated the increased warmth as they sat in silence. Though still quite upset that she hadn't told him any of the evening's revelations until he had confronted her, he still deeply cared for her. He felt a little hurt and betrayed.

"Who else knows about this?" he asked. "Paige? Alton?"

"Nobody," she replied quietly. "Just you and me."

He sighed.

"Are you mad at me?" she asked tentatively.

"Yes."

Crap. "Do you still love me?" she queried with some hesitation. Her heart was in her throat as the seconds ticked silently by.

"Yes," he finally replied. "If what I feel is real, then yes."

Good, very good. "It's real. It has to be," she confirmed.

But he frowned and challenged, "Why? Why does it have to be real?"

"Because if it's not, I don't think I could handle that."

He turned to look at her with an odd expression, not quite sure what to make of her answer, but not liking the implications of it, either. He paused, then shrugged and inclined his face to softly kiss the skin of her pale neck.

She smiled contentedly and quickly turned to face him, pressing her lips against his. She tried to kiss him passionately, but he abruptly pulled away.

"No, not like that. Not right now," he insisted. "I'm still angry with you for not telling me all of this already."

Her lips tightened into a thin line. *He's been upset with me so much lately. First, Devon Archibald, and now this. Dammit to hell,* she thought.

"Fine," she replied forlornly, but quickly kissed him on the lips before he could object.

He conceded that and shrugged into his leather jacket. She removed her arm from around him long enough for him to put on his jacket, but he moved away from her before she could embrace him again.

He's going to make me pay for this, I suppose, she considered darkly. "What's restitution going to cost me?" she asked half-playfully.

He looked at her with a serious expression. "I'm not entirely sure yet. But I know one thing for certain."

She frowned. "Yes?"

He pointed to his head. "You're going to help me unblock these memories. I want to see what happened that day and night when I was eight."

She inhaled her breath sharply and countered, "Caleb, no. Not that. There's nothing to be gained by that now."

But he shook his head defiantly and demanded, "I'm already having flashbacks. I had a horrible one in the garage tonight and another one back in the kitchen earlier. So, I don't care how you do it, but make it happen."

She was taken aback by the strength of his insistence and silently considered him at length. *His eyes are so determined, so intense. What if I can't?*

"I'll try."

"Promise me," he insisted with an arched brow.

She frowned. "I promise," she conceded unhappily. Somehow.

He rose from the bench and turned his back on her. "I'm headed back. I'm cold," he stated and began walking back towards the estate.

She rose quickly to follow, but inwardly she was concerned by his suddenly dark demeanor. *I hope this is just a passing phase. But then, what can I do except try to help him through it?*

She was devoted to him and determined to get her light-hearted Caleb back somehow.

I won't give up on him when he needs my support more than ever, whether or not he realizes it himself.

* * *

Nearly a week had passed since Caleb found the banquet

photograph of his mother and Katrina. By that Friday he had at best remained stoic regarding Katrina's failure to inform him about his past, though inside he still felt a tumult of emotions.

And while it had been difficult for Katrina to view and sense his continued displeasure on a daily basis, she had remained pleasant and understanding in addition to giving him his space and leaving him to his own diversions. The problem was that it had been tearing her apart with guilt, frustration, and sadness. And as was her nature, she bottled up her emotions and concealed them from him.

In keeping with her self-imposed quiet suffering, Katrina chose to divert her own attentions to anything that would keep her mind or body occupied. She cleaned out the basement wine cellar, sorted her files and financial records, and emailed a host of vampires from around the world who sought her out. By that Friday evening, her welcome diversion was in the form of shopping.

Caleb spent the official start of the weekend grading history exams at the new dining room table. As with a number of pieces of furnishings at the estate, the large oak-finished table had been delivered in the past few weeks. A lot of former furniture had become a casualty of the battle between Chimalma and Katrina the past December.

He considered that he was sitting in the very room that had nearly been the location of his death. And though it was with discomfort that he recalled those dark events, it failed to deter him from grading exams in the room. It was the roomiest tabletop in the house and ideal for spreading out paperwork.

He paused from grading long enough to glance down at the photograph that had started the argument with Katrina a week ago. In the past few days, no flashbacks occurred, and he had begun to wonder if the effects were dulled by his frequent glances at the photo.

A pang of sadness passed through him as his eyes passed over the younger vision of his mother. He glanced with a sigh at the short-haired brunette version of his mate, then known as Amber.

Why didn't you just tell me? he wondered before returning to grading.

A few minutes later the doorbell rang. He stretched and yawned on his way to the front door, and unlike a previous occasion when opening the front door nearly earned him a crossbow bolt in the chest, he made the effort to look through the door's peephole. To his pleasant surprise, he saw one of his favorite people standing in the glow of the twin front porch lamps.

He swept the door open and beamed at the short, petite young woman dressed in form-fitted jeans and a Ramones concert t-shirt who quickly launched into his arms, knocking him back slightly with her momentum. Paige Turner was a spunky force of nature, and he was proud that she considered him a younger brother since their exploits together.

She kissed him lightly on the lips, lingering just a moment longer than would be plutonic, and whispered, "Hey kiddo, missed you."

His grip tightened around her midsection with both arms as he pulled her small body close to his, feeling as if a sudden weight had been lifted from him merely by her presence.

"God, I've missed you," he whispered desperately in her ear.

Paige considered his warm, but almost troubled greeting and pulled away from him only slightly so her penetrating blue eyes could gaze into his. His attention darted to her trademark blonde hair, styled in a straight bob, reminding him of a Charleston dancing girl from the 1920s. He had learned it was a style she had originally worn during those days before she became a vampire. It was yet another characteristic he loved that made her so different from anyone else he had ever known. There was no way Paige Turner could ever blend absently into a crowd.

"Are you okay, tiger?" she asked with a narrow-eyed expression. She had anticipated that he would be happy to see her, but she had vastly underestimated the intensity of his greeting.

He forced a smile and nodded. "Sure, just glad to see you after what seems like forever."

She rolled her eyes. "It's only been a little over a month, silly. But I decided you've been getting into trouble a lot since I was last here. So, here I am."

Paige was well informed of how the episode with Devon Archibald and the subsequent agreement between him and Katrina had negatively affected the young man before her. Additionally, she was concerned about the recent visit from the two vampires who had visited him at the college. Despite some personal challenges in her own life and reassurances by Katrina over the phone, she needed to check on him herself.

Caleb's too important to me. I told him in December that his interests are also my interests.

He grinned at her warmly, and then noticed a young man standing on the front porch, which startled him.

"Oh, sorry," she apologized, sensing his reaction. "This is my date."

Caleb shook hands with the slim, mid-twenty-something-looking fellow standing before him. He wore black jeans and a concert t-shirt for some band called The Red Letters. His short, spiky, jet black hair was tossed in an unkempt manner and reminded Caleb of a famous lead singer from one of his favorite rock bands.

"Hi, I'm Caleb," he offered. "Um, aren't you the lead singer for—"

"Green Day?" the man asked with a grin. "No, sorry, man. I wish!"

Paige groaned. "Caleb, this is Gil Yeager. While he's not in Green Day, he's the former lead singer for an underground LA band called The Red Letters."

Gil appeared amused, but she added with a sour expression, "He just likes it when people think he's Billie Joe Armstrong, hence the copy-cat appearance."

"Aw, c'mon babe," he pleaded, "You know I love Green

Day. They rock!"

She shook her head and returned her attention to Caleb. There was something about his demeanor that bothered her. She ushered Gil into the entry so she could close the front door, taking a moment to relock it.

Old habits, she considered. "Where's Katrina?"

"Out," Caleb replied dismissively. "She should be back soon. In the meantime, come in and relax. When did you get into town? You've got to stay with us while you're here, of course."

He led them into the main living room at the back of the house and gestured for them to be seated. Paige and Gil plopped onto the large leather couch in the middle of the room, while Caleb sat on the edge of a leather recliner.

"How about something to drink?" he asked politely.

"Yeah, man. You have some beer around by any chance?" Gil asked eagerly. "It was a long flight, and I'm bone dry."

Paige rolled her eyes and shook her head. "You mean, other than the four beers you had during the flight?"

"You're in luck. We've got some Samuel Adams," Caleb recalled, to which Gil energetically responded with a thumbs-up. He looked to Paige with a raised brow, uncertain if to ask her about blood since he wasn't sure if Gil knew about her true nature or not.

"It's okay, he knows," she responded to his unspoken question. "And I'll have a type A-positive, if you have it."

His eyes darted to hers with sudden recognition that his own blood was that type. He raised an eyebrow playfully and asked with a grin, "Will that be fresh or chilled?"

She smirked slyly. "Refrigerated will be fine, thanks. For now." She deliberately extended and playfully displayed her fangs at him.

He went into the kitchen with a grin. As he opened the door leading into the basement wine cellar, he heard Paige's voice in the background: "I'll just give him a hand. Oh, and the nearest bathroom is off the main hallway just down that way, if needed."

Caleb descended the concrete stairs leading to the lower level where Katrina kept her wine selections, some storage, and of course, a refrigerator stocked with plastic packets of various types of human blood. It was her food pantry, of sorts. He'd no sooner opened the refrigerator door when Paige suddenly appeared behind him in a blur. However, he had halfway expected her to follow him after her comment to Gil. "So, I see my babysitter has a new client," he commented nonchalantly as he picked out a bag of blood and closed the refrigerator door.

She frowned, grasped him gently by his upper left arm and turned him around to face her. "Babysitter only has one client, and you already know who that is," she reassured him with a sly smile.

"Boyfriend then?" he asked.

She took the bag of blood from him and turned to walk upstairs. "More like my boy-for-right-now-friend," she replied as he followed her back into the kitchen.

"You know, you're not your usual happy self, kiddo," she noted while removing a drinking glass from the cabinet. As she poured the blood into the glass, she heard his pulse increase slightly. "What's been going on?" she asked.

"I just thought that since Gil knew you were a vampire you had chosen a mate," he ventured in an attempt to defer the topic of his situation with Katrina. While he would have liked to confide in her for her perspective, he didn't want to antagonize Katrina by revealing details she might want kept between the two of them.

She considered his comment as she heated the glass in the microwave. "Nah, the reveal was purely a mistake, really. I outed myself during a late night tumble between the sheets. Lusty moments bring out our fangs and flashing eyes, you may recall. Gil seemed like a nice guy despite a rather strong marijuana habit, so I didn't want to just kill him. And although he's not the brightest bulb in the socket, he's a really great fu—"

He glanced at her with wide eyes as she corrected herself

midsentence, "…bed partner. And his blood's pretty sweet, though that's probably due to all the weed he smokes."

He smirked at her while shaking his head slightly, retrieving two cold beers from the refrigerator.

"So, a lead singer for -- what's the name of his band?" Caleb asked.

The microwave went off, and she withdrew her glass of warm blood. "The Red Letters. They broke up about three weeks ago," she said.

"Creative differences?"

She scoffed. "Yeah, the drummer got creative with his use of heroin a few weeks ago and overdosed, and the bass player got creative in a bar fight and ended up in county jail that same week. The lead guitar player got upset with the whole situation and filled an opening with another band in San Francisco. Then there's the creative streak Gil gets, until the pot runs out, that is. But that's life in a rock band for you, I guess."

"Oh," he muttered. He was completely confused and had no idea how someone as cute, desirable, intelligent, and capable as Paige could wind up being paired with Gil. But despite being so close to her, it wasn't really his place to say anything.

Life is strange, he considered.

It was at that odd moment that he focused on how fortunate he was to have Katrina in his life. However, he was upset with her for sparing Devon Archibald's life and still angry for her not telling him about his past. He had always thought their meeting was serendipitous, rather than merely her checking up on an old interest. But nothing changed the fact he was in love with her. Never mind that she not only saved his life as a child, but saved his life on numerous occasions as an adult as well.

Paige noted Caleb's distracted demeanor and could only guess at the nature of his thoughts. She waited for him to lead the way out of the kitchen. As he passed, she poked him in the ribs with the tip of her index finger and whispered,

"Sometimes it seems like all the good guys are already taken."

He smirked at her off-handed compliment and led the way into the living room where Gil was patiently waiting for them on the couch.

* * *

Katrina drove particularly fast down the highway on her way back to the estate as "Fake Plastic Trees," by Radiohead, played on her car stereo. Despite the sedate nature of the tune, she still felt somewhat edgy, so the feeling of the car's velocity as it propelled her down the highway helped to channel those feelings for the moment.

Her thoughts mulled over her current situation with Caleb. She had been particularly patient with him the past few days, but she had decided she was hardly going to hang around the house waiting for him to forgive her. It was bad enough that he was already upset over the issue with Devon in Marietta, but adding the unexpected revelation about his past had really tipped the scales against her.

Kind of crappy timing on the photograph.

At least she sought refuge in personal interests as an escape mechanism, such as the brief shopping trip she had gone on that night. She had looked at some new women's suits that were on sale, but found nothing in her size in the color she wanted.

She browsed the shelves of one of Atlanta's largest bookstores until she found a few romance novels that intrigued her. While she had always taken time to read, she now had a lot more time on her hands with Caleb avoiding social interaction and activities with her.

He's just being difficult, she reflected darkly. *No, it's like he's deliberately rubbing it in.*

At least that's how it felt to her. Like anyone, she didn't appreciate being shut out from someone important to her, even if she had been at fault. It wasn't as if she had done anything deliberately to hurt him. She had merely failed to reveal something she had intended to tell him all along but for which she was waiting for just the perfect time.

She sighed irritably while reflecting on how fate had conspired against her on that matter. How was she supposed to know that he would go digging through old pictures his mother had collected? Better yet, finding the sole photograph she allowed to be taken of herself as Amber Simmons?

Geez, I must be cursed, she thought acidly as she weaved in and out of slower traffic on the busy highway.

It was so hard being patient while waiting for Caleb to work the angst out of his system. She felt confident that she had communicated well enough how she had been protecting him as a child from an abusive father.

So that makes me the hero in this story, right?

"It wasn't like I was going to waltz into the house and tell his mother, 'Oh, hi, Mrs. Taylor. Thanks for the use of your garage today. And don't worry about that wife-abusing and child-beating husband of yours, I just killed him. The body's out in the garage, but I'll bury that for you. Now you can carry safely on your way through life. Oh, and yes, I'm a vampire, but please try not to say anything about that, okay? I'll be on my way now. And be sure not to dial 911 as I'm leaving. Nice meeting you,'" she muttered.

She shook her head while reconsidering her relations with Caleb and decided she just might have to say something to him if he didn't snap out of his funk in the next week or so. The situation was killing her, and she was only willing to let matters stew for so long before confronting them. It was in her nature, after all.

Although being somewhat morose and melancholy seems to be in my nature a lot lately too.

She sighed with resignation as her car entered the addition, and she made her way down the dark, winding street, eventually arriving at the estate's driveway.

* * *

Caleb idly chatted with Paige and Gil about California and their flight to Atlanta. After a time, Gil pulled a partially battered pack of cigarettes and a lighter from his jeans pocket and slipped a cigarette from the pack. Caleb wasn't sure what his mate's rules on smoking in the house were, but neither he nor Katrina smoked. However, Paige quickly spoke up before Gil flipped the lighter open.

"Uh, Gil, no smoking in the house," she interjected smoothly. "Maybe you could take that out back for us?"

"Yeah, sure, babe," he replied amiably, rising from the couch.

"The back porch is through the dining room there," Caleb offered while pointing towards the back of the house.

Once Gil departed and they heard the back door close, Paige looked at Caleb with a mix of amusement and curiosity. She patted the couch cushion next to her a number of times with her left hand. "Come sit with me, and tell me what's wrong," she offered lightly.

He considered the perky blonde vampire with a tentative expression. "Kat and I kind of had a disagreement of sorts, that's all."

"Yeah, I already gathered that from a recent phone call with her," she replied. Her eyes narrowed, and she asked in a curious tone, "Caleb, did you forget I'm a vampire?"

"What? Of course not," he replied in a confused tone.

"I've been listening to your heartbeat since arriving, particularly when I mentioned you weren't your usual cheerful self. I also noted the change in the dilation of your pupils from all the way across the room. So, come on over here and sit down, and tell me why you seem upset. But don't make me ask you twice, okay, tiger?"

He moved slowly to sit down next to her, slightly unnerved by her intense stare.

"Katrina mentioned you two had a pretty heated disagreement, but I failed to get a call from you about it, which I found sort of strange, kiddo," she explained. "We usually talk about everything. In fact, you haven't called me at all recently, despite my leaving you repeated voicemails. So, in the four or five minutes it's going to take Gil to get back, you need to have told me a little bit about it. Now, spill."

He smiled briefly at Paige's popular catch phrase, but reverted to a more serious expression and ventured tentatively, "Well, it all started with a photograph of my mother that I found by accident in the garage when I was going through some things."

"I don't get it. Why would that cause an argument?" she asked in a confused tone.

He swallowed, wondering if Katrina would be upset with him for saying more. "It was a photo taken when I was only a child, back when my mother worked at Columbus Mortgage. She and a few others won a contest for receiving a college scholarship for their children, and there was a group photo taken with the lady who owned the company. She had personally sponsored the giveaway, you see."

Paige frowned and shook her head while trying to discern the substance of the issue. She could tell he was clearly uncomfortable talking to her about it, but she didn't know why. "Can I see the photo?" she asked.

Caleb sat where he was and, folding his arms in front of his chest, stared past her to the dining room nearby. She watched his eyes and turned to look in the direction he was staring.

Darting into the dining room, she picked up the picture lying next to the exams he had been grading. She scanned the image, noting that the woman on the far left had eyes that reminded her of Caleb's. The other faces were rather ordinary looking, until her eyes fell upon the face of someone she recognized. Her eyes widened with surprise.

"So, Katrina knew your mother?" she asked. "And she didn't mention it to you, which instigated an argument?"

"Sort of," he conceded, fearing to say more. "I guess that's sort of silly, isn't it?"

Yeah, unusually silly. But there's got to be more to this than meets the eye. Her eyes darted back to Caleb, who appeared very tense and even less pleased than a few moments ago.

"What aren't you telling me about this?" she asked with narrowed eyes as she walked slowly back into the living room with the photograph in hand.

"There's things I don't recall from my youth, Paige," he hedged. "And I'm having some flashbacks, which started when I first looked at that photo. Although actually, I suppose I had a couple even before seeing that, but didn't realize they were related."

Paige's mind raced to try and put the facts together in some meaningful fashion, but she was still having trouble. She stood before him and noticed him glance at his watch nervously.

"Kat should be back anytime now," he ventured.

Is he relieved about that, or worried? She sat down next to him and stared into his pale blue eyes with concern. "Are you okay, kiddo?"

"Not really," he answered with a weary expression.

They heard the back door open, and Gil walked into the room muttering, "Well, it's not as cold out there as I thought it would be, but it's still way worse than winter in L.A."

Paige suddenly wished she hadn't brought Gil to Atlanta with her. But she wouldn't have been comfortable leaving him alone in California until she had a better idea of his trustworthiness. When she turned her head again, Caleb had risen from the couch and was heading back towards the reading chair.

More than anything, she wanted to know the full story of what was going on between him and Katrina, but Katrina's absence coupled with Gil's presence was complicating matters.

"Hey man, any chance I could snag another beer?" Gil queried as he plopped down on the couch.

Paige rolled her eyes and glared at him. "How about 'please?'"

"Huh?" he asked obliviously, and then smirked in recognition. "Yeah, please, dude?"

She bit her lower lip and managed to keep from growling as she looked at Caleb with a visibly strained expression. "He calls everyone dude, Caleb. It's so cute that I almost hear it in my sleep sometimes."

Caleb stifled a laugh while shaking his head and heading towards the kitchen. "No problem," he replied easily, though he wondered how long it would take before Paige lost her composure. As he entered the kitchen, he thought he heard the garage door opening. A few seconds later, Katrina appeared in the kitchen seemingly out of nowhere wearing a frown as she glanced into the living room.

"Hi, Kat," he greeted her amicably. "Oh, Paige and Gil just got here an hour or so ago."

"Gil?" she asked curiously as she moved towards Caleb, suddenly noting his unusually pleasant demeanor. It was only hours earlier when he had still seemed somewhat distant from her, not that she didn't appreciate his upbeat attitude change.

He detoured from the refrigerator to approach her and bent his head up towards her while puckering his lips. She arched an eyebrow and met his lips in a quick kiss.

"She didn't mention him to you, either?" he asked. "Gil's her date."

"Oh," she replied absently. She recalled Paige mentioning dating someone recently, but she failed to remember his name. At the time, she thought that Paige's news seemed more incidental than substantive.

And I've had my hands full lately.

Caleb reached out gently to take her hand in his, looking up into her eyes with a mix of distress and concern, "Two things. First, I've been thinking about us, and I hope you know how much I still love you, even though I haven't been very pleased with things lately. You've done so much for me in the time I've known you, Kat. I realize that I should be more appreciative about that. I hope you'll understand, and I suppose I wouldn't blame you if you were upset with me."

Her eyes rose with surprise, but she appreciated his sudden and sincere acknowledgement of his recent attitude towards her. It also helped to soften the feelings she had been contemplating on her return home that evening. A hopeful feeling flowed through her, but she was concerned by the other emotions reflected in his eyes.

"And?" she prompted by squeezing his hand in hers lightly.

"Well, second," he broached uneasily, "I've really tried to keep our recent disagreement to ourselves for the most part."

She noticed Paige was suddenly standing in the doorway to the kitchen with a photograph in her right hand. "Howdy, Red," she offered with a tight-lipped smile.

"Hi, Paige," Katrina acknowledged, realizing the photo was the one that had started the troubles between she and Caleb. "Always good to see you, though I didn't realize you were coming to town. How long are you here for?"

"Not sure yet," she replied and turned her attention to Caleb. "Why don't you forget that beer for now and help Gil bring the luggage up to one of the spare bedrooms?"

Caleb released Katrina's hand as he glanced sidelong at Paige. His eyes darted back to Katrina, and she smiled wanly at him and nodded.

"Go ahead, my love," she replied with resignation.

He gratefully slipped from the kitchen into the living room, not particularly wanting to be around when they had their discussion about the photograph. It was still a difficult enough topic for him to discuss just with Katrina.

Paige waited until she heard Caleb and Gil in the front entry area before she addressed Katrina. "What's going on, Red?" she insisted emphatically. "First there's the situation with Devon Archibald, and then the visiting vampires on campus. And since last Saturday, Caleb quit returning my calls, and all you've said is that you two were fighting. On top of that, I felt like he's avoiding me. Come to think of it, you've been pretty downtrodden and unusually distant in our conversations, as well. So, I called Alton, and he didn't seem to know anything about it, which is odd because you normally tell him everything."

Katrina felt irritated that Paige came all the way to California just to confront her about things, although some of that might be because she was altogether avoiding the topic with both her and Alton. The issue had been her little secret for so many years, and she had hoped Caleb might be the only person in whom she would need to confide.

After another moment of no response from Katrina, Paige continued assertively, "I decided to come check on things firsthand and maybe surprise Caleb, but I'm the one being surprised because he greets me like I'm his last, best hope or something. Then our boy's all tight-lipped and won't say anything, and that bothers me, Red. Finally, I've got this photograph of you with his mother from way back when. So now it's time to spill."

"Let's go for a walk," Katrina urged as she led the way towards the door leading out into the back yard. She determined that her friend seemed genuinely concerned and perhaps deserved an explanation. There was also no denying that Paige had an important vested interest in Caleb, which merited the information more than most.

Paige followed her friend, laying the photograph on the dining room table as she passed by. Once outside, she fell into step beside her friend and waited patiently. The two vampires walked through the darkness of that cold, moonless evening until Katrina reached a stand of pine trees in the furthermost part of the property. She turned to Paige with a serious expression and related the history of her first meeting with Caleb following her aborted suicide attempt nearly twenty years prior.

Paige listened raptly, her surprise turning to shock as the story unfolded. Although she had only known Caleb in recent months, she had no difficulty envisioning him as a curious blue-eyed child who unknowingly helped a vampire under the guise of aiding a supposed angel from Heaven.

She shared Katrina's outrage at how Caleb had been abused by his father and sympathized with her decision to kill Ted Taylor. And she was touched by Katrina's desire to help

Caleb and his mother following Ted's disappearance, as well as Katrina's generosity to provide for Caleb's college expenses. But most of all, she was amazed that Katrina had been able to hypnotize Caleb as a child, never having thought it was possible to do so to a human, much less with such success.

She was still wide-eyed by the time Katrina finished speaking, merely shaking her head in disbelief. She had once marveled at the close, loving relationship that Caleb and Katrina had settled into, but the complete story made it seem incredibly fateful. And it made their eventual pairing once he had reached adulthood seem like something from a Hollywood film rather than reality. However, she disagreed with Katrina's decision to wait so long to tell him about the past, even while appreciating her reluctance.

Still, she had a full understanding as to why Caleb had been so upset.

"Holy crap, Red!" Paige exclaimed. "My fangs nearly popped out of my head, and I can only imagine what Alton would say."

Katrina nodded and sighed deeply, feeling as though a heavy burden had been removed from her shoulders. She was suddenly happy she had told her friend everything and hadn't anticipated that such relief was even possible, given the subject. Still, she wasn't sure what her close friend and former mentor, Alton, would say.

I'll cross that bridge later.

Paige warmly reached out to embrace her tall friend and asked, "What can I do to help?"

Katrina wrapped her arms around the young woman who was like family to her, rested her chin atop the short blonde's head, and asked with a sigh, "Do you know anything about hypnotic memory modification?"

Paige arched one eyebrow in silence.

Gil was sitting alone on the couch when Katrina and Paige walked into the living room. Caleb appeared from the kitchen with a fresh beer and placed it on the coffee table for Gil, unaware the two women were standing at the side of the room near the dining room.

"Thanks, dude," Gil offered.

"Sure," Caleb replied and stopped upon seeing the two women standing off to his left.

Paige walked purposefully up to him, and her short arms slowly encircled him in a warm embrace. She inclined her head upwards so her lips were near his ear and whispered, "I had no idea before about yours and Katrina's history, but I understand completely now, kiddo. I'm always here for you."

She kissed him on the side of the cheek warmly, lingering for a few moments before pulling away from him. It was an uncustomary emotional gesture for the normally playful and eccentric vampire, and her actions meant the world to him. He smiled gratefully, feeling both satisfaction and relief wash over him that his guardian finally knew the truth about him and Katrina.

"Thanks, babysitter," he quipped in a whisper.

Meanwhile, Gil looked up with a mix of surprise and curiosity. "Hey babe, what's with the body pressing going on there? I thought you said he was your adopted brother."

"Hush, Gil," Paige admonished as Katrina looked on with a wry expression.

Caleb separated from Paige's embrace, moved to stand next to Katrina, and held her hand while interlacing their fingers together. "Gil, I'm proud to introduce you to Katrina," he said while glancing up at Katrina with a smile. "She's my mate."

Gil's eyes narrowed slightly as he looked at Katrina and clarified, "Hiya, Katrina. So, you two really are a couple then?"

Paige rolled her eyes, popped Gil on the back of his head lightly with the flat of her palm and chastised, "Yeah, Gil, a couple. Remember when I told you about vampire mates on the plane? Like common-law spouses but without rings?"

He grinned and nodded, "Oh, yeah. Well, that's a relief. You had me worried for a minute there, babe."

She shook her head with a tight-lipped expression and observed dryly, "He calls most women 'babe,' by the way. Though I recently expressed to him how I really *hate* that."

"Nice to meet you, Gil," Katrina offered with an amused nod from where she stood, not wanting to remove her hand from Caleb's. It felt like it had taken so long finally to get back to that point with him.

"Same here," Gil replied as he raised his beer bottle in salute and drank.

The four of them stayed up visiting, learning more about Gil and how Paige and he had met while she was out on the town club-roving. Around midnight it was obvious that both men had grown tired, though Gil's response might have been due to the volume of beers he had consumed. And while Katrina and Paige were both night dwellers by nature, a silent signal between them prompted a mutual herding of their partners to their respective bedrooms.

In the sublevel room, Katrina showered first and lay on top of the king-sized bed reading a novel. Caleb stifled a yawn as he exited the bathroom wearing a pair of dark sweatpants and the pendant Katrina had given him at Christmas. He paused for a moment to admire her in her satin pajama pants and form-fitted sleeveless top. Her long red hair was combed out smoothly and draped across her shoulders like a flowing mantle.

She's a vision of beauty, he resolved, feeling affirmation that despite their recent differences she was undoubtedly the love of his life.

Katrina glanced up from her book and smiled at him before returning to read again. She uncrossed her legs at the ankles and stretched her bare feet out before her. He walked to the end of the bed and began massaging her feet gently.

"Ooh, that feels wonderful," she purred. "But you don't have to do that. I know how tired you are."

"Eh," he replied. "I want to do something nice for you."

She smirked and returned to reading her novel. *That certainly works for me.*

After a few minutes of ministrations, he said, "Kat, I've been thinking about Paige's active night life. I mean, I feel bad enough you have to spend your days cooped up here in the estate. Then in the evenings you rarely go out unless you and I do something together. Don't vampires need to roam through the night to exercise or something?"

"I work out in the home gym," she replied off-handedly. "Besides, our stamina and constitution don't require exercise in the same way humans do."

Must be nice. He considered the topic from another perspective. "Aren't you bored, though? I mean, if you wanted to roam around town all night I'd understand."

She frowned and glanced up at him from over her book. "Do you honestly want me to spend my nights away from you?" she asked.

He massaged one foot at length while mulling that over. "Well, maybe not every night. But I feel guilty that I may be keeping you from enjoying life while you wait around for me. And even then, I can't stay up all night with you because I need at least five or six hours of sleep so I can make it through work the next day. Half the time, you spend the night lying in bed next to me, and you don't even need more than two or three hours of sleep every few days."

"I like watching you sleep. It's soothing to me to listen to the rhythm of your heartbeat, my love," she replied simply. "It's a meditative experience, really."

He wasn't sure how to respond to that, and instead just continued to massage her other foot and ankle. "But if you wanted to go out—" he began.

"Prowling around town? Skulking in the shadows for victims?" she offered in an amused tone.

"Well..."

She nodded as she turned a page in her novel and only glanced up at him briefly. "Thanks so much to Hollywood once again. Caleb, do you think for a moment I miss 'the old days' when much of my time was spent scoping out blood sources? Some of the best developments to our kind include large refrigerators and regular blood deliveries. I'm just like any other human you know, for the most part. I like reading, Internet surfing, watching television and films, shopping, and a host of other diversions. Sometimes I even like pursuing business interests or part-time careers. For the most part, I'm very content with things."

"For the most part?" he asked as he ran his hands up and down both of her calves.

She paused from reading, relishing the feeling of his firm fingertips. "Well, I have enjoyed our Find Caleb sessions, despite the most recent troubles at the wildlife preserve," she mused with a smile. "But I understand if you're kind of turned off by that for a while."

He nodded, happy to hear she enjoyed his attempts at meeting her hunting need. However, he silently admitted he was wary about elaborate Find Caleb sessions following the encounter with Devon Archibald. But he made a mental note to continue plans for the abandoned construction site.

After a moment, he looked up and stared at her in a penetrating fashion, admiring how beautiful she was. *She's a red-haired vision of loveliness. She's perfect, and I can't believe how fortunate I am to be with her. Although it's true that I'm still not entirely pleased about everything that's happened lately.*

After a moment, she looked up with a quizzical expression and asked, "What is it?"

He swallowed, stopped massaging her ankle and replied, "I was just admiring. You have to be the most beautiful woman I've ever seen, Kat."

She grinned broadly, placed her novel aside on the nightstand, and beckoned to him with the crook of her index finger. "Come here."

He crawled onto the bed, perching next to her. She reached out to grab him by the arms, rolled his body onto the bed next to her, and draped her leg across both of his. He lay on his back looking up at her as she softly kissed him on the lips a number of times, to which he responded eagerly and felt a sense of excitement wash through him.

"Do you know how many vampires would love to have you?" she asked endearingly.

"For dinner?" he countered with raised eyebrows.

She chuckled. "No, silly. For a mate."

"Very kind," he replied, although he wasn't sure if he necessarily agreed with her. But then, he didn't know many vampires, either.

Her expression turned somber as she perched over him, staring down into his blue eyes. "I'm serious, my love. You proved your worthiness for that kind of role by age eight, and then solidified it again last December. Do you know how many vampires never meet a human as dedicated and devoted as you, even over a period of centuries?"

Not that I considered you for the role of mate at age eight.

He nearly blushed. "Thanks, Kat. I'm proud to be your mate."

She smiled back at him and placed a warm kiss on his lips.

After lying in silence in her arms for a time, he felt he needed to revisit a topic. "I'm ashamed to admit that I laid the guilt on a little heavily this past week, Kat," he conceded. "While I'm not okay with what happened, I've also held a bit of a grudge against you this past week. You didn't deserve that, and I apologize."

"But you're still unhappy?" she asked.

He shrugged, admitting, "I'll move beyond it eventually. But I still want to know what happened, and I need my memories back to do that properly."

She respected his resolve, even if she disagreed with it. "Well, I suppose I'll forgive your angst-ridden indulgence from this past week."

Grateful for her understanding, he kissed her in appreciation.

A series of exchanged kisses ensued as they embraced in silence, each enjoying the intimacy of being with the other. Finally, she sighed and searched his face with a distant expression. *If only we had more time together.* Time passed so quickly for humans, and she was quite fond of the one cradled in her arms.

He regarded her silently and considered inquiring about her thoughts, but she spoke before he had the chance.

"You would probably make a remarkable vampire, my love," she muttered under her breath in a manner that, even with their close proximity, he almost missed.

His eyebrows rose, and he looked into her eyes with unabashed intensity as his mind contemplated the scope of her comment. She noted his expression and heard his pulse increase marginally, and the corners of her mouth upturned with veiled amusement.

"We won't speak of this further," she stated firmly. "But yes, the thought has crossed my mind on occasion. Although I've never turned anyone before." She tapped him on the end of his nose lightly with her fingertip. "But you have many human years ahead of you, and I probably shouldn't have mentioned the topic."

He tried to put the subject aside, but felt compelled to ask, "If I became a vampire, what would that mean for us?"

She paused, and then reached down to pinch the pendant around his neck between her fingertips. She raised it up until it was suspended before his eyes. "You're mine forever, Caleb," she answered resolutely.

He actually shivered as her words sunk into his mind. *Hers forever.* The thought was simultaneously thrilling and ominous. Despite his love and adoration for her, forever was a long time to contemplate.

He wrapped her hand in his as she held his pendant and rose to meet her lips with a passionate kiss. She pressed him back down onto the bed and nipped at his lower lip as she kissed him. Within moments, she felt his hand probing underneath her knit top, and his fingers gently caressed her breasts.

A tantalizing shiver ran through her as she turned his body to lie on top of hers while continuing to kiss him. Acting upon her signal, he used one hand to shift his sweatpants off while she slipped from her pajama pants. He kissed her passionately and endeavored to please her tenderly. Then time stood still as darkness blanketed them from the cares of the outside world.

After Caleb fell asleep, Katrina glanced at him in the darkness and pulled the covers up to his neck so he didn't catch a chill. She slipped out of bed, pulled her pajama pants and sleeveless top back on, and made her way upstairs to the first floor. She found Paige in the front entry room, curled up on one end of the couch with her feet pulled beneath her as she lounged against the arm rest. Katrina grinned at her friend's attire: a pair of black Lycra biking shorts and a black cotton t-shirt with the image of a large, red, flaming skull on the front.

"There you are," Paige greeted her.

"Sorry," Katrina offered as she commandeered the other end of the couch, draping one leg over the edge of the cushion. "Took a little longer than expected."

Paige smirked and ventured slyly, "Make-up sex is great, isn't it?"

"What makes you think—"

The blonde vampire looked away and interrupted, "Fine, whatever."

"Yes, it's wonderful, actually, particularly after a couple of weeks or more," Katrina conceded with a sigh.

Paige smirked and affirmed, "Yep, thought so."

The red-haired vampire shook her head. "So, what's the scoop on Gil?"

Paige recounted everything that she had told Caleb earlier. "So Gil has two women in his life: me and Mary Jane."

"Ah, but do you have feelings for him?"

Paige considered that with a slight frown. "Somewhat, but it's still too early for me to say for certain."

The two chatted at length about a host of other topics, including the upcoming spring break trip to England that Katrina had in mind for her and Caleb. That led to a discussion of their favorite European destinations, and Paige revealed her desire to revisit Italy and Greece following the few decades since her last visit. Since then, most of her time had been spent in North or Central America, and she welcomed a change of scenery. But with needing to observe Gil for the time being, she was putting off any vacation plans.

"Why not take him with you?" Katrina asked.

"I need to wait to find out if he's on any watch lists before he applies for a passport," Paige explained. "I'm still researching his background, but it wouldn't surprise me if he's had some trouble with the law in the past for—"

"Drugs," Katrina interjected.

Paige nodded and chuckled. "Yeah, he's kind of a pot-head. But I can probably break him of that eventually, if I wanted to."

Katrina nodded and hoped everything would work out for her. It had been years since anyone had caught her friend's eye, although Katrina had a sneaky suspicion that someone like Caleb might have been on her radar under different circumstances.

Fortunately, she trusted Paige implicitly, and the thought of her former pupil's friendship and innocent affections for Caleb no longer made her jealous. Besides, few were as devoted as the young man in her life.

"Hello? Earth to Katrina," Paige interrupted with a snap of her fingers. "Lost you there for a minute."

Katrina jolted from her reverie with a smirk and remarked, "Okay, I'm back now, Houston."

"So what are you going to do about Caleb's memory?"

Katrina quietly considered a response. "I was thinking about trying to use the same hypnotic technique to undo what I did nearly twenty years ago."

Paige's eyebrows rose. "You can do that?"

The red-haired vampire shrugged. "I can try. I've never actually faced something like this before. In fact, I haven't hypnotized anyone else since then, either. I was surprised when it worked the first time, actually."

"We could call Alton for his advice," Paige ventured.

Katrina countered, "Or I could try myself first and see

what happens."

"So, when are you planning to try?"

"Sometime soon. He seemed pretty insistent about it again tonight, actually."

Paige shrugged. "Okay, why not tonight?"

"Now?"

"Sure, why not?"

"He was pretty tired earlier," Katrina hedged.

"And that matters?" Paige retorted pointedly. "Maybe it's better when his mind is more receptive to it. I dunno, like when he's already tired?"

Katrina conceded that the idea seemed logical and peered at the clock across the room. Nearly two hours had passed. "Fair enough."

"Can I watch?" Paige asked. Katrina shrugged and nodded.

The two proceeded into the dark sublevel chamber where Caleb was sleeping. After closing the door behind them, the two vampires quietly navigated their way across the room through the darkness until Katrina sat on the edge of the bed next to Caleb while Paige stood near the foot of the bed, watching intently.

"Caleb?" Katrina asked gently as she caressed his forehead with her fingertips. "Wake up, my love."

He murmured something unintelligible and stirred. His eyes fluttered open. "Kat? Is everything okay?"

"Yes, everything's fine," she replied softly. "But I need you to wake up for me, okay?"

"B-but why?" he stammered as he rubbed at his eyes, straining unsuccessfully to look up at her in the darkness as she leaned over him. He was barely able to make out her form in the nearly pitch black conditions.

"I'm going to try the hypnosis removal," she offered.

"Awww, Kat, can't it wait until morning?" he groaned and rolled over on his left side while trying to pull the covers over himself again.

She rolled her eyes, pulled the sheet and comforter down

to his waist and insisted, "No, my love. I need to do this while you're vulnerable."

His eyes shot open as he clawed to grasp at the covers. "What?"

She quickly corrected herself. "I meant, susceptible. It may be easier that way."

He sighed and rolled back over to stare at her dark silhouette as she sat next to him.

"Maybe you could sit up for me?" she suggested.

He sat up in bed lazily, and she was suddenly pleased he had pulled his sweatpants back on since leaving him earlier. She wasn't comfortable parading her mate around naked in front of Paige, or anyone else for that matter. Reaching behind him, she pulled his pillow up to rest against the headboard. "Lean back against the pillow."

He sighed again and leaned into the pillow while pulling his legs up underneath him to sit Indian-style before her. Then he crossed his arms before his bare chest.

"Just keep staring into my eyes and try to relax," she instructed as her eyes began glowing bright emerald.

He watched her eyes and yawned, while shivering slightly from the cool air in the room. He noted that Katrina's eyes continued to glow more and more brightly.

They look like beautiful emeralds floating in a black sea.

After a few minutes his breathing relaxed, but he shivered again as a chill reverberated through his body. A fleecy blanket was abruptly wrapped around his upper body, startling him.

"Sorry, kiddo," Paige offered to his left.

He broke his gaze with Katrina and glanced to his left. "Paige?"

Katrina made an exasperated sound and growled, "Caleb, please concentrate. Paige is just supposed to be observing quietly."

He smirked in Paige's direction. "Glad you could make it to our little séance."

He felt the bed move slightly as Paige scooted next to him

and pulled her knees up to her chest. "Happy to be here, actually."

"Could we please get back to business?" Katrina asked with an exasperated sigh.

"My bad," Paige whispered while nudging Caleb slightly.

"Sorry about that," he added quietly as his gaze returned to Katrina's glowing eyes. He felt Katrina's hand pat him lightly on the inside of his thigh and withdraw again, leaving him feeling much more comfortable while wrapped in the comfy blanket.

After staring into Katrina's eyes for an undetermined period of time, he felt his eyelids grow heavier. He could have sworn that her eyes were actually pulsing, becoming brighter.

"Think back to your childhood, Caleb," she whispered. "Think of your back yard, and your toys, and the garage."

He tried to recall his childhood and immediately recalled images of opening gifts at Christmas when he was just a boy. He flashed on an image of riding his bike from the front yard out into the street during late spring or early summer, though he couldn't recall how old he had been. He thought of his mother baking cookies and pies at the holidays, followed by his father coming home from work and the smell of alcohol.

"Think of your garage, Caleb," she urged soothingly.

Caleb's flashbacks shifted, and he was able to see the inside of their old garage, including the tools and old car parts his father left lying around. He saw the old car covered in the dirty plastic tarp that his father had renovated for years when he was a child. He recalled the times he sneaked beneath it to peek at things just out of curiosity.

Caleb no longer saw Katrina's glowing orbs, and instead flashed to a time when the garage seemed somewhat scarier. He breathed in sharply as he flashed on a vision of his father lashing out with a belt at him and the searing pain across his left arm. The pain was fresh, but it felt like a stabbing dagger instead of simply a leather belt.

"Pain!" he shouted as his eyes went wild, and he kicked away from Katrina abruptly, nearly catching her in the chest as he flailed away with his right foot while his left foot dug against the mattress. He sprang to one side as his foot finally impacted the mattress beneath him, and he flung the blanket from around him in a sudden lurch.

"Caleb!" she shouted, trying vainly to reach out for him.

But Paige was closer and faster and was able to wrap her arms around his torso, trapping his arms to his sides as he tried to launch his body past hers. He bounced against the mattress, shutting his eyes tightly against the images which still flashed before him.

"Stop!" he pleaded. "Just stop, I changed my mind. No more!"

Paige's eyes were wide with shock as she held him against her body. Her gaze darted over to Katrina, who quickly recovered and was stretched across the bed alongside him.

Katrina held his face between her hands, whispering, "It's okay, my love. You're safe. We're stopping."

He nodded and quietly lay there, no longer trying to fight against the strong arms that held him in place like iron bands. Paige relaxed her embrace and unwound her arms from around him.

"I'm so tired," he murmured raggedly into the comforter pressed against his face.

Katrina's mind raced as she tried to understand what had just happened, but she suspected that questioning him about it at that moment would prove both unwise and fruitless. She kissed him affectionately on the forehead, and Paige assisted her with maneuvering him back under the covers in the center of the bed.

The petite vampire gathered his pillow and slipped it beneath his head for him. "Try and get some rest, kiddo," she whispered.

Both vampires moved off the bed and stared at each other silently with wide-eyed expressions.

"Please don't leave," he mumbled quietly.

They glanced down at him, and then Paige looked back at Katrina. "You call Alton," she suggested. "I'll stay with him for now."

Katrina nodded with a resigned sigh, picked up the phone handset near her computer hutch, and preceded upstairs up to the first floor while Paige lay down beside Caleb.

"Babysitter's right here, tiger," Paige whispered as she laid her arm over his huddled form. She kissed him lightly on the back of his head.

"Thanks," he whispered.

Her mind raced to understand what had just happened. She had never seen anything like that from him before, and she realized it was going to take more than just amateurs to assist the young man in reconciling his memories. She just hoped that Katrina realized it and that Alton advised her friend of the same.

Within minutes, Caleb drifted off into an exhausted, dreamless sleep.

CHAPTER 4

Imperfect Pairings

When Caleb's eyes fluttered open, the room wasn't as dark as before, and he realized from the dim glow that a lamp had been turned on somewhere across the room. He was lying on his stomach, and one side of his face was pressed into his pillow. Upon trying to move, he winced as his neck and upper back muscles ached in protest.

"Oh, crap," he moaned.

He rolled onto his back and rubbed his eyes. Feeling the bed jiggle slightly, he removed his hands to see Katrina staring down at him. She leaned over him with her hands planted on each side of his body and kissed him lightly on the lips.

"Good morning, sleepy head," she greeted with a warm smile.

"Mm, morning," he murmured.

"Feeling better?" she asked.

His mind quickly recalled the events from the night before, and he frowned. "Oh, that's right. I think I'm okay."

She continued to hover over him as she studied his features, and he noticed she was already dressed in jeans and a long-sleeved turtleneck. "Wha-what time is it?" he stammered.

She glanced at the clock across the room. "Almost ten-thirty, my love."

"Geez!" he exclaimed. "I need to haul my butt out of bed then. I don't want be rude just lying here all day."

But she pressed her palm against his bare chest and pushed him gently back onto the bed. "No hurry, it's Saturday. And Gil only roused an hour ago," she reassured him.

He relaxed somewhat and studied her eyes for a moment. He could spend hours gazing into those beautiful orbs.

The corners of her mouth upturned slightly in amusement. *He has that mesmerized expression again.*

He deliberately blinked and looked past her face to regain his concentration. "What's next?" he asked.

"I called Alton last night after your outburst," she replied. She related how Alton had listened intently to her story of meeting Caleb as a child, as well as all the events that transpired, including taking the dead body of Caleb's father with her that night to bury him in an undisclosed location. Her former mentor had been very patient and waited until the very end to ask clarifying questions.

Finally, he had remained so silent before speaking again that Katrina had feared he had hung up on her. He explained how tricky hypnosis was and ventured how difficult it might be to alter what she had done.

"Alton said he knows of a vampire in London who's a long-time practicing psychiatrist who might be able to help you," she said. "Although he'll have to provide details later. He suggested we might be able to address that when you and I visit him on our trip to England."

"That's kind of him, of course. But I'm curious what he said about our real initial meeting?" he asked pointedly.

Her expression was unreadable as she fell silent for a moment. "He was sympathetic, actually," she recalled. "But he was very intrigued and said that it answered a few questions he had about your and my relationship. I'm still not sure what he meant by that; he was terribly hedgy on the subject. But he did have a message for you."

Caleb's eyebrows rose. "Yeah?"

She smirked. "He used that term of his again. He said, 'Tell Caleb that, to be brutally honest, I'm concerned for him and want to help as much as possible.'"

He smiled at the use of their special phrase "brutally honest" to indicate the sincerity of his comments versus merely being polite. Katrina studied his reaction carefully and wondered if there were more to the message than what had been stated.

"That was very kind," he replied.

She decided not to press the topic. "You gave Paige a bit of a scare last night too. She's very concerned."

He grinned shyly. "Really? She's a good friend, and a great guardian. We're tight."

"Even closer, I think," Katrina observed and kissed him softly on the lips. *But I'm okay with that level of friendship, she conceded fleetingly, so long as it remains a friendship.*

"Hungry?" she asked.

"Sure!" he replied brightly.

She shook her head. "When are you not?"

He adopted a mock-insulted expression, and she used her hand to dishevel his hair even more than it already was. "Okay, now you need to get that cute butt of yours out of bed," she prompted with a sly smile.

"How about breakfast in bed?" he countered with a smirk.

She arched an eyebrow in a challenge and swiftly wrapped her right arm underneath and around his waist. Pulling him from the bed with a lurch, she swung his body around until his toes touched the carpeted floor. He nearly lost his breath and teetered unsteadily as he landed on his feet, but she steadied him with her arm still wrapped securely around him, for which he was grateful.

"Wha—" he started, but she crushed her lips to his.

His arms encircled her waist, and he pulled her towards his body as they kissed. "I'll be up soon," he promised.

She pressed against his body and countered, "I sense

you're already up."

What a nice way to start the day.

He flushed slightly regarding his body's excited reaction as she pulled deliberately away from him. She moved in a blur to appear at the top of the stairs, glancing back over her shoulder with a smirk. The door slid shut behind her, leaving him standing in silence.

"Damn, she's fast," he muttered with a grin, shaking his head.

After he showered, shaved and slipped into a pair of jeans and a Georgia State baseball sweatshirt, he proceeded upstairs and immediately smelled the fresh scent of pancakes. He smiled with sincere appreciation as he noticed Katrina flipping fresh pancakes over a griddle.

Paige stood next to her, watching with an amused expression, while Gil sat at the kitchen bar counter eating a stack of three large flapjacks.

Katrina glanced at Caleb from over her shoulder as he walked closer to the stove. "Ready for some pancakes?"

Paige looked at him with a raised eyebrow and an expression of awe and asked, "When did all this cooking stuff start?"

He grinned. "Just recently. Kat's a great cook, actually."

Katrina smiled appreciatively as Paige reached out to pull Caleb into a sideways embrace with her left arm. She gave him a quick peck on the cheek. "How ya feeling this morning, kiddo?"

"Better, thanks," he offered as his right arm quickly slipped around her waist to complete the hug.

Katrina slipped three pancakes onto a large plate and handed it to him. "Eat up," she quipped.

"Mmm," he hummed, and plopped onto a barstool next to Gil. "Morning, Gil. How'd you sleep?"

Gil's eyes played over to Caleb's fresh pancakes, and he looked back over his shoulder at Katrina.

She anticipated his request and asked, "How many, Gil?"

"Three, please," he replied gratefully before returning his

attention to Caleb. "A good night for me last night. Pretty sore in some places when I woke up, though. But it was the good kind of sore I wouldn't pass up again tonight, if you catch my drift."

Paige shook her head as she moved across the kitchen to fill a drinking glass with water. She sat the glass down in front of Caleb while glaring at Gil. "A little too much info, Gil."

Caleb smirked as he drizzled syrup on his pancakes. "Couldn't agree more, Paige." He dug into his pancakes with a vengeance and complimented his mate, "These are great, Kat!"

She neatly slipped a fresh stack of pancakes on Gil's plate with her large spatula and lightly ran her fingernails down the back of Caleb's neck in silent response, causing him to shiver pleasurably.

"Yeah, these are good, Katrina," Gil offered. "Thanks."

Paige used Caleb's momentary distraction to slip a forkful of his syrupy pancakes into her mouth with an appraising expression. "Tasty, actually," she offered with surprise.

"Want some?" Katrina asked her with a smirk.

"Make 'em with blood, and I'll consider it," the spunky vampire replied.

"Major gross," Gil muttered around a mouthful of pancake.

Paige popped him playfully on the back of the head with the flat of her hand and teased, "Ha! Just wait until you try burning some stinky dead animal meat in my kitchen again."

"So, what are we doing today?" Caleb asked.

"How about we go around town and take in some sites?" Gil suggested. "We can all hang out together."

Caleb stopped chewing and looked sidelong at the young man with upraised eyebrows while Paige just rolled her eyes.

"The ladies are vampires, Gil," Caleb reminded him. "Remember? Sunlight bad, nighttime good?"

"Oh, yeah," Gil replied foggily. "Sorry, they just seem so normal that I forgot about that."

Katrina gazed wide-eyed at Paige, who slowly reached out

her hand towards Gil's neck from behind him as if to choke him while glaring into the back of his head.

"How long have you known Paige exactly?" Caleb asked warily while noting Paige's reaction out of his peripheral vision.

"Oh, just a few weeks now," Gil replied as he continued eating his pancakes, oblivious to the shaking motion Paige was making with her closed fist behind his head.

Katrina stifled a laugh and interjected, "Maybe Caleb can take Gil out for the day to scope out some activities for tonight."

"Please, take him away already," Paige muttered.

Gil chuckled, not realizing Paige was actually annoyed with him.

Caleb defrayed any further aggravation on Paige's part by offering, "I'll show Gil some of downtown. Like Kat suggested, we'll locate some potential hot spots for this evening. How's that?"

Before long, the two men were on their way. To Caleb's satisfaction, Katrina had been kind enough to let them take her Audi out for the day. He drove them past a number of areas of interest in the Atlanta area, including some historic plantation homes, museums, the Centennial Olympic Park, Civil War locations, the Atlanta Zoo, and a host of other noteworthy attractions.

He stopped at a number of interesting locations with the hopes of piquing his West Coast visitor's interest. However, Gil seemed most intrigued by the heart of the city itself and was curious about the locations of some of the city's most popular clubs, particularly ones catering to alternative rock.

By mid-afternoon, Gil asked to stop at a bar or pub to grab a beer and a bite to eat. Caleb began a quick search on the car's GPS for possible locations, but Gil pointed to a random bar just up the street.

Caleb realized that they weren't in the safest part of town, but relented after sensing the enthusiasm in Gil's demeanor. The bar was a reasonably maintained establishment called

Brandy's whose parking lot teemed with sport utility vehicles and pickup trucks.

In fact, Caleb took note of the fact that their sports car was the only actual car in the parking lot. A large-framed fellow with mustache and crew cut parked beside them and gave them a long, wary look as he walked past their car to head into the bar.

By the time the two of them crossed over the threshold of the front door, Caleb wondered how poor a choice they had made. The customers consisted mainly of what appeared to be gritty, hard-nosed types.

Even the furniture looked nearly as worn and hard as the clientele, relegated to a variety of scratched oak tables and chairs that looked as though it was generations since they had been refinished. The stools lining the worn-looking bar were vinyl-covered, though most had cracks and tears in the material.

George Strait blared from a jukebox across the room, and some older model televisions mounted above the bar displayed rodeo, monster truck, and boxing events.

Most of the faces in the room looked up at the two newest patrons with expressions ranging from amusement, to wariness, and even mild disgust. Obviously, despite the inclusion of their leather jackets, Caleb's college sweatshirt and Gil's Green Day concert t-shirt failed to impress anyone.

"We should go," Caleb urged with a wary expression.

"No way man, I'm thirsty," the suddenly willful young man from California retorted as he strode purposefully up to one of the available wooden tables. He pulled out a worn chair and plopped down.

"Just great," Caleb muttered as he followed and pulled up a wooden chair opposite him.

A short, blonde waitress who appeared in her forties wearing faded jeans and a polo shirt with the bar's name on it stopped by their table with a slightly raised eyebrow. "You two stayin'?"

Caleb looked across the table at Gil, who was taking in the

décor in the room and sighed. He glanced at the waitress, noted her nametag and replied, "Well Peggy, it kind of seems that way."

The woman shrugged. "Just thought I'd better ask first. What can I get you?"

Gil immediately popped up with an order for a Modelo Especial on tap, and Caleb ordered a bottle of Samuel Adams.

"I'll be back in a minute," the waitress responded. "Menus are on the table."

As Caleb reached for one of the worn-looking menus, he heard a chortle from the table next to theirs where three burly, rough-looking guys were sitting, including the large-framed man with the mustache who had preceded them into the bar. Their laughing was followed by a deep voice razzing, "Hear that, Wes? No salt or lime to go with that Modelo for the punk-rocker."

A round of chuckling ensued, including some cursing, followed by the response, "Hell, I haven't heard about anyone ordering old Sam Adams since he died at the Alamo!"

The history professor personality inside Caleb cringed painfully. It always incensed him when people made such inaccurate historical references.

Still, it wasn't as if the guy would care to know that Sam Adams was actually a reference to Samuel Adams, a prominent founding father from the American Revolution. It would just escalate tensions, which was precisely what Caleb didn't need at the moment.

"Well, ya' old bastard, I guess you'd know since you were there!" another teased.

A round of laughter ensued, followed by the thumping of empty beer mugs on a tabletop. One fellow boomed, "Peggy! Another round of Buds for the real working men over here!"

The waitress appeared with Caleb's and Gil's beers, plopped them onto the table, and barked at the men, "Keep your shirts on. I'll get to you in a minute!"

The men grumbled and returned to talking shop.

Peggy's demeanor became somewhat more professional as she regarded Caleb. "You boys ready to order something from the menu?"

"Any recommendations?" Caleb asked with a hopeful expression.

She regarded him with a sober expression and suggested, "Drink here, eat somewhere else."

"Maybe just a burger, well-done, and some fries, please," he requested politely as the waitress scribbled on a small notepad.

Peggy looked at Gil. "And for you?"

Gil's face turned oddly introspective. "So, about the nacho platter. Is it pretty good?"

Her expression turned a mix of sour and amused, and she retorted, "You been to the state fair before and ordered nachos?"

Gil shrugged. "Yeah, I guess so."

"Well, these ain't as good as those," she replied.

Gil frowned with distaste and offered, "Uh, yeah. Well, I'll just have the same as him, well-done on the burger, too."

The waitress smirked as she wrote on her pad, and then silently walked back towards the kitchen. Gil and Caleb simultaneously exchanged curious glances, and one of the burly fellows at the nearest table muttered to his buddies, "Five dollars says they can't even finish eatin' those greasy burgers."

Caleb ignored the comment, took a swig of his beer and asked, "So Gil, what do you think of Paige so far?"

The rocker considered his question. "Well, she's a free spirit, you know. But I like her, and she's a hell of a lot of fun out clubbing. And damn, she rocks that body, man. But you probably already know that, eh?"

Caleb frowned. "Not really, Gil. I haven't been out clubbing with Paige. At least, not yet. She keeps threatening to get me out on the town, though. And as for rocking her body, we're almost like family, you know. She means a lot to me, but we're not like that."

153

Gil glowered and took a long pull from his beer.

"What?" Caleb pressed.

"Well, it's just the way you two act," Gil began carefully. "Listen, I ain't an idiot, Caleb. You're not her family, after all, no matter what she says about being like a sister and all that. And then there's the way she pressed against you last night. Damn, Caleb. My buddy Skeet has a sister, and they don't look at each other the way Paige does you. Although Skeet and his sister aren't all that close, I guess. Hell, I don't know. I just know nobody ever looked at me like that before, dude."

Caleb felt a pang of concern run through him.

"Gil, you've got it all wrong," he countered. "Paige, she's really more like a sister to me. I mean, I really care about her. But I'm not a threat to you and her. It's cool."

Gil took another swig of his beer and cast a glance to the men at the nearby table who were distracted with fresh beers from Peggy. He regarded Caleb with a more relaxed expression and grinned, "Hey, no problem, Caleb. I get it."

But he sensed something from Gil and lowered his voice as he leaned across the table. "No Gil, you don't. You've got it all wrong about Paige. She's like my guardian angel, a protector. I mean, she's saved my life on at least two separate occasions since last fall. I owe her my life, for God's sake. But I want her to be happy, and if you do that for her, then I'm all for it. Got it?"

Gil responded with a quick nod and half-grin before being distracted by something across the room.

Caleb observed him looking pointedly at the old jukebox along the back wall and watched him get up from his seat. He immediately suggested, "Hey Gil, I'd just leave well enough alone there if I were you. We'll finish eating and head out of here, okay?"

But Gil seemed determined and insisted, "Man, this lame bumpkin scene is killing me. We're gonna change the sound around here, at least while we're stuffin' our faces."

Caleb just shook his head and watched as the young man strode confidently over to the old jukebox and sorted through the available titles. He fed dollar bills into the jukebox, and there was a pause as titles loaded. In a matter of moments, hard rock began to play, starting no less than with Green Day's "When I Come Around."

"Just great," Caleb remarked under his breath before taking a swallow of beer and casting a wary glance at the rowdy fellows seated nearby. The men were talking, but paused as the music blared. Their narrowed eyes followed Gil all the way back to the table, glaring at him as he sat down.

"Friggin' punk rock shit," one of the men growled. "I told Butch he shoulda kicked that damned old jukebox to the curb years ago if he wasn't going to pack it with more country."

Caleb took a swig of beer and silently considered how quickly they could make it to the exits if things turned ugly. Fortunately, the men seemed to be content to just curse and complain, rather than take any action.

Moments later, Peggy arrived with their burgers and fresh beers, and she seemed more upbeat for some reason.

"Here's the burgers, guys," she announced. "And good job on the music. Nice to hear something else besides George Strait or Brooks and Dunn for a change."

She departed quickly, leaving Caleb and Gil exchanging surprised expressions. Both shrugged and returned to their burgers and beers. Everything seemed more sedate for a short time until they were almost done eating. That's when the three guys at the nearby table divvied up money to pay and rose to leave. Each of them made a point to brush up against either Caleb's or Gil's chairs while walking past.

"Friggin' yuppies," grumbled the man with the dark bushy mustache and crew cut as he banged into the back of Caleb's chair while passing.

Caleb discreetly rolled his eyes at the comment. It wasn't as if either he or Gil looked anything like young urban professionals, particularly dressed as they were. *Ignorance is definitely bliss with some people.*

"Redneck bastard," Gil muttered under his breath as the guy walked away.

The man turned abruptly to grimace at Gil, demanding, "What was that, punker?"

Gil swallowed his bite of burger and started to say something, but Caleb cut him off with, "He said 'better eat faster,' that's all."

The burly fellow sneered, shook his head, and cursed under his breath while continuing to the door to leave. Caleb relaxed somewhat once the last man walked out and looked over at Gil with barely contained contempt.

"Are you anxious for a bar fight or something?" he chastised. "Those guys are just blowhards. Geez, let's just eat and get the hell out of here."

Within minutes, Caleb finished his beer, and both of them declined another refill when the waitress stopped by with their bill.

"I hope you weren't bothered by those guys who were in here," Peggy suggested. "They're just a bunch of complainers who usually shoot off their mouths. Butch, the owner, threatens to ban them from this place, and they usually simmer down."

Caleb thanked her and took care of the check with cash, making sure to leave a generous tip for Peggy. Barely ten minutes after their biggest fans had left, Caleb and Gil were exiting the bar out to what was a sunny, warmer-than-expected February afternoon.

"Gil, next time, I get to pick the bar," Caleb remarked absently.

Everything seemed fine, until they spotted the three troublemakers from the bar standing around Katrina's car at the side of the building where they had parked. Caleb shook his head in near disbelief as he stared at the throng of men, only to realize the guy with the mustache and crew cut was relieving himself onto the Audi's right rear tire.

A surge of anger ran through him, but he managed to keep himself in check as he walked slowly towards their car. The man zipped up his jeans, and all three men started laughing as they cast incendiary glances towards Caleb and Gil.

"Hey, assholes!" Gil snapped as he walked a little faster than Caleb towards the car.

"Just get in the car, Gil," Caleb warned, deactivating the alarm with the key remote.

But Gil was already approaching the three men with his fists balled up tightly.

Caleb swore under his breath as the mustached man barreled forward while Gil shifted next to the car. Gil barely had time to lift his fist before the man punched him in the gut, causing him to double over.

"Aw, crap," Caleb growled as the other two men moved deliberately towards him.

Everything happened so fast after that. Caleb barely realized that one of the two men had swung towards him, but he managed to pivot his body, only catching a glancing blow to the left side of his head.

Something shot through him, like a cross between a flashback and an electrical surge. The memory of Devon Archibald's attack on him at the wildlife preserve replayed in his head like a lightning flash. Only this time, instead of fear, he felt intense anger and resentment. He was tired of being attacked, and since these guys weren't vampires, an important notion occurred to him: they were only human, which made them beatable.

Reactions began to flow in his body without the need to think as some of the combat training Katrina had drilled into his head activated. Of the two men approaching him, the second fellow, a red-haired man, aimed his fist at Caleb's stomach while his buddy recovered his balance from the initial missed punch.

But Caleb grabbed the red-haired man's forearm with his left hand while slamming his clenched fist into the front of the man's throat. The assailant immediately gasped with a choking sound, and fell forward onto his knees onto the asphalt parking lot.

The first man, a bearded guy with curly hair, recovered and punched Caleb in the lower back around his kidneys.

Pain shot through him, but it was bearable and nothing like the pain from Devon's assault, so he had enough stamina to whirl and catch the man in the side of the nose with the back of his right elbow. Caleb heard a crunching sound as his elbow slammed into the bearded man's face, followed by a shriek as the guy reached up to cup his face with both hands.

One glance at Gil revealed he was quickly losing in the brief melee of fists flailing between the two men. The mustached man made a quick punch to Gil's jaw, sending him banging into the side of a beat-up old pickup parked next their car. The young rocker slumped groggily down to the asphalt after that.

Caleb rushed forwards to side-kick at the mustached man's left knee, sending the yelling thug to the ground. Caleb landed punches against the left side of the guy's head and jaw, requiring only three sharp blows before the guy fell unconscious onto the blacktop with a heavy thump.

Caleb was spun around from behind, glimpsing the red-haired man who he'd hit in the nose with his elbow. Blood still ran down the guy's mouth and chin as his fist landed against the left side of Caleb's face, popping his head backwards. The man weighed into Caleb with a left blow to his ribs, but Caleb maintained concentration on retaliating by foot-sweeping him.

As the red-haired man fell backwards, Caleb slammed the flat of his foot into his head, knocking it back against the pavement with a thud. All the fight ebbed from the thug as he rolled onto his side moaning and grasping at the back of his head.

Caleb breathed heavily while glancing around for witnesses as he grasped Gil by his arm and helped to steady him as he rose. Gil shook his head slightly, seeming to recover his wits and looked at Caleb with a surprised expression.

"Where the hell did you—"

"Just get in the damned car!" Caleb yelled as he felt warm blood running down into his left eye.

"Shit, no, dude! I better drive," Gil insisted as he picked

up the keys from the pavement near the front of the car. "Dude, your face is bleeding wicked bad."

Caleb cursed and fell into the passenger seat of the car as Gil raced around to the other side, hopped into the driver's seat, and revved the engine. He peeled out of the parking lot and into the late afternoon light traffic.

"Shit! I'm not even sure which way is home," he complained.

Caleb managed to remove his blood-covered sweatshirt, wadded it up, and used it to press against the bleeding side of his face as he attempted to discern their location. He glanced at the GPS, punched the preset for home, and barked, "Just follow the GPS!"

"Okay, just chill," Gil snapped. "Don't get all cracked out on me, dude."

Caleb grumbled under his breath, wishing he had some ibuprofen or something for the pounding in his head. He shifted slightly in the seat to test his back and ribs, but didn't think anything felt broken or out of place. Still, most of his body ached, and his right knuckles were throbbing. He glanced sidelong at Gil, who had a bloody lip and bruises on his face, but otherwise seemed okay.

What a sight-seeing trip, he thought darkly. Katrina's sure as hell not going to be happy about this, he considered as an afterthought.

It only took about twenty minutes for them to make it back to the estate, though that was partly due to the fact that Gil enjoyed speeding down the highway at any opportunity.

The car lurched into the driveway, and Caleb activated the garage door opener, muttering, "Just leave the car out. We have to hose down the tire and fender, remember?"

"Yeah, sure," Gil replied absently as they got out of the car and walked into the garage.

Katrina and Paige sat in the living room at the back of the house sipping glasses of warm blood and discussing the prospects of the prospective territorial claims needing to be declared by Katrina around Atlanta.

The quiet was broken as Gil burst into the kitchen, announcing grandly, "Ladies, your knights have returned! Hey, Katrina! Your car is one bitchin' machine!"

Both vampires cast curious glances at each another and turned to stare at Gil as he walked into the living room. Gil hastily tossed the car keys across the room towards Katrina, who neatly caught them in one hand over her head without even glancing at them.

Both vampires were transfixed, studying the bruises and cuts on Gil's face.

Paige demanded, "What the hell happened to you?"

"Oh, shit, man," Gil began excitedly. "We just got a beer and burger, and so these three rednecks were bitching about our music. Then..."

While Gil rambled about their adventure, Caleb sneaked behind and past him through the kitchen and made his way down the main hallway to the sublevel chamber where he could clean up and tend to his bleeding face.

As Gil rambled on, both vampires abruptly sniffed the air, and Katrina cast a sidelong glance at Paige with a knowing look in her eyes.

Caleb's blood, she determined.

Paige seemed to sense the same conclusion, because she jumped up from the couch and held up her hand for Gil to stop talking. "Wait!" she insisted. "Where's Caleb?"

"Caleb?" Gil asked. "I dunno. Maybe he's hosing off the car tire."

She frowned with confusion, but Katrina already sped past her and was following the blood scent trail through the house.

"Car tire?" Paige asked with narrowed eyes. "Why would he—"

"One of those assholes peed on the car," Gil explained.

Paige sighed and demanded, "Where were you two again?"

Gil started to speak, but Paige grabbed him by the arm and led him into the kitchen saying, "Never mind. Let's get you cleaned up first. And don't bleed all over the new carpet; Katrina's had it less for than a month."

* * *

Caleb removed his bloody t-shirt and dropped it to the tile floor atop his blood-soaked sweatshirt. As he washed his face in cold water, the bathroom door knob rattled. Then came an immediate knocking sound and Katrina's voice.

"Caleb? Caleb, are you okay?" she insisted with concern.

"Fine. Everything's fine," he reassured her, "I'll be out soon."

Outside, Katrina exhaled a deep breath and shook her head. *Yeah, right. That's typical guy talk for, "I'm hurt and don't want you fussing over me."*

"Open the door right now, my love, or I'm breaking it down," she ordered.

Caleb winced from her tone and held a damp washcloth over the left side of his face where it was still bleeding. He unlocked the door and turned back to the sink to the freely flowing cold water.

The door opened, and Katrina literally towered over him from behind as she looked into the mirror to see his face. "Turn around, Caleb," she insisted gently, grasping him by the shoulders and pivoting him around.

She examined his hand, noting the cuts and bruises on his knuckles and pulled the washcloth away from his face. She gazed upon the gash above his left eyebrow, the cut on his right cheek, his bleeding lip, and the bruises on his face. "Oh, Caleb," she gasped softly.

Paige appeared behind Katrina, scrutinizing Caleb with a clenched jaw and steely expression. "How many?" she demanded tersely, her blue eyes flaring angrily.

"Three," he replied as Katrina took the washcloth from him and rinsed it in the cold water. "But don't worry, we gave as good as we got."

"We?" Paige dubiously challenged. She had not noticed

much damage to Gil, which made her think it was less Gil and more Caleb doing the fighting.

Katrina used the washcloth to dab at the cut above his forehead and moved forward to roll her tongue over the wound to seal the cut. The taste of his blood sparked a momentary pang of thirst in her, but she quickly suppressed it.

"Well, Gil helped," Caleb insisted.

"Hold still," Katrina complained as she held his face in place firmly and returned to sealing the cut.

"Do you think they followed you?" Paige asked.

"Don't know. They were still lying on the parking lot when we left," he replied absently, appreciating Katrina's ministrations as the pain in his face ebbed.

Katrina pulled away from him and looked at her mate with surprise. "Really?"

He nodded. "Yeah, really. I got tired of being beat upon by everyone, it seems."

She raised a curious eyebrow, while Paige considered him with an introspective expression.

"Who started it?" Paige asked.

As Katrina returned to lick at another cut on his face, Caleb considered the question briefly and replied, "They did. The waitress said they were troublemakers. Hell, they were pissing on the car when we went out to the parking lot. I tried to avoid a fight, but there it was."

Katrina listened closely to his response, but felt that something was missing from his story.

"Hey, is Caleb okay?" Gil asked, popping his head into the bathroom.

"We're working on that," Paige replied. "Gil, Caleb's a little hazy on how that fight got started. Care to enlighten us?"

Caleb started to speak up, but a hard look from Katrina quieted him.

"Well," Gil hedged, "those guys harassed us in the bar and attacked us after we left."

Paige pressed, "You didn't happen to antagonize them, did you?"

"Aw, c'mon, babe," he retorted. "Just 'cause some tumbles happened at our band's club gigs, you think I started this?"

"I'm just saying, you're good at pissing people off, Gil," she remarked. "Quite a few of the performances your band gave ended up in fists flying. Bouncers tended to get busy around you."

Gil smirked. "You've got some pretty good moves in a fight, too."

But Paige wasn't amused. "Yeah, well, you don't, as I recall. And you appear to be in pretty good shape compared to Caleb right now, too."

He puffed up his chest a little and shot back, "Oh, so now it's my fault just because Caleb caught some more action than I did? What if I did a better job dodging fists than he did?"

"*Gil*," Paige warned.

"Hey, chill. Anyway, babe, I always told you I'm a better lover than fighter," he continued, to which she scoffed derisively.

"Lame, Gil. If you can't finish them, don't start them!" Paige snapped.

He made a sour face. "Well, old Caleb here sure took care of those bastards. Hell, he was wiping the floor with 'em!"

Katrina heard Caleb's teeth clench, and she whipped her head around to address Paige and Gil in a flat voice, "Take it upstairs. We're busy here." She didn't like what she was hearing, although a similar stream of thought as Paige's had occurred to her, as well.

Gil took a deep breath, exhaled, and left.

Paige moved past Katrina to stroke Caleb on the less injured side of his face with her fingertips lightly. "Nice job, kiddo," she complimented. "And thanks for looking out for Mister Trouble."

"Yeah, sure," he replied with a slight nod, although he wasn't particularly enthused about taking Gil out on the town again anytime soon.

Paige disappeared in a blur, leaving Katrina and Caleb alone in the bathroom.

"I'm proud of you, my love," Katrina offered. "Remember after the attack that night in the forest, when I said that if Devon were a human the results could've been quite different?"

Caleb nodded.

"Humans didn't fare so well against you today. And someday, vampires won't find you as easy a target, either," she remarked sagely.

"Good. I'm tired of playing the victim," he remarked acidly.

But his tone made Katrina frown, and she considered it would be important to observe him as his combat training progressed. Attitude was important, but so was control. She momentarily wondered at the condition of the three men who he had fought, as well as whether or not they might have reported Caleb to the police.

Her experience had shown that often enough the victorious victim could end up appearing as the perpetrator if the loser pressed charges first.

But then, I'll deal with that if I have to. Dead men tend not to press charges.

"I want to lie down for a while," he remarked as a growing sense of exhaustion began to flow through him. "Got any aspirin?"

After a welcome nap, he lay on the bed on his right side beneath a blanket, Katrina curled up alongside him. The room was dimly lit from a table lamp across the room, and he was unsure what time it was.

"Feel better, my love?" she inquired gently.

He yawned. "Yep. How long was I asleep?"

"About four hours," she answered. "It's almost eight o'clock now."

He was surprised by that and stretched to sense how sore he felt. While achy, he felt better than expected. He paused to appreciate lying next to Katrina and would have preferred to stay there for the rest of the evening.

But he recalled Gil had wanted to go clubbing that night to some of the alternative rock venues they'd noticed earlier in the day. Then the mid-afternoon encounter with the men at the bar replayed in his mind, and he sighed.

"Thinking about earlier?" she asked, running her fingers through his hair lightly.

"Yeah," he replied. "And how I need to get up, take a shower, and change."

"We can stay in tonight," she offered.

He would have liked that.

"Sounds nice, but I promised Gil," he countered. "Besides, you and Paige have been cooped up at home all day while we were out picking fights—"

"You didn't pick it, you finished it," she interjected mildly.

He nodded and conceded, "Okay then."

She reached around from behind him to pat him his chest with the flat of her hand, one of the few places he wasn't sore, and suggested, "Let Paige take Gil out. We can curl up with a movie in the theater room or something."

He considered that for a moment and quickly warmed to the idea. But a pang of guilt flowed through him. "That's a nice idea, but I wouldn't mind taking you out tonight. That is, if you don't mind my looking like I was dropped out of the back of a speeding truck," he said, deliberately injecting some enthusiasm into his voice.

She chuckled and kissed the back of his neck. "You might want to look in a mirror, my love," she recommended. "I worked on you while you slept, and your face looks pretty good to me."

His mood brightened as his fingers probed his face tentatively, realizing he felt no scars. In fact, his face was only mildly sore in places. He wondered how long she had spent using her saliva to heal his face. "Is your tongue tired?" he teased.

She giggled. "It was worth it, my love. There's no bruising or scars, but you might want to avoid any more fights over the next few days until your facial tissue heals fully."

He smiled and rolled over to face her. He puckered his lips, and she kissed him. "Thanks, Kat. I'll try to stay out of fights, but just for the next few days," he teased.

Her eyes narrowed. "Yes, you will. Because I'll be the one doing the fighting for you in the foreseeable future."

"Just the foreseeable?" he inquired playfully.

Her eyes narrowed slightly. "Forever. Except when you refuse to let me and, of course, when you seek trouble while I'm not around."

"Hey, sometimes trouble finds me before you can arrive," he challenged.

She conceded the truth of his statement and kissed him on the tip of his nose. "Touché," she capitulated. "And while I admit I wouldn't mind going out tonight, we'll only stay out for a short time. Paige and Gil can pull an all-nighter if they want, so we'll take separate vehicles."

Caleb smiled wryly. "Yeah, I better hose off your car first."

She grinned. "No need. Paige made Gil do that earlier, actually."

"Good," he replied irritably.

She frowned. "Tell me, did Gil do something to draw you into that fight?"

He considered the question, not particularly wanting to lay blame on Gil, but admitting the man's behavior hadn't helped their situation and may have antagonized the men further. "Those guys were real troublemakers, Kat," he explained. "But I'll admit that Gil did antagonize them a little bit. Hell, maybe I should've never let us walk in there in the first place, so it's partly my fault too."

She shook her head at her mate's attempt to defray blame and let the topic drop. However, it didn't engender much appreciation for Gil in her opinion, either. "Okay. Go start the shower, and I'll join you in a minute," she suggested as she removed her arm from around him.

"Hmm, maybe I'll rethink my plans for tonight," he

ventured suggestively.

Please, tempt me, she thought as she watched him get up. It was only the past day or so that he had begun to warm up to her again after the Devon and photograph issues. She felt that she needed to work particularly hard on smoothing the rough edges of their relationship.

A couple can only endure so much conflict at one time.

Though it wasn't any lack of resolve on her part that bothered her; it was her concern that he might give up on her first, and she couldn't bear the thought of that.

Caleb changed into a pair of black casual slacks and royal blue sateen shirt, and then went upstairs. Katrina had gone to the master bedroom on the second floor where she kept many of her more elaborate outfits, and he was anxious to see what she picked to wear for their evening out. And of course, he was looking forward to Paige's being part of the event.

Caleb went to the kitchen, observed Paige standing next to the bar counter, and stopped in amazement. She wore a red key-hole halter dress that perfectly fit her petite frame and ended halfway between her upper thighs and her knees. She spun in a quick circle for him.

The crossed spaghetti straps at the back revealed her smooth, pale skin, and she accented the outfit with some strappy, spike-heeled shoes and ruby earrings. Her outfit, coupled with her 1920s hair style, gave her the edgier, modern appearance of her life as a former flapper. While he smiled appreciatively at her, he noted a somber expression on her face.

"Howdy, Miss Sassy, Sexy, and Supernatural," he greeted her. "You look amazing, Paige."

She smirked in classic Paige fashion and retorted, "Well, well, if it isn't our newest resident street fighter and upcoming bar room brawler himself. And yet, you have that subtle out-on-the town look tonight."

He was happy that her quick wit seemed intact, but noted she still seemed more subdued than normal. "Too ordinary looking?" he asked self-consciously.

"Hardly, tiger," she assured him. "Everyone in clubs nowadays is trying to look either too Hollywood or like a rock star, but it's overdone and over-rated. I happen to like men with a subtle and confident look; you don't see that as much anymore."

"Thanks," he replied with bolstered self-confidence before assessing her more closely.

She watched him curiously as he walked up to her and reached out with his two index fingers to lift the corners of her mouth into a forced smile. She deliberately revealed sharp-looking fangs against the backdrop of her otherwise beautiful white set of teeth.

"I'm going to make you laugh tonight, and there's not a 'fang' you can do about it," he teased.

She grasped both of his index fingers in her hands and pulled them away from her face. "Oh, that was a bad one. You deserve a bite to the neck," she mock-threatened.

He wiggled his index fingers playfully as she held onto them.

"You're looking a lot better than when I last saw you, kiddo," she observed softly.

"I took a lickin' from Katrina since then, you know."

She winced, but smiled.

"Another bite earned over that one?" he ventured with raised eyebrows.

She looked at the ceiling briefly through narrowed eyes while shaking her head. "Nope," she replied matter-of-factly. "Just tickling!" With that, she released his index fingers, only to move in a blur and begin tickling his ribs. Despite a twinge of soreness, he flailed and twisted as he tried to evade her wriggling fingers.

She wrapped her arms around his midsection from behind and continued to dig her fingers into his sides. He laughed and struggled, while she evilly giggled. He was amazed at how spry and balanced the vampire was in a pair of heels.

After a few seconds she stopped, but continued to hug him to her body closely for a minute or so longer. He tried to catch his breath while chuckling to himself as a happy feeling surged through him over the playful exchange.

Mission objective number one accomplished, he mused.

"I needed that," she whispered before releasing him.

He frowned slightly, curious as to the reason behind her comment.

"So, where are we going tonight?" Gil asked with a curious expression, appearing suddenly from the living room. He had changed into a pair of leather pants and a tight-fitted, gray and black shirt. It made Caleb think of the trendy, devil-may-care California club scene.

The young rocker stared at Paige with raised eyebrows and a grin on his face. Clearly, he liked what he saw. She looked back at him with a forced smirk.

"Wow, babe," Gil offered. "You look like one of those sexy women from a rock video."

She frowned momentarily and shrugged. "Thanks, I think," she offered while observing Gil's attire with an appraising expression. "You look like the classic vision of a Hollywood rocker tonight, Gil," she added.

Caleb recalled her earlier comments about club attire and glanced at her with a mildly concerned expression.

But her demeanor turned abruptly cheerful, and she changed the subject. "Well, getting back to our plans for tonight. First, we get something for you two to eat," she ventured. "I'm thinking someplace Asian."

Caleb frowned. "Since when do you pick restaurants?"

"Shush!" she mock-admonished, placing her forefinger against his lips. "I happen to know of a little Asian restaurant and bar not far from here, and the online reviews are great. So, then we head to a downtown club called The Gecko Room for some alternative rock and dancing."

"Sounds good. And guess what? Remember when you promised me last December that you wanted to get me out clubbing with you someday?" Caleb recalled with a smirk. "That day has finally arrived."

She beamed with sincere satisfaction. "Yeah, I did, didn't

I?"

He grinned back at her as Gil watched both of them suspiciously. The young rocker interjected, "Let me tell you, Paige rocks on the dance floor, dude."

"Aw, she rocks anyway, floor or no floor," Caleb quipped with a smirk.

"Thanks, tiger," she replied with a grin. "And I'm anxious to see how you do out there yourself."

Caleb wrinkled his nose. "Yeah, well, one of my ex-girlfriends said I look like a Muppet when I dance."

Paige chuckled. "I'll have you know, I happen to like Muppets," she admitted shyly.

"Is that like Kerbett the toad?" Gil asked with knitted brows.

"That's Kermit the frog, fry-brain," Paige corrected him irritably with a roll of her eyes.

Caleb was getting the distinct impression his vampire guardian wasn't exactly enjoying her time with Gil lately. He admitted the two didn't seem like a likely pair, though it wasn't really his business to say so. He just wanted Paige to be happy, no matter whom she dated.

"Oh, yeah," Gil replied awkwardly.

"Oh, Caleb? Do you have a minute?" Katrina called from the front part of the house.

He adopted a curious expression as he headed in that direction. He stopped at the foot of the stairs leading to the second floor and looked up to the top. What he saw nearly caused him to lose his breath.

Katrina stood at the top of the stairs with a smirk on her face as she appreciated his reaction. She was dressed in a bright blue sequin halter dress with a plunging neckline and open back that fit her like a glove.

Her red hair was straight, flowing down her back like a beautiful ruby river. He took note of the strappy blue high-heeled shoes and sequin clutch purse, which finished off the ensemble perfectly. He forced himself to take a breath as he stared up at her sexy vision.

"You like?" she asked, having clearly observed his complete reaction like a scientist studying a test subject. His response pleased her, and she reveled in having captured his attention completely.

"You-You're stunning," he stammered with a grin.

"Thank you," she beamed, slowly stepping down the stairs towards him. "You look handsome and tasty all at the same time, yourself."

She savored the fact that he stood there simply watching her approach, like a deer transfixed by the stalking of a predator.

Of course, that's exactly what I am, she considered with satisfaction.

She was particularly pleased to see something other than disappointment or resentment in his eyes after all that happened between them recently.

He was mesmerized by her sexy appearance as she descended the stairs and felt a surge of pride run through him. She's my mate and mine alone.

He felt other, more animalistic urges rise in him as well.

She stopped before him at the foot of the stairs and bent down to kiss him on the lips. He eagerly responded and reached out to grasp the sides of her waist with both hands. She felt the magnetism in his kiss, and a surge of satisfaction passed through her.

Oh, this is good. I should've worn this for him a long time ago.

Her arms draped around his neck to rest atop his shoulders, and she pressed another kiss on his lips. She felt his arms begin to enfold her and smirked into his kisses. "Now, now," she admonished playfully. "We have an entire evening ahead of us."

He wasn't thinking at all about the evening ahead, instead feeling other immediate desires rise in his body. But she removed her arms from around his neck and gently disengaged his hands from around her waist so she could step back.

"Later, my love," she promised.

He merely nodded and stared at her hungrily. Wow. She

looks completely irresistible.

Paige appeared around the corner to view the pair and grinned with admiration. "Nicely done, Red," she complimented.

"Ditto, Paige," Katrina replied in kind.

"Whoa," Gil said with widened eyes as he rounded the corner to view Katrina's outfit. "Smoking hot, Katrina!"

"Thank you, Gil," she replied appreciatively.

"Both the ladies look smokin' hot," Caleb interjected, to which Paige smiled thoughtfully.

The four gathered their jackets and proceeded to the garage. Katrina suggested Paige and Gil take the rental car so that she and Caleb could return earlier in the evening if her mate grew too tired. Paige gave a pained expression, but conceded the merits of her suggestion.

Knowing that Caleb enjoyed driving her Audi, Katrina encouraged him to drive them to the restaurant. While her goal was to please him, she particularly wanted to make him the center of the universe that evening. She hoped he could recapture some of the thrill he had experienced when they had first started dating last fall.

She feared that their recent disagreements were taking a negative toll on their relationship and wanted to plant new, enjoyable memories that night.

Caleb was somewhat tired but drove them to their destination capably, though much of the credit went to the impeccable aid of the car's GPS. He barely stifled a yawn as he walked around the car to open the door for Katrina.

The Lotus Garden was a trendy, chic Asian restaurant catering to a sophisticated, yet youthful, crowd. It was bustling with customers, though, much to everyone's relief, Paige had called ahead to make reservations earlier that evening.

The four of them were seated at a table where the food was prepared tableside in an entertaining, uniquely oriental fashion. The two vampires placed Caleb between them, while Paige placed Gil to her opposite side. During the meal, they chatted about the atmosphere and the merits of Saki over other alcoholic beverages while the chef prepared their food in miniature courses. As was common with vampires, the two women picked at their food, which consisted exclusively of vegetarian items.

Katrina paid close attention to Caleb throughout the meal and often placed her hand over his, or draped her arm around him affectionately. He appreciated it and made an effort to return her attentions in kind.

Paige also noticed the improved relations between Caleb and Katrina with a degree of satisfaction, feeling that her interventional visit to Atlanta was continuing to be quite successful. However, she found it difficult to concentrate upon Gil fully, inwardly feeling a pull to Caleb in ways that bothered her slightly.

In the end, they all had a thoroughly enjoyable time, and Paige took care of the check. From there, they proceeded to the alternative rock club, which wasn't far from the restaurant.

Upon their arrival at The Gecko Room, the parking lot was nearly crammed with vehicles, and they had to park in a nearby overfill lot. It was an unusually cold night in Atlanta; the north wind had steadily increased throughout the evening. Caleb and Gil hugged their vampires close to them as they made their way to the front of the building, both oblivious to the fact that neither vampire was affected by the cold.

A crowd of people lingered outside the entrance, and it appeared there might be a wait, but two large-framed men stationed at the door immediately noticed Katrina and Paige and beckoned to them to approach. Caleb and Gil shrugged at each other and followed behind them.

In a matter of minutes, after Caleb paid for everyone's cover charge, the four were in the midst of a sea of humanity. Both men appreciated the warmer interior.

The alternative rock music blared as the dance floor was alive with undulating bodies. An alternating series of neon lights created a surreal atmosphere, and the cavernous interior seemed to magnify and echo the cacophony of music coupled with the dialogue of patrons.

Tables lined the periphery of the main walls, and two separate lengths of bar were arrayed to the each side of the large room. It was apparent significant funds had been spent preparing the club for efficient function as well as atmosphere.

The environment was almost complete overload to Caleb's senses, not having frequented clubs since well before he had dated his ex-girlfriend, Melanie, nearly a year ago. However, Gil seemed quite at home in the surroundings. Meanwhile, Katrina's and Paige's attentions seemed heightened by the crush of humans crowded around them.

"Must be like a massive feeding pen to them," Caleb whispered with dark amusement, having noticed the women's reactions.

Katrina stopped in front of him, swept her left arm around his waist to draw him against her, and touched her lips to his ear. "Yes, but you're the only one I want to drink from tonight."

His eyes widened with surprise as they walked together, having been shocked that she could have somehow heard his whisper over the din surrounding them.

Katrina silently conceded that her thirst was rising by the minute amidst the humans surrounding her. She heard a thunder of heartbeats among the pounding of the music, and the varieties of scents from the various bodies pressing around her was like standing in the middle of a human-scented candle shop. Still, she concentrated and focused on the singular scent of her mate.

Within seconds she picked out his heartbeat among the others, and her senses zeroed in on him from beside her as she breathed in and selected his body's scent. She held her breath for a lingering moment and softly exhaled.

Paige bobbed to the music as they made their way to a small booth in the back corner of the establishment that was being vacated by a group of twenty-somethings. Paige and

Katrina received a mix of subtle glances and outright stares from people in the club, both men and women.

Gil seemed unaware of the scrutiny, but Caleb picked up on it with unusual clarity. Granted, the two vampires were extremely beautiful, but it was as if other people were magnetically drawn to them.

Minutes later, they were seated at a small corner booth, and Paige swayed to the heavy dance music. A young waitress with long blonde hair appeared at their table, and she took a moment to stare at the two vampires with a wide-eyed expression before speaking.

"Hi. Welcome to The Gecko Room," she offered courteously. "I'm Cindy. Can I get you something?"

"Sex on the Beach," Paige blurted.

Katrina glanced at Caleb and insisted, "Choose for us, my love."

"Two mojitos," he ordered with a grin, to which Katrina nodded with approval.

"Orgasm for me," Gil said.

"Great, I'll be back soon," Cindy replied with a courteous smile.

A particularly energized dance beat began, and Paige began swaying to it. She grinned and rose from her chair. "Come on, Gil," she beckoned while grasping his hand in hers. "Let's cut a rug."

"Wha—" he started to say, but was pulled behind her with a lurch towards the dance floor.

Caleb chuckled as he watched them go and looked around the room to take everything in. As he scanned to his left, his eyes eventually fell upon Katrina's beautiful emerald eyes, which focused on him like lasers. The corners of her mouth were upturned slightly as her penetrating gaze bore into his pale blue eyes, causing a shiver down his spine.

His eyes widened, and he smiled back at her innocently. She felt a surge of desire run through her, both for his body and his blood, and momentarily considered again how he appeared like defenseless prey caught in her gaze.

She leaned slowly towards him until her lips were just inches from his.

"You're so intense," he whispered, feeling an almost palpable energy emanating from her.

"Kiss me," she insisted.

He leaned across the distance between them and brushed his lips against hers. Then her lips locked onto his, and he immediately felt her fingers pressing against the back of his neck. He reached one hand across the table towards her, and her hand met his halfway and interlaced with his fingers.

Despite the pounding beat of the music and the cacophony of voices around them, he felt that the only person in the room was Katrina, as if everything else was just indecipherable background noise.

Suddenly, her lips were no longer touching his, and he realized that he'd closed his eyes. He opened them, only to see Katrina's face hovering an inch before his. Her eyes glowed back at him with telltale signs of either desire or hunger, or both. His mind raced at how drawn he was to her, despite the distraction of being in the midst of a sea of people.

"I'm really focused on you right now," she muttered loudly enough over the noise that he could hear her.

"It's like you're—" he began in a near whisper.

"Hunting," she completed with a feral grin.

Another shiver cascaded through his body, leaving him speechless. He could only recall one previous occasion when he had sensed such strong energy and emotion from Katrina. It was the night that she and Alton had returned from their first confrontation with Chimalma, after they had raced back to the estate to check on him because he and Paige had been assaulted in the estate by mercenaries. Katrina had stood at the foot of the stairs gazing up at him in the dark, appearing more vampire-like than at any time he had recalled.

She was staring at him in that same manner. It was powerful, and he craved to be the center of her attention.

"Stalker," he teased.

"Guilty as charged," she countered slyly.

He blinked once and whispered earnestly, "I love you."

She smiled back at him, and he saw her fangs extend ever so slightly below her lip line. She closed the distance to him quickly, and he felt her lips at his neck. For a split second, he felt her fangs press against the soft flesh of his neck, and then retract. He took a sharp intake of breath, and held it, waiting to see what she would do. But she merely kissed him and sat back to regard him with a predatory smile.

"I love you, and I shall have you tonight," she issued as part challenge, part promise.

He caught sight of glasses in his peripheral vision and glanced up to see their waitress placing mixed drinks on the table. Cindy smiled down at Caleb, but her eyes quickly darted to Katrina, and her expression became more reserved. A wary expression, he realized.

"Just give a wave when you're ready for me again," she offered to Caleb intently, as if she were concentrating on keeping her eyes on him alone. She departed into the crowd, although at a faster pace than one might normally expect.

"You spooked her, I think," he whispered, realizing that Katrina could hear him as clearly as if they were speaking in a quiet room sitting next to her.

They picked up their drinks and sipped, and she smiled at him and leaned towards him.

"Cindy senses a predator," she answered simply. "Some humans are more perceptive than others. She's more sensitive to such things. In a baser setting, she might be a survivor."

"Survival of the fittest?" he asked.

"Exactly."

"Whereas I would be caught," he quipped with a grin.

She appeared smug and countered, "You already have been; you just haven't realized it yet."

He cast a wide-eyed smirk back at her and sipped his drink again. It tasted wonderful.

I'm happy to be caught by her.

He considered the revelation about his forgotten

encounter with Katrina as a child, followed by the disagreement he had with her over Devon. But instead of a resurgence of resentment, anger, or aggravation, he felt a satisfaction that she was his mate and that he was hers. And while he might still be concerned about those topics, he suddenly realized his love for her was stronger than those issues, and it made him feel a surge of combined happiness and relief.

"Happiness for me is loving you and being loved in return," he whispered as he lovingly gazed into her eyes.

She looked up suddenly from sipping her drink, and a bright smile formed as she stared back at him. "Thank you," she mouthed silently.

Gil and Paige appeared at the table, though he appeared slightly out of breath while she seemed perky and energetic. Paige slipped into the booth at Caleb's right and swept up her drink in one fluid motion. Her lips sipped at the edge of her glass delicately, and she smirked at Caleb.

"Having fun, kiddo?" she asked with a sparkle in her eyes. She had discreetly noted the interaction between him and Katrina from across the room and divined the exchange between them. She also easily recognized the signals Katrina was giving off. Stalking the poor kid.

"Oh yeah," he replied emphatically with a grin and a nod as "Ava Adore," by Smashing Pumpkins, played.

"Man, this place is slammin'!" Gil exclaimed before taking a swig of his drink.

Paige rolled her eyes and looked at Caleb with renewed vigor, almost like a kid with a new toy. The blonde-haired vampire's eyes darted over to Katrina's for a mere second, and she saw Katrina's imperceptible nod that only a vampire's quick vision would catch.

She challenged Caleb, "Come on, you big overgrown Muppet. Let's dance!"

Caleb laughed and allowed her to drag him by the hand through the crowd until they reached nearly the center of the dance floor. Katy Perry's "Firework" began to play as Paige bopped to the music. Caleb relaxed his body and subtly shadowed her movements. She grinned brightly at him, and he smiled back, fully appreciating the happiness emanating from her. Fortunately, the music was easy to dance to.

He admired Paige's fluid movements, marveling at how the beautiful woman before him was such an instinctive dancer. A brief pang of guilt ran through him as he also admired how sexy she looked, her red dress accenting her shapely form. *I'm supposed to think of her as a close friend or an adopted sister.*

He moved closer to her and said, "It's great to see you so happy."

She smirked appreciatively. "It's definitely the company."

"I'm just glad to be here," he shot back.

"I'm glad you are too," she agreed with a penetrating stare and a gleam in her eyes.

They both grinned and kept dancing. After a few minutes, Caleb noticed that Paige was garnering the attention of a number of fellow dancers, both men and women. He grinned at her knowingly, and she frowned at him for a moment before sweeping the room of her newfound fans.

Another popular song started, and they adjusted their movements to match the beat. Caleb was having a great time, and he was happy to see that Paige seemed to be, too.

After the second song finished, "Right Round," by Flo Rida, started. Paige smirked and looked deliberately past Caleb with a nod in his direction. He raised an eyebrow and turned to see Katrina standing behind him swaying provocatively to the music.

Her body moved in a smooth, feline manner that was both fluid and sensual all at the same time. He moved his body to the music with hers, although in a much more subdued fashion.

A number of eyes in the room locked onto Katrina with a mix of curiosity and mesmerism. But she maintained an eye lock on Caleb as if he were the only one in the room. Her eyes flashed bright green for a split second, and his gaze was drawn to them immediately. He wanted to get lost in her beautiful eyes.

She moved closer to him as her body synchronized with the music and reached out with one hand to caress the back of his neck. He blinked only once, and when he opened his eyes, she moved even closer to him, nearly rubbing against him.

He felt strong desire rise in his body, and his breathing became heavier. Her penetrating eyes became the only thing he saw, and before he knew it the song had ended.

In one fluid movement, she moved to his side and slipped her arm around his waist, leading him away from the dance floor and to their table. It was as if he were floating in a partial daze, and he felt strangely at peace as she guided him away.

As he passed a number of people in the crowd, he could have sworn they deliberately parted to let them pass. A few moments later, she kissed him on the lips, and he felt the booth's cushion at the back of his legs. He sat down with a near plop and reached for his drink absently as he stared into Katrina's emerald eyes.

"Well done, Kermit," Paige quipped with a grin. "Nice dancing for a Muppet."

"Thanks," he muttered as he brought his glass to his lips to drink. Just the taste of the mojito seemed to help revive his senses, and he felt less like he was in a haze after a moment. He glanced over to Paige, who was grinning at him like a Cheshire cat.

"Somebody still looks a little dazed," she giggled. "We'll do that to you if you let us."

"Glamour?" he asked as his wits returned.

"Not exactly. At least, nothing that strong or involuntary," Katrina explained. "More like a willing state of meditation."

"Cool," he replied with a smirk as he looked across the table and noticed for the first time that Gil wasn't with them. "Where's Gil?"

"The men's room, like, a quarter of an hour ago," Paige

muttered with a shake of her head.

"Is he okay?" Caleb asked with concern. "Maybe I should go check on him."

Paige wrinkled her nose, shook her head and replied, "Oh, I'm sure he's feeling fine by now. And don't go looking for him, that is, unless you bring a pizza with you."

He raised his eyebrows with surprise and insisted, "No way. You're sure?"

"Yeah," she replied with a wane smirk. "I strolled by the men's room doorway while you and Katrina were on the dance floor. I could smell the weed from outside."

Caleb shook his head and bit his tongue rather than say what he was thinking: *How can Gil even think about smoking a joint when he has Paige here to spend time with? The guy must be crazy.*

Their waitress stopped by to bring a fresh round of drinks and promptly departed with a practiced demeanor. Paige looked around at the other patrons, casually scanning the room, and grinned. "Well, I'm going dancing some more."

The spritely vampire bopped onto the dancing floor alone, quickly garnering the attention of men around her. Within seconds, she was dancing with a muscular, twenty-something man. Katrina smirked and cast a thoughtful glance at Caleb, who sipped at his fresh mojito.

"Having fun, my love?" she asked with a smile.

He smiled back and replied thoughtfully, "Yeah, actually this is great, Kat."

The remainder of the evening was uneventful, although Caleb and Katrina shared additional dances. A much mellower Gil returned to the dance floor not long after Paige and sought her out to dance with her throughout most of the remainder of their time there. Much to Caleb's surprise, Paige didn't seem overly annoyed with Gil and took occasional opportunities to dance with other patrons as the mood struck her. She caught his eyes on one occasion, winking at him while flashing a bright smile.

Sometime after midnight, Katrina sensed Caleb was growing tired and suggested they leave. He accepted the idea gratefully, and they bid hasty goodbyes to Paige and Gil, who remained to continue their reveling. Katrina paid the outstanding tab for the four of them, including a healthy tip for their wary waitress, and led Caleb from the club.

The night was quite cold and windy as he wrapped his arm around Katrina's waist on their walk back to the Audi. He held the door for her as she slipped into the passenger seat and leaned in to kiss her warmly on the lips. She laid her purse aside in the console area and freed her hands to reach out for him.

"Thank you for a wonderful evening, Kat," he offered tenderly. It was a thoroughly enjoyable and memorable night, and he was grateful that everything had gone so well between them. It reminded him of happier times when they had dated last fall before vampires like Chimalma and Devon Archibald interrupted their lives.

"I haven't been so kind to you lately, but—" he started, but she pressed her lips against his and wrapped her hand behind his neck to pull him towards her.

He reveled in the heated passion of her kiss and knelt before her in the open car doorway as the cold wind pressed in around them. Her mouth was so warm and comforting against his, and he leaned further into the car against her. She wrapped an arm around his shoulders protectively and continued to kiss him.

A hunger rose in her that was so strong she almost couldn't resist its calling. She yearned for his body and his blood simultaneously and knew she had to stop kissing him, or she might take his blood there and then. Fighting the strong desire, she gathered her resolve and shifted her body without warning.

Much to his surprise, she rapidly rotated him into the passenger seat as she slipped out through the compact doorway. He had no time to react before she snatched the seatbelt and snapped it into place around him.

"What?" he protested, but she pressed her fingertip to his lips to silence him.

"I'm taking you home. Fast," she stated with faintly glowing eyes. She shut the door and disappeared from sight.

Before he could turn his head, she had opened the driver's side door and plopped into the seat. While shutting the door with one hand, she buckled her own seatbelt with the other. The car's motor roared to life and, within seconds, she shifted into gear and the Audi zipped down the nearly deserted city streets.

"You've made me very happy tonight, Caleb," she murmured as her eyes glanced at him with a predatory glint. Her right hand reached out to him, and she ran her fingernails against his cheek lightly and across the soft skin of his neck.

He shivered with delight and smiled back at her. *This vampire captured my dreams and made them come true.*

The drive back to the estate from downtown went by in a blur as rock music played on the car stereo. Katrina's right hand reached out occasionally to run her fingers through Caleb's hair, or massage at his neck, or simply brush against his cheek. When they happened upon a stoplight, she craned her neck towards him and kissed him deeply, albeit all too briefly.

He started to say something, but she interrupted, "No, my love. Say nothing."

He grinned at her and remained silent, but his mind was racing with a mix of curiosity and rising excitement. His adrenaline flowed freely, and his body's earlier tiredness began to abate.

The time passed so quickly that, before he realized it, they were pulling up the estate's driveway and into the expansive garage. Katrina opened the driver's side door and disappeared from view. Her door barely had time to shut before his was opening and she was standing aside waiting on him. He marveled at that and started to exit before realizing he was still buckled in.

She giggled as she slipped the high-heeled shoes from her feet and gathered them in one hand with her purse. He removed his seatbelt and exited the vehicle, blushing slightly. While kissing him on the lips briefly, she shut his door for him as he stepped aside. She planted a firmer kiss on his lips and herded him towards the door leading into the house.

Dropping her shoes on the floor in the hallway, she sped into the kitchen to disengage the alarm and toss her purse onto the counter. He had barely followed her into the kitchen before she wheeled on him and kissed him passionately. As she kissed him, she unbuttoned his shirt and tossed it over the back of a kitchen barstool.

He stared into her eyes, glowing brightly back at him. "Hungry?" he asked tentatively.

She nodded.

"Can I get you some blood?" he inquired with a smirk.

She nodded her head again.

He turned around to get into a cabinet for a glass, but she grabbed his wrist to stop him. She drew his arms against him and pressed her lips to his right ear. "Fresh, not reheated," she insisted as her body pressed against his from behind.

He swallowed and inquired playfully, "Perhaps a deer?"

She growled and murmured, "Perhaps you."

He smiled and felt her lips press against his neck to kiss him. Her teeth nipped at the supple skin, and he breathed in sharply. His body's excitement grew, and he turned to meet her lips.

Both felt a heated wave of passion as they kissed at length.

After a few moments, she herded him out of the kitchen and down the main hallway. He made a playful attempt to turn around, but she spun him back the other direction and tickled him on the ribs to usher him before her. When he arrived at the doorway leading down to the chamber, she wrapped her arm around his waist and pulled him through the doorway with her in a sudden lurch.

He felt his body sailing into air, realizing she had leapt with him down to the floor of the sublevel area by jumping over the stairs entirely. He landed beside her gently as she tightened the arm's vice-like grip around his waist to keep him from landing hard. He barely had time to catch his breath before she propelled them both towards the nearby bed, only to have their bodies bounce on top of it twice before coming to a stop.

He recovered quickly and rolled over on her to kiss her lips deeply. She responded in kind and slipped from her dress as their lips met. He fumbled with his own belt, but she reached up to pinch the end of his nose, pressed her mouth to his, and drew the breath from him in one quick intake.

He felt the world go dark, followed by the sensation of his body's landing on the bed with a bounce, and drifted on a momentary light-headed sea of euphoria for an indeterminate period of time.

When he regained a keener sense of awareness, he realized his clothes had been removed, and he felt Katrina's naked body lying against his. He smiled slyly, having recalled her using that trick on him once before, which he conceded was an ingenious and effective maneuver for a vampire. His eyes focused on her face amidst the darkness, only to see her staring back at him.

"Welcome back, my love," she whispered before kissing him. "Now, about dinner," she ventured with a smirk.

He nodded and felt her mouth move to his neck to kiss and nip at him. His excitement rose quickly, which she appreciated with a chuckle.

Her mouth latched onto the side of his neck near his jugular vein, and she pressed her hand against the side of his face to avert his gaze. He grinned at her sense of urgency and reached around to massage her lower back with one hand. He ran his other hand across her bare bottom and pinched her skin slightly.

She lurched with surprise and grabbed at his hand with her free hand as she straddled him with her body. As the surface of his neck grew numb, he felt her pressing fangs before the process was complete, and he froze in place.

She snickered into his neck, holding her fangs against his skin. *The predator has control now*, she thought with satisfaction.

After he remained still, she retracted her fangs and proceeded to numb his skin with her tongue.

"Simply vicious," he teased.

She deliberately pressed her nude body against his, baring her breasts against his chest, which only increased his excitement. She chuckled into his neck again, followed by penetrating his skin with her fangs.

He gasped from the sudden sensation, which was thankfully pain-free. He lay very still and felt his blood being deeply drawn from him.

He felt a momentary sensation of light headedness and the feeling of floating in a quiet sea of contentment. She slowed her drawing of blood, and his awareness slowly began to return.

He relished the closeness that he shared with her as she fed upon him, feelings of communion, passion, warmth, and love.

Time seemed suspended as he lay beneath her body and vaguely felt her mouth covering his neck. The suckling and slurping sounds continued for a time and then slowed. Eventually, the noises ceased entirely, and he felt her tongue pressing against his skin to seal his bite marks. Then she laid her head against his chest and kissed his bare skin.

"You're everything to me," she murmured. "I'll love you forever, Caleb." Being with him made her so very happy, and she wanted to make him as happy as she felt.

He nodded and wrapped his arms around her body. He loved her dearly and wanted to be hers forever.

She fills a huge, empty niche in my life.

"I love you too, Kat," he whispered, kissing the top of her head. Then his thoughts turned more amorous, and his excitement rose again as her body lay against his.

He lightly ran his fingers across her lower back then across her bottom and down her thigh. She shivered slightly, and he tried to roll her over to lie atop her.

"Mmm," she hummed contentedly and allowed him to roll her onto her back.

He kissed her and cupped one of her breasts with his hand.

"I'm all yours," she whispered playfully as her legs slowly wrapped around his lower body.

Then time stood still.

Later that night, Katrina dried Caleb off with a towel following their shower together.

He felt exhausted and drained of energy as he leaned into the wall with both arms stretched outward. As if in confirmation, he swayed slightly. "I feel like I'm going to fall over," he mumbled.

She smirked. "You've had a long day. First, fighting with bar patrons, then out on the town half the night carousing, and finally drained of a little blood by a vampire. All in all, a pretty full day, I'd venture."

"Well, when you put it that way," he agreed as he took the towel from her and wrapped it around his waist.

She removed two towels from the linen cabinet, wrapped one around her body, and dried her hair with another as she watched him depart the bathroom.

I simply adore you, she thought as she appreciated his lean, muscular form.

He slipped on a pair of sweatpants and nearly fell onto the bed. Moments later, Katrina exited the bathroom to slip on some panties and a long, cotton nightshirt. Then she turned off the lamp on her nightstand and crawled into bed.

She nestled next to him, pulled the covers over them, and kissed him on the back of the neck. Within a few minutes, she heard his breathing fall into a regular pattern and determined that he had fallen asleep.

She lay next to him for some time afterwards, thoughtfully considering how much better they had been getting along the past day or so. She had no doubt that it was in no small part to Paige's arrival and efforts.

However, given Caleb's altercation in the bar parking lot, she questioned the inclusion of Gil into their midst.

Returning to happier thoughts, she let the topic drop and

snuggled closer to Caleb as she drifted off for a brief respite of sleep.

CHAPTER 5

Visitors and Violations

When Caleb woke on Sunday, he discovered quickly that he had slept until midday, which earned a round of teasing from Paige. However, Katrina was pleased he had slept that late, knowing how exhausted he had been from the previous day's events.

Sunday was spent lounging around the house, although by early evening Caleb offered to grill some steaks and potatoes for him and Gil. Then the four watched the film Public Enemies in the theater room.

On Monday, Caleb returned to work, pleasantly noting that at least he had no evening classes to teach; those were only on Tuesdays and Thursdays. The day seemed to last longer than normal because he had some quiz grading to do before he went home for the day.

He knew that he would be too distracted by his house guests if he dared take the work home. By early evening, an unexpected visitor arrived as he continued grading at his desk. Paige appeared at his office doorway with a sly grin and wearing a pair of form-fitted blue jeans and turtleneck sweater.

"Hey, tiger," she greeted in a perky voice. "So, this is Professor Central, huh? You about to finish up for the day?"

He smiled up at her from his chair. "Hey, Paige. Yeah, this is the place, my home away from home. Thankfully, I'm almost finished. What brings you around?"

She shrugged. "I'm just wondering if you might want to run an errand with me after work."

He was intrigued. "Okay, I'll bite. Where to?"

She leaned against his door frame and adopted an innocent expression. "Oh, nothing major, really. But while I'm thinking about it, would you mind loaning me your car keys?"

"What?"

But she merely held out her empty, open palm. Then she snapped her fingers impatiently. "Come on, come on. Keys, please."

He laughed and tossed her his car keys, which she snatched out of midair and turned to leave. "Thanks! I'll be right back, so just stay put."

He chuckled and shook his head as his mysterious friend disappeared from view, followed closely by sound of the nearest exit doors abruptly opening and closing. Her actions had piqued his curiosity, but he returned to grading quizzes so they could leave soon.

Minutes later, she returned with a satisfied expression, but he noted she was without the car keys in hand.

"Hey, what about my keys?" he asked.

"Oh, Gil's taking your car back to the estate," she replied off-handedly. "I sure hope he doesn't get my directions confused. I mean, I printed off a Google map for him, after all."

"Gil was here?" he asked. "Didn't he want to go with us on the errand?"

"Nah, but then, you know how Gil is," she replied evasively as she plopped down in the guest chair beside his desk and inspected the items and décor in his office.

Actually, I don't, he mused, but let the topic drop for the time being.

"Go ahead, finish grading. Let me watch the young history

professor in action," she urged while perusing the titles of books on the nearby shelf.

He shook his head slightly, and then shrugged and returned to grading. Within another thirty minutes he had finished and stacked the quizzes into an orderly pile. As he filled his backpack with take-home items, Tanisha stopped by his open office doorway on her way out of the building.

"Goodnight, Caleb," she offered as she shifted her leather satchel to her left hand while reaching into her shoulder purse for her car keys.

"Oh, Tanisha, there's someone I want you to meet," he beckoned, rising from his desk and gesturing to Paige.

Tanisha smiled at him and took in Paige more fully as her attention shifted. Paige's bright blue eyes stared into Tanisha's with amusement as a smirk played across her face at the woman's mild surprise. However, Tanisha maintained her cool sense of grace and immediately extended her right hand to take Paige's in a polite grasp.

"Paige, I'm proud to introduce you to my friend and colleague, Dr. Tanisha Browning," Caleb offered. "She's our highly regarded Professor of Women's History. She's also a priceless mentor to me since I started at the college."

He turned his gaze to Tanisha with a wide grin and offered proudly, "Tanisha, I'm happy to finally introduce you to Paige Turner. She's like an adopted sister to me and one of the dearest people in my life."

Paige's eyes darted to him for only a split second at the grand introduction, but quickly refocused her attention back to Tanisha.

"Well, I'm pleased to meet you, Paige," the petite, hazel-eyed professor offered with an appraising smile. "Caleb neglected to tell me that he had an adopted sister."

"It's a dynamic title, of sorts," Paige replied as the two women released hands. "That's to say Caleb and I are like family, and he's also very dear to me."

One of Tanisha's eyebrows rose ever so slightly. "Oh, I see. I thought at first you might be related to Katrina."

Paige frowned with genuine curiosity. "Really? Why would you think that?"

"Although there's a difference in height, I sense you both have similar qualities," Tanisha observed with a glance at Caleb, who by that time regarded the sudden change in the nature of the conversation warily.

"Purely a coincidence," Paige replied easily. "But then, Katrina's a long-time, close friend of mine, so perhaps we've rubbed off on each other a little bit."

"Perhaps," Tanisha accepted politely. "It's a pleasure to meet you, nonetheless. Any friend of Caleb's is a friend of mine."

Tanisha glanced at him and prompted, "I'd better run, Caleb. Desta has a recital this evening, and Richard and I promised we wouldn't be late for it."

"Tell Desta I'm pulling for her," he offered as Tanisha headed for the building's exit.

When the door shut behind her, he released a heavy sigh. For some reason, he felt as if he had just dodged a bullet.

"She's perceptive," Paige observed. "You'll need to watch yourself with that one, kiddo."

Caleb countered, "She's a good friend, Paige, not a threat."

But she turned to face him fully. "Not to you, to her. If she even guessed about our true nature…"

He swallowed hard, understanding her meaning all too clearly. It hadn't been long since Katrina had nearly threatened to kill Tanisha for similar reasons. Concealing their existence was the first concern in every vampire's mind. Even the normally playful Paige became lethally serious as the topic surfaced, which unnerved him somewhat.

"Don't worry. I know," he replied dutifully. "Katrina's already warned me."

Paige seemed satisfied and didn't press the issue further. Instead, she recovered her previously playful smile and demanded, "Okay, enough stalling. Let's hit the road."

Caleb nodded and turned to collect his backpack when

Paige's cell phone buzzed.

The petite vampire fluidly slipped it from her waist and flipped the cell phone cover open with a flourish. "What's up, Red?" she asked.

He looked up at Paige, and her eyes glistened brightly as she gazed back at Caleb with a penetrating look. "Well, I'm glad Gil was able to follow directions. And yeah, our boy's right here," she confirmed. "Sure, everything's just fine. If you don't mind, I need to kidnap him from you for a short time tonight. I have an errand to run that he's going to accompany me on before we head back to the estate."

"Our boy?" he asked with raised eyebrows.

Paige grinned at him and continued, "Nah, tell Gil to go ahead and eat. Yes, I'll make sure Caleb eats before we come home. His jacket? Yeah, I'm on it. It's hanging on his door hook as we speak." She rolled her eyes, nodded her head, and used the fingers and thumb on her left hand to make the symbol for someone being very talkative.

He barely restrained himself from laughing out loud at that.

"Yes, I'll tell him you love him," she replied. "Okay, you overprotective nag, we need to get going now." She flipped the cell phone shut with a sigh and slipped the device into the holder at her waist. "She loves you, by the way," she offered before ushering him out of the office and locking and shutting the door behind them as she slung his backpack over one shoulder.

He chuckled while slipping into his leather jacket. As the two of them walked through the parking lot to Paige's rental car, he commented, "Hey, it's not kidnapping if I go willingly, you know."

A cold wind blew from the north, and she casually wrapped her right arm around his waist as they walked. "That's true, I suppose. At least for now, that is," she alluded.

What an odd comment, he noted warily. Just where are we going?

She activated the remote on her keychain to unlock the

doors to her black rental sedan and followed him around to the passenger side as she heard his pulse increase in a slightly agitated manner.

He opened the door and pulled the seat forward so she could toss his backpack into the back seat. Then he pushed the seat back and turned to stare at her with a curious expression.

"So, where are we headed, anyway?" he inquired after reconsidering her odd, earlier comment.

"You trust me, don't you, kiddo?" she asked gently.

He didn't even need to consider her question. He trusted Paige with his life and had done so on a couple of occasions in the months he had known her.

The corners of his lips upturned, and he replied earnestly, "Of course, silly. You're my surrogate vampire, my guardian. I trust you completely."

She smiled warmly, stepped closer to him, and popped a kiss against his cheek. Then she held the passenger door open and said, "Good, you should. So, get in already, and we'll hit the road."

He got in and fastened his seatbelt, and within minutes, they were speeding onto the nearby highway entrance not far from campus. She played some rock music to break the silence as they traversed the cold February evening.

Ten minutes later, he noticed they were traveling north on highway 75 out of Atlanta, and his curiosity increased.

When Caleb noticed their exit at the South Marietta Parkway, his heartbeat increased noticeably. The only reason he could divine for coming to Marietta was a less than desirable one, and he gritted his teeth.

"Where are we going, Paige?" he demanded sternly, despite having a bad feeling that the answer had to do with Devon Archibald.

She glanced over at him and replied, "I just need to stop by to visit with someone for a few minutes, so relax. After all, it's not often you and I get to go someplace alone together. Just think about where you want to go for dinner tonight."

She was relieved that she had been able to assuage his curiosity for as long as she had. It was a good testimony to the degree of trust they shared. However, she hoped he would be agreeable from that point on since he obviously had an idea of why they were in Marietta.

He silently fumed for a time as they continued through the city streets.

"Nice little town, actually," she commented agreeably as she realized they were getting closer to their destination. She had memorized the MapQuest directions before leaving the estate to pick up Caleb.

He merely grunted and mumbled, "Except for one resident, in particular."

She failed to contain a smirk at his acidic wit, which she found amusingly out of place coming from someone who normally maintained such an upbeat and cheerful disposition.

When they pulled into Devon's driveway, Paige noted that his car was already there. She had called him earlier to arrange their visit and was encouraged that he seemed agreeable.

Though they had interacted via email a couple of times, this was her first occasion to meet the vampire in person. Fortunately, Katrina had given her very detailed information about him and his background.

"We're here," Paige announced calmly. "We're simply going inside to chat for a few minutes, and then we'll leave. Okay?"

He reached for the door handle, but withdrew his hand and turned to look at Paige. "I think I'll stay here. You go ahead."

She chewed her lower lip and considered the situation for a moment before shrugging and exiting the car. After shutting her door, she walked calmly around to the passenger side of the vehicle and opened the door for him to exit. But he kept his seatbelt on and crossed his arms across his chest defiantly as he sat silently staring straight ahead.

Paige reached into the car and grasped the bicep of his right arm in her small hand and squeezed until she had a firm grip on him.

"The reality is you're going in with me. So, how about a deal, tiger?" she offered plainly. "I'll play nicely, if you will."

His jaw clenched, and he turned to stare at her with incredulity as he recalled how she had used the same declaration with him when she had first met him last fall. He realized there was likely no arguing with her, but it galled him that she would force her will upon him. She knew full well how much he hated Devon Archibald.

"Fine," he replied levelly, conceding there was little to be gained from causing a scene.

She released his arm and adopted a pleasant expression as she waited for him to release his seatbelt and exit the vehicle. As she shut the door and used the remote to lock the car, he stepped aside to look around the mostly dark neighborhood as the cold north wind whipped around him. He noted the area didn't appear in decline, but it was an older-looking neighborhood.

"Are you scared?" she asked gently. It occurred to her that some of his anger could be masking a sense of fear, although she only detected moderate wariness from him.

"Just irritated," he admitted as he stared up at the house before him. It appeared somewhat ominous at night despite the warm glow from the front porch light.

Why the hell did Paige have to bring me here?

"We have a very reasonable agreement with Devon," she reassured him. "And besides, I'm a burgeoning alpha. I can handle my own against a vampire, if needed."

He frowned at the spunk that she exuded under the circumstances and recalled how scary she had been at the estate when interrogating an intruder last December.

He shivered slightly at either that memory or the biting wind, or both. "He's huge, Paige," he recalled quietly as events from the night at the wildlife preserve replayed in his memory.

"Babysitter's on duty, so don't worry," she replied. "Now quit stalling."

He felt her hand pat the small of his back gently, and he slowly walked up the driveway towards the house. He stopped at the foot of the small front porch for a moment and sighed, but he felt the gentle pressure of Paige's hand at his back again.

He glanced back over his shoulder at her with a dark expression, but she merely stared back with mild amusement.

"Something funny?" he asked.

"Sorry, but Katrina's so right. You're really cute when you're annoyed," she observed with a smirk.

He rolled his eyes and felt her arm encircle his waist as she pulled him forward to stand before the front door with her. She reached out and rang the doorbell once.

A moment later, the door opened to reveal Devon Archibald wearing a pair of faded blue jeans and a black t-shirt. He towered above both of his visitors, but had a pleasant smile on his face. "Please, come in," he offered as he stood aside for them to enter.

Caleb took a moment to stare up at the tall, muscular vampire. He intended to allow Paige to enter first, but he felt her arm press him forward, and she followed him into the small entry area.

Devon closed the door behind them, and then held his hand out to shake Caleb's politely. "Welcome to my home. I hope you'll permit me the courtesy of starting our introductions over by shaking your hand in a gesture of mutual respect and civility."

Caleb wasn't happy to be there, but he conceded that there was no reason for him to be rude in the vampire's own home. He extended his hand, only to have it disappear in Devon's. But the vampire grasped his hand with a courteous degree of pressure and shook.

"Pleased to meet you, Mr. Taylor," Devon offered formally.

"Likewise, Mr. Archibald," Caleb replied, feeling a little silly. "You can call me Caleb, I suppose," he added.

"Thank you," the towering vampire replied. "And please

feel free to call me Devon."

Afterwards, the vampire moved to shake Paige's in turn. "It's nice to finally meet you in person, Paige."

"Likewise, Devon," she replied. "And thanks for seeing us on short notice. I hope that didn't create any hardships for your schedule."

"Not at all," he replied, gesturing towards the living room for them to enter. "Please make yourselves comfortable."

As they entered the living room, Caleb scanned the room warily before sitting next to Paige on the couch. He took particular interest in the pastoral paintings depicting wildlife and outdoor scenery, and he frowned at the seemingly domestic setting before him. His throat suddenly felt dry, and he coughed into his fist to clear his throat.

Devon started to sit down, but glanced at Caleb when he heard him cough. "Caleb, would you like something to drink?" he asked. "I have Coca-Colas in the fridge."

His eyebrows rose. "You do?"

Devon nodded as Caleb found himself feeling somewhat surprised by the revelation. It was his favorite cola, though perhaps Katrina had tipped him off to that.

"Well, um, please," Caleb stammered. "That would be nice, thank you."

"Glass or can?" Devon asked.

"Oh, a can would be fine, thanks."

Devon looked to Paige, but she shook her head. "No, nothing for me thanks."

The large vampire disappeared around the corner, and Caleb looked at Paige with upraised eyebrows. She nodded back at him reassuringly.

Well, he seems polite enough tonight, Caleb thought.

Devon returned with an open can of Coke and handed it to Caleb.

"Thanks," he replied, accepting the beverage. "Much appreciated."

Devon smiled pleasantly and sat in the reading chair opposite from them. "What brings you to grace my doorstep tonight?" he inquired.

"Caleb and I thought it would be a good idea to meet you in person," Paige began. "I'm not sure when I'll be leaving town, and I didn't want to miss the opportunity."

Devon appeared thoughtful while steepling his fingers before him. "I'm surprised Katrina didn't join you," the large-framed vampire observed. "I thought perhaps with Caleb being present for our first official meeting..."

She smiled in a manner that wasn't reflected in her steely gaze and casually placed her left hand on Caleb's thigh, of which Devon took immediate notice.

"I'm Caleb's guardian, his surrogate vampire. So, I have the latitude to act in his best interests as I deem necessary," she explained while looking at Caleb. Then she glanced at Devon. "Providing I don't run contrary to Katrina's wishes, of course."

Katrina had spoken at length with Paige regarding what she had said to Devon concerning their agreement, and she felt it important to mirror Katrina's words as closely as possible to avoid confusion.

"Of course," Devon replied with a nod.

"I was hoping you might tell me a little about yourself," she prompted. "That is, unless you feel uncomfortable discussing such personal matters with us."

Devon considered the two of them for a moment and told them much of the same background story he had related to Katrina, though he glossed over the details of his relationship with Nadida.

Caleb found his tale somewhat intriguing from a historical perspective, and he almost forgot his anger at Devon during the recollection. Paige had already heard the story once from Katrina, but displayed respectful interest as the tale was relayed.

"And here we are," Devon finished and turned to Caleb. "But before we speak further, I'd like to offer my apology for attacking you that night at the preserve. I thought you were prey, but I should have curtailed my hunt after you declared yourself a vampire's mate. For that, I am particularly sorry, and I hope you'll accept my apology. And while the offer stands no matter your response, I harbor no resentment if you decline. In my past, I've been hated by people who didn't know me for who I truly was, and yet I haven't allowed it to make me a bitter person."

Caleb remained thoughtfully silent for a moment. "Yes, I can see where, in your past, you may have been hated by others simply because of the color of your skin, which is certainly reprehensible. But then, you weren't hunting them as food at the time, either. Despite that, and hatred aside, does the rabbit not dislike the wolf by its very nature?"

Devon's eyebrow rose in a degree of surprise and appeared introspective as he considered Caleb's response. Paige's hand tightened ever so slightly on Caleb's thigh, and she glanced at him with a slight frown.

Interesting. I hadn't looked at it quite that way before, she mused.

But before anyone spoke, he continued, "But I'm willing to accept your apology in the spirit in which it was offered. However, while I can't guarantee we might ever be friends, I can certainly agree to be polite and respectful in the future. And I appreciate the gesture of your apology."

Paige looked sidelong at her young charge with a curious expression, admiring his diplomatic craft. Devon, too, seemed impressed.

"Thank you," the towering vampire replied. "And yes, I can agree to polite and respectful dialogue from this point. I'm confident Katrina would encourage that, as well."

Caleb took a swig of his Coke as he glanced at a picture of an elk on the wall to his left. While he wasn't feeling as angry or anxious as when he arrived, he wasn't feeling overly happy about being there either.

"There's something else, actually," Paige interjected. "There's a small matter of your blood supply."

Devon looked taken aback and corrected, "I'm afraid you're misinformed. I don't maintain a blood supply here."

"Exactly," she agreed. "But if you're going to be around

Caleb much, then I insist you do. I don't want you encountering him when you're hungry."

Devon nodded with understanding, but countered, "That's a rather expensive prospect for me, you understand."

"I appreciate your circumstances," she said. "I was there myself not so many years ago. However, I'm prepared to carry your delivery and blood supply expenses under my account at no cost to you."

Devon looked up with genuine surprise, and even Caleb cast a perplexed glance at his blonde-haired protector.

"Why?" he asked carefully. "Why would you do that? I mean, forgive me if I seem suspicious, but you have no direct vested interest in my agreement with Katrina, so I'm not sure what your incentive might be."

The corners of Paige's mouth rose, and she casually draped her left arm behind Caleb's lower back. "Understand: I'm Caleb's surrogate vampire. That means his interests are now my interests," she explained as her blue eyes penetrated Devon's.

Caleb smiled and placed his right hand on Paige's upper thigh.

"And that's all the incentive I need," she added with a glance at Caleb.

Devon's eyes went between Caleb's and Paige's faces, and he nodded, as if in understanding. "This is all very unusual to me," he observed. "I haven't met other vampires such as you and Katrina, and not merely because you're alpha females, either."

There was a brief pause as the dark-complexioned vampire considered the situation. "I appreciate your offer, and I accept. Are there conditions with this gift?"

Paige nodded and answered, "Just that you look after Caleb as called to do so and never allow your hunger to pose a threat to him."

"Done," Devon replied easily. "And thank you."

"You're welcome," she said, once more the perky, carefree vampire. "I'll email you when the first delivery is scheduled.

Oh, and always feel free to call my cell if you have questions regarding most anything, particularly matters concerning Caleb."

She rose from her seat, and Caleb followed suit behind her. "Now, I better get him to a restaurant. He's not pleasant to be around when he's hungry, either," she quipped. "He's mostly stomach, you understand."

Devon grinned, shook the short vampire's hand and turned to Caleb to shake his. "I'll show you to the front door."

Caleb found that to be an interesting prospect given the front door was visible from where they stood, but perhaps it was just southern hospitality or something. Nevertheless, he was happy to be leaving, although he conceded the visit had gone better than he had expected.

As Devon opened his front door and stepped aside for them to pass, he offered, "Thank you for stopping by, and please come again anytime. Although I'm away at work a lot, so maybe call ahead of time so you don't waste a trip unnecessarily."

They nodded, and Caleb offered, "Well, feel free to visit our home as well. That is, if you happen to be in the neighborhood. And thanks for the cola."

"You're welcome, and thank you for the offer, Caleb," Devon replied. "But keep in mind what I said about hating blindly. I've seen what it can do to a person."

Caleb nodded with a polite smile.

Devon added, "But I'll also consider your hunting analogy, as well."

Paige and Caleb stepped outside into the cold night air as Devon watched them walk away. The front door shut quietly as they neared their car.

"Well, the vampire-human summit went pretty well overall," she said.

"Summit, huh? He tried to eat me not long ago, you may recall," he pointed out as she unlocked the car doors with her remote.

202

"I might also have under different circumstances," she countered slyly as she followed him around to the passenger side.

But he returned her sly expression with one of his own and quipped, "You know, under different circumstances, I just might have let you."

Her bright blue eyes stared mischievously into his for a moment. She grinned at him and playfully ushered him into the passenger seat with a flurry of her hands. "Don't tempt me," she challenged as she softly patted him on top of the head with the palm of her hand, and then shut his door.

She got into the driver's seat and started the car. Then she paused and turned to Caleb with a smirk. "I'm a wolf, you know. And yet, you don't hate me by nature, do you, Mr. Rabbit?"

He grinned and downed the remainder of his Coke before placing the empty can in the in-dash cup holder. He turned to her and replied matter-of-factly, "Ah, but I adore you, Ms. Wolf, because you're a friendly wolf."

"Think so?" she countered with a raised eyebrow. She grinned, gunned the engine, and whipped out of the driveway and down the street. Once they were navigating through the main streets of the town, she glanced over at him and asked, "Okay, Rabbit, where do you want to eat dinner then?"

He considered that at length and finally replied with a sneer, "Pizza buffet."

"Pizza buffet?!" she demanded incredulously. "Do you know how strong the stinky, dead, burned meat smell will be in there?"

He remained silent, but grinned back at her evilly.

"This is payback, isn't it?" she asked with a sour expression.

He chuckled and replied, "Yep."

"Evil bunny," she muttered and sped onto the highway headed back towards Atlanta.

Once in Atlanta proper, she took him to a pizza place with a dinner buffet and nursed a cola while watching him eat.

Despite the strong scent of cooked pepperoni, sausage, and all manner of meats in the air, she relented to nibbling at a slice of cheese pizza and some salad just for show. In the end, they had an enjoyable visit together and chatted and laughed just like two best friends enjoying each other's company.

Afterward, they returned to the estate, where Katrina was watching some television in the back living room.

Caleb squatted down to kiss Katrina on the lips as she lay on the couch holding the remote control. One brief smell of him told her exactly where they had been.

"Pizza and a lingering scent of...Devon's home." She noted the latter with narrowed eyes.

"That's right," Paige interrupted before he could be grilled further. "We had a brief meeting, which went very well, I might add."

Katrina looked up at Caleb, her right arm snaking out to encircle his waist and asked, "Indeed?"

He sighed, leaned against her while squatting on his knees and replied, "Yeah, it went pretty well, actually."

"How about some random vintage of blood for the pizza-beleaguered vampire?" Paige suggested dryly.

"Sure," he replied with a grin. "You too, Kat?"

"No, thank you," she replied and released her arm from around him so he could rise. Once he disappeared into the kitchen, Katrina focused her attention on Paige fully. "Why did you take him there without me?" she demanded in a whisper.

Paige positioned herself next to the couch, planting both hands atop her slim hips. "Think about it, Red. You're already in the doghouse for the agreement with Archibald in the first place. This way, I got to meet him, and Caleb didn't have to blame you for dragging him there. I get to be the bad guy instead of you for a change. Or are you so ready to be back on the skids with him so soon after your romantic redemption last night?"

Katrina was taken aback by her frank assessment, but she conceded that her friend made some good points. It was true that she was very happy with how things had gone between her and Caleb the previous night, and she didn't want things to change. "Okay, points well made, actually," she admitted. "I suppose thanks are in order."

"None needed, Red," Paige countered with a shrug. "It was nice to spend time alone with him, actually."

Katrina nodded. She knew how much Paige adored Caleb, and a little time alone with him was probably reasonable. "By the way, tomorrow's the day I'm announcing my territorial claim, and I'm pronouncing you and Devon as Caleb's protectors."

Paige nodded. She was fully aware that Katrina and Alton were working on that, but was still a little surprised that Katrina was willing to make such a public declaration given how private and reclusive she had been over the years in the vampire community.

"By the way, where's Gil?" Paige asked.

"In the theater room," Katrina replied. "He was bored and wanted to watch some new vampire movie that Caleb recently added to my film collection."

Paige rolled her eyes, not typically a fan of Hollywood vampire films. Although, she admitted the romantic one with the young male vampire who fell in love with the clumsy brunette teenager was rather endearing. Although that one also had werewolves, and everyone knew that werewolves weren't real. She plopped down on a nearby upholstered chair with a sigh, draping one leg lazily over the arm rest.

After a few minutes, Caleb returned with a glass of heated blood for Paige, who gratefully accepted it. "Thanks, kiddo."

He slipped his shoes off and went to lie down beside Katrina on the oversized couch. The red-haired vampire smiled gratefully, wrapped her arm around him, and even handed him the remote control.

"Surf away," she remarked and kissed him on the cheek.

"Yeah, but no vampire movies tonight, okay, sport?" Paige remarked before sipping from her glass and reflecting on the evening's events. "Pizza buffet, of all places," she mumbled sourly, only to hear Caleb chuckle in response.

* * *

On Tuesday, Caleb was once more at work teaching history classes, meeting with students, and mingling with the daytime world over which humanity presided. During occasional free moments, he considered the meeting the previous evening between him, Paige, and Devon.

The towering vampire had surprised him somewhat by providing access to an entirely different side of his personality, as well as by sharing his intriguing life story. He had been quite critical of Katrina's decision to spare Devon's life, but he felt a glimmer of sympathy for the vampire. At the very least, he was willing to wait and see how things progressed.

During the early afternoon, he checked his personal email account for messages. Among the usual spam was a message with the header, "Declaration of Territorial Claim," which Katrina had BCC'd him on. As he read the message, he found himself holding his breath.

Greetings Fellow Night Dwellers,

I bid you peace and well wishes from Atlanta, Georgia. In the interest of good relations and cooperation, I hereby inform you that I am officially claiming and declaring the city of Mableton, Georgia, as sovereign territory under my personal jurisdiction, including a small portion of the city proper in downtown Atlanta. The specific area claimed downtown relates to the campus of Robert Fulton Community College and an area of two miles radius surrounding the campus property. Individuals under my sanction and protection include my human mate, Mr. Caleb Taylor, and his vampire protectors, Ms. Paige Turner, and Mr. Devon Archibald. In addition, the culling of humans within and around my stated territories should be curtailed to avoid unnecessary scrutiny and/or visibility to myself and our kind.

I appreciate your cooperation in observing my claim, and I welcome advance notification of planned visits into or through my territory to avoid unnecessary misunderstandings. Thank you, and may your hunting by fruitful.

Regards,
Katrina Rawlings of Mableton/Atlanta, Georgia, United States

After he finished reading the message, he sat back in his desk chair and looked out his office window. The human world beyond continued on its merry way through life, completely oblivious to the fact that part of their city had just been claimed by a vampire. The very thought seemed surreal to him. However, in the same manner that he had become accustomed to the idea of his having been claimed by a vampire, so too would he to this latest revelation.

The question was, would others kindly observe Katrina's declaration? More to the point, what would happen if they didn't?

He tried not to contemplate the latter question at length. Instead, he picked up his desk phone and dialed the estate. On the first ring, the phone was picked up.

"Hello?" Katrina inquired.

He smiled at the sound of his mate's voice. "Hi, Kat. I just read your message a few minutes ago, very nicely written," he said, closing the door to his office.

"Thank you, my love," she responded with a pleased tone. "Were you surprised?"

"Actually, yes, I was," he said. "It's somewhat eerie to think about everybody's being oblivious to the declaration. It's like secretly asserting that someone has just claimed your property, and you're completely oblivious to it."

She chuckled at his analogy. "Sorry that we didn't have a chance to discuss it beforehand, but Alton conveyed a sense of urgency about getting that out. He believes the recent notoriety of our experience with Chimalma will encourage additional unexpected visitors unless we quickly establish some ground rules."

"Hmm, that's a good point, I suppose. But I have a quick question or two," he said. "What about vampires who don't have email? And what about vampires whose addresses you didn't have access to?"

There was a silent pause.

"Excellent questions, my love. There's always the possibility of an occasional transient visitor from the off-line ranks of our kind. But at least an effort has been made on my part. The Internet makes things so much easier for us, as a matter of fact. And as for those whose addresses I didn't have access to, some of the recipients may pass my email along to others. But I'll also post the message on some of the secure blogs and chat rooms that our kind utilize."

"You have chat rooms?" he inquired with surprise. "What next, vampire dating services?"

"Very funny, my love," she replied dryly. "But yes, we're quite active online despite being a diverse and often reclusive community."

"Do vampires Tweet?"

"Tweet? Oh, ugh, I hate Twitter."

He chuckled. "Yeah, me too."

"How's your day?" she asked.

"Oh, okay, I suppose," he replied. "But I wish I were home with you right now."

"I wish you were here too," she purred.

"Well, I'll be home right after class tonight," he promised.

"Great," she replied. "And I'll have some paperwork for you to sign, as well."

"Paperwork?"

"Later. Have a good remainder of the day, my love," she replied and hung up.

He frowned as he pulled the handset away from his head and stared at it with a bland expression. *I hate it when she does that.*

* * *

Later that evening, once Caleb had arrived home, he dropped his backpack next to a chair in the dining room. He glanced into the living room and noticed Paige lying peacefully on the couch with her hands folded across her stomach as a black and white classic movie played on the television.

He observed the steady rise and fall of her chest, wondering if she were asleep. It would have been the first time he had ever caught a vampire sleeping.

He moved slowly and quietly towards the end of the couch until he neared where her head rested. From his vantage he was able to see that her eyes were closed.

He reached out to grasp at her shoulders to startle her, but at the last moment her hands darted out to grab him by the lower arms. She propelled him forward, pivoting his body in a semi-circle until he landed on top of her.

"Gotcha'!" she hollered as her hands tickled him about the stomach and ribs mercilessly.

He laughed and thrashed, desperately trying to wriggle from atop her and onto the floor. Seconds later, he was having trouble catching his breath, and she stopped abruptly.

The petite vampire swiveled into a sitting position and pulled him next to her on the couch. He finally managed to inhale a deep breath and wrapped his arm around her shoulders.

"I thought I had you there for a minute," he said once he caught his breath. "You looked completely asleep."

"Actually, I was napping," she conceded. "But I heard you the minute you entered from the garage. Still, I'm a pretty good actress, eh?"

"Academy Award-winning," he agreed. "Hey, where's Gil?"

"He went out for cigarettes about an hour ago," she recalled. "I'm sure he's trying to find his way back about now."

He shook his head and offered with a sigh, "Should I go

looking for him?"

"Nah, he'll call when he's desperate enough," she said. "Besides, Red's waiting for you in the study. Something about paperwork. Better be careful, kiddo; she seemed pretty angry."

He looked at her sharply. "Angry?"

"Yep, you better take her a glass of blood as a peace offering," she advised. "Maybe a little massage on her shoulders when you go in. After all, couldn't hurt to start off on a positive note."

He nodded as his mind raced as to why Kat might be angry with him. "Yeah, good idea. Thanks."

He rose from the couch, made his way down to the wine basement to retrieve a packet of blood and heated it in a glass in the microwave.

After a few minutes, he went down the dark central hallway on the first floor until he reached the outer door to Katrina's study. The door was slightly ajar, and he could see enough to determine that she was sitting at her desk looking over some paperwork. But instead of just entering unannounced, he knocked on the door frame politely.

"Caleb?" she asked. "Please come in."

She smiled up at him when he entered, and he offered the best hopeful expression that he could muster as he walked towards her desk. Unfortunately, his heart was beating more rapidly than normal, though he was certain she had already determined that before he entered. Once again, she had the advantage over him.

He sat the glass down carefully, making sure to avoid any of the papers strewn across the desktop. He moved to stand behind her and reached out to massage her shoulders gently between his fingertips. She leaned her head back and moaned with pleasure from his efforts.

"How was the rest of your day after I spoke with you?" he asked carefully. *She didn't sound angry earlier today.*

Katrina frowned. "Caleb, is everything okay?"

"Me? Sure, just fine," he reassured her, his fingers rubbing a little harder as he tried to discern why she would be upset with him, although she didn't seem terribly upset with him at the moment.

She reached up to grasp his hands and swiveled in her leather chair to face him, looking up at him with a curious expression. "Is there something I should know, my love?"

His mind raced as he swallowed hard and replied, "Um, I don't think so."

She narrowed her eyes as she continued to hold his hands in hers.

He rolled his eyes and conceded, "Look, I don't know what I did, but I'll confess if you'll just tell me what I did wrong. Can we just get this over with, please?"

She looked at him as if he were insane. "What are you talking about?" she demanded.

He looked into her eyes with his mouth agape, saw the confusion on her face and asked, "Aren't you angry with me for something? Paige said—"

She interrupted him with an amused expression, "Paige is having some fun with you, my love. I'm not angry at all. But thank you for the massage, as well as the warm blood. I was getting a little hungry."

The feeling of relief surged through him like a blast of cold air on a hot summer day. A new mission flashed in his mind, and he tried to pull his hands away from Katrina's, growling, "Oh, I am so going to kill her!"

But she laughed, held onto his hands, and stood up from her chair. "Okay, okay, you can kill her in just a minute. While you're here, I want you to sign some things for me."

He stopped tugging and let her steer him into the chair. She picked up the glass of blood, took a sip of it, and pointed to some papers on the desk before him. "Just sign those two where you see the yellow highlight," she instructed him, resting her left hand atop his shoulder.

He picked up the ink pen lying to the side of the papers and looked over them for a moment. "What am I signing?" he asked.

She savored another sip of blood and replied, "I'm adding you onto one of my bank accounts as a co-owner, as well as requesting you to be added to one of my credit cards as joint-owner. It will make things so much easier for you when we go to Europe."

He looked up at her and shook his head. "You don't have to do that, Kat," he insisted. "I don't want your money."

She smiled down at him fondly. None of her previous mates had ever refused her gifts, particularly the monetary kind. But Caleb was in a different class altogether, making all the previous ones seem like frauds and interlopers. The sole exception was her human husband, Samuel Lawnder, of whom Caleb reminded her a great deal. *Sometimes it takes five hundred years to find true love again*, she mused as she licked her lips and set the glass on the desk.

"Kat?" he asked with upraised eyebrows. "Are you okay?"

She broke from her reverie and bent down to kiss him on the lips warmly.

"I love you so very much, " she whispered and kissed him again.

He sensed a slightly metallic aftertaste from the hint of blood on her lips and murmured, "I love you too."

She deliberately adopted a mock-stern expression, placed her hands on her hips, and ordered, "You're my mate, so what's mine is yours. Now, sign."

He smiled up at her with an appraising expression, impressed with her stern visage. "You're so sexy when you do that," he commented and turned to sign the forms.

While his attention was focused on the paperwork, she grinned slyly. I know, and you love it.

Then she turned serious and pointed out, "You need to realize that having the strength of proper funding in some parts of the world is essential to ensure safe travel. And it can get you out of a lot of delicate situations with a minimal amount of questions."

He put the ink pen down and turned his head to glance up at her with a grin. She reverted her facial expression to a more sedate one.

"Thank you," she offered pleasantly. "I'll let you know when your credit card arrives."

Suddenly, Paige popped into the room from around the corner and teased with a mischievous grin, "Hey, tiger. Think you could heat up a glass of blood for me, too?"

"You hellion!" he blurted and leapt from out of the desk chair with a lurch, leaving the chair spinning in his wake as he charged towards the doorway. Paige disappeared down the hallway with Caleb in close pursuit.

Katrina giggled at the sound of their footsteps rushing down the hallway and observed, "'Hellion.' I like that one." She shook her head with amusement and muttered, "Ah, how I missed the sound of children playing in a house."

Abruptly, the phone rang, and she picked up the cordless handset from the desk with a flourish. "Hello?" she asked. "Hi, Gil. Yes, I'll send someone to lead the way back. Where are you?" She paused a moment longer and said, "Got it."

She moved to the open doorway and yelled down the hallway, "Gil's at the Quick Mart about five miles away and can't find his way back!"

"Well, crap!" Paige exclaimed irritably.

Katrina paused and heard Paige venture hopefully, "Um, Caleb?"

"Hey, he's your boyfriend," he countered.

Katrina grinned.

"Come on, kiddo, at least drop me off so I can drive the car back," she pleaded.

Following a brief silence, Paige added, "Come on! Back rub?"

"We'll be back soon, Kat!" came Caleb's booming voice.

Katrina chuckled, heading back to her desk to finish preparing the forms. She was very pleased that everything seemed to be going so well for a change. Then she frowned and wondered how long that would actually last.

* * *

By Saturday, an important first-time event was about to take place between Katrina and Caleb. It was February 14th, marking their first Valentine's Day together. Caleb had been thinking about the prospects of that particular occasion because it was a holiday that seemed uniquely suited for a vampire with the color red and the symbolisms of the human heart.

He made sure to acquire a romantic greeting card, of course, but he also tried to think creatively regarding his gifts for Katrina. He even managed a little something for Paige, the second-dearest woman to his heart.

Caleb spent the day at the college assisting with a community outreach project to curb domestic partner abuse. He answered phones at the call center and helped prepare lunch for community members attending the free seminars and workshops. As a victim of abuse himself, he felt it was important to reach out to others suffering under abusive circumstances, understanding fully how helpless and lost a person could feel. He was grateful that his and Katrina's relationship was nurturing, respectful, and violence-free.

By the end of the day-long event, he eagerly made his way home. Upon his arrival, he noticed that Paige's rental car was nowhere to be seen, and he entered the house only to be greeted with the sound of silence. However, he did smell the scent of one of his favorite cuisines, barbeque.

"Kat?" he inquired as he slipped the backpack off his shoulder and sat a paper sack full of gifts on the dining room table.

Upon hearing only silence, he laid aside a small, shiny red gift bag covered with red tissue paper and a greeting card. He sat out a small square gift wrapped in silver wrapping paper, followed by a single red rose accented by baby's breath in a slender crystal vase. He left the remaining two gifts in the sack at the other end of the table.

He walked into the kitchen, only to see Katrina standing before him wearing a black mesh gown open to reveal a matching g-string. Her long red hair cascaded down across one shoulder, and her emerald eyes glinted in the dim kitchen lighting as she smiled at him alluringly.

"Happy Valentines' Day, my love," she murmured in a sultry voice. "Do you like?"

She had shopped for just the right outfit to entice him. And while it seemed somewhat cliché, she sought to appeal to his baser desires before offering a more sentimental gift to him later.

"Oh, you're ravishing," he whispered with a growing sense of desire. He crossed the distance to her and bent his head up slightly to kiss her on the lips.

She reveled in his response and offered, "Gil and Paige are out for the evening, so the house is ours for a while. I hope you like what I've catered for you."

His mouth watered from the scent of barbeque, and he appreciated how much of a sacrifice she was making to allow it to permeate through the house. "Oh, it's wonderful," he replied with a grin.

"Are you hungry?" she asked playfully.

He silently nodded.

"Food, or fun first?" she asked with a smirk.

He grinned, took her by the hand, and started down the hallway with her in tow. But then he stopped, turned, and led her back into the dining room. While the desire to make love to her surged through him, he made a deliberate effort for patience in order to present her gifts to her first.

She followed him into the dining room and observed the array of gifts before her. She picked up the vase with the rose and took a moment to savor its sweet fragrance. Setting it down, she opened the romantic greeting card. It included a poem about true love and his own handwritten note, *To my true love: the woman of my dreams, the fulfillment of my desires, and the angel who watches over me. My life, my blood, my body for you. I love you. Your mate, Caleb.*

She closed the card, her heart melting over his sincere declaration. She gave him a smoldering look and pressed her lips against his in a passionate kiss.

He grinned with satisfaction. So far, so good.

She placed the card on the table with a look of satisfaction and removed the tissue paper from the red gift bag. Reaching inside, she removed a small gift set of cherry blossom-scented body lotion, creams, and shower gel. It was her favorite scent and, she had discovered, Caleb's as well.

"Perfect. How did you know that I needed some more of those?" she asked and glanced down at the remaining small, silver-wrapped box.

He picked it up from the table and placed it in her hands with a hopeful expression, prefacing, "The best for last."

She removed the paper delicately from the box to reveal a soft, black leather casing. Her fingers slowly pivoted the lid open, and her breath caught in her throat at the sight of two perfect emeralds suspended from gold earring posts.

"Oh, Caleb, they're beautiful," she whispered appreciatively. She felt a small pang of guilt as she realized that they must have cost him a great deal of money, given their exquisite cut, clarity, and size.

He beamed with satisfaction and offered, "When the light catches the gems just right, they remind me of your beautiful, glowing eyes."

She was both impressed and deeply touched and turned to embrace him. She nestled her nose against his neck, kissed his supple skin and moved to his lips.

"I love them," she murmured. "And I love you."

They held each other at length, relishing the closeness. Then she pulled away from him, gazing into his eyes with approval. It was definitely a memorable Valentine's Day for her, the first in so many years. And now it was her turn to make it memorable for him.

She took him by the hand and suggested, "Now, come with me. I have something for you to unwrap. It's a gift I think you'll find keeps on giving."

He grinned and gratefully followed her down into the sublevel chamber.

During Katrina's five centuries of existence, she had mastered a number of talents and skills, including the refined art of lovemaking. And while Caleb was no novice to sex, she reveled in the opportunity to explore a number of techniques that were wholly new to him.

Following their intimate time together, during which time Katrina made him work up an appetite, she served him a wonderful barbecue dinner. She also gave him a new Rolex wristwatch, engraved on the back with his initials. He had been shocked to receive such an expensive gift on Valentine's Day.

Later that evening, they changed into comfortable clothes and lay on the couch together watching a romantic comedy in the living room. Before long, they heard Paige and Gil returning from their evening out, and Caleb quietly slipped from Katrina's arms, kissing her on the cheek beforehand. She smiled and pinched him on the rear as he got up, resulting in his smirking back at her.

"Take your time," she offered quietly as her attention returned to the movie.

"I'll put the flowers in some water while you go upstairs to shower," Paige's voice emanated from the kitchen. "I'll be up before long."

"Sounds good, babe," Gil replied eagerly as he strode through the kitchen.

Caleb leaned against the kitchen door jamb, casually folded his arms across his chest, and watched her retrieve an empty glass vase from one of the cabinets. She began arranging the dozen roses in it, then glanced up at him with a curious expression.

"Nice flowers," he observed pleasantly.

She smiled wanly. "Yeah, that was sweet of Gil, actually."

"What else did he get you?" he asked carefully, uncertain whether it was a good idea to ask.

She wrinkled her nose. "Lingerie. Black lace with pink accents, and skimpy, of course. I asked him to take it upstairs with him when he went up to shower."

"Hey, you have the body to wear it, so be happy," he offered with a smirk.

She shrugged and ran water from the tap into the vase. "True, I suppose."

He regarded his friend soberly, realizing she wasn't particularly happy. A pang of sadness ran through him, and he was suddenly pleased he had made the gesture to do something nice for her. He had the feeling a surprise was exactly what she needed at the moment.

"I took him to dinner at a nice seafood place downtown," Paige said as she set the vase of flowers on the counter. "Reservations were hard to come by, but I sort of charmed my way into one last week, since I had anticipated we'd still be in town. Gil was really happy about that. Food is definitely one way to his heart."

"Have time for one more surprise tonight?" Caleb asked as he stared into Paige's pale blue eyes.

She grinned at him and replied slyly, "A surprise? From you?"

He feigned an indifferent shrug. "Maybe." He glanced in the direction of the dining room and waited patiently.

Her expression immediately turned playful, and she darted past him in a blur into the dining room. "Are both of these mine?" she asked happily with a tone reminiscent of a child's at Christmas.

"Yep," he replied, following her into the dining room to watch. He glanced over to the couch and noticed that while Katrina still lay there, she had cocked her head to one side to listen more closely.

Both gifts were wrapped in bright red paper, one the size of a small jewelry box and the other about one foot square. Paige picked up the larger box, shook it, and tore the wrapping off in a flurry of hand movements. She popped the cardboard box open to reveal a black t-shirt. When she shook it open to look at the front, it had a picture of two white fangs with blood dripping from them and a slogan in white letters reading Got Blood? below the fangs. She giggled, held it up to herself, and glanced at him.

"I love it!" she exclaimed with a gleam in her eyes. "It's so me!"

She set the t-shirt down and smirked as she picked up the smaller box. That one she took the time to open delicately at each end and slowly remove the wrapping paper from around it. It was a small, black velvet jewelry case, which she deftly popped open with her fingers. Inside was a sterling silver bracelet with an inscription.

She beamed at him and removed the bracelet to place it on her wrist. The engraving stated: *Happy V-tines to my guardian & babysitter. Luv, Caleb.*

"Oh, Caleb, I love it," she offered and moved in a blur to wrap her arms around him in a warm embrace.

He embraced her happily. "Happy Valentine's Day, Paige."

"They're both perfect," she assured him softly. "Thanks, tiger."

"You're welcome. I'm really glad you like them."

"The t-shirt is too cute," she added. "And if it wasn't for Red, I'd kiss—"

"Oh, shut up, and kiss him!" Katrina barked with exasperation from the living room.

Paige giggled and reached her head up to kiss him on the lips discreetly. He responded in kind and gave her a big hug, lifting her off the floor momentarily.

"You're the best, kiddo," she said, her blue eyes seeming to sparkle in the light. She was touched and particularly loved the bracelet, suddenly realizing she hadn't received a gift so special and sentimental from anyone in a very long time.

He smiled, watching as she gathered up the small jewelry box and t-shirt and walked back through the house with a huge grin.

"Nice earrings, Red," Paige remarked as she passed by the living room and glanced in at Katrina.

"Thanks, Shorty," Katrina replied. "All right, now get back in here and snuggle with me before I get jealous...kiddo," she teased Caleb.

He shook his head with a smirk and dutifully proceeded back towards the couch. He beamed with contentment that it was a memorable first Valentine's for the two most important women in his life. But as he started to lie next to Katrina, she held up her hand and regarded him with a conspiratorial expression.

"It seems you have one last item to open," she prompted.

He looked at her with a puzzled expression and glanced around the room for anything resembling a gift or envelope. "Really? Where?"

She smirked and pointed to the cabinet doors on the entertainment center across the room. He walked over and opened them, revealing a small, rectangular gift wrapped in shiny blue paper. He picked it up and noted that it felt rather weighty. He glanced over at Katrina, who was watching him intently, and slowly unwrapped the gift.

After removing the paper, he was left with a plain, white cardboard box. She put the television on mute and waited as he removed the box lid. It contained an eight-by-ten dual-picture frame made from sterling silver.

He parted the frames, revealing two photographs. The one on the left was Katrina in the sexy, blue sequin dress she had worn the night they went clubbing. The photograph on the right was of Paige, wearing the red dress she had worn that night. Both were smiling in their photos, and each had signed their pictures.

Katrina wrote: *To Caleb, my love forever. Kat.*

Paige wrote: *Always watching out for you, kiddo. Love, Paige.*

He was so proud to have those photos, and he looked up at Katrina with surprise. "These are wonderful! I've always wanted a picture of each of you. But I thought that vampires don't give out their photographs." The entire time he had known her, she had consistently refused to allow her picture to be taken.

She nodded. "We don't, typically." She momentarily considered how much trouble a simple picture of herself as

Amber Simmons had caused her recently. But then, this was different: it was for Caleb.

"But you're special, kiddo. So we made an exception," Paige announced from the other side of the room.

His head turned in time to see her grin and blow him a kiss before disappearing back upstairs in a blur.

Suddenly, Katrina was standing next to him, and she wrapped her arms around him from behind in a warm embrace. "Happy Valentine's Day, my love," she whispered before kissing him on the neck.

He smiled with delight and realized it was indeed the best Valentine's Day he'd ever had.

* * *

Another week passed, and Caleb had gotten used to having two additional house guests. It was almost like Gil and Paige had taken up brief residence with them. While he enjoyed having Paige close by, part of him wondered how Gil liked the extended visit.

The young aspiring rocker had seemed restless the past couple of days and, while polite, had acted more distant towards him when they chatted. More often than not, Gil and Paige spent their nights out on the town, only to return home long after Caleb had gone to bed. Katrina seemed quite comfortable hosting their extended visit, so he merely continued with his weekly routine.

On Friday, he was pleased that his afternoon at the college was a short one, because he was anxious to initiate his third installment in the Find Caleb series. He decided to move forward with his plans for the construction site. He anticipated that it would prove easy to navigate due to the dormant state of the late-February foliage.

He had some surprises up his sleeve and had purchased a couple of lengths of climbing rope, as well as the gloves and accessories required for climbing and rappelling . One positive aspect of his challenges for Katrina was his growing familiarity with the inventories of the local sporting goods stores.

By late afternoon, he left the college with a trunk load of equipment. He arrived at the abandoned site before sunset and parked his car well off of the road behind a stand of pine trees.

Once he had unloaded his gear from the car, he set everything in place. Darkness fell two hours later, and he ate a sandwich and some chips he had brought out to the site. Then he dialed the estate's number from his cell phone, and someone picked up after only two rings.

"Hello?" Paige answered.

"Paige?" Caleb asked. "Where's Kat?"

"Hi, tiger," she replied. "Oh, she's finishing some laundry. Hey, we've been wondering when you're coming home. Any problems?"

"No problems," he answered proudly. "Tonight's another installment in the Find Caleb series for Kat."

"Sounds good. Where's tonight's exciting episode taking place?"

"An abandoned construction site not far from the estate, actually," he explained. "I have an idea to give me an edge this time."

"Ha! Good luck, kiddo," she replied. "Hold on, I'll get Katrina."

He gnawed apprehensively at his lower lip at her tone and heard what sounded like wind rushing into the receiver at the other end. *Damn, vampires are fast.*

"Caleb?" Katrina asked. "We've been wondering about you. Do you have to work late tonight?"

He grinned. "Nope, I'm calling to inform you that it's time to play another installment of Find Caleb tonight."

She giggled. "I was wondering when you'd spring one of these on me again."

He appreciated her upbeat tone. "I'm at a place not far from the estate tonight. Do you remember the abandoned construction site not far up the highway?"

She was silent for a time.

"The place with the three-story frame and the overgrown landscape?"

"That's the one."

"Time limit?" she asked simply.

"Coming by car?"

"Nope, running," she answered. "It's not far, and it's a great night for a run. I'll just ride back with you."

He nodded and glanced at his illuminated watch facing. "Okay then. Twenty minutes from right now."

She chuckled. "Better get ready...here I come!"

The phone went silent, and he pulled his cell away from his ear to stare at the display. He shook his head and muttered, "Someday I'm going to get in the last word."

He ran a quick pattern of spreading pre-worn clothing through the trees to diffuse his scent in multiple locations before heading to his staging location. He appreciated the lack of wind on that moonless, cold night as he pulled on some snug-fitting leather rappelling gloves and checked the straps on his climbing harness.

The lack of wind would prevent his scent from being spread in one direction, giving him more opportunities to move around. He was determined that the evening would mark his first successful evasion from Katrina within the specified time limit.

He glanced at his watch and tried to determine if ten minutes were enough time for her to cover the few miles. Standing near a small copse of pine trees, he listened for any unusual noises. He could see the dim glow of a street lamp to his left in the direction of his parked car, and on a whim, he took out a small pair of binoculars to survey the area.

As he sharpened the focus settings, he saw Katrina standing near his parked car. He held his breath as he watched her scan the area slowly, then take a deliberate deep breath and hold it. He smiled, realizing he was actually viewing her in the act of hunting him. A feeling of exhilaration shot through his body at the thought of being hunted, and his heartbeat increased rapidly. He glanced at his watch again, realizing that roughly two-thirds of the time limit had expired already.

A nervous feeling formed in his stomach as he watched her, estimating it would take only minutes for her to run through the area looking for him. It could take scant seconds more to get to him once she spotted him.

Katrina slowly moved out of the illuminated area and into the trees where he had scattered some of his clothes and in a direction that put her at a right angle to his current position. The analogy that immediately came to his mind was of chumming the water when trying to attract a shark in the ocean.

He experienced a strange moment of complete clarity in which he weighed the skills of his opponent and was very happy this was a playful game and not a matter of life and death.

He determined he had spent enough time in one position and slipped his binoculars into a small nylon satchel clipped onto one of the rungs on his climbing harness. He moved in the direction of the partially constructed building while trying to muffle the noise of the metal rings attached to his harness.

He was making good time while moving very quietly, but the toe of his hiking boot caught on a discarded piece of lumber that was partially buried in the ground. All the metal rings on his rappelling harness jingled like an alarm all at once, and he winced with frustration, only barely managing to avoid cursing out loud.

Suddenly, Paige appeared out of nowhere. She moved at a quick pace, grabbed him by the upper portion of his left arm, and hauled him forward at a dead run. His eyes widened to the size of saucers with surprise until he realized who it was.

"Way to go, Mister Ninja!" she exclaimed as she half-pulled him along. "Where did you learn how to sneak, Bugs Bunny cartoons?!"

"Where the hell did you come from?" he demanded, barely managing to keep his footing alongside her as they ran towards the abandoned concrete structure looming ahead.

"I just had to see this for myself," she replied with a chuckle while slowing down to match his pace. "Can't you run faster?" she demanded.

His heart raced as he ran as fast as his feet could carry him, his harness rings jingling loudly. He stole a glance back over his shoulder, but didn't see Katrina anywhere. He wasn't sure how long they had before she would appear, but he knew it had to be quick.

The two of them made it onto the building's lower level slab, and he turned on a red-lens flashlight just to avoid running into anything that might be lying around. The concept of stealth was completely lost at that point, and instead he merely tried to run out the clock.

Of course, Paige had no problems seeing in the dark, and she pulled him from behind as she headed in the direction of the open concrete stairwell.

"Hurry! Get to the top floor!" she barked as she grasped his rappelling harness in one hand and half-carried him up the stairs with her.

In less than a minute, they made it up to the third floor. Caleb ran over to the side of the open-walled structure and gazed down to see if Katrina were down there yet. Paige appeared at his side and pointed off to the left of where he had been staring.

"She's just left the tree line, kiddo," she noted. "And we've got less than a minute before she's up here with us."

His eyes darted around and spotted the coiled up length of rope he had tied to a concrete support column earlier in the evening. It was one of a few ropes he had pre-staged on both upper floors. He interlaced the rope into his rappelling harness hurriedly.

Paige grinned as she watched him. "I was wondering about that harness," she observed with amusement. "At first I thought it was just part of your costume."

He paused only a moment to give her a withering look and muttered, "Costume, my ass. I used to rappel in college, you know."

She giggled, took the coiled end of the rope, and tossed it over the edge of the building. After cocking her head to one side, she nodded. "Say goodbye now," she said. "You've got about four seconds."

He grinned, grabbed her around the waist, and quipped, "Got to have my good luck charm!"

"What?!" she demanded incredulously. But she was distracted as Katrina came into view with a smile and announced, "Ha! Found you!"

He waved one hand in a half-salute and tightened his grip around Paige's waist. Unfortunately, his dramatic exit was ruined as he half-stumbled over the edge of the building with her in his arms.

"Awww, CRAAAAAAP!" she shouted as the two of them disappeared from view.

"Caleb!!" Katrina screamed, rushing to the edge of the building. She watched them with a mix of surprise and helplessness, her heart in her throat.

They plummeted downwards like a rock as Paige gripped him tightly, but he managed to right them properly. He hadn't anticipated a passenger, and despite the relatively light weight of the petite vampire, he had to compensate for the added weight while also controlling the feed of the rope in spurts through his gloved hands.

They hit the ground with a bounce, and he fell somewhat off-balanced to one side, causing them to fall over onto the cold, hard ground.

"Ooof!" he grunted, rolling across the ground and releasing his grip on Paige.

The blonde-haired vampire rolled to a stop next to Caleb, lay still for a few seconds, and complained, "Well, that sucked."

"Okay, so it's been a while since my last rappel," he admitted with a groan while arching his back.

"More practice, Mr. Bond," she rebuked in a mock-evil voice as she gingerly rotated her right shoulder.

Then the timer on his watch went off with a series of beeps. A second later, Katrina towered above them with partially glowing eyes.

"You two idiots could've killed yourselves!" she barked while kneeling down to check on her mate.

Paige sat up absently rubbing her thigh and retorted, "Hey, Indiana Jones here was the brains of this operation! I was just the baggage on this flight."

But Caleb chuckled happily and exclaimed, "Awesome! I finally won!"

Katrina stared at him as if he were crazy and shook her head. "I did Find Caleb before the timer went off," she noted with an air of superiority.

"Ah, but you didn't 'tag' Caleb," he countered, sitting up and brushing the dirt off his leather jacket.

"He's got you there, Red," Paige interjected with a smirk.

Katrina looked sidelong at her friend and chastised, "Oh, and what are you now, the referee?"

She stuck her tongue out at Katrina and got up to brush at the seat of her jeans.

"Hey, thanks for the assist," Caleb offered to Paige with satisfaction. "You get half the points on that goal."

She grinned and reached over to dishevel his hair. "Anytime, tiger."

Katrina sighed with resignation, merely happy that neither of them was injured.

As the two vampires turned to walk away, Caleb prompted, "Hey! Um, how about a hand with the clean up?"

They stopped, looked at each other, and then back at Caleb.

"What do you think, Red?" Paige asked. "Gil's probably fine back at the house."

Katrina smirked. "Well, he did actually win tonight, I suppose."

"Great, thanks!" he replied. "Maybe you two could go through the woods to retrieve my clothes hanging up in the trees?"

The two vampires exchanged amused glances.

"Better yet," Paige clarified, "you get your own clothes, and we'll get the ropes and other equipment from in and around the building."

"Besides, I still have to pick up my heart from the third floor," Katrina retorted.

"Oh, all right," he replied sourly.

Paige and Katrina victoriously smacked each other's open palms in midair as they walked towards the concrete structure, appreciating their easier task.

"I really didn't know he could rappel," Katrina noted quietly.

"Ha! I still don't," Paige snickered, and then added seriously: "He's full of surprises, though, and with some additional training…"

"Oh, don't encourage him," Katrina chided, but smirked. She was proud of him for trying, despite the anxiety it had caused her.

Meanwhile, Caleb proceeded into the nearby woods with a sigh. *At least I won this round, he considered proudly.*

However, he realized his victory was partially due to the aid of another vampire. He wondered if he would ever really be prepared to confront vampires on an equal footing.

* * *

Saturday morning, Katrina spent time sorting through emails. It seemed that her recent territorial declaration was the focus of conversation in the vampire community, and some were wondering if she were creating some form of organizational structure. A few vampires were even interested in joining such a structure under the right circumstances.

owever, Katrina had hoped her initiative would serve as a subtle deterrence rather than an open invitation, and it annoyed her that the declaration was only partially successful. She discussed her concerns with Alton, but he seemed rather amused, conceding that such a result had been within the spectrum of possibilities.

Funny, she thought irritably. *Alton never mentioned that as a possibility leading up to my decision.*

Alton reassured her they would discuss it further when she and Caleb came to England in March. It occurred to her that their trip to the United Kingdom was taking on more and more significance, which wasn't encouraging.

In the meantime, Saturday afternoon Caleb learned the proper techniques for basic knife-fighting from both Katrina and Paige, including some advanced combat techniques. After a few hours of repetition, both vampires were impressed with his ability to observe and duplicate the methods demonstrated, though Katrina intended to test him every few days to ensure his continued competency.

Early on, Gil asked to participate, but after only a short time was relegated to being a stand-in for demonstrations rather than a student.

That evening, the four of them went out to dinner and then perused the downtown Atlanta area for impromptu diversions. For Gil, that primarily amounted to seeking out prospective clubs and bars that looked promising. Once they were downtown, Gil recalled conversations with patrons at the previous weekend's club activities about a couple of bars that sounded interesting to him.

Paige rolled her eyes, but conceded to let Gil lead the way. However, Caleb's limited experience with Gil engendered a wary sensibility regarding the former rock singer's choices and decisions.

Fortunately, the two bars that Gil selected were in reputable sections of the downtown area, which relieved Caleb. The first was a popular bar named Atlanta Tap, frequented by a number of the college students and the urban twenty-something crowd. The music was loud, and the atmosphere was lively, and the four of them stayed for a couple of hours. However, the mood and conversation between Gil and Paige seemed somewhat distant and tentative.

The second bar, Downtown Blues, presented them with a mostly thirty-something or older crowd. It was styled with rock and soul music memorabilia and hosted a live classic blues band. The bar offered a number of locally brewed beers, as well as a decent selection of food on their menu. Caleb and Gil took the opportunity to order something to eat, while Katrina and Paige contented themselves with watching them while nursing their beers and appreciating the live music.

While Paige hardly ignored Gil, her attention was often subtly distracted as she observed the interactions between Katrina and Caleb with satisfaction. Her blue eyes caught Caleb's as he and Katrina laughed at a joke he had made, and Paige winked at him approvingly.

One of the primary reasons for her journey to Atlanta had been to determine what was happening between Katrina and Caleb, and she had not only done that, but also managed to aid in mending a rift in their relationship. She reflected on how she had been able to lay the groundwork to help mend the social rift between Caleb and Devon Archibald.

Additionally, she had learned so much more about Caleb's past and why Katrina had been so drawn to him initially. Finally, she was able to spend some long-overdue quality time with Caleb. All in all, it had been a productive and informative visit to Atlanta, and she was content to have helped the two people who were perhaps most dear to her.

They're like family, she affirmed.

After a couple of hours, everyone agreed it was time to leave. While Gil excused himself to use the restroom, Caleb paid the tab for everyone as Katrina and Paige left the bar to wait outside for them.

On his way to the exit, Caleb saw the merits of a restroom break before joining the women. As he passed through the initial men's room door, he overheard Gil speaking somewhat loudly. Gil's somewhat angst-ridden tone of voice caused him to pause just inside.

"...so this scene is lame and getting lamer by the minute,

dude," Gil complained. "Everybody's nice enough, I guess. But Paige has turned out to be a real drag for a vampire."

Caleb's eyes widened as he listened to the conversation, and a momentary feeling of shame ran through him as he reflected on his eavesdropping. But then, the conversation suddenly seemed important enough to override his social sensibilities.

"What? Hell yeah, Skeet, a frickin' real vampire! Fangs, super-fast speed, the works. Oh man, I think I can snap a pic with my cell, and I'll show you her teeth. Dude, they're real. I ain't freakin' lyin'!" Gil blurted excitedly. "It's like I'm some kind of 'blood on tap' for her, but she always has a way of erasing the teeth marks so they don't show."

Caleb realized that his own rule number one had been broken, and though he never recalled Paige's mentioning the rules for her own companions, he was nevertheless confident that was a universal one.

One was never to reveal the true nature of a vampire's existence to anyone, no matter the emotions or motivations driving such an inclination. Katrina stressed that rule above all others as the most important to maintain the safety of a vampire. Anonymity was their best friend in a twenty-first century world where humanity probably wasn't ready to deal with the realities of vampires among them. And yet, somehow he wasn't entirely surprised that Gil seemed oblivious to that fact.

"You want to see a picture?" Gil asked. "I guess I could try to snap a pic, if she'll let me. But Dude, you'll just bitch about how it looks like makeup and photo editing."

Gil paused. "Really? Yeah, I remember Doug. He works over at that rag magazine, right?"

Another pause. "A thousand bucks for one picture? Ah, hell, are you trippin' me?!"

Caleb's anger flared as he realized where Gil's conversation was heading.

"Hell, yeah," Gil said. "That would pay some serious rent for me, dude. And with me between bands, I need all the spare Benjamins I can lay my hands on. Besides, she doesn't even read the *Inquirer*. She'll never know. And hey, would they pay for additional shots?"

Caleb started to burst into the room and yank the guy's cell phone from his hand, but paused as Gil said something that stopped him in his tracks.

"What's she like? Ah, hell, she's a great lay," Gil replied emphatically. "But it ain't like I'm hookin' up prime time with her, either. She can be bossy and kind of bitchy at times. Paige is more of a nighttime gig only, if you're followin' me. And there's this guy I think she has a torch for or something. I dunno, it's shit!"

Caleb had tried to reassure Gil that Paige was only a friend.

Then again, am I the one getting the wrong picture?

He pushed that thought from his mind and instead refocused on the situation at hand. He stormed into the room, fuming over the gall of Gil's indiscretion, and saw the young man looking back at him with wide-eyed surprise. Caleb walked directly up to Gil, reared his arm, and punched him squarely in the face with a balled-up fist.

He winced as his knuckles were impacted slightly by the leading edge of Gil's teeth.

"Shit!" Gil exclaimed after recovering from the blow. "What the hell?!"

"Don't even think about doing that, asshole!" Caleb demanded.

Gil glared back at Caleb abashedly and stammered, "Hey man, chill! I was just joking, you know?"

Caleb considered punching him again, but then shook his head, spun around, and walked purposefully back out of the restroom. He stalked back though the bar and exited out onto the street, still shaking his head with aggravation.

His mind raced with a host of emotions: fear that humans would find out about Paige and Katrina, anger that Gil was such a creep, and concern that the balance of another human's life was essentially in his hands based upon "the rules" he was supposed to follow. Another realization struck him.

Maybe there are two people's lives in my hands. Surely, that other guy -- Skeet? -- will have to be addressed as a loose end or something.

An anxious feeling formed in the pit of his stomach, but his concern for the two dearest women in his life far outweighed his reservations at that moment.

Katrina and Paige were idly chatting, and both looked up with curiosity as Caleb approached. They immediately noted the troubled expression on his face, and their countenances turned more serious.

Paige sniffed at the air, and her eyes went immediately to Caleb's right hand and his bleeding knuckles. Katrina noted the scent and Paige's attention, and her eyes quickly focused on his hand with a curious expression. Caleb blinked once slowly, looking at each woman in turn, and absently flexed his sore right hand.

"Bars are dangerous places for you, it seems. Is everything okay, kiddo?" Paige asked. "And hey, where's Gil?"

He frowned. "He's still in there...probably still talking on his cell, I think."

"Caleb?" Katrina ventured with concern evident in her voice. She could tell by his distracted expression that he was troubled, and she was confident that his knuckles hadn't been injured by accident.

He looked at Katrina only for a moment before his gaze focused on Paige fully. "Listen, there's something you need to know about Gil. I'm afraid he's just not right for you."

But Paige misinterpreted his comment with a smirk. "Is he taking a hit from a joint in there? He's kind of a pothead at times."

"That's not the problem, believe it or not," Caleb replied before staring into her bright blue eyes in penetrating fashion. He fell silent, not exactly sure how to proceed.

Katrina watched silently, waiting for him to say more, and suspected the news wasn't good.

"Go ahead, tiger," Paige encouraged as she grasped him

gently by the shoulders and directed him towards a small, darkened alley close by. "Tell me more."

The three of them relocated down the dark, narrow alley a short distance away, although Caleb glanced warily into the darkness.

"We're alone," Katrina assured him with a gentle brush of her hand across his back.

Caleb's eyes darted briefly to Katrina's before settling his gaze on Paige. "Rule number one was broken."

Paige's eyes widened with surprise, and Katrina pressed closer to Caleb to place a supportive hand on his shoulder. By the look in his eyes she knew he hadn't been the one who broke the rule.

"Tell us what you know," Paige encouraged in a serious, yet reassuring voice as she continued to grasp Caleb gently by the upper arms.

He quickly recited everything that he had overheard from Gil and tried not to include any of his own reflections or emotions so as not to influence the presentation of facts.

He focused on maintaining eye contact with Paige in the same manner that Katrina did with him on occasion to give the vampire the opportunity to gauge his emotions further. It wasn't as if he were trying to mislead anyone, but he wanted Paige to know he was both serious and forthcoming with everything. During his recollection, Paige occasionally squeezed his shoulders in an encouraging fashion, which he appreciated.

But the one item of information he deliberately left out was the accusation that Paige had affections for someone else. He wasn't sure the topic was wise to mention at the moment.

Paige frowned momentarily as she detected a change in his body language, but patiently listened as he described his own animated response towards Gil. Both vampires adopted amused smirks when he recounted punching Gil in the face.

When he finished, he stood silently and felt Katrina's fingernails stroke the back of his neck in soothing fashion.

Paige removed her hands from his shoulders and softly cradled his face between her warm palms. She stepped up to him and placed a light kiss on his forehead. "I know how hard this must be for you," she offered tenderly. "But thank you for having the courage to come forward."

He nodded while she cradled his face in her hands. "I won't let anyone or anything threaten you or Katrina, if I can stop it."

Paige smiled in a warm, appreciative manner, and softly, yet deliberately, kissed his lips. A small charge seemed to pass through her as their lips touched, and for a split second her eyes widened with surprise.

He's a good kisser.

She was also struck by the sincere, protective nature of the young man, as well as the fierce sense of dedication he had shown to her. As humans went, she had never met anyone quite like Caleb before, which only added to his aura of intrigue.

Katrina's eyebrows rose slightly, but she said nothing. She felt a momentary pang of jealousy, but quickly reined it in given the nature of the topic at hand. She shared the preeminent concern of any of her kind to protect their identities from humanity.

However, Caleb blushed slightly from Paige's intimate appreciation as he stared back into her deep blue eyes.

"Thank you for protecting me, kiddo," she offered before releasing his face and adopting a far more serious expression.

He offered a tentative smile back at her and cast a sidelong glance at Katrina to gauge her reaction to the kiss.

Katrina noted the silent inquiry in his eyes, and her arm reached out to encircle his shoulders supportively. "It's fine, and I'm very proud of you, my love," she offered in a soft voice.

Paige looked up at Katrina with a hard expression. "Red, I need a flight ready to leave for California sometime tonight. Think you can set that up for me?"

Katrina nodded. "I'll see to it."

Gil exited the blues bar and looked around searching for them as he rubbed his jaw with one hand. His face was still reddened slightly where Caleb had punched him. Paige stepped out of the alley into his line of sight, and the young man grinned sheepishly.

"There you guys are. Why've you been hanging out in the alley?" he asked nonchalantly. "Where to next?"

Paige turned to glance at Katrina with a serious expression and whispered humorlessly, "We'll be returning late to the estate."

Katrina nodded, and Caleb swallowed hard at the steely look in Paige's eyes. One of the rare times he had seen that look was following a mercenary attack on Katrina's estate when he and Paige had been sequestered.

Paige had done an excellent job of protecting him, and he recalled that gaze as she had interrogated one of the surviving mercenaries in Katrina's garage. A shiver momentarily played down his spine at the vivid and disturbing memory.

"You okay?" Katrina whispered with concern.

He merely nodded and watched the exchange between Paige and Gil intently.

"We're going to break away from these guys," Paige offered to Gil in a suddenly light-hearted tone. "They're lightweights and want to head back to the estate."

Gil grinned in semi-relieved fashion as Katrina and Caleb stepped out of the alley and back onto the sidewalk.

"Yeah, old Caleb doesn't seem to be the out-all-night type. I think he's a little on edge tonight," Gil agreed with a scowl and nod of his head towards Caleb.

Paige took Gil's arm and glanced back over her shoulder at Katrina with a resolved expression. "Don't wait up for us. We'll catch a cab home."

A chill flowed through Caleb as he wondered if it were possibly the last time he might see Gil. But then, he felt renewed anger that Gil sought to reveal Paige and, quite possibly, Katrina.

As Paige and Gil walked down the street together,

Katrina's left arm wrapped around Caleb's waist, and she turned them in the opposite direction. She picked up his right hand in her own and lightly sucked on his bleeding knuckles so her saliva would seal the scrapes.

"I probably just sentenced someone to death," he muttered with cold realization as he appreciated the numbness forming around his knuckles.

But she pulled him against her in a side-hug and countered, "No, Caleb. He committed suicide. There's a difference."

Caleb frowned at her semantics and sighed. He stopped walking and tilted his face up to her lips to kiss her. She eagerly responded and initiated one of her own.

"I love you," he offered sincerely. "And I would never betray you. I'll take your and Paige's secret to the grave if I have to."

She smiled in genuine admiration. "No need to worry. I already know that, my love. And so does Paige."

Katrina drove them back to the estate in relative silence as Caleb considered the evening's events. The topic he had omitted from Paige in his recounting of Gil's betrayal returned to the forefront of his mind.

Was Gil right about Paige caring for me in more than merely a friend-like or sister-like manner?

The thought burned in his mind like a bonfire and filled him with anxiety. It was a sensitive topic, and he knew that he needed to tread carefully with it.

Katrina sensed his tense mood and glanced over at him with concern. "What's wrong, my love?"

"Gil said something else on the phone tonight," he recalled carefully. "Something I didn't tell Paige."

She frowned and cast another curious glance at her mate. She wasn't certain what the subject was, but she sensed it wasn't good.

Reaching out with her right hand, she caressed his left cheek with her fingertips. "You can tell me, my love," she encouraged. "Perhaps I can help."

He swallowed, glanced at her, and looked out through the passenger side window at the darkness permeating the glow of the street lamps.

"Gil told his friend that he thinks Paige is 'carrying a torch' for someone else. He was pretty upset about that. He said as much to me at the bar the other day, but I tried to reassure him that wasn't the case. I told him that she and I were just close friends, like family, and that I didn't present a threat to him for her affections."

Katrina remained silent as she considered Caleb's revelation. She wasn't hearing anything that hadn't already crossed her mind. The situation was rather complex and required careful handling on her part. Multiple serious relationships were at stake if the issue were allowed to be mismanaged, and she didn't want that to happen, either for Caleb or for her best friend.

"Paige is quite fond of you," she explained carefully. "She cares for you a great deal, Caleb. I'm not naïve about her affections for you, you know. It bothered me at first, but I'm confident she poses no threat to our relationship. Would I be mistaken about that?"

He felt a surge of concern run through him, and he replied hastily, "No. I'm yours, Kat. You're my mate, and I've never been happier in my life. But I also care about Paige. I love her, but not in the same way that I do you."

Katrina sensed the sincere and honest nature of his response, and a feeling of reassurance coursed through her. "She's an attractive, and yet playfully quirky woman," she ventured. "It's easy to see her allure."

He reached out to grasp Katrina's hand as she gripped the console gear shift. "You're beautiful, intelligent, kind, and generous, Kat. How could I ever ask for more?" he insisted before drawing her hand to his lips and softly kissing her skin. He resolved there was nothing he would ever do to tarnish his commitment to her.

She nodded, sensing the earnest nature of his declaration. It sent a warm, reassuring feeling through her. "I'm happy to hear that, my love. Though I don't doubt your intentions."

He continued to hold her hand while casting a quick glance at the profile of her face as she drove. The muscles appeared taut across her high cheekbones. "I love you, Kat."

They continued down the highway in silence for a time longer, until Katrina exited the highway near Mableton.

"Do I need to mention this to Paige?" he asked warily. He was adrift in foreign territory like a boat on an open ocean and needed guidance.

Katrina paused. "No, there's no reason to now. It would only upset her further, I think. She has to focus on getting Gil back to California and addressing him and his friend--"

"Skeet," he prompted.

She looked sidelong at him with a darkly amused expression. "Yeah. Skeet."

The car wound its way down the sparsely lit county roads as Caleb silently contemplated the grim task that was before Paige. But then, she was a vampire; the very act of killing was second nature to her. He tried to imagine himself killing Gil in a measured, calculated manner, and found that he was having trouble envisioning that.

Does that make me weak or cowardly?

"A planned killing would be hard," he whispered absently.

Katrina squeezed his hand supportively as their car entered through the gates of the Pine Valley addition. She didn't want to tell him that such things got easier with time, given an appropriate motivation or necessity. She also didn't want to tell him that most vampires, herself included, actually enjoyed aspects of killing. It was a predator's pleasure and part of their very nature.

And yet she would have added that his own life was never safer around either her or Paige, despite the constant desire for taking blood that always lay just beneath the surface. Instead she let her grip on his hand speak of her concern.

"I wish Paige didn't have to go," he murmured. He reflected on how much easier life had been with Paige around. She was a part of their extended family unit, not to mention a key friend and protector for him.

Katrina pulled the car into the garage, and her eyes quickly darted to his. "Actually, me too," she offered. She understood that Paige's arrival at the estate was instrumental in helping to mend her relations with Caleb. There were so many reasons why Paige was an important part of their lives.

Caleb unbuckled his seatbelt and looked at Katrina, who had turned off the ignition and remained in the driver's seat staring out through the windshield as if transfixed on something before her.

"Kat?" he asked. "Are you okay?"

She broke from her reverie and turned to glance at him with a smile. "Me?" she asked innocently. "I've never been better," she replied.

"You sure?" he asked as he opened the door and started to exit.

Her expression turned sly, and she challenged, "Sure. That is, sure I'll have your blood tonight if I beat you to the door into the house."

He grinned broadly and spurted from the car, racing towards the door leading to the interior of the house. She moved in a blur, pursuing him like a cat chasing a mouse. As he nearly reached the door knob before her, her hand darted out at the last second and firmly grasped his wrist. She deliberately spun him around before her and caught him in her arms as he slightly lost his balance. Then she leaned down and kissed him with passion.

"Got you," she declared.

"I wouldn't have it any other way," he replied before wrapping his arms around her waist and applying a warm kiss of his own to her lips.

They were lying together in the sublevel chamber by the time Paige and Gil finally returned to the estate. Katrina had made the impromptu arrangements for a charter flight to California on Sunset Air for them and left the boarding information on the dresser in the room Paige and Gil shared.

Katrina heard Gil question Paige about the abrupt return,

but he seemed relieved to be leaving. The two of them slipped out just prior to dawn to make their way to the airport. Fortunately, Sunset Air took elaborate measures and precautions to ensure that their vampire clients wouldn't be threatened by daylight if the flight arrived after sunrise.

Katrina deliberately let Caleb sleep through their departure per Paige's wishes. The young vampire was never one for long goodbyes, and the nature of Caleb's conflict with Gil the previous night had suggested that such plans were for the best.

Once Caleb woke, dressed, and went upstairs, he knew that Paige and Gil had already left to return to California, but part of him still felt disappointed to discover the house so quiet and empty.

He gave Katrina a big hug as she made his brunch, clearly her favorite and most accomplished meal to prepare for him, and she tried to offer upbeat conversation to occupy her mate's thoughts.

She was all too aware of how Paige had quickly formed a prominent presence in their lives, making the youthful vampire's absence all the more poignant.

They spent the day doing laundry, reading alongside each other on the couch, and generally appreciating their shared companionship.

As the evening approached, Caleb sat at the dining room table sorting through his materials for Monday's classes. He looked over to the couch where Katrina was comfortably reclined and prompted, "Kat, I wonder how Paige is doing."

"She'll call or text us when she can," Katrina replied as she lay on the couch reading a novel. "But I need to warn you, we probably won't be hearing from her for some time. No email, texting, or phone calls. And I suggest you refrain from contacting her as well."

He looked up with surprise. "Why?"

"It's a delicate matter she has to address, my love," she replied in a dark tone. "Think about it. If there's an investigation of some kind, she needs to avoid any communication trails leading up to, or following, the event. It's for our protection, really."

He stared at her as the weight of his Saturday night thoughts returned to the forefront of his mind. He was momentarily surprised that those thoughts hadn't preyed upon him before that and wondered if he had subconsciously blocked them out until then. His musings were followed by a degree of embarrassment at seeming so dense regarding the topic. "Oh, sure," he replied sheepishly. "That makes sense, of course. Sorry."

There was a rush of air near him, and suddenly Katrina was standing next to him. He started slightly, and she placed a gentle hand on his shoulder as he sat at the table.

"Don't be sorry, my love," she offered. "This is something new for you. Just try not to dwell on it and realize that Paige will contact us again when she feels it's safe to do so."

He nodded. "Okay, then."

She caressed the back of his neck with her fingernails, causing a soothing sensation to permeate his neck and shoulders. He arched his back slightly forwards, and she lightly ran her nails down his back. A satisfying shiver ran through his body, and he momentarily considered how wonderful life was with her, followed by how peculiar it was that such happiness could be coupled with the dire thoughts of another human's demise at the hands of a vampire. It was a truly odd dichotomy, and he was scarcely able to believe how logical it all seemed or how easily reconciled.

* * *

Paige was a patient person, and it was Monday evening before she chose to broach the subject of her concerns with Gil. She met him at a trendy restaurant in town, LA Bohemia, that was frequented by rock bands and Hollywood types who wanted to be seen with rockers. The prices were expensive, but naturally Gil counted on her to pick up the tab.

She wore a black leather jacket, a Garbage concert t-shirt,

and fashionable jeans as she waited in a leather booth in a corner of the main dining room. When Gil finally showed up at the table smelling of inspiration in the form of marijuana, she shook her head slightly. She was pleasant as he offered a quick hello, but she rolled her eyes when he wasn't looking as he sat down in the booth across from her.

"Hey, babe," he began tentatively. "Thanks for meeting me here tonight."

I'm not going to miss that whole "babe" thing, she considered grimly. "Sure, Gil," she replied easily while toying with the straw in her glass of cherry Coca-Cola. "No problem at all."

A waitress showed up to take Gil's drink and food order and departed before he continued his chat with Paige.

"So, uh, I was wondering if you were feeling better since Sunday," he ventured as off-handedly as he could manage in his innately abrupt manner.

She looked across the table at him with a slight frown. "Better? I'm fine, Gil. Why do you ask?"

He shifted uneasily in his chair and nodded. "Well, you know. Things were a little quiet on the plane home, and I thought you didn't feel good or something. I mean, we took off out of Atlanta pretty fast, and all."

She nodded, sipped her cola sedately, and offered, "Well, you didn't seem to care for Atlanta that much. And I got the impression that you and Caleb weren't getting along very well, among other things."

He looked up sharply and then back down to the beer before him. "Caleb? Nah, we're good. Good dude, big heart, and all. Why? Did he say something to you?"

Paige listened to Gil's heartbeat among the music and voices of patrons around them. She heard it increase abruptly and knew she had touched just the right nerve. "Oh, not so much," she replied. "It was just a feeling, that's all."

He seemed to relax suddenly and took a big swig of beer. "Oh, well, of course not. I mean, I'm cool with you and him, you know."

Her eyes darted to Gil's sharply, and she pressed, "Cool

with what, Gil?"

"You know, how tight you two are," he said with a lopsided grin. "Hey, it's no problem having a guy on the other coast and all. We rockers, we get that better than anyone, you know?"

What the hell? she thought wildly as she gazed across the table at him. "Gil, Caleb and I aren't an item," she insisted. "He's a friend, like part of my extended family."

He shrugged. "Yeah, sure. Like I said, no problem."

"He belongs to Katrina, Gil," she said with an edge to her voice. "Got it?"

His eyes widened slightly, and he took a swig of beer. "Got it, babe," he replied with a nod of his head.

She rolled her eyes and suppressed a growl, not really believing his response. But she refused to bother further with the topic since there were more pressing matters on her agenda.

The truth was that she loved being around Caleb and already missed his presence since her return to California. In the end, the issue seemed to her to be a moot point.

But then, if that's true, why is the topic still nagging in the back of my mind?

"So, maybe we can change the subject, okay?" she pressed in a more conciliatory tone.

He nodded agreeably.

"Good," she said. "Now, what would you like to talk about?"

He considered the question for a moment. Finally, he nodded and proposed in a semi-practiced tone, "Okay then. How about pictures? I noticed you and Katrina both gave Caleb a picture for Valentine's Day. I wouldn't mind having a picture of you, you know."

She smiled pleasantly, but mused, *Here we go then.*

"What kind of picture?" she asked before sipping at her Coke and glancing casually across the room to scan the other patrons so as not to intimidate him.

He paused. "How about something with your smile?

Maybe something with a little fang showing? You know, something classic?"

Caleb was right after all, she thought darkly as her gaze returned to rest on Gil's somewhat anxious-looking features. "Classic, huh? Yeah, I can see the appeal of that," she replied. "But you wouldn't show it to anyone else would you?"

He looked up only briefly and then back down to his beer again and shook his head. "Me? Nah. I mean, who would believe it anyway, right?"

She scowled and offered, "Who, indeed?" However, she also knew a lie when she heard it, and Gil was a terrible actor. *Come to think of it, Gil's a terrible singer in reality, as well. Pretty soon, he's going to become a distant memory.*

They sat together in relative silence while Paige swayed to the rock music playing in the background above the din of conversation among the patrons. Gil happily accepted another beer when the waitress passed by, and Paige stared back at him thoughtfully.

"So, how about a picture sometime soon?" she offered, lifting her glass to her lips.

His expression brightened somewhat, and he looked up with a renewed sense of curiosity. "Really?" he asked. "You'd be down with that? I mean, that's great and all. I'm just surprised."

She smirked with a gleam in her blue eyes. "I'm absolutely full of surprises."

His food arrived, and he seemed almost gleeful as he dug into a plate of sausage pasta alfredo. Paige made a sour face at the pronounced scent of garlic wafting in her direction and sighed. Her thoughts went back to a time when she had counseled Caleb on selecting meals with less garlic because it generated a pungent flavor to the taste of his blood. Of course, she wasn't particularly interested in feeding from Gil at that moment, which was partially colored by her disappointment in the former rocker's personal judgment as of late.

"So, when's a good time for you?" he inquired

energetically.

She regarded him for a moment, paused to sip from her glass, and ventured, "Oh, I'm pretty flexible. What's your schedule looking like? I realize you're trying to get a spot with another band or find some other job options."

He chewed a forkful of pasta at length. "Well, no new prospects for now, but Skeet's helping me out with looking, you know. I've got the feeling something's gonna turn up real soon, though."

She tried to appear nonchalant. "Skeet's helping you out, huh? Friends can be helpful sometimes. And how is Skeet doing these days?"

Gil smirked, took a drink of beer, and replied, "Ah, you know Skeet. He's good. You know, he's got some cool connections."

Paige frowned and countered, "I can't say that I know him. You forget that I've never actually met Skeet, Gil."

He looked up from his plate with a slightly dumbfounded expression and recalled, "Hey, that's right. He's cool. I should set up a meet with you sometime soon. He'd like that, actually. I told him a lot about you."

The corner of her mouth upturned ever so slightly. "Oh?"

Gil stopped chewing his food for a moment and looked up sheepishly. He immediately reassured her, "Well, yeah, I mean being that we're an item, and all. Just the normal stuff, you know?"

She nodded. "Oh sure, the normal stuff."

He smirked awkwardly and returned to shoveling more pasta into his mouth. He tapped his fork against his plate a couple of times as he chewed and made an effort to look around the room as if distracted, but Paige heard his heartbeat increase slightly for a moment, almost anxiously.

"Hey, how about a drive along the coast? It's great weather for a night out," she suggested congenially. "Cool breeze, the sound of surf."

His eyes blinked as he considered the idea. Then he grinned, took a swig of beer, and replied, "Yeah, sounds good."

"Maybe Skeet would like to join us," she suggested. "Then I could meet him. He sounds like an interesting guy. And if he's such a good friend of yours, better to meet him now than later."

Gil shrugged as he chewed his food and nodded. "Yeah, sure, babe," he agreed. "He's got a soft top on his Jeep, too. It's killer for cruising the coastline. I could have him meet us somewhere."

Paige nodded affirmatively and smiled. "A soft top on his Jeep. Sounds perfect."

A couple of hours later, Paige dropped her car off at her condo, and Gil called Skeet to arrange for their meeting. Then she and Gil took his car to Skeet's house in Eagle Rock near Glendale. The house was an older, single-story home with a detached one-car garage to the side. Gil parked his older model Chevrolet Malibu in front of the house in the street and turned to Paige with a grin.

"Man, this rocks," he offered. "You're gonna love Skeet."

She nodded, and the two of them made their way through the recently mowed front yard as she scanned the immediate area for anyone who might be watching. Fortunately, there wasn't anybody hanging around outside at that time on a Monday night. She noted that Skeet's late-model red Jeep was parked in the driveway.

Gil rang the doorbell in the yellow light of the front porch and waited. Paige stood with her arms folded casually in front of her and leaned against one of the wooden banisters holding up the small porch.

A lanky, curly haired man about Gil's age and dressed in a pair of jeans and USC Trojans sweatshirt appeared in the doorway with a grin. Skeet immediately reached out with his right hand to grasp Gil's, pulled him to him in a quick, brotherly hug with the other arm around his shoulder, and laughed. "Hey, bro! Long time!"

"Dude, this is Paige," Gil offered with a grin as he gestured behind him to the blonde-haired young woman.

Skeet's eyes brightened somewhat, and he half-waved at Paige. "Wow, hey, Paige. Gil's told me a lot about you. I've been dying to meet you."

She smirked and gave a little wave with her right hand before concealing it beneath her other arm crossed before her. "Nice to finally meet you, Skeet," she replied in a friendly tone.

Skeet stared at her for another moment, as if looking for something in particular, but Gil broke his reverie by starting to walk forward to enter the house. However, Skeet put a hand to his shoulder and countered, "Hey, the place is a real mess, man. I've got a lot of inventory lying around inside, if you know what I mean."

Paige frowned slightly, but Gil smirked with recognition and nodded. "Yeah, dude. Sorry about the short notice. But hey, we're going out to the coast tonight anyway. So, you ready?"

Skeet nodded, closed the front door, and took the time to lock two sets of deadbolts before turning to follow Gil. The three of them made their way over to the Jeep, and Gil held the passenger door open for Paige. She got into the back, while Gil and Skeet took the soft top down and stowed it. They pulled out of the driveway and made their way towards the coast.

By the time they reached the ocean, it was pretty late, but the evening was beautiful and the temperature perfect for a drive.

"So Skeet, what do you do for a living?" Paige asked as she leaned forward and propped herself between the front seats.

Skeet smirked. "I'm kind of in business for myself. I guess you could say I'm into natural supplements."

Gil stifled a laugh and asked, "Hey, dude, you have any of that natural stuff with you?"

"Glove box," Skeet replied as he sped around a slower car in front of them.

Gil opened the glove box and pulled out a roll of papers

and a small plastic bag.

"Ahh, natural supplements," Paige acknowledged with a smirk. "I get it."

"Business is great, too," Skeet added proudly. "Man, I wish I was a doctor, then I could write out prescriptions to people."

Paige smiled supportively, thinking, Somehow, I should have guessed.

Gil primed the cigarette lighter on the dash and rolled a quick joint. He lit up and took a large draw, then offered the remainder back to Paige. She declined, and Gil handed it off to Skeet.

After a short time driving along the coast, Paige pointed to a scenic turnout bordering the small cliffs looking out towards the ocean. "Hey, let's drive along there," she directed them.

The road was almost completely devoid of other cars at that time of night, and Skeet effortlessly pulled the Jeep onto the road. He reached out his hand to Gil, who passed another lit joint to him. Skeet took a long draw, laughed, and leaned his head back against the driver's seat head rest as he steered the vehicle.

"Man, this is the life!" he shouted as the cool night air flowed past them.

Gil took a long draw on his own joint and laughed. "You got that right!"

"You guys better be careful smoking that stuff, you know," Paige offered loudly.

Gil just shook his head and retorted, "Ah hell, come on, babe!"

Skeet scowled. "Yeah, why's that? This stuff never hurt nobody."

She nodded knowingly, noticing the upcoming sharp curve, and explained loudly, "You have to keep a clear head. After all, you just never know when life will throw you a dangerous curve."

"What?" Skeet asked.

Paige reached swiftly over to Gil with her right hand and grasped the back of Gil's neck. She slammed his head forward into the dash, knocking him unconscious, and Skeet shouted, "Hey! What the fu—!"

She moved in a blur to grasp Skeet's head from behind and neatly broke his neck with a quick snap. She grabbed the steering wheel over with her right hand while pressing Skeet's body forward, causing the man's foot to press against the accelerator and increasing the speed of the vehicle. The Jeep swerved slightly for only a second until she stabilized their course.

She directed the vehicle towards the looming cliff railing and, at the last second, leapt out of the back of the Jeep as it crashed through the railing. The car sailed over the edge of the cliff until finally arcing downwards in a steep plummet.

Paige managed to land on the balls of her feet, rolling her body against the pavement while using her leather jacket to cushion her as the momentum from her forward velocity abated. A huge explosion bellowed from beyond the edge of the cliff, and she glanced around quickly to see if any other vehicles were in the vicinity.

After a moment, she raced over to the edge and peered down into the night, seeing only the burning remains of the mangled Jeep as the ocean lapped at the rocks below. With her keen vampire vision, she was able to see that both bodies were still in the vehicle, which was exactly what she had hoped for.

A wave of disappointment washed over her, and she shook her head for a brief moment, feeling almost sorry for Gil and his friend. The young rocker hadn't been that bad a guy overall, and she felt somewhat conscience-stricken by what she had just done.

"If only you'd been more honest with me," she muttered absently and turned to race from the area. "And I really hate the term 'babe!'" she growled.

But she realized that the matter had been more than simple honesty. It was a grave matter of maintaining her anonymity among a planet full of humans, and the fact that Gil took that for granted while trying to profit from it was inexcusable in her mind. There were limits to her sense of compassion, and Gil Yeager had exceeded them.

As she raced away from the crash site across the coastal landscape, her mind wandered back to thoughts of Caleb and how fortunate Katrina was to have someone like him in her life. Of course, he was a part of Paige's life as well, but it was a different sort of relationship. A pang of jealously flashed through her, but she quickly stifled it.

Sure, I'm fond of Caleb. Hell, I love the little guy. He's not a bad kisser, either.

But the evening's earlier conversation with Gil at the restaurant replayed in her mind, and she wondered why the misguided former singer was so convinced that Caleb had been something more than just family to her. Then she wondered if somehow she had been the one who had the wrong impression about that issue, after all. It was a sense of doubt that scared her a little bit, actually.

Maybe I should stay away from Caleb for a while, she resolved gloomily as she made her way back towards the city.

An odd feeling pervaded through her at that thought. For someone who had always been so independent and self-sufficient since her turning in the early 1900s, Paige was suddenly surprised to find that the idea filled her with a sense of longing and melancholy. The confusion she felt over the matter struck her with a mix of shock and aggravation. Suddenly, her traditionally simple vampire life was becoming somewhat complicated, and by a human, no less.

I love Caleb, but that's a good thing. Right?

She knew she would have to lay low for a time until she was certain there were no ties back to her for Skeet's and Gil's deaths. It was a blessing of sorts, because it would give her time to reflect on the issues, and her feelings, surrounding her relationship with Caleb.

But a part of her wanted to stop and call him on the phone to talk to him. Just the sound of his voice might cheer her up. It was nearly magical, the manner in which he always managed to make her smile or laugh. Of course, she realized it would be some time before it was safe to contact him again.

Then again, maybe it's better if I don't.

The complications fueling her intense emotions were both confusing and annoying.

"Well, crap," she muttered irritably, speeding through the night on her way back to the city.

Paige Turner didn't appreciate complications, particularly those involving relationships.

CHAPTER 6

England

The sole communication that Katrina and Caleb received from Paige following her departure from Atlanta was a brief text message she sent to Katrina's cell phone indicating she had arrived home safely.

And while Katrina found that to be perfectly normal and expected, Caleb was less pleased with the development. However, he reluctantly honored his promise to his mate not to attempt further communications with Paige until an appropriate time had passed. The problem was that the term "appropriate time" was far too arbitrary for his satisfaction.

Still, life proceeded, and he was once again preoccupied with the progression of the spring semester and all the associated functions of teaching at a community college. He spent a great deal of spare time drilling with Katrina, refining his mastery of self-defense techniques, including his recently acquired knowledge of knife fighting.

He admitted that she had been correct in stressing that, while firearms were effective, the proliferation of sharp, bladed objects made them more important for weapons training.

On the social front, Katrina and Caleb spent time with William and Tanisha Browning. Caleb was pleased that his mate enjoyed visiting with the Brownings and their excursions to dinners and evening events attending plays and films. They even went out dancing at a local club one Friday evening in early March.

Caleb had enjoyed seeing Tanisha really let her hair down that night and had been amused to see a much less controlled version of his friend as she danced heatedly with her husband. Tanisha later kidded him that if he ever said anything to their peers, she would blacklist him from future social events. Of course, Katrina was quite a sultry dancer when she wanted to be, as on one occasion when she had lost herself in the moment, grinding against his body.

The weeks passed quickly as Caleb prepared for their upcoming trip to England. Katrina helped him confirm that his passport was in order and made the arrangements for their flight to, and hotel stay in, London. She was an excellent, detail-oriented planner, one of her many admirable traits. He marveled at the amazing woman who had selected him as her mate and thanked the Fates for the day he had met her.

However, the day that his memory held as their first meeting was not necessarily accurate, and he looked forward to the opportunity to have his memory restored completely. Though potentially emotional, he wanted to understand the true nature of their initial meeting. He hoped that the doctor whom Alton had recommended was indeed as good as the reputation that preceded him.

It was a Friday afternoon in mid-March and the last day of Caleb's obligations at the college prior to the weeklong spring break. He chatted excitedly with Tanisha in his office as he crammed items into his backpack and tidied up his desk. She sat in his guest chair, listening with amusement as he described the anticipation of his first overseas journey.

After a quick goodbye and Tanisha's good wishes for a

safe journey, he hurried out to his car and barely noticed the drive home as he appreciated the spring temperatures and late day sunshine.

He pulled into the garage, and the door had barely closed behind his car before Katrina appeared at his driver's side door. She kissed him and smiled brightly as he rushed from the car, forgetting his backpack in the passenger seat, and hurried into the house to finish packing for their trip. With a pleased smile, she calmly reached into the car, pulled out the backpack, and carried it inside behind him.

She had spent the entire day packing while he was at the college so she would be available to help him with his own preparations. Her assistance included watching over him to ensure that he didn't forget anything important, such as his passport, new exclusive joint-account credit card, or his collection of notes and brochures on London that he had assembled meticulously during the past month.

Additionally, she made arrangements for Devon Archibald to check in on the estate a few times during the week. She also left word with the security system monitoring company to make Devon the primary local contact at night, but to respond immediately to any daytime alarms.

Within a couple of hours, evening arrived in full. Caleb finished packing, and Katrina made a call to Sunset Air to send a car to pick them up. One of the company's additional services was to arrange for secure transportation to and from the airport, if desired. In order to avoid leaving their car at the airport, she had quickly decided the added cost was well worth it. Their luggage would be automatically processed and loaded on the plane.

"Are you ready?" she asked with a smirk as she noticed Caleb glancing at his watch for the third time in less than twenty minutes.

"Me?" he asked innocently, folding his arms across his chest. "Oh, sure. Yep, ready to go."

"You're adorable," she observed with a smile as she regarded his nervous energy. He had a contagious sense of wonder and anticipation about him, which she found endearing.

You're definitely keeping life both fun and interesting for me.

Katrina's cell phone rang, and she gave the Sunset Air driver a temporary access code to enter the neighborhood gate. Then she manually opened the driveway gate to allow access to the front of the estate.

Minutes later, a black limousine pulled up in front of the house, and Caleb hastily carried their luggage to the back of the car. His heart was beating fast as he anticipated what he hoped was the journey of a lifetime with Katrina.

* * *

Their aircraft was a three-engine airliner specially outfitted with oversized fuel capacity for non-stop transatlantic flights. The interior of the plane was laid out in a series of special oversized compartments reminding Caleb of miniature hotel rooms. Each compartment had locked and closed portal windows and was tastefully furnished using lighter colors. In the center of the room were four large seats facing a large flat-panel display inset into the wall panel.

The already roomy seats were fastened together in pairs so that a set of two could be turned into one large area, much like a small sofa. Mounted before each seating space and appearing to be adjustable forward, up, or down, was a small oak-finished table. Suspended directly above each of the four seats was a console with an individual drop-down LCD display, reading light, adjustable air vents, and buttons to summon attendants or control the display.

Set behind the single row of seats was a small bed and a large overhead storage compartment. Next to the bed was a small doorway leading into a private bathroom, including a small shower. All in all, it appeared to be a comfortable setup for long-term flights. Katrina had reserved an entire compartment for them, though Caleb had no idea exactly how many other passengers might be on the flight in the other compartments, if any.

She sat next to him in the set of two seats closest to the outer wall of the fuselage. She noted the curious expression on his face as he viewed the interior of their compartment.

"Geez, this is nicer looking than any plane interior I've ever seen," he observed with awe. "It's like our own little apartment. There's even a bed back there."

She grinned at him, pulled up the seat arm that was barring her from snuggling next to him, and commented, "That's right. This is your first time on a Sunset Air charter flight. It's unlike most anything humans are used to, for obvious reasons."

He scooted closer to her and placed his hand on her thigh. "Are there any other passengers on the flight?" he asked as the aircraft's engines roared to life.

"Passengers are asked to please buckle their seatbelts, remain seated, and secure any loose cargo until we're airborne," announced a pleasant female attendant's voice over a small speaker set into the console above them.

So much for snuggling, Katrina thought. *Maybe later.*

The two of them buckled their seatbelts as she replied to her mate's question, "I sensed three vampires and one other human."

"The human would likely be a--"

"Companion, most likely. Although I discovered one of the pilots is human, as well as two of the flight attendants."

He nodded at the information and felt the plane begin to move. His grip tightened on Katrina's thigh, and he inhaled deeply. He had never flown overseas before, and while not scared, he was a little nervous as to what to expect.

She noted his increased grip and turned her head sharply to look into his eyes. "It's your first time flying, isn't it?" she asked.

He offered a shy smile as he returned her gaze and shrugged. "Well, over water," he conceded. "I've usually traveled via trains, buses, or cars. My mother and I didn't travel a lot, except for short car trips. Money was tight for us when I was growing up, and flying around the country was pretty much out of the question. When I relocated to Atlanta for college, I drove down from Ohio, mainly to have my car available. My college baseball team flew a couple of times, but those were just short flights. So, this is my maiden flight over water. Kind of strange and lame for someone who's twenty-six years old, isn't it?"

She smiled back at him and noted how endearing his expression appeared to her. Sensing a sort of vulnerability in his eyes, she stretched her left arm across his shoulders supportively. "Not at all," she reassured him. "Are you nervous?"

"Nah," he retorted casually, though there was a tightness in his voice. "Although it's a big ocean we're going to be flying over, and I'm not too keen on swimming in it."

She looked at him with amusement. "So, you don't care for the ocean then?"

He frowned. "Well, I'm not fond of deep water at all, really. I can't swim."

Her smile faded as she took in that important fact to file away for future reference. Her protective nature kicked in, and she reassured him, "Well, there's no swimming on this flight, so you're in luck. And besides, Sunset Air has one of the safest flying records in the industry. It's one of the few airlines where the safety of its passengers really is their first priority."

A man's deep voice resonated over the intercom, "Ladies and gentlemen, we're preparing for take-off. Please fasten your seatbelts at this time and remain seated until we're airborne. We'll announce when it's safe for you to move around your cabins. Thank you for flying Sunset Air."

Caleb rechecked his seatbelt and glanced over to ensure Katrina was buckled in. He looked up at her with a tight-lipped smile and gazed around the cabin as if seeking a distraction of some kind. She reached out to grasp his right hand in hers and noticed that his palm was slightly moist.

Ah, he's a little nervous after all, she considered with a smile.

She found it somewhat endearing and made a mental note to be particularly reassuring towards him.

"So, Sunset Air only caters to vampires, don't they?" he asked absently.

Katrina nodded and explained, "Well, they're vampire-owned for a reason, but they cater to human customers using a separate fleet of aircraft. They're a legitimate business focused on a profit-making venture, after all. It's just that their vampire-supportive fleet specializes in safe, relatively anonymous, sunlight-free transportation. It's one reason why their fares are so exorbitant. Of course, the amenities are numerous as well."

He nodded silently as the aircraft seemed to shift abruptly. He thought it must be taxiing across the runway to prepare for take-off. Though, without a window view, it felt to him like riding in a closed box on wheels.

Minutes later, he felt a sensation of acceleration, and his body was pressed back into the seat cushion. He felt a tell-tale uplifting, tickling sensation in his stomach, as well as a feeling of being lifted upwards at an angle.

He continued to feel that for a time, until the plane seemed to bank again before leveling off. In the end, it was a smooth and pleasant experience, and he sighed appreciatively.

"There. We're in the air now," Katrina commented softly with a small pat on his shoulder.

"Ladies and gentlemen, this is Captain Richard Webber speaking," announced a deep, male voice over the loudspeaker. "We're airborne now and will continue non-stop to London. We welcome our human passengers and request on behalf of your safety that you please stay in your assigned cabins. Our staff will be happy to provide for any and all your needs, and we hope you enjoy the flight. Thank you for traveling with Sunset Air."

Katrina unbuckled her seatbelt, but Caleb merely stared up at her with a curious expression. "Let me guess," he ventured as he folded his arms before him. "That must have been the vampire pilot."

She smirked at his reaction. "Now, now. Humans are guests just like the vampire passengers. It's just that our kind are hesitant about mingling openly with humans in these circumstance. Please don't take it personally."

"But you can leave the cabin, right?" he pressed with a hint of annoyance in his voice.

Her eyes quickly darted to him, and she looked over at the nearby plasma display nonchalantly. "Well, yes, I suppose I could. They do have a bar area set up for vampires to socialize in." But she brightly countered, "However, I plan on spending the flight here with you, enjoying my mate's company. It's our first real traveling experience together, after all."

He frowned slightly, but then shrugged and unfolded his arms with a sigh. "Yeah, I suppose it's nice to have some privacy together," he acknowledged with a half-smile.

She grinned slyly, reached over to unbuckle his safety belt, and tilted her head towards his to kiss his soft lips. Following a couple of additional kisses, a light knock sounded at their cabin door.

"Come in," Katrina replied.

A tall, brunette woman wearing a Sunset Air stewardess uniform peeked into the cabin with a pleasant expression and asked, "May I offer you warm towels?"

"Yes, thanks," Katrina replied as she sat up in her seat beside Caleb.

The woman entered, and Caleb noted that her nametag read Trish. She presented Katrina with a warm, moist towel using a pair of tongs and repeated the process for Caleb. He appreciated its warmth and happily rubbed his hands and face with it.

Trish asked about food and drink preferences, to which he asked for a menu and a Coca-Cola, while Katrina asked for a glass of wine. The stewardess departed, and Caleb set his towel aside on the small adjustable table before him.

"Kat, what else are you expecting to do while we're in London?" he asked. "I get the impression this is part business trip."

Very perceptive, she silently acknowledged. "Alton mentioned there are some vampire-related matters he wanted to discuss with me," she explained. "I'm not entirely clear on most of the details, but it appears a rift is forming in the vampire community. The implications are still being determined, although I can't help feeling that Alton is one of the leaders representing one side of the issue."

He considered that for a moment. "He wants to recruit you, doesn't he? Isn't that part of why he offered to set up the meeting for me with the vampire psychiatrist?"

She frowned, not wanting to consider her former mentor's actions as being so base or manipulative, but conceded there might be a hint of accuracy to her mate's assessment. "It's possible that Alton only wants to get my impression of things, but it's more likely that he wants my assistance in some form," she said. "However, he's becoming fond of you, and I think he sincerely wants to try and help if he can."

"Well, that's nice of him, at any rate," he conceded with a shake of his head. "I'm feeling both nervous and hopeful about meeting with- What's his name?"

"Dr. Roehl Guilhelm," she supplied. "According to Alton, he's supposed to be one of the best in his field. I did some preliminary research, and he does appear to be an actively practicing psychiatrist."

Caleb nodded, hoping again the doctor was as good as his reputation. He really wanted to get his blocked memories back. Somehow he felt as if some sort of important closure could occur, at least regarding his father, if not also for his initial meeting of Katrina, or rather, Amber. "That's good to know," he replied absently.

A few minutes later, Trish returned with wine, cola, and a menu, which Caleb perused at length before ordering a deli sandwich. Much to his surprise, it tasted freshly prepared. He and Katrina watched a recent blockbuster action film on the display and read novels they had brought in their carry-on luggage.

He was amazed by the friendly, attentive service provided on the flight and became so acclimated to the smooth in-flight conditions that he felt comfortable taking a shower and napping in his reclined seat. Although Katrina was amused that he didn't feel so relaxed that he would concede to napping on the comfortable-looking bed.

"Fear of unexpected turbulence rolling me out of bed," he had countered with a yawn.

Soon afterwards, she took her turn in the shower, after which she noted he had fallen deeply asleep during her brief absence. She settled down to do some more reading while listening to some music on a set of headphones connected to the console above her.

When he woke, he realized that he had slept nearly six hours and was hungry. After a quick perusal of the menu, he was served an early morning breakfast of eggs, pork sausage, and Belgian waffles while Katrina enjoyed a warm glass of human blood. In a brief simultaneous exchange, each viewed the other's meal with mild disdain.

"Mine smells tastier than yours," he bragged with a smirk.

"You smell tastier than either," she observed with a predatory grin, to which he smiled and returned to his platter of food.

"You want a little nip?" he asked playfully as he poured hot syrup over his waffles.

"I would, but I've decided to spare you for later," she replied suggestively.

He merely smiled and shook his head. It was nice to be desired, despite the fact that he was the intended meal. He suddenly realized how comfortable he had become with being a vampire's mate in just a matter of months and how much he relished his role in Katrina's life. It was a source of both great pride and personal satisfaction.

As their plane approached the British Isles, the sun had already risen, and the human pilot who took control of the aircraft invited Caleb to the cockpit to view their approach to the mainland. As he approached the cockpit he noted all the other cabins had been closed and the bar area was devoid of patrons. He found the cockpit view fascinating and couldn't help but wonder what adventures awaited him as he observed the looming land mass of Great Britain. Upon his return to their cabin, Katrina glanced up at him from her mystery novel.

"Enjoy the view?" she asked with a smirk, though she easily detected how pleased he was.

He bent down to kiss her. "It was great! And I suspect I've got you to thank for that, as well."

"While you were napping earlier, I slipped out and let it be known it was your first transatlantic flight, and the other vampires and crew were kind enough to oblige my small request."

He smiled warmly as he sat down next to her, once again touched by his mate's seemingly endless kindness. "Thanks, Kat. You're the best."

She adopted a mock-smug expression, returned to reading her novel, and agreed, "Yes I am, in fact. And don't you forget it, my love."

It was mid-morning by the time the plane landed at a small airport just outside of London. They remained in the plane at length while the aircraft taxied into a completely blacked-out hangar, its doors closed to preclude any sunlight from entering. A special ramp was brought alongside the plane, and the few passengers disembarked.

They grabbed their carry-on luggage and proceeded through the quiet central hallway leading towards the front of the plane, though the only people they encountered were the human pilot and their two assigned stewardesses. Caleb shook their hands and thanked them for their service and safe flight, and each person seemed flattered and slightly taken aback by his friendly and appreciative manner. Katrina followed suit, though merely nodding, smiling, and thanking the crew for their hospitality and service.

"Such a friendly, polite young man," the captain whispered to the two crewwomen standing next to him.

"Cute couple," one of the women muttered, causing Katrina to smirk as she descended the ramp next to Caleb.

Two black limousines with tinted windows were already idling near the plane with their brake lights on, indicating their passengers were loaded and ready to depart the hangar.

One lone black limousine remained near the bottom of the ramp. Its rear-most passenger side door was open, beside which a tall man wearing a tailored suit stood arrow-straight. His right hand was crossed neatly against his left hand as he stared ahead of him observing their descent to the concrete floor of the hangar. A man dressed in a traditional chauffeur's uniform stood next to the rear bumper of the vehicle as airport employees transferred the luggage from the aircraft into the car's trunk.

Caleb noticed Katrina's change in posture to a more aggressive stance as she deliberately walked a little ahead of him towards the man standing next to the car's open door. The dark-haired man seemed momentarily taken aback by Katrina's forward bearing, and he blinked once as he stared back at her.

"Ma'am," the man offered deferentially with a nod. "Welcome to London. My name is Simmons, ma'am. Mr. Rutherford sends his regrets that he couldn't meet you in person. He sent me to ensure that you and Mr. Taylor are properly escorted to your hotel."

The chauffeur approached Caleb and gestured towards his and Katrina's carry-on luggage, which he took and stored in the trunk for them. He nodded politely to Caleb, returned to the rear of the vehicle, and watched the other airport staff who were loading two remaining luggage items.

Katrina raised an eyebrow. "I see. And you're part of the security detail for Mr. Rutherford?"

The man nodded and replied in a crisp English accent, "Yes, ma'am."

Caleb knew better than to interrupt the interaction taking

place and stood quietly behind and to the left of Katrina. He found his mate's sudden change in demeanor to one of immediate authority curious, but perhaps not surprising. She was an alpha vampire, after all, and she had no idea who the man was.

"Expecting trouble, Simmons?" she asked pointedly as she looked in the direction of the chauffeur, who closed the trunk and moved to the driver's side of the vehicle. He stood quietly, apparently awaiting word to proceed with the departure.

"Not expecting any, ma'am," Simmons replied crisply. "Mr. Rutherford merely wanted to ensure that your journey to the hotel was without incident given that it's daytime."

Caleb's eyes perked up with the recognition that the man fully understood he was addressing a vampire.

"Then I appreciate your service today, Simmons," Katrina replied politely. "Let's proceed."

Simmons nodded to the chauffeur and held the car door open for them. Caleb glanced back to the airplane, but all the people had suddenly disappeared from the area, leaving them seemingly alone in that part of the hangar.

Katrina touched Caleb lightly on the shoulder to urge him forward to enter the back of the car before her. He ducked into the back of the limousine and scooted over to the far side of the seat to allow her to enter. She slid onto the seat, and Simmons closed the door. He got into the passenger side of the front compartment, leaving Katrina and Caleb alone in the roomy rear compartment of the vehicle.

Caleb looked out the passenger side of the car and noticed the hangar doors were opening, allowing the two limousines ahead of them to depart. A few moments later, their own limousine pulled through the hangar and into the daylight, although the darkly tinted windows kept any ultraviolet radiation from penetrating.

He looked out the car window at the airport buildings and hangars and found that things looked very similar to the airports in the United States.

Katrina extended her left arm across the open expanse of space towards him and pulled him back to the center of the car next to her with one swift motion. He chuckled as he slid across the leather seat towards her and tilted his head up to kiss her.

"Welcome to London, my love," she offered. "Don't worry about the view for now. It will begin to look more scenic and noteworthy once we leave the area around the airport."

"That man, Simmons," Caleb noted curiously. "He reminds me of a secret service agent."

"Alton likes to hire former British military and intelligence service members in his security ranks," she told him. "Their experience and discipline lend themselves well to Alton's preferred style of performance and leadership."

He nodded. "You looked rather authoritative there for a moment, as well."

She shrugged and hugged him to her. "It was important to establish the pecking order with such types. They respect that, and it removes any role ambiguity."

He smirked. "I think I like you better this way."

She smiled back slyly and kissed him on the cheek. "Of course you do. But then, I've already established our pecking order, haven't I?"

He shook his head, rolled his eyes, and patted her thigh with his hand. He took a moment to take in the interior of the vehicle and realized that a small LCD display was built into a central console before him. There appeared to be a small bar and built-in cooler, and a leather seat was situated on each side of the console facing towards them. The interior would comfortably seat five, he noted.

"Nice ride," he said. He was impressed with the luxuriousness of the vehicle and anticipated that it must have cost a small fortune.

"One of Alton's," she noted. "I'll bet they even stocked the fridge for us."

He reached across to open the small refrigerator and

found two bottles of chilled Coca-cola along with two plastic vials of chilled blood. He took out one of the Coke bottles, opened it, and took a swig. His dry throat appreciated it, and he looked up at Katrina.

"Want some cold blood?" he asked with a grin.

She frowned for a moment and reached over to the console to open a small wooden panel. Inside was a set of two clear drinking glasses, which were heated by elements surrounding the interior of the small storage area. A brief wave of heat flowed out of the interior towards them.

"Wow," he said with surprise. "Preheated glasses. Never seen that before."

She nodded, but closed the door again without removing a glass. "I seem to recall his telling me about installing heated glass holders in his cars. Novel idea, but I'm not terribly hungry right now," she replied, although she took the Coke bottle from him and took a small swig before handing it back to him.

Once they left the area surrounding the airport, the scenery looked somewhat rustic, though the most notable aspect was that they were riding down the opposite side of the road from what was normal in America.

Caleb decided to not look forward, half expecting to run into an oncoming vehicle. As if sensing his personal challenge, Katrina ran her fingers down the back of his neck lightly, which caused him to shiver slightly.

"Try looking at the passing scenery instead of forwards for a time," she suggested. "It takes a little getting used to, I'll admit."

As they approached the outskirts of London, Caleb noticed that the buildings were a mix of the most modern constructions combined with architectures of less descript design. It was almost like one could see the varying generations of English architecture all combined into one stretch of the city. However, a number of homes and buildings really didn't look that different from designs found in the United States or Canada.

Once downtown, he wished that he could open a window to see a lighter version of the scenery around him, rather than the darkly tinted imagery, but he naturally didn't want to do anything to harm Katrina. He anticipated that he could stand outside of the hotel for a time once they arrived and checked into their room.

Again, Katrina seemed to sense his thoughts. "I'll see if Alton knows someone who can take you out for some daytime touring of the city. It would be a shame for you to only see the place at night."

He grinned back at her as he briefly turned from the window. "You're sure vampires don't read minds? Thanks, I'd love that."

She smiled in response and appreciated the engaged manner in which he tried to take in the passing scenery. Their trip had been very successful thus far, which pleased her. She was determined to make the trip as relaxing, fun, and enjoyable as she could manage, despite her daylight limitations.

As they proceeded further into London proper, the city became an anomaly unto itself. There were many modern buildings sporting both professional and creative architecture interspersed with sites of historical antiquity, and all were crammed into a metropolis thriving with both people and traffic. Certainly, most major cities supported a blend of architectures from varying periods, but London was the historic heart of Great Britain, and it was laid out in its glory for the world to see and traverse.

When they arrived at the hotel, Summit Towers, in the heart of the business district, Caleb was impressed by appearance of the fifteen-story building. The frontage offered a stately elegance that also appeared very modern.

As the building loomed above them, he noted that the glass around the first and second floors, as well as the three top-most floors, appeared tinted, while the other floors appeared to have traditional glass. He wondered if that were to accommodate vampire guests more easily, though Katrina hadn't mentioned that the hotel catered specifically to vampires.

The limousine pulled onto a small access road leading around the periphery of the building and proceeded to a gated entrance into an underground parking garage that was manned by a uniformed security guard. Their limousine was admitted after a brief exchange between the guard and chauffeur, and they proceeded into the well lit garage. Following a couple of brief turns around concrete pillars, the vehicle came to a stop before a faux street entrance, appearing much like the street-side entrance of the hotel.

Two uniformed hotel staff approached the car immediately, and the chauffeur provided access to the trunk. Simmons exited the vehicle, swept his gaze around the garage meticulously, and then opened the rear passenger side door to allow Katrina and Caleb to exit.

Katrina slid out of the car, visually swept the surrounding area herself, and stood aside for Caleb to exit. As he left the car, he was amused by the hotel's replica entrance and noted that their luggage was quickly being removed from the limousine's trunk.

A short, middle-aged man with a neatly trimmed mustache and wearing a tailored white business suit approached Simmons and nodded politely. Simmons gestured towards Katrina deliberately, and the man shifted his focus to her with a professionally practiced smile.

"Welcome to Summit Towers, madam," he offered in a stately English accent. "My name is Jenkins, and as the daytime manager, it would be my pleasure if you would allow me the privilege of checking you into the hotel. May I inquire as to the name on the reservation?"

Katrina smiled pleasantly. "Reservations for Mr. Caleb Taylor and Ms. Katrina Rawlings."

The man's eyes widened only slightly before returning to their previously practiced state. He clasped his hands in front of him and inclined his head towards Katrina deferentially.

"My apologies for this unnecessary delay, Ms. Rawlings,"

he apologized. "I wasn't informed that you were already on your way to us this morning. I am aware that your reservations have already been processed, and I'll see that your luggage is taken to your suite immediately. We're very pleased to have you stay with us, and rest assured that your every need will be attended to immediately. You have only to ask, and it shall be addressed. If it pleases you, I'll program your key access cards."

Katrina raised her own eyebrows with slight surprise at the elevated form of address from the man. "Of course. Thank you, Mr. Jenkins."

Caleb looked up at Katrina, who maintained an impassive expression as she turned to follow Jenkins into the hotel lobby through the small entrance. He shrugged and followed behind her as Simmons closed the car door and nodded brusquely to the chauffeur.

Caleb nearly stopped in his tracks as he entered the posh hotel. The flooring was mostly polished white tile, while other areas were polished oak. The walls were white plaster with matching wood lining the lower part of the wall, the effect both stately and regal at the same time.

Large plaster columns inlaid with Greek-looking symbols were scattered throughout the interior of the vast lobby, and crystal chandeliers with imbedded lights hung from high vaulted ceilings, which were themselves inlaid with white plaster designs outlined in painted gold trim. Polished oak furniture complemented the décor, as well as leather couches and reading chairs placed throughout.

Sleek lamps decorated polished wood end tables near the chairs and couches, and a variety of stylized classical artworks hung in various open wall spaces.

Jenkins moved behind a polished wood counter with marble inlay. A young woman wearing a business suit with hotel crest on her jacket stood at the main desk, and she quickly cast a curious glance at both Katrina and Caleb before turning her eyes downward to the countertop.

Caleb frowned, wondering why she seemed so subdued.

She briefly glanced up at them again, and he smiled at her.

She returned his smile shyly, then returned to some paperwork set before her. Katrina glanced at him with a raised eyebrow, and he shrugged innocently before moving to stand beside her.

"Your luggage is being moved to your suite as we speak," Jenkins offered as he produced two gold key cards and handed them over to Katrina. "These will work for any of the special services rooms, elevators, and of course, your own suite."

Katrina took the keys and handed one to Caleb.

"We're so very pleased that you're staying with us, Ms. Rawlings and Mr. Taylor," Jenkins offered. "Now, if you'll permit me, I'll show you to your suite."

Katrina nodded politely and smirked at Caleb, who wore a telltale tourist expression as he tried to take in everything at once. They both turned to follow Jenkins across the beautiful lobby towards the nearby elevators.

They entered the elevator together, and he regarded them with a respectful smile as he inserted a pass card and pressed the button for the fifteenth floor, the topmost in the hotel.

"Your room key is required for the car to go to the top two floors," he informed them.

The elevator doors opened to reveal a regal hallway decorated much like the lobby with polished wood paneling at the lower portion of the plaster walls. There were stained oak tables with mirrors above them and flanking fabric-backed chairs at intervals along with curtained windows. Caleb cast a quick glance up to Katrina as she comfortably passed the first window, and he noted the window panes were all tinted with what he guessed must be a UV-dampening coating.

Their suite was at the end of the long hallway furthest from the elevators, and Jenkins commented, "There are only four suites on this floor, so I'm hopeful that you will enjoy a quiet, relaxing atmosphere."

The manager gestured to Caleb for his room card, neatly swiped the lock and opened the large door leading into Suite 1504. He handed the card back to Caleb, encouraging them to enter ahead of him with a sweeping gesture of his arm.

The living room was as roomy as the one at Katrina's estate. The furniture was a mix of oak and leather-covered chairs and a comfortable-looking couch. The rich carpet was thick-piled, complementing the décor with an air of regal comfort. The far wall was a series of large pane-glass windows coated with the same tinting as the hallway glass, each flanked by heavy drapes for privacy at night.

"Wow," Caleb muttered with a degree of awe, to which Jenkins offered a sincere grin. A pang of embarrassment passed through him, and he silently admonished himself for acting like a little kid who'd never seen a hotel room before. *Come on, act like you've been off the farm more than once in your life.*

"I'm happy that you approve," Jenkins offered congenially, but with a tentative glance at Katrina.

"Very nice, indeed," she agreed with a simple nod.

The bedroom was spacious, and a lengthy dining room sporting an eight-seated varnished table held court at the back of the suite before another series of large windows. A small study next to the dining area hosted a stocked wet bar.

"I'll leave you now, but please let me know if there's anything at all I can do to accommodate your needs or make your stay more enjoyable," Jenkins offered with a polite nod to both Katrina and Caleb. He quickly exited, pulling the door closed behind him.

Caleb walked over to the living room windows, staring in silent wonderment at the city beyond. Katrina walked up behind him, wrapped her arms around him, and kissed him warmly on the cheek.

"Very cool. I'm actually in London," he murmured before turning his attention back to his mate. "This is simply unbelievable, Kat."

She beamed, so very pleased he was happy. "And it's just the beginning, my love."

"Hey! I can see the London Eye from here," he exclaimed as he stared out the large window.

She raised both eyebrows as she looked. She absently curled her arm around his waist as she glanced through the window, grateful the coated glass allowed her to appreciate the daytime view with him, even though the coating made the view appear somewhat duskier than the early daytime hour that it was.

The London Eye was indeed a sight. The large circular wheel was part of a Millennium landmark competition in the late 1990s. Its perimeter was surrounded by glass-encased viewing pods, which allowed for spectacular views of the city. Caleb grinned as he observed it in the distance and turned to glance up at Katrina with an inquisitive expression.

"Yes," she replied with a smirk. "I'll make sure that you get to go up in it, both at day and night."

He chuckled and tilted his face upwards slightly towards her while elevating himself on his toes to kiss her lightly.

"You're the best, Kat," he complimented, to which she kissed him in return as she tightened her grip around his waist.

She relished their closeness at that moment and fully appreciated how easy it was to love him. He made her so happy, so content with her life. "Come on," she offered while reluctantly releasing him. "Let's call Alton. He'll want to know we've arrived."

She walked to the nearest phone in the living area while Caleb continued to absorb the view of the city. Soon afterwards, the two of them shared a shower and changed into fresh clothes. Being in casual tourist mode, both chose jeans. However, where Caleb wore a plain cotton shirt, Katrina selected a fleecy turtleneck sweater. While the temperatures were cold outside, neither needed their jackets as they didn't intend to go outdoors, never mind that Katrina would find the experience lethal from the UV radiation emanating through the clouds.

They proceeded into the hotel elevator and took it to the

first sub-level floor, which was one story below ground. Alton had informed Katrina that the hotel and his office building were connected via an underground passageway, making it ideal for vampires during daylight hours.

They had no sooner exited the elevator car and proceeded down a short length of carpeted hallway when a lone, smiling figure appeared at the end of the empty corridor.

Alton Rutherford stood a few inches over six feet and appeared quite the English playboy in a pair of dark gray dress slacks and white, long-sleeved silk dress shirt. He had forgone a tie, but still looked sharply attired by the addition of a designer leather belt and dress shoes. His late thirty-something appearance was complemented by a solid body frame, short dark hair, and piercing hazel eyes.

While Caleb didn't know exactly how old Alton was, he knew the vampire was older than Katrina, and she had lived over five hundred years.

Like Katrina, his unusually pale skin tone was nearly radiant, though not stark enough to set him aside from the human environment around him. In London, it wasn't as if people walked around sporting a natural tan. But Alton's pale complexion hardly detracted from the attractive specimen who likely turned many a woman's head in his direction.

Katrina immediately moved to embrace Alton warmly, each smiling at the reunion. It had been months since they had last seen each other, just prior to Katrina's and Caleb's nearly lethal confrontation with Chimalma.

As they parted, Alton pressed a kiss to her cheek, eliciting a playful smirk. While her close friend and former mentor had never been a romantic partner, she felt strong affection for him.

"Welcome to London, my dear," he offered. "I'm glad you're here."

"It's good to see you as well," she replied.

Alton turned his full attention to Caleb and extended his hand. Caleb returned the firm grip in kind, but felt the elder vampire pull him towards him in a brief, fraternal embrace. Katrina raised an eyebrow at the exchange, noting Alton's unusually affectionate greeting towards her mate.

"Hello, young man," Alton greeted. "It feels like a long time since we've seen each other. Strange, isn't it?"

Caleb smiled brightly as he pulled away from the tall vampire and looked up appreciatively into his eyes. He welcomed the warm greeting and marveled at how natural the exchange felt for him. He had confided many things to Alton during the past few months. The vampire's advice and knowledge of Katrina's background had proven quite helpful in strengthening his relationship with her. Not to mention the fact that his continuing understanding of alpha vampires was due in large part to Alton.

The three exchanged small talk regarding the overseas flight as they walked down the span of corridor leading into a small lobby at the other end. Aside from a couple of conservative-looking couches, reading chairs, and contemporary tables, the only other central element was two elevator doors. Devoid of other people, the area seemed eerily quiet.

"Kind of handy having a connecting corridor between the hotel and your office building," Caleb noted as he glanced at Alton.

"Sensible and convenient for our kind, wouldn't you say?" he replied.

"Indeed," Katrina agreed. "Did you enter into a partnership with the hotel to arrange this?"

"Oh, yes," Alton replied with a smirk. "In fact, I bought the hotel almost a year ago."

"Cool," Caleb noted. "Which must explain why some of the hotel's floors have coated glass."

Alton pressed a return button for the elevator. "Precisely. London's well on its way to becoming a central hub for our kind, all the better to ensure that accommodations are easily available. The Tube is another element of that, in fact. It's mostly underground, allowing virtually unlimited travel throughout the city without ever exposing oneself to sunlight."

Katrina's eyes narrowed suspiciously at the off-handed comment, but Caleb appeared aloof to Alton's reference as he looked up to view the elevator car's floor on the LCD panel before him.

What exactly is Alton up to now? she wondered.

A few moments later they boarded the elevator, and Alton pressed a series of codes into a keypad mounted next to the control panel. The elevator continued on an uninterrupted rise to the fifteenth floor, one level below the topmost floor of the building.

"And did you find your room in order?" he inquired politely with a glance at Katrina.

She frowned slightly. "Yes. In fact, it's much grander than the suite on the Website."

"Well, some of the suites are reserved for V-VIPs," Alton noted simply. He took a moment to appreciate the perplexed expression on Caleb's face before adding, "Vampire VIPs, that is. Oh, and your stay is being comped, as well."

"Now, Alton," Katrina protested.

The elder vampire raised his hand and interrupted, "No. I won't hear of it. You're my guests on this trip. Besides, it is my hotel, after all."

Katrina merely inclined her head. "Very kind, Alton. Thank you."

"Yeah, thanks Alton," Caleb added. "The suite is amazing. I've never stayed anywhere quite so grand." He glanced up at Katrina with a guilty expression and amended, "Except for Kat's estate, naturally."

She smirked at her mate and lightly ran her fingertips across the back of his neck. "It's your estate now, too, you know," she corrected him gently.

He shivered slightly at her caress while Alton chuckled.

Moments later, the elevator doors opened to reveal a professionally decorated and carpeted hallway appearing much like any elegant office building. The sound of a nearby phone's ringing added to the subdued sound of people chatting, while a nearby office emitted the sound of rapid keyboard typing through the open doorway. Alton led the way out of the elevator and down the length of short hallway before turning a corner to a longer stretch of carpeted corridor much like the one behind them.

As Caleb glanced into some of the open offices they passed, he noted men and women dressed in professional suits who reminded him of a corporate law firm he once visited back in Atlanta. A tall, blonde woman wearing a business suit halted in an office doorway to wait as they passed.

He observed with a wide-eyed expression that she had piercing green eyes like Katrina and was holding a steaming mug of what appeared to be blood. The woman smirked as he passed, and he briefly glanced behind him to see her watching him with amusement.

Caleb reached out to tug on Katrina's hand to get her attention and muttered, "Hey, did you just see—"

But she silenced him with a slight frown and silently mouthed, "Sh."

Alton glanced back at Caleb over his shoulder with an amused expression. "Yes, Caleb. I employ a significant number of vampires in this office facility. However, they're discreetly limited to the uppermost floors for the most part."

Katrina considered that revelation, which only added to the growing sense of curiosity stemming from his earlier comments regarding accommodating vampires in the city. *I had no idea he was employing vampires on a large scale.*

Her friend had said nothing about it in their recent interactions, and she wondered how long the development had been in practice.

Finally, Alton led them through oak double-doors that proceeded into a spacious office with a large window looking out upon London's financial district. The room was the size of a small hotel suite, complete with a wet bar to one side and a large oak conference table surrounded by ten high-backed leather chairs. A plush sofa sat along the opposite wall with an oak coffee table set before it. Ceiling-high oak bookshelves lined each of the two side walls, some shelves open and containing books, while others sported finished cabinet doors that concealed their contents.

Set before the large window was a wide oak desk with two large, high-backed leather chairs set before it. Alton gestured to the seats with one hand while closing the office doors and moved to the wet bar in a blur of movement.

"Blood, Katrina?" he asked as he rummaged beneath the bar counter, producing two crystal glasses. He filled them with blood from a chilled container in a small refrigerator.

"Yes, please," she replied with a glance towards Caleb. *I'd prefer Caleb, but it seems that will have to wait for later.*

"Coke, Caleb?" Alton asked as he produced a simple drinking glass with ice without waiting for a reply.

"A little early in the day to be hitting the hard stuff, isn't it?" Caleb quipped with a grin as he walked directly to the open, film-coated window to gaze out upon the city.

Alton stared at Caleb's back and raised a curious eyebrow, perplexed by his quip. Katrina smirked and cleared her throat slightly to get her mate's attention. When Caleb turned around to gaze at her, he immediately noticed Alton's sober expression and his grin quickly faded.

"Sorry. That would be very kind, thanks," he replied quietly.

Alton shook his head slightly as he produced a glass bottle of Coca-Cola and neatly popped the metal cap off with the flick of his thumb. As he poured the contents over ice without even glancing down, he heated the two glasses of blood in a microwave located below the counter with his free hand.

Caleb marveled at the stately vampire's almost off-handed, precise, smooth movements. *Wish I could to that.* He moved across the room to accept the neatly filled glass from Alton's outstretched hand.

"Thanks so much," he said, to which Alton merely inclined his head with a smirk.

"Certainly," the vampire replied as he retrieved the two heated crystal glasses of blood from the microwave. He effortless glided across the distance to Katrina and offered one of the glasses to her with a purposefully dramatic sweep of his arm.

"M'lady," he offered in a gentlemanly tone as she reached out to accept the glass with a charming smile.

"Thank you, kind sir," she replied gracefully. "Show off," she added with a wink.

He chuckled and returned to sit behind his desk, while Caleb sipped at his cola and perused the articles displayed on the oak bookshelves along one side of the office. A small, unnamed wooden sailing ship in a glass bottle caught his eye.

"So, you'll be sightseeing this evening, I should think," Alton ventured to Katrina before taking a sip of the warm blood from his glass.

She nodded and swallowed a mouthful of blood. "Yes, but that's not the topic I'm interested in at the moment, I'm afraid. Why don't you tell me more about this little business you're running here? I always thought you were into corporate investments."

"I am," he said. "Vampires are long-lived beings and are wonderful for implementing long-term investment strategies. Wouldn't you agree?"

She cast a sharp glance at her former mentor before her eyes darted across the room in Caleb's direction.

"How many vampires?" she pressed quietly.

Alton's eyes flickered to hers and then to Caleb as he answered, "For investment management? Seven."

"And what about vampires employed for non-investment purposes?" she pressed with a raised eyebrow.

He hesitated for a couple of seconds. "Eighteen, for now."

She stared into his eyes in piercing fashion, but remained silent. *I should've suspected as much. What are the others being used for?*

"Hey, this looks like the *HMS Victory*," Caleb finally spoke up. It took him a number of minutes studying the details of the model ship while searching his naval history knowledge for a name. "That was Horatio Nelson's flagship during the Napoleonic Wars at the Battle of Trafalgar in the early 1800s."

Alton broke his stare with Katrina to glance over at Caleb with an amused expression. "Well played, my boy. However, that vessel is the *HMS Agamemnon*, reportedly Nelson's favorite ship. It was at the Battle of Trafalgar in 1805. Still, you were correct that Nelson's actual flagship was *HMS Victory*, also at Trafalgar."

Caleb raised his eyebrows appraisingly and nodded, pleasantly surprised at how close his venture had been. While American history was his specialty, he sought increased knowledge in world history too. He moved to peruse the leather-bound books above the model ship as he sipped at his Coke, oblivious to the hushed conversation taking place across the room.

Katrina observed her mate for a moment in silent admiration. *My charming, handsome historian,* she considered with a slight smile before returning her gaze to Alton. "So, what are the other vampires busy doing?" she whispered too low for Caleb to overhear.

"Before I answer that question, there are some things you and I should discuss first, privately."

Caleb glanced over at the two vampires with a sour expression, all too aware that the hushed whispers were intended to exclude him from the conversation. He hated secrets, but had learned it was best not to challenge his mate at such times.

Instead, he sighed with resignation. *So, it looks like this will be a "working vacation."*

He had hoped that he and Katrina would be able to have an enjoyable getaway together, as well as perhaps be able to get to the bottom of his blocked childhood memories.

"You want to talk business, and I'm in the way, aren't I?" he mused out loud as he placed his nearly empty glass on the bar countertop.

Katrina looked up with a mildly guilty expression, while Alton simply smiled in a disarming manner that might charm a charging rhino.

"Perhaps you could stroll the corridors a little bit, dear boy," he suggested. "There are excellent views of the city from multiple large windows situated along the hallways. We won't be long, and you two can resume your discovery of London in earnest."

Caleb shook his head as his presumption had proven correct. *Vampires and their secrets. Still, who could blame them? It has to be habitual to have lived this long in secrecy, right?*

"I'll come for you soon, my love," Katrina promised with a penetrating stare. "And I appreciate your patience." She felt a momentary pang of desire course through her as she registered his scent and the sound of his heartbeat from across the room.

Caleb smiled in silent reply and turned to exit the room, closing the door behind him. As soon as the door shut, Katrina raised her voice to a normal conversational level.

"What is it you want to tell me, Alton?" she insisted with a hint of irritation in her voice. "You were more than kind to sponsor Caleb's upcoming visit to Dr. Guilhelm, but I knew there was another reason you wanted me here. I promised Caleb a vacation, you know."

Alton sighed. "I assure you, I'm not trying to hijack your holiday. So, as always with you, I'll simply cut to the chase."

She scowled at her friend's prescient, yet sardonic, wit.

"Recently, there's been a shift in vampire politics abroad. I'm part of a select group of our kind who are interested in collaborating at global levels to curtail events like what took place with Chimalma last year," he explained. "The 'other' vampires on my payroll are helping to scope out certain unsavory elements among our kind in and around central Europe who have turned hostile in opposition to the new venture. In fact, you could say that tensions are rising among us, depending upon from which side of the fence the venture is being viewed."

Katrina sat motionless as a statue as she absorbed everything that he told her. Somehow she wasn't surprised by his revelation, but she was certainly dismayed. While she respected her former mentor's reaching out to her for support, it caused her to pause. Granted, she felt a definite sense of obligation after all he had done for her last year, including nearly losing his life himself. Nevertheless, she resisted the idea of getting involved in global vampire politics.

"Alton," she began with a sigh. "My mate and I barely survived a battle with an ancient one of our kind, and frankly, I'm more interested in sitting this venture out."

He regarded his former pupil with an expression of stoic patience as he considered her reaction. "Katrina, I'm not drawing you into a war," he countered. "I just want you to keep an open mind and perhaps attend an upcoming gathering in Europe during the summer with me. There's a group of stakeholders who will be in attendance, or at least their designated representatives. It's really just a preliminary project proposal to gauge interest among the major players of our kind."

Her expression turned to one of surprise. "You mean, a vampire summit of sorts?"

"Perhaps that's a good description," he considered. "But your presence would be a powerful symbol among the attendees. After all, you not only foiled a global vampire murderer, you've declared a territorial claim in a major American metropolitan area."

Her temper flared as she realized the implications of his last statement. "A territorial claim that you suggested, I might add."

"And a good one, nonetheless," he reassured her calmly. "Most vampires wouldn't want to challenge your authority or show up unexpectedly. That makes things safer for Caleb, you realize."

"Yes, yes, we've already been over that," she replied impatiently. "But once again, you've guided me into uncomfortable waters."

Alton stared into Katrina's eyes and deliberately softened his expression, once again adopting a disarming visage.

"Stop trying to charm me," she admonished. "It won't work. I'm wise to you after all these years, you know. Well, for the most part, anyway."

"I suppose the only person who can charm you is roaming the hallways as we speak," he speculated with a grin.

She smiled in silent reply as she sipped at the blood in her glass. *Yes, he does have that magical quality. When I allow it, that is.*

She realized that she was only partially correct. There was very little she could actually deny Caleb if he asked.

* * *

Caleb casually strolled down the formally corporate hallway on his way to the next available window to gaze upon another part of the city. Fortunately, Alton was correct that the views were actually quite amazing from such heights. But it only hastened his desire to pick a direction and start walking. Then he felt guilty and berated himself for being so dense.

It's not like Kat's going to be able to just start roaming the streets until evening anyway.

He would have liked to call or text Paige about their arrival and share his initial reactions to London, but he dutifully followed Katrina's advice to avoid contacting her.

Caleb passed a vampire in a business suit as his mind returned to what he and Kat might do to pass the time until evening. It wasn't as if he wanted to experience all the sights without her, despite the added benefit of improved vision during daylight. He kept walking, not really paying attention to the hallway before him.

Although it's not as if she'll have any problem seeing at

night. Are some of the museums even open at night? How about tourist attractions?

Suddenly, he looked up and found himself staring at a solid, metal-reinforced door that looked more like an armory entrance than an office access. He frowned and looked at the information panel posted on the wall next to a numeric keypad and badge scanner. The panel read, Data Center.

"Where all the vampire geeks are kept, I presume," he muttered with a chuckle.

"Hey," spoke a gruff British voice from behind him. "Who are you? What are you doing there?"

Caleb spun around to see who was addressing him and noted two tall men in dark suits standing at the end of the hallway from where he had wandered. They were both pale and solid in stature. With one glance into their slightly glistening eyes, he realized they were vampires. He watched them guardedly, feeling a sense of panic rise inside, and his eyes darted around him nervously as he instinctively searched for an immediate exit. The two vampires watched him intently and began moving slowly, deliberately towards him in an almost stalking manner.

"Stop!" echoed Alton's commanding English accent from somewhere nearby.

Alton and Katrina appeared at the end of the hallway some distance behind the two vampires, who both froze in place at his command. Caleb noted that Katrina's arms were folded before her as she wore a stern expression, while Alton seemed almost amused by the scene before him.

"This is Mr. Taylor," he explained. "He's a personal guest of mine and shall share courtesy access with Ms. Rawlings to the upper floors of the tower during their stay in London."

"Sorry, Mr. Rutherford. But we didn't notice them on the sign-in roster," one of the vampire's explained.

"Er, yes," Alton replied. "Well, that's my fault, actually. I escorted them up personally."

Both of the suit-clad vampires nodded towards Caleb

and turned to depart the hallway heading away from him and past where Katrina and Alton were standing. The tall, pale, blonde woman wearing a dark business suit that Caleb had seen earlier appeared behind Alton and Katrina and smiled in a practiced, professional manner. Aside from being quite attractive, she had green eyes, much like Katrina's.

"Ah, Ms. Kendrick," Alton greeted the woman. "Would you please be so kind as to escort Mr. Taylor to the best viewing locations on the upper floors? Then bring him back to my office and add their names to the guest roster, please. We wouldn't want any future misunderstandings, now, would we?"

"It would be my pleasure, Mr. Rutherford," the woman replied in a dutiful, practiced manner and employing an accent that sounded Danish or German.

Caleb offered a sheepish grin and shrugged his shoulders with resignation at Katrina while she smirked at him and shook her head. She turned to follow Alton back around the corner, leaving Ms. Kendrick standing at the end of the hall with a welcoming expression.

He walked towards the woman with a tentative look on his face, extended his right hand, and offered, "Hi, I'm Caleb. Pleased to meet you."

She smiled genuinely, shook his hand, and replied, "Marla Kendrick. Pleased to meet you, Mr. Taylor."

"Caleb," he corrected her gently.

"Of course, Caleb," she accepted while studying him curiously. "Please feel free to call me Marla."

He nodded, and she gestured with her hand in the direction of the hall behind him. He turned to walk alongside her and glanced up to look into her green eyes. They definitely reminded him of Katrina's, though he realized that they were paler somehow, almost washed out, and yet distinctive in their own way compared to a human's.

"Our immediate destination is further back and to the left," she explained, frowning slightly as she noted him observing her closely. He deliberately averted his gaze to avoid seeming rude.

Once Marla directed him to a few windows on two other sides of the building, he noticed that the city was quickly being covered by gray clouds, suggesting oncoming rain. She explained that sunny skies were hard to come by in London in the early spring and for him not to be too disappointed if it did rain quite a bit during their vacation.

He sighed, and they returned to Alton's office. Marla waited to shut the office door behind him before departing. Katrina turned to observe him from where she sat as he entered the office, and Alton gestured to the empty seat next to Katrina.

As he sat, she smirked at her mate and teased, "Welcome back, trouble-maker."

"Hey, I was just standing there quietly minding my own business," he retorted innocently.

"I'm sure you were," she accepted diplomatically. "But then, you already have quite a track record for that sort of thing."

"Oh sure," he muttered with a roll of his eyes to the ceiling. *Geez, how ridiculous. I can't even walk down a hallway without being accosted by vampires.*

"I'm just saying," she gently teased. *You're so cute when you're perturbed, my love.*

He glanced up at her curiously. *Sounds a lot like something Paige would say.*

Alton curtailed a smile and interrupted the exchange. "Well, what do you think of my little office building?"

"Quite impressive, actually," Caleb complimented. "And far from little."

"I do hope my vampire associates didn't alarm you too badly," the vampire added with a twinkle in his hazel eyes.

"Rather intimidating, under the circumstances," he replied. "But I'm sure they're quite friendly once you get to know them."

The corners of Alton's mouth upturned slightly with amusement, but his eyes narrowed as he stared back at Caleb.

"Friendly? Not even on their best days, young man," he admonished mildly. "And Ms. Kendrick?"

"Very cordial and polite," Caleb replied diplomatically and looked into Katrina's eyes appraisingly. "But Kat has more beautiful green eyes."

Her eyes glistened, and she spanned the distance between them in a blur to kiss him on the lips. *You know just what to say.*

He smiled back at her, even as he jolted slightly from the nearly instantaneous appearance of her face before his.

Alton changed the subject in stride. "Would you permit me to treat you to lunch? Are you hungry?"

Caleb thoughtfully considered his stomach for a moment and shrugged. "Sure, I could eat."

"He can eat, all right," Katrina retorted. "Most anytime, in fact." It was amazing to her how his appetite was almost as resilient as a vampire's constitution.

Caleb cast a withering look at his mate before adopting a solemn expression. "Sounds nice, actually. And it's not like we can really explore the city until dark anyway. I presume you know somewhere close that's daylight-friendly?"

Alton's eyebrows rose. "As a matter of fact, I do."

The restaurant he had in mind was located on the tenth floor of the office building. It was called Shakespeare's and commanded a respectable view of London via the huge windows that extended from the high ceilings to within two feet of the floor. As with the fifteenth floor, the windows appeared to be coated with an ultraviolet-resistant material.

The dining room was nearly half full, the chatter inside presenting a lively atmosphere without seeming noisy. Most patrons wore typical office business attire, and none of them stood out as being vampires upon Caleb's cursory glance, although he readily admitted that he was no expert in identifying vampires on sight.

The pressed white tablecloths were a notable quality of the elegantly decorated dining area. The lighting was bright but not distracting, and the finished wood floors added a sense of warmth to the otherwise polished appearance of the room.

They were promptly approached by a middle-aged man wearing a black suit, who appeared to be the maître d'. Caleb felt a little underdressed for his surroundings and glanced up at Katrina with an uncomfortable expression, and she did a double-take over the look on his face. He made a subtle gesture with his fingers as he pulled at his shirt slightly, to which she smiled.

"You look fine," she reassured him in a quiet voice before subtly teasing him, "Besides, Americans usually dress notoriously casual when abroad. Britons and Europeans have grown to expect it."

His eyes widened as he glanced up at Alton, who was doing his best to restrain himself from laughing out loud.

"Mr. Rutherford, how nice to see you, sir," the maître d' greeted crisply.

"And you as well, Mr. Gibbons," Alton replied politely. "I realize we have no reservations, but my friends are just in from America, you see. Could we perhaps encroach upon a table for lunch?"

The man seemed genuinely amused by Alton's query and insisted, "Perish the thought, sir. We always have a table for you."

"Very kind, I assure you," Alton said with a smirk and looked over to Katrina and Caleb with a broad grin.

Katrina's eyebrows rose with amusement, and she cast a brief glance to the ceiling. *Oh please. You probably own the place.*

"Please, follow me," Gibbons offered and turned to lead the way into the restaurant.

Meanwhile, Caleb was quite impressed and placed his hand in the small of Katrina's back for her to proceed behind Alton. *I may be underdressed, but my chivalry is still intact.*

The table they were led to was in the corner of the dining room furthest from the front of the restaurant and had a spectacular view of the city from the glass windows that flanked the table. Gibbons held Katrina's seat for her as she sat between Alton and Caleb, her back to the rest of the dining room, thereby allowing her the best view of the city. The table was also comfortably far away from other diners.

Gibbons placed a cloth napkin across Katrina's lap with a flourish and offered menus to each of them. Another waiter appeared seemingly from nowhere to fill their empty water glasses, while a waitress appeared to place fresh-smelling warm bread and small plates on the table.

"Perhaps some wine, sir?" Gibbons suggested to Alton.

"Indeed," the stately vampire agreed. "Bring us the 1900 Bordeaux, please."

Gibbons' eyebrows rose for only a moment, but he nodded. "I'll see to it myself, sir."

Katrina looked at Alton sharply, and even though Caleb was uneducated regarding wines, he realized that something that old must cost a fortune.

"It's a special occasion when friends come to visit," Alton offered simply as he reached for a slice of the warm bread.

Caleb watched the dark-haired vampire smell the bread as if categorizing it and break off a bite to chew it slowly as he looked directly at him. "Try some, it's really quite good," he insisted. "Baked daily, actually."

Katrina's eyes narrowed slightly, but she reached out for a piece of the still-steaming bread and inhaled slightly as she held it before her. A small smile crossed her face.

Caleb selected a slice and smelled it for a longer duration than either vampire, fully appreciating the fresh-baked scent of it. His taste buds watered as he broke off a bite and popped it into his mouth. Another bite quickly followed as the flavors came alive.

Gibbons returned with the wine, uncorked it, and offered the tasting to Alton. After a moment, the vampire nodded with approval, and the maître d' served Caleb and Katrina. Then, as quickly as he had appeared, Gibbons departed.

Alton savored the scent of the wine for a moment and

took a small sip. Katrina did the same, and Caleb waited until last to taste. The flavor was full and rich, yet with a hint of bitterness to it. Caleb silently conceded that he wasn't exactly a connoisseur of fine wine.

"An added benefit of our kind: our senses allow for a fuller appreciation of things in small quantities," Alton prompted Caleb. "I don't miss my human experiences at times such as this," he added as he watched the young man with a degree of amusement.

"Stop teasing him," Katrina admonished mildly.

Caleb frowned as he considered Alton's comment. "And just when was your last human experience?" he asked before taking another small sip of his wine.

Katrina's eyes darted to watch Alton as a sly smile formed on her lips. The stately vampire's eyes narrowed and bored into Caleb's with sudden intensity. He remained both still and silent for a few moments, as if half-studying the young man. Then his face resumed an almost bored-looking expression, and he took a moment to sip his wine.

Alton deliberately waited until Caleb took a drink from his water glass to reply, "Sometime in 1216, actually."

Caleb choked on his water as his mind reeled over the sudden revelation. Katrina's hand instantly patted him on the back, heedless of the risk of someone's noticing as she moved in a blur. She gave Alton a dirty look, as well.

"Eight hundred years ago?" Caleb whispered excitedly as he tried to keep his voice low. His mind was still reeling from the vampire's admission. He'd always anticipated that Alton's age was a little older than Katrina's, but not by nearly twice.

"Ah, but it seems just like yesterday," Alton replied with a grin as he took another sip of his wine. The vampire's disposition darkened somewhat as he stared out across the view of the city, and he amended, "Actually no, it seems like eight hundred years ago, and I still don't miss being human."

"Incredible," Caleb muttered as Katrina rubbed his back lightly with the palm of her hand. "That's nearly a millennium."

He struggled to wrap his mind around the concept, not yet having fully reconciled the idea of having a five hundred-year-old mate in Katrina.

"Rubbish," Alton complained. "I'm still a couple of centuries from a millennium yet."

Caleb merely stared across the table at Alton with wide eyes. He averted his gaze to stare out of the window as Gibbons reappeared to take their orders.

Katrina ordered a fruit and herb salad, while Alton ordered a cheese and cracker assortment, claiming to have eaten a late breakfast. Gibbons looked at Caleb, who tried to collect himself enough to think of something to order. However, his memory of the menu suddenly failed him.

Just as Katrina began to speak up, Alton interjected on Caleb's behalf, "The young man mentioned something authentically English. Bring him a Cottage Pie."

"Very good, sir," Gibbons replied and quickly departed.

"Caleb?" Katrina asked softly as she reached out to grasp his hand in hers. "Are you okay, my love?"

Her hand felt soft and warm in his, and he was momentarily jarred from his scattered thoughts. He blinked slowly and looked first into her eyes before turning his attention back to Alton.

"1216?" he asked again with disbelief.

The corner of one side of Alton's mouth rose slightly. "I joined the ranks of our kind the year after the Magna Carta was signed. Henry III rose to the throne of England that year at the age of nine."

Katrina squeezed Caleb's hand in a gesture of support as she studied his features and listened to his heartbeat. She hadn't expected her friend to reveal such information so abruptly to him and wondered what caused him to do so. *I'll certainly ask him later.*

"It's just so unreal to me," Caleb stammered. "It's like something magical and -- and ominous all at the same time. It makes my brief lifetime seem insignificant by comparison. I'm merely a blink in your existence."

Katrina immediately frowned with disapproval, squeezing his hand and fiercely whispering, "Don't you dare think that, Caleb Taylor. You're the most significant and wonderful development that's happened to me in centuries. You made me want to live again."

He was taken aback by Katrina's tone and winced slightly as she squeezed his hand to a nearly painful level. She immediately noted his reaction and cursed under her breath as she released his hand.

He pulled it into his lap and massaged it with his other hand as he stared back at her morosely.

"I'm sorry," he apologized in a subdued voice. "I didn't mean—"

"No, my love, I'm the one who's so very sorry. You have every right to your feelings," she insisted. "Please, I didn't mean to hurt you."

She reached out to his hand tentatively, and he allowed her to hold it gently between both of hers. She ever so lightly, and with deliberate effort to be careful, massaged his hand for him.

She berated herself for having hurt him, despite its being an accident. Even after so many years, she occasionally neglected to consider how easily humans could be injured by her kind, even inadvertently.

Alton viewed the exchange silently, but with a hopeful expression. "I've never seen a human and a vampire matched so perfectly before," he whispered with an uncommon tone of reverence. "You're an anomaly, Caleb, and not just for Katrina either."

Caleb regarded Alton curiously.

The vampire read his expression and body language and explained in a subdued tone, "Human mates are actually as common as vampire mates for our kind. However, very few human-vampire pairings are successful for long periods without conflict, or the human's being turned into a vampire, or being killed. And yet you and Katrina have been through more challenges and potential relationship pitfalls than any previous pairing that I've ever heard of, and you're still together. No, not just together, truly devoted to each other. That surprises me, to be brutally honest."

Katrina's eyes darted to her former mentor and narrowed dangerously.

But Alton continued unabated by the warning signal. "And then there's you specifically, Caleb: successfully paired with a vampire mate and supplemented by a vampire surrogate. I would say two guardians, but Devon Archibald is only temporary by agreement. That's never happened to my knowledge, and I know a lot about vampire culture."

"And?" Caleb beckoned. He wanted to know more and gain additional insight into the scenarios placed before him.

"And," Alton answered with an uncustomary blank expression as his hazel eyes bored into Caleb's directly, "I can't wait to see what happens next. Though very little would surprise me. Or would it?"

Caleb shivered slightly from the distant and empty expression in Alton's eyes, and he deliberately averted his gaze to stare out the window upon the expanse of city before them.

Further discussion was interrupted by the arrival of their meal. Alton deliberately lightened the mood by discussing the various points of interest that Caleb and Katrina needed to visit while in London. He offered the services of two of his human staff to escort Caleb through the city during the day, so he could take advantage of some locations that either weren't open at night or didn't offer viable vantage to human eyes in darkness.

Katrina considered the merits of the idea, and while it saddened her that she couldn't experience some things with her mate, she nevertheless wanted him to see as much as possible on their visit.

Caleb enjoyed the conversation, as well as the meal. His cottage pie was comprised of minced beef and vegetables topped with mashed potato, and he found it both delicious and filling. Alton assured him that it was a traditional entrée that he had frequently eaten as a human, though he offered few additional details regarding his human lifetime.

"The shepherd's pie was excellent," Caleb offered with satisfaction as he ate the last bite on his plate.

"Cottage pie," Alton clarified.

"Isn't it pretty close to the same thing?" he asked.

"Cottage pie is made with beef," Alton explained in a practiced manner. "Shepherd's pie is made with mutton."

"Oh," he muttered, filing the information away. "Either way, very tasty."

"Just like you, my love," Katrina offered with a sly smile. *Very tasty*, she silently added as she contemplated time back at the hotel with him. *And sexy*, she amended, considering additional options for their quality time together.

Caleb yawned after finishing his second glass of wine, though both vampires seemed completely awake and unaffected.

"Tired, my love?" Katrina asked.

He nodded and stifled another yawn. *Geez, I could fall asleep on the floor right now.*

"It's probably the wine coupled with a full stomach and jet lag," Alton suggested.

"Speaking of wine," Katrina prompted. "How did you know there was a 1900 Bordeaux available?"

Alton smiled brightly. "Oh, didn't I mention? I own the restaurant."

She rolled her eyes and muttered, "It figures."

Thought so.

Then she humorously contemplated Caleb's weariness and whether she would have to carry her sleepy mate back to the hotel room or not. In the end, he managed to walk out using sheer willpower, and she couldn't help but smile at him endearingly as she wrapped her arm around his slim waist protectively.

Okay, sleep, then sex, followed by "tasting Caleb," she determined while following up on a previous train of thought.

CHAPTER 7

Revelations

Caleb woke in their hotel suite a few hours following their return from lunch with Alton. The elder vampire had been correct that their flight, combined with the food and wine, had caused him to feel incredibly exhausted.

He rolled over onto his back and immediately stared into Katrina's beautiful eyes.

She smiled down at him warmly while perching on one elbow next to him. "Welcome back to the world of the conscious, my love." Her fingertips tenderly brushed against the side of his cheek, causing him to smirk from the tickling sensation.

"Watching me sleep, I presume?" he asked before stretching and yawning.

She half-shrugged. "You're the best view in the hotel."

He shook his head. "I don't know, there's always London through the windows."

"I've seen London. I can't get enough of you," she said simply and kissed him on the lips.

"You're spoiling me. Badly," he warned.

She smirked playfully and teased, "Don't worry, I'll put you in your place if you get out of hand."

He rolled his eyes at her and glanced at his wristwatch. It

was already early evening. "Wow, I slept five hours!"

"Just in time for evening, actually," she offered.

He shook his head slightly at the late hour and asked, "So, are you ready to go out on the town for some sightseeing?"

Her eyes flared bright green for a second and she replied, "Once I'm done with you."

"Done with me?" he asked carefully.

She smiled slyly. "You got your sleep. Now I want blood and more."

While initially caught off guard, it took very little motivation to interest him for more amorous prospects. He was amazed by the level of passion she raised in him, almost at will. He felt a mix of adoration mixed with animal magnetism coming from her. It was like standing before the sun: blissful warmth that burned into you if you stood too long before it or got too close. But it was a blissful burning, the kind that you wanted to yield to and embrace.

So he did, and time stood still for them.

Later, a numbing sensation formed in his neck as he lay on the bed, glistening with sweat. He was still catching his breath as he subtly felt Katrina's fangs pressing into him. It wasn't painful, thankfully, more like increased pressure forming in his neck. He heard the telltale slurping sounds indicating that she was feeding from him.

No, not feeding. Communion.

And he was only too happy to oblige. He let his mind wander on a euphoric tide, which ended much sooner than he wanted. When her head lay against his chest, her mane of hair tickling his skin, he opened his eyes and wrapped his arms around her.

"I so love you," he whispered.

She kissed his chest with soft lips and murmured, "My love. My reason for existence."

They relished the precious moments, lying together in contented silence.

Following a shower and changing into fresh clothes, they

headed downstairs to begin their excursion into London. The weather was still cold and cloudy, but at least the rain had ceased, allowing them the opportunity to take pictures using Caleb's camera.

While the city was breathtaking to view from the hotel and Alton's office building, it was another thing entirely for Caleb actually to walk through it. The city was alive at night, transformed from just a large metropolis to something mysterious and eternal, teeming with people from all walks of life.

The sights were amazing. Their view from inside the London Eye was impressive. Of course, while the stores were still open, they also did some souvenir shopping. Then they proceeded to get Caleb something to eat at a popular downtown restaurant named Bankside, not far from Southwark Cathedral. Katrina contentedly watched him eat, and they discussed their next destinations that evening.

Afterwards, they went through parts of the city to view key sights such as Buckingham Palace, Big Ben, and the Thames River itself. Katrina even posed a couple of times with Caleb as friendly passersby were willing to snap the photos for them.

As much as she enjoyed the touring, most of her satisfaction came from watching Caleb's reactions and sharing in the excitement of his experiences. It was so easy to see how much fun he was having, and it filled her with genuine happiness.

It was while appreciating his interest in a granite-mounted statue of the Duke of Wellington on horseback that she caught the glimpse of something out of the corner of her eye. Her keen vampire vision focused on a pale man in a dark overcoat who was watching them from about a hundred feet away while partially concealed in the shadow of a nearby building. However, once the figure realized he had been sighted, he quickly disappeared from view.

I wonder if he's one of Alton's vampire staff? Katrina wondered with a narrow-eyed expression.

Caleb looked up at her curiously, but she smiled at him as if nothing had happened. Instead, she made a point to stay close to him and be more aware of her surroundings without raising her mate's suspicion. Fortunately, the remainder of their nighttime excursion was pleasantly uneventful.

As they made their way back to the hotel via the London Tube, she snuggled into his arms as he held her closely beside him, earning a number of envious-looking stares from fellow passengers.

All in all, it's a perfect evening, Caleb mused as he closed his eyes to rest.

This has been wonderful, Katrina thought happily as she scanned the train car's nearest passengers in precautionary fashion.

As soon as they carried their armload of shopping purchases into the suite, they freshened up, and Caleb collapsed into bed. Katrina lay beside him, lightly caressing his back while gazing out the large bedroom window into the night and out onto the city.

She recalled the events of their excursion, but also played back the brief discovery of the mysterious vampire observer. The stranger's actions hadn't seemed hostile, merely curious.

Probably one from Alton's cadre of employees. I'll ask him about it tomorrow.

Caleb woke early on Sunday to find Katrina gazing upon him fondly as she lay beside him. A glance out the bedroom window revealed gray clouds and some light drizzle. However, it didn't detract from his excitement of knowing that he was waking up in London.

"Morning, Kat," he offered with a sleepy grin.

"Good morning, my love," she replied warmly.

She started to kiss him, but he held up his hand to cover his mouth and shook his head.

"Oh, not yet," he protested and quickly rolled out of bed to patter into the bathroom as she regarded him with a raised eyebrow.

A few moments later he returned to bed and offered her

a minty fresh-breath kiss. She smirked following their kiss and shook her head.

Always so thoughtful, she mused.

"Fresh breath for a fresh day in London," he quipped. "What's on today's agenda?"

"Well, there's a couple of museums located near the hotel that aren't open in the evening, so perhaps you can visit those today. We'll see other sites together this evening," she offered.

He glanced outside again before returning his gaze to her. "I'm no meteorologist, but isn't it safer for you on cloudy, misty days like today?"

She smirked. "Somebody needs to watch more Weather Channel. Despite the clouds, the sun projects very powerful ultraviolet radiation that penetrates them, and it would still damage me. It's an easy misperception by most people. UV radiation isn't in the visible spectrum for humans, but vampires can sense it quite readily in much the same way you can feel heat emanating from an oven."

"Oh," he replied sullenly. He hated the idea of spending the day without her, but he certainly didn't want her to be injured, either.

She reached out to caress the side of his face with her fingers in soothing fashion. "It's okay, my love. I don't want you to be cooped up here in the hotel all day. Besides, I'm used to the limitation, and it will be evening before you know it. There's a lot to see, and we'll only be here a week. Please, go enjoy, okay?"

"Well, okay. But I won't enjoy it as much without you."

"You're very sweet," she acknowledged appreciatively.

He wished that he could do something nice for her before he left, but it wasn't as if he could order breakfast in bed for her. An idea struck him, and he smiled slyly. She frowned at him with a curious expression as he lay back down onto the bed and turned his head slightly away from her.

"Hungry? How about a little nip before I get ready?" he

offered.

She smiled at his thoughtful gesture. Her eyes briefly flashed, and she advanced upon him to kiss him deeply, warmly.

I'm such a lucky woman. He's so giving, especially of himself.

Her mouth moved from his lips to the side of his soft neck, and she kissed him ever so gently a number of times with appreciation. Her lips parted, her tongue pressing against his skin. He waited patiently as the numbing sensation spread throughout his neck.

"Thank you, my love," she whispered. "You fulfill me in so many ways."

She held her tongue against his skin for another brief moment, and then extended her fangs into him. A wave of ecstasy passed through her as his blood trickled past her lips, into her mouth, and down her throat. She caressed his scalp with her fingertips soothingly and deliberately controlled the rate at which she drew blood from him.

Knowing that he was preparing for a day of sightseeing, she made sure to take only a small amount from him, just enough to fulfill her morning craving. There were few words she could use to describe the satisfaction that partaking in him brought to her. Human blood was sweet, but all the sweeter when given freely and with love.

The time passed all too quickly, and she carefully retracted her fangs and used her saliva both to seal and heal his bite marks so nobody would be the wiser.

Despite his aversion to the idea of touring London alone, the day passed quickly for Caleb as he visited two museums close to the hotel. He ate in one of the museum cafes and continued his perusal until later that afternoon.

He was amazed by the diversity of people that he saw as he walked around the exhibits and quickly understood how popular the city was for tourists. By four o'clock, he hurried back to the hotel. Upon entering the suite, he found Katrina sitting on the couch watching television and using her notebook computer.

After he freshened up, he and Katrina went out on the town. They went to a different local restaurant so that he could eat dinner someplace new and afterwards took in a play at the Her Majesty's London Theater. It was a rendition of Andrew Lloyd Webber's Phantom of the Opera, and they had a wonderful time.

The remainder of the evening was spent seeing various sites of interest and walking arm-in-arm together while appreciating each other's company. Time flew by, and soon after midnight, Katrina redirected them back to the hotel so that her mate could get a decent night's sleep. And though it felt like a brief evening out for a vampire, she felt the quality of their time made up for its length.

The next day was Monday, and Caleb woke very late in the morning to find himself alone in bed. He stretched, yawned, and happily reflected on the previous night's events. Despite the closed the bedroom door, he heard Katrina talking in the living room beyond.

"...he just woke up, in fact," he heard her comment when he strained to hear what was being said.

Okay, so I'm nosy, he conceded with a shrug.

A few moments later, Katrina appeared in the room with a swoosh of air and a sweep of the doorway. The gust of air actually blew his hair around slightly before she appeared at the bedside.

"Good morning, sleepy-head," she murmured before placing a soft kiss on his lips.

"Hey, morning breath alert," he warned, but was too late to make a difference.

She merely shook her head. "A few hundred years ago, there wasn't any such thing as morning breath. Just breath. And a morning waking with breath was a good morning."

He pursed his lips as he considered the historic logic of her statement, admitting, "You certainly have a way of putting things in perspective."

She gave him an endeared look. "You better get up and around; breakfast will arrive soon." She noted his curious expression and explained, "Alton thought you would appreciate an authentic English breakfast. Oh, and he made an appointment for you."

She explained that Alton had scheduled for him to meet with Dr. Guilhelm that evening. He hoped that the accomplished vampire psychiatrist would be able to unlock his blocked childhood memories. And while he was adamant about recovering those memories, he still felt a sudden rush of anxiety at the prospect. *But I'm not going to get cold feet, that's for damn sure.*

He shaved and dressed and was ready to eat the breakfast that had arrived just minutes prior. Katrina watched with amusement as he gazed upon the large platter containing eggs, bacon, sausages, fried bread, mushrooms, and baked beans.

He wrinkled his nose and looked up at her with shock. "This is a traditional English breakfast? Mushrooms? And baked beans?"

She laughed so hard from his semi-horrified expression that tears streamed from her eyes. In the end, he ate the eggs, bacon, and part of the sausages and picked at the rest just to be polite.

Overall, not too bad, he reflected.

He passed the time perusing the local shops and interests within a block of the hotel while Katrina spent most of the afternoon visiting with Alton about his new European project intended for the upcoming summer. When evening arrived, Katrina would accompany him to see Dr. Guilhelm.

Much as Caleb expected, and as was typical when he was apprehensive about something, the afternoon passed rather quickly. By the time the sun began to set and early evening arrived, he returned to the hotel suite to find Katrina sitting on the couch channel-surfing.

He put down a small sack of novelties he had purchased and plopped down on the couch next to her. After a quick exchange of kisses, he glanced at the television and pointed to the screen as the channel changed.

"Hey! Wasn't that a *Doctor Who* episode?" he asked excitedly.

She peered at him curiously, shook her head and replied, "Not sure. And anyway, we don't have time for, um—"

"*Doctor Who*," he supplied happily.

"Ah. We've got to head across town for your appointment. Then we'll get dinner afterwards, okay?"

He shrugged. "Okay."

The journey was expedited via the London Tube, and they arrived nearly thirty minutes early. The five-story office building was actually used for a variety of businesses, which included small medical practices. Dr. Guilhelm's office was on the fifth floor and reminded him of the small office that Alondra Vargas, actually Chimalma, had maintained in Atlanta during last fall's adventure.

The small seating room outside of the doctor's main office was eerily similar in size and layout. A brown-haired, human receptionist greeted them, acknowledged their appointment and asked them to sit in some chairs on the other side of the room.

Caleb looked up at Katrina with a frown and made a comment regarding the odd coincidence in setting. Her expression turned serious as she whispered, "Something like that's simply not going to happen to you again. I promise no vampires will be messing with your mind or body. Except for me, of course."

He sighed with his arms folded across his chest, and she placed a comforting arm across the back of his shoulders as they sat next to each other.

After a few minutes, the doctor's interior office door opened, and a tall figure with teal eyes and silvery blond hair looked at Caleb with an inviting expression. The fellow appeared to be in his late forties and had gaunt features and a lean body. Aside from his overly pale complexion, the only attribute even hinting at his true nature was that his eyes appeared somewhat brighter than normal.

"You must be Caleb," he ventured calmly. "I'm Dr.

Guilhelm, and I'm pleased to meet you. Alton said to expect you. And Ms. Rawlings, I presume?"

"Katrina," she offered as she rose to shake his hand firmly.

Dr. Guilhelm shook Caleb's hand in turn and gestured towards his dimly lit office. "Please come in, Caleb. Would you mind if Katrina remained out here for the time being?"

He looked up at her, and she smiled supportively and nodded her affirmation.

"I'll be right outside if you need me," she assured him and noticed the doctor smile and nod subtly in agreement.

"And Ms. Prescott, you may clock out now," Guilhelm politely instructed his aide. "I won't need you back here until tomorrow afternoon at the regular time."

"Yes, sir," the woman acknowledged with a respectful tone. "Good night."

"Good night," he replied as Caleb walked past him to enter the office.

A few minutes later, he perched on the edge of a brown leather couch placed against the back wall of the office. A series of forest photographs was displayed in three large frames above the couch. A leather reading chair sat across from the couch, in which the doctor sat with his legs crossed.

Caleb scanned the office and noticed the window behind the doctor's large oak desk looked out upon a nighttime view of the city beyond. Overall, it was much more comfortable than Vargas' office and far more warm and inviting.

"Kind of a classic look in here, Doc," he offered with a hint of anxiousness. "Do all psychiatrists use the same office furniture catalog? Or maybe it's a standard layout?"

The doctor smiled, briefly and nodded. "Chapter three of the psychiatrist's manual, actually."

Caleb sighed and smirked.

"Are you feeling nervous, Caleb?" Guilhelm asked calmly with a supportive, non-threatening expression.

Caleb swallowed. "No. Well, actually, yes. But I'm okay."

"Ah, but if you really were okay, you wouldn't be here,

would you?" the vampire asked with a grin.

Caleb looked up with a surprised smirk and chuckled despite himself. "You're not a real psychiatrist, are you?"

The doctor grinned reassuringly. "Actually I am, but I've found humor usually lightens the mood, and you seem to enjoy a little levity."

"I can see that," Caleb agreed good-naturedly as he absently rubbed his fingertips against each other. "And yeah, I like humor."

"That's good. So, why not tell me a little about yourself?" Guilhelm encouraged. "And then a little about what it is you're trying to recall."

Caleb described his background at a cursory level, but soon found himself going into further details about his childhood and abusive father. He was surprised how easy it was to talk to the doctor, and he effortlessly described his introduction to Katrina last fall, including the occasional flashes of memory flaring at odd occasions.

He described the flashbacks after having discovered the old photograph of his mother and Katrina, then Amber, at the company banquet. Occasionally, the doctor asked simple questions for clarification or additional details, but mostly listened patiently. By the end of his recollections, Caleb found himself feeling oddly at ease and had even stopped fidgeting.

"Caleb, have you ever undergone hypnosis therapy?" Guilhelm asked once Caleb had finished.

"Nope, never."

"Well, I'm going to try something that's very straightforward and pain-free," the doctor began. "It's just to gauge how significantly your memory may be blocked. And if the conditions are viable, I'll see what I can do beyond that. Perhaps I can nudge them free for you. All you need do is sit back and relax."

Caleb nodded, and the doctor stared at him in a sedate manner. Guilhelm's eyes began to glow mildly, and he offered in a reassuring voice, "Now just stare into my eyes, Caleb. And don't be nervous. My eyes are calm, and friendly, and inviting…"

Within moments, Caleb was concentrating on Guilhelm's teal eyes. They were entrancing and soothing, and it made him feel a little sleepy. Suddenly, he saw only teal eyes before him. He heard Guilhelm continue talking, asking him to think about his childhood. Random memories from his youth flooded his mind. The doctor's voice continued to soothe and guide him as he remembered back to various childhood events. Again, the teal orbs filled his vision, blocking out everything else. And the memories continued to flash in his mind.

He described his visions in a subdued voice, explaining the scenes and recollections playing out in his mind. But at some point, he was unable to recall whether he were speaking aloud, or merely thinking, or both. Yet the memories continued to flood through his mind. After an undetermined period of time, he saw something new from his childhood seemingly appear before his eyes. At least, the vision seemed new. He didn't recognize the scene, which included a sunny day in his old backyard in Ohio.

Was it summer?

Everything was so vivid in the vision.

I played with my toys, and I saw something blurry kicking up dust in the field near our house. A door opened and slammed shut abruptly. It was the old garage next to the house. I ran to investigate. Caleb watched events play out through his own eyes as he entered the musty garage with a curious expression.

I went into the garage, and I think I heard moaning somewhere. Was it an animal? The sound came from the tarp-covered old car that Dad worked on sometimes. I knelt on the floor and peeked underneath the oily old tarp. Caleb gasped. *I saw a person, or something that looked like a person! There was a stinky, burnt smell, too.*

There was a woman's voice, a quaky-sounding woman's voice. Was she hurt? What was she doing under the car? Then additional flashes of conversation with the woman. *She's an angel? From heaven? And she needs help soon! I ran back into the house for a pencil and some paper and returned to the garage. It was a secret, the angel.*

Angel Amber said not to tell anyone, not even Mom. A long series of numbers followed. He needed to get to a phone and call the number and give the angel on the other end of the phone some more numbers. What were all the numbers for? Did God use all those numbers too?

I waited for a truck to arrive. God sent a truck? The delivery angel, Angel Bruce, although he looked like an ordinary man, left a plastic box with me. Why did the angel need for me to write my name on a clipboard? Don't angels know everybody? I rushed the box to the garage for Angel Amber. She told me to leave for a while, so I did. More playing with toys, watching television, and eating lunch. Then Mom made cookies. It was evening, and I had to go check on Angel Amber after supper. But Dad was angry after work, and he drank more of the stinky bottles of beer. He got angry again. Lots of shouting, and Mom started crying. Then Dad hit me when I kept asking about Mom. The pain hurt so much. He likes hitting, I think.

I went into the garage and wanted to see the angel, but I'm upset. Angel Amber asked me questions from under the car. Wait! Dad's coming! He looked angry, and I was scared. Ow! My arm was bleeding, and I cried. There's a woman standing in front of me. Who is she? She's Angel Amber? Dad's really mad and doesn't like Angel Amber. The angel hit Dad! She's putting me outside, out of the garage. But Dad's going to hit the angel with a big metal bar! Angel Amber grabs Dad by the neck, and he falls onto the floor. Angel Amber wants to look at my arm because it's still bleeding. She kisses it, and it feels funny, but better. She says the angel magic will fix it. She wants me to look into her eyes. She has pretty green eyes. I feel sleepy. Then I'm playing in the back yard with my toys. I see the angel carrying something over her shoulder as she walks through the empty field near our house. And Dad's gone...

Caleb gasped as he fell back against the cushion of the leather couch, still staring into Dr. Guilhelm's calm face. His heart was racing so fast that he thought it might burst from his chest.

"Are you okay, Caleb?" Guilhelm asked quietly with a concerned expression. "How are you feeling?"

Caleb blinked once and nodded dumbly. "Um, yeah," he stammered. "Confused..." He actually remembered meeting an angel named Amber. *It's like everything just happened.*

Everything's still so fresh.

Guilhelm merely nodded silently and waited.

"Angel Amber was Katrina," Caleb mumbled almost to himself. "She killed...She saved me from my dad."

Guilhelm nodded again. "Caleb, you found something that was hidden away inside your mind. You must realize that these new memories, though valid, are as you would have interpreted them as a child. They are yours either to embrace or reject, but either way, they are your own. I suggest that you patiently take the time to go over them in your mind."

"They're so vivid, like they just happened," Caleb rambled.

"In essence and to your conscious awareness, they just did," the doctor explained. "What are you feeling right at this moment?"

Caleb rubbed at his eyes and felt wetness on his face. Guilhelm handed him a box of tissues, and he blew his nose.

"I'm not sure," he began unsteadily. "I'm free from Dad, though. Forever."

"Caleb, your memories can be very powerful, and I want you to think about your feelings surrounding them. You have some difficult images to digest and may want to consider further visits with me. I'll be more than happy to help," Guilhelm offered.

"What next?"

"Most of all, you should talk to Katrina about your memories openly and honestly. I also want you to call me if you have any questions or concerns, day or night." Guilhelm handed him a business card. "I put my personal cell phone on here, and you shouldn't hesitate to call me anytime. After all, I'm a vampire, and I don't sleep much."

Caleb smirked at the quip and took the card. Guilhelm rose from his chair, but motioned for him to remain where he was. "I'm going to step out for a few minutes so you can collect yourself in quiet," he explained. "But I'll be outside with Katrina if you need me or her."

Caleb nodded, and the doctor quietly slipped from the

office.

Katrina rose as soon as Guilhelm exited. She had an expectant expression on her face, and the doctor motioned for her to remain quiet. Once he pulled his office door to, he whispered, "We're done for now. He seems fine and is collecting himself at the moment. I was successful in releasing his memories, and I suspect he remembers everything that you blocked. But time will tell, and he may need to visit with me in the future. I told him that he needs to think about his feelings and to talk to you about them. I gave him my card, but I'll give you one too, just in case. Call me anytime, especially if you sense that something is wrong."

"Can I see him now?" she asked with concern. *My God, it's been nearly three hours!*

He held up his hand tentatively and suggested, "Give him a few more minutes alone. Then you can peek in on him."

"Um, just let me know what I owe you, and—" she began a little unsteadily. Her mind was racing with concern for Caleb.

"No," Guilhelm countered. "This one's *pro bono*. Alton told me a little about your circumstances, and I'm just happy to help."

"Pardon me for being suspicious, but why?" she asked carefully.

Guilhelm smirked. "I see what Alton meant when he warned me about your protective and cautious nature. Not that I'm criticizing, mind you."

She scowled. *Alton, you blabber-mouth.*

"For one, he seems like a fine young man. I'm sincerely pleased to help you, actually. Alton conveyed how very important Caleb is in your life. And frankly, I don't get to see many vampire hypnosis patients, particularly vampire mates. This was a sort of professional opportunity for me," he explained. "You did a pretty good job, by the way. But I'd stay away from hypnotizing humans in the future. It's quite tricky."

She sighed and shook the doctor's hand. "Yeah, I found that out the hard way."

Guilhelm smiled and nodded.

He certainly seems like a thoughtful being for a vampire. How unusual. "I've got to hand it to you, doctor," she said. "You're a first in my book, as well."

"First vampire psychiatrist?"

"No, first time I met a psychiatrist who does *pro bono* work," she teased. Fortunately, a hopeful feeling began to replace the anxious ones of a few minutes ago.

Guilhelm shook his head and smirked. "Cute. Tell you what, I'll make a few phone calls from out here while you go in to check on him."

Katrina nodded and gently opened the door leading into the office. She slipped into the office and noticed Caleb rubbing at his eyes while sitting on the couch. *He's been crying.*

She suddenly felt anxious, wondering what his first reaction would be to her following the restoration of his memories.

He'll know for certain that I'm the one who killed his father.

He blew his nose into a tissue and looked up at who entered, thinking it was Dr. Guilhelm again. Instead, he saw Katrina, only this time, there was another figure in his mind whom he instantly recognized. His mouth dropped open with a degree of astonishment.

"You're Angel Amber," he whispered as he rose from the couch. He had seen the photo of Katrina as a short-haired brunette, but now the face in that picture was actually real to him and not just a blank space. "You called me Angel Caleb. I remember that, too," he added.

She smiled tentatively and promised, "You're still an angel."

"You saved me," he whispered in a shaky voice. "Thank you, Angel Amber."

Katrina felt a tear slip from the corner of her eye, but it was swept aside by the velocity of her movement as she lurched towards him. She wrapped her arms around him and pulled him to her in a warm embrace. "You never have to thank me," she whispered soothingly. It was a far better reception from him than she could have hoped.

"I love you," he whispered into her ear as his arms encircled her waist.

"Oh, how I love you too, Caleb," she whispered. "Completely and forever."

* * *

It was very late by the time they left Dr. Guilhelm's office. Katrina asked if Caleb wanted to get something to eat, but he declined, insisting that he wasn't very hungry. Instead, they rode the Tube back to the hotel.

During the journey, he kept glancing at her furtively, though she only regarded him supportively or tried to ignore it altogether. His expression was a mix of wonder and confusion, as if he were trying to discern something perplexing.

Caleb wondered about the vivid nature of his new memories and how the woman in them was both different and familiar to him. The freshness of his visions coupled with the current timeline generated a confusing temporal dichotomy.

He kept trying to reconcile both periods in his mind, almost as if trying to get his mental bearings. Equally confusing was the host of feelings accompanying the process, a confusing mix of shock, apprehension, wonder, appreciation, and love.

They sat together quietly on the couch once back in the suite, holding hands as Katrina leaned her head against his shoulder. Sometime later, Caleb's stomach abruptly reasserted itself with a growl. Katrina smiled and ordered a cheeseburger, fries, and Coke for him through room service, hoping it would serve as a form of comfort food.

Later, she quietly watched him eat with her chin propped up on her upraised palm as her elbow perched on the dining area table. He smiled wanly at her and seemed to be much more at ease. Occasionally, he glanced up at her thoughtfully.

"You seemed much taller in my memories," he ventured between burger bites.

She smirked. "You were much shorter then. Though I'm still taller."

He nodded with a smirk, continuing to eat.

After dinner, he took a shower, and Katrina called Alton to fill him in on the details from the session with Dr. Guilhelm. The stately vampire listened quietly, finally advising her to keep an eye on Caleb and to try to make him comfortable. *Yeah, like I need another opinion on how to look after Caleb.*

"Did you check with your vampire contacts and staff on whether they were observing us the other night?" she asked, quietly changing the subject.

"I checked, and nobody has seen you in town, nor have they sought you out," Alton replied. "But that doesn't mean some rogue vampire living in the city didn't just happen upon you. London's an old, populated city, and it's conceivable that there are a number of anonymous vampires lurking in the vicinity," he added.

Katrina conceded the plausibility, but experience had taught her that a little paranoia was healthy. "Well, thanks for checking, anyway."

"Listen, Caleb mentioned wanting to see the city during the day. Perhaps I could offer two of my best human staff to accompany him on a tour tomorrow? It would be a great opportunity for him to see the daytime sights under the guidance of locals who also happen to be accomplished in the area of security. Not that anyone is particularly seeking him out, mind you," he ventured.

She frowned, but conceded the viability of the idea. "Hm, no thugs, though," she insisted. "I don't want him to feel overtly guarded."

"Rob and Lynne Fuller are an unassuming married couple who just happen to be two very promising agents on my staff. And they might welcome a respite from their normal duties," he suggested. "I think that Caleb would like them, in fact."

"You're employing married couples now?" she challenged.

"Ah, but they work well together," he countered. "And I made an exception in their case. They each have useful backgrounds."

"Very well," she replied guardedly. "But I want to meet them before Caleb does."

He chuckled. "Fine, fine. You can interview them in the morning. Just call me when you're ready."

"Thanks, Alton," she offered sincerely. "Until morning then."

As she hung up the phone and listened to the sound of Caleb's shower, she appreciated that Alton was trying to be helpful. Then her thoughts turned back to Caleb, and she wondered if the past were finally on its way to being reconciled between the two of them.

Only time will tell, I suppose.

* * *

The next morning, Caleb woke to Katrina's arm draped across his chest. She was staring into his eyes as he glanced over to her, and she smiled.

"Good morning, Angel," he greeted with a sleepy expression. His freed childhood memories from the previous night's session with Dr. Guilhelm were still so vivid.

She grinned and patted him on the chest lightly. "Good morning, my love," she replied.

"This is nice," he mumbled. "I could get used to all the room service, nice hotels, traveling the world, not to mention plentiful spending money. No worries, no limits, and complete freedom. It's surreal for me, really. Heck, it's easy to forget what day of the week it is."

"It's Tuesday, and I can make this come true for you

every day if you want," she baited with a raised eyebrow. "Just say the word and it's yours."

He chuckled and rubbed his sleepy eyes. "Don't tempt me."

She stared into his eyes intently. "Just say yes, and I'll make it happen," she whispered.

"Kat," he stammered with a serious expression, "I can't just…I mean, I have a job, a career to nurture. There's retirement to plan for. Hell, in a couple of years, I'm gonna need a new car, for Pete's sake. You can't just—"

She raised an eyebrow. "Oh, but I can. And I will. Just tell me that's what you want."

He swallowed, taking a moment to contemplate what she had just offered to him. It was like something out of a Hollywood film or fantasy novel. He considered the thrill of it all and the freedom. But he would feel terrible, like the world's worst mooch. A shameless, greedy leech of a person.

It's her money, not mine.

His pride wouldn't allow such a thing. As much as he wanted to say yes, he simply couldn't with a clear conscience.

"That's very kind," he replied. "But I can't."

"Why not?"

He frowned. "It's just wrong," he explained. "What you're doing for me here in London is already too much."

She sighed. *Male pride*, she fumed. *Still, his heart's in the right place, I suppose.* "Do you know how many people would've already faxed resignations to their employers by this point?" she teased.

He adopted a more thoughtful expression. "Sorry, it's just not me."

"Well, I don't want you to feel uncomfortable. But let me know if you change your mind. The offer stands, and I'm not going anywhere."

He nodded as he stared down at the comforter draped over them. She reached up to grasp him gently by the chin and turned his face towards hers.

"We're going to travel more, you know," she resolved.

"And you have to get used to the fact that I'm going to dote on you."

He smiled back at her and winked. *You're the best.*

"So, what's on today's agenda?" he asked.

"I'll know more later this morning," she answered mysteriously, rolling over to the opposite side of the bed to get up. "Why don't you order something to eat while I'm getting ready?"

"Okay," he replied, stretching lazily in bed as she went into the bathroom to shower.

He slipped into a pair of jeans and t-shirt and was sitting at the dining room table eating a recently delivered breakfast by the time Katrina appeared in the room with a burst of speed. She blew him a kiss and smirked at the plateful of food before him.

"I'll be back soon, my love," she offered as she hastily departed the suite.

She called Alton on her cell phone as she made her way towards the underground passageway between the hotel and his office building. He assured her that the Fullers would be waiting to meet with her.

As soon as she walked into Alton's office, she began her assessment of the two humans before her. Rob Fuller was her height with short brown hair, brown eyes, and a fit, muscular build. His bearing suggested prior military experience.

Lynne Fuller was somewhat shorter with blonde hair, blue eyes, and a lithe, toned build. Katrina detected that both of them were watching her as closely as she was observing them, and she offered a slightly predatory smile. It seemed to surprise both of them, which pleased her.

Alton raised a curious eyebrow at her. "Katrina, I'm pleased to introduce Rob and Lynne Fuller. They're two of my best staff." He gazed at the Fullers in turn, offering, "Ms. Katrina Rawlings. She is Caleb's mate."

Neither of them looked at Katrina in a challenging manner, but each seemed quite interested in her reaction to them.

"Rob was British SAS and later served as a British secret service agent. He's been in my employ for three years," Alton began. "Lynne was MI-5, specializing in intelligence gathering. She's been with us for two years."

"Weapons training?" Katrina asked as she regarded Lynne Fuller.

"Small arms and martial arts," Alton supplied. "Carries a Beretta 9mm pistol."

Her gaze shifted to Rob Fuller. "Your background tells me what I need to know, except perhaps weapons of preference?"

"Steyr 9mm pistol," Rob replied easily. "And combat boot knife."

"Tourism experience?" Katrina asked with a straight face.

The Fullers exchanged curious glances, and then Rob smirked while Lynne stifled a laugh through her bright smile. Katrina allowed a slight smile to form on her lips.

Good sense of humor. Caleb will like them, I think.

"Thank you for agreeing to look after Caleb," she offered politely as she reached out to shake their hands. "It's a pleasure to meet each of you."

Their demeanors relaxed further, and Alton raised an eyebrow with intrigue over the brief exchange. "Well, they're yours for the day," Alton offered. "They'll escort Caleb back to the hotel by evening, unless you request earlier, of course."

Katrina nodded with approval, and the Fullers subsequently accompanied her back to the hotel suite. Rob and Lynne politely stood just inside the suite's entry area while she went to find Caleb, who was perusing the Internet on his laptop in the dining room.

He glanced out the large picture window onto the city beyond. Once again, it was overcast, and some drizzle started to fall. It looked somewhat cold and foreboding to him, in fact.

"Back already?" he asked as she walked up behind him and bent down to kiss his lips. "Are we staying in today?" he asked.

"Staying in?" she countered. "If we waited on nice weather in London in March, you'd never see most of the sights, my love. Instead, there are two people I'd like you to meet."

He gave a puzzled look as he closed his applications and shut down his laptop. He followed her into the living area, where he noticed the Fullers standing near the door. He glanced up at Katrina curiously, though he moved forward to shake their hands in turn.

"The Fullers will be showing you some of the sights in the city today," Katrina offered. "They work for Alton, who's been kind enough to offer their tour guide services to you. As Londoners, they have the inside scoop on the best places to visit."

"Hi, Caleb. I'm Lynne," offered the blonde woman with a friendly smile as she shook his hand.

"I'm Rob," offered the dark-haired man with a polite expression as they shook hands. "Happy to make your acquaintance."

Caleb found them quite charming, aided in no small part by their British accents, similar to how he felt when he had first met Alton. Katrina assessed her mate's reaction closely, quite pleased to sense his relaxed body language and melodically calm heartbeat.

"Excellent," Katrina observed. "I think you're in very capable hands, my love. You'll be able to take daytime pictures of some of the sights, and then they'll have you back by evening so you and I can go out on the town together."

"Great! I'll get my coat and camera," Caleb blurted as he headed towards the bedroom.

"You should only need a light jacket, Caleb," Rob suggested while watching Katrina. "We'll take the Tube around town to avoid being in the elements as much."

Katrina nodded at him in silent approval.

Caleb called back from the bedroom, "Hey, we can also scope out Tube stops where Kat would be able to access sites without being—" He abruptly fell silent, unsure if the Fullers were aware that they were working among vampires. *Surely, Alton would have told them,* he mused.

"They know about us, my love," Katrina called to him in an amused tone.

He reappeared with his camera and black leather jacket in hand. "Good. We'll be able to pick out sites that allow access through the Tube system without ever being in daylight. Maybe we can plan to see those sites together tomorrow." He looked up at his mate with an endearing expression and asked, "Sound good?"

She smiled broadly and quickly kissed him on the lips. "Sounds wonderful, my love. Have a good time, and mind Rob and Lynne's advice, okay?"

He smirked and feigned innocence. "Me? I'll be the picture of the model tourist."

She arched one eyebrow and murmured, "Mm-hm."

Rob and Lynne cast quick glances at each other as Caleb opened the front door and proceeded into the hallway. As Lynne passed him, Rob silently nodded to Katrina in a reassuring manner and turned to follow the others down the hallway.

Katrina stood in the open suite doorway for a few seconds before closing it behind them. She hoped that Caleb left his unexpected penchant for trouble back in Atlanta.

Still, it's just sightseeing, right?

* * *

Caleb enjoyed getting to know Rob and Lynne as they proceeded to various points of interest throughout the city. He didn't ask, but realized that if Alton employed the couple and Katrina approved of them, the Fullers were likely much more than just a timid, married couple who were showing him around town.

They're probably agents, or something, he mused.

Still, he didn't want to seem rude by asking, and instead

merely kept the conversations light and friendly.

Besides, we're here on vacation anyway. It's not like we're on a mission or something. The mission portion of the trip ended with Dr. Guilhelm last night.

His mind momentarily wandered to last evening's revelations regarding his memories of meeting Katrina as a child and the death of his father. He had been scared by what might be revealed in his memories, but was actually relieved by what he had learned. Granted, he found the vivid images disturbing as they related to his father's demise, but it wasn't as bad as he feared it would be. Many other unblocked memories of his father included numerous cases of physical or verbal abuse, and he hated the man for it.

I'm glad he's dead, he considered darkly.

He realized there was a time not so long ago when such thoughts would have disturbed him. *But that changed after I met Katrina. Should that concern me, or perhaps encourage me?*

"Caleb, is everything okay?" Lynne asked as she sat next to him on the Tube. Rob glanced discreetly past his wife to study him as well.

Caleb broke from his reverie and felt himself blush slightly. "Sorry," he replied with a sheepish grin. "I was just caught up in some other thoughts for a moment. I'm having a great time, though. Thanks so much."

She smiled at him supportively and nodded.

The three ate a light, afternoon lunch at a quaint English pub called The Cross Keys, where Caleb tried a tasty ale on tap and enjoyed a traditional English sausage entree. Later, they went by Buckingham Palace to view the queen's impressive elite guards on duty.

They took some outdoor photos of old buildings, including Parliament and the Courts of Justice on the Strand, and of course, Big Ben, the London Tower Bridge, and the London Eye. The Fullers kindly took photos of him standing before those sites as well. He thoroughly enjoyed their company and forgot they were anything more than a charming English couple showing him the sites.

He also called Katrina a couple of times during the day to check in and noticed on the last call that his cell phone battery was waning.

I'll be back in a few hours to recharge it.

By late afternoon, they were once again riding the Tube on their way across town. When they exited the train, there was a large crowd of people in the underground boarding area, and Caleb had to squeeze between people. He shared a smirk with Lynne as both of them were brushed aside by a man carrying a violin case who seemed in a hurry.

"Probably just a mobster late for a hit," Caleb joked loudly over the din of voices around them.

"Gonna rub somebody out, eh?" Lynne quipped with a smile, to which he grinned and nodded.

Rob suddenly grabbed the sleeve of Caleb's jacket, and he looked up to see him focused on something along the far wall across the terminal.

"Bloody hell," Rob muttered under his breath, catching Lynne's attention.

She abruptly stopped and turned to look at both of them as Caleb's eyes spied a tall, pale man wearing a gray leather jacket staring back at them with slightly glowing brown eyes.

"Go!" Rob urged to Lynne. "Get Caleb topside into daylight!"

Lynne grasped Caleb's left arm and pulled him towards the nearby escalator heading upstairs. He saw Rob's arm sneak inside his jacket.

"Keep moving, no matter what, Caleb," Lynne urged as she pressed at his back, glancing over her shoulder in the direction of her husband.

"But Rob—" he protested.

"Rob's fine. He'll be fine," she urged and pushed him onto the escalator. "He knows what to do."

Somehow Caleb doubted that. He had been attacked by vampires before and knew how utterly futile it felt to combat them.

At the top of the escalator, Caleb heard a brief gunshot,

followed by people screaming. Lynne looked behind her, hesitating. She turned to Caleb with a desperate expression and ordered, "Get up to street level and call Alton or Katrina! Just stay in the daylight, no matter what!"

Caleb nodded and hurried towards another escalator leading further upstairs.

He stopped after ten feet to look back, but Lynne had already disappeared downstairs. He turned to continue to the escalator, but spotted a tall, blond man wearing a dark suit coming down the escalator, urgently pushing past people as he descended. Caleb noticed his complexion was very pale, and the man glanced up with slightly glowing violet eyes.

Crap, another vampire!

Crowds of animated and scared-looking people were pouring upstairs even as people upstairs were frozen in place wondering what had happened. Instead of getting on the escalator in the direction of the other vampire, Caleb turned towards a small corridor leading away from the area.

He quickly proceeded down the abandoned, tiled corridor. It ended in a metal door with a push-bar handle, which he hit at full force as he hurried forwards. Instead of leading upstairs, the concrete steps led down. But rather than backtrack and risk running into the vampires, he proceeded downstairs. At the foot of the stairwell was another heavy, metal door, which he barreled through like the previous one.

He entered into a dimly lit concrete corridor, realizing he'd likely made a bad mistake. The door shut behind him with a metallic thud, and he whirled around with a horrified expression as he grasped at the metal door handle and pulled. It didn't budge an inch.

"Damn!" he cursed and peered tentatively down the darkened corridor before him.

His hand flew to his belt to withdraw his cell phone, and he flipped the face open, muttering, "Hope I get a signal."

He tried scrolling through his contact list, and then stared at the blank screen with a puzzled expression. He tried actuating the power button a couple of times, to no avail. He removed the battery, reinstalled it, and tried turning the phone on. Again, nothing.

Worse than no signal. No charge.

He slipped his dead phone away in its carrier and walked carefully to the end of the corridor where it opened into an underground subway tunnel. There were only occasional dim lights placed in the ceiling, giving the tunnel an eerie ambiance.

"Pick a direction," he mumbled, finally turning right.

He walked for a short distance in hopes of finding another side corridor that might host another potential exit, but found the tunnel continuing in a slightly curved fashion. He heard the sound of a train in the distance, which grew progressively louder.

Anxiously looking for a place to step off the track area, he quickened his pace forwards. He thought it was too far away to turn back and was relieved when he found a small alcove set in the wall that appeared big enough to squeeze his body into. Thankfully, the niche was more than adequate, though he was less than enthused by the feel of the moist, cold concrete at his back.

The oncoming roar of a train drew closer as he remained in the niche. A rumbling accompanied the noise until a train sped by his location with a roaring rush of air. He clamped his hands over his ears and tightly shut his eyes until the train passed. Stepping from the niche, he proceeded onwards. His mind wandered back to the fate of the Fullers, and he prayed they were okay. He struggled to focus on his present situation instead of allowing his growing anxiety to get the best of him.

Caleb soon arrived at a branch in the tunnel, and he was forced to choose between right and left. He took the left tunnel, walking at an increased pace.

The tunnel was much quieter until he heard the roar of another train in the distance, which failed to grow louder and eventually faded away. Time passed, and he finally located a small side corridor leading away from the tunnel. It looked like the passageway that had brought him into the tunnels, but seemed older and less utilized.

The brick wall appeared antiquated, and there was only a single light at the front of the corridor. He considered abandoning it for another further up the tunnel, but instead removed a keychain flashlight from his pocket and flipped it on.

Proceeding into the narrow passageway, he failed to hear any noises or voices.

It's probably a dead end up here, he mused.

After a short walk, the corridor led into a small, open area that appeared completely abandoned. However, he noted a newer looking leather couch that one might find in an office waiting room or lobby.

That's strange, he thought.

He shined his small light around the approximately twenty-foot square room and spied a small niche. He walked to it, noting a deteriorated metal door set into the wall. The handle appeared antiquated, and an old deadbolt lock was set into its dingy metal facing. He tried the handle, but the door was secured in place.

"It figures," he groused. "Probably just goes to the Land of Oz or Alice's rabbit hole, anyway."

He sighed and dejectedly headed back to the tunnel. When he arrived, he turned right and proceeded onwards. Not long afterwards, he heard another train in the distance, which grew progressively closer.

He shrunk into another alcove formed by two large concrete pillars until his back pressed against the cold, damp cement wall. The rumbling of the approaching train reverberated through his body via the ground and wall behind him.

The train sped by with a screeching and whooshing roar, a gust of air sweeping over his body as it passed. He shut his eyes tightly to the onslaught and waited a few seconds longer once the train had passed before opening his eyes again.

"Crap, that's loud!" he cursed as the sensation of the train still seemed to vibrate through his body.

Gathering his wits, he proceeded down the tunnel towards what he hoped would be another boarding area where he could rejoin humanity.

He proceeded into the barely lit darkness and concentrated on keeping his footing, pausing occasionally when he thought he heard a rustling sound around him. His nerves were on edge, feeling as if at any moment a vampire would rush out of the darkness at him. He hated the idea that he was essentially weaponless and felt vulnerable due to both his reduced visibility and increasing disorientation.

After a time, he heard another quickly approaching rumbling in the distance. He hastily sought another niche in the tunnel wall and pressed his body into the space.

The train roared past him like the previous ones, and he gritted his teeth while closing his eyes until it passed.

Once the train was gone, he opened his eyes, took a deep breath, and proceeded up the dismal tunnel. He had quickly grown to despise the subterranean detour and was anxious for it to be over. He proceeded down another lengthy stretch of dimly illuminated tunnel and avoided yet another approaching train.

Following its passing, and after a much longer interval, he heard another train approaching and sought another niche in the wall. The increasing rumbling noise and accompanying vibrations unnerved him, and he forced himself into the nearest wall space.

"Damned trains!" he shouted with frustration.

The train whooshed by with a roar and a bone-jarring reverberation. He closed his eyes tightly and waited as the air rushed past his body, which shook from the tremulous vibrations working their way through his muscles and bones.

Caleb released a deep breath he'd been holding, feeling weary from his seemingly never-ending journey, and slowly opened his eyes again once the train had passed. But instead of staring into the darkness, he was staring into a black cotton sweater. His eyes widened from the scent of cherry blossoms, and he quickly looked up into Katrina's glowing emerald eyes.

"You're such a handful sometimes," she lightly chastised him, but with an adoring expression on her face. She deliberately hid her relief at finding him safe, having feared the worst when she learned he had disappeared near the tunnels.

His arms immediately wrapped around her waist, pressing her against him in a bear hug. "You don't know how freakin' glad I am to see you," he muttered.

She smiled down at him, fully appreciating his firm embrace, and wrapped her arms around him protectively as she felt his rapid heartbeat thrumming from deep within his chest. However, she also detected the tension in his body and realized just how alarmed he must have been over the situation. *Of course, hearing him yell in the tunnel was a good indicator of that.*

"Are the Fullers okay?" he asked. "I heard gunshots before Lynne went to help Rob."

"They're both fine," she assured him. "Alton called me while I was on my way to find you. The vampire attacked Rob, but was deterred by a gunshot wound to his neck. By the time Lynne arrived to aid her husband, the injured vampire had escaped into the tunnel."

"What about the other one, the blond vampire?"

"There was another?" she asked. She hadn't recalled Alton's mentioning two vampires on the phone.

"Just how did you manage to find me down here?" he asked, continuing to hug her a moment longer. He savored the comforting feel of her body and scent of her cherry blossom lotion.

"My love, I could find you in a city packed with people," she replied simply. "How much easier would it be in an empty subway? Besides, I also heard you shout, and a faint trace of your scent was flowing through the tunnel."

"I'm so glad you're a predator," he mumbled gratefully.

She chuckled at his odd comment and shook her head slightly before craning her neck down slightly to kiss him. While reluctantly separating from their embrace and stepping back into the dark tunnel, she reached down to his belt, smoothly slipping his cell phone from its carry pouch. She flipped the facing open with her thumb and noticed it was powered off.

"Dead battery," he explained irritably.

She nodded. "Explains why we couldn't reach you," she observed. "And why Alton was unable to triangulate your location from it."

"Pretty typical, isn't it?" he asked with a sigh. In all the excitement over their arrival in London, he had forgotten to place it on the charger.

She handed his dead phone back to him with a smirk and asked, "Ready to get back to civilization?"

He glanced up into her eyes, noticing they weren't glowing as much as a few moments ago. Realizing that she must have been upset when she found him, he smiled, pleased to have a mate who cared so deeply for him.

"Hell yeah, I'm ready," he insisted as he grasped her hand and began walking. Then he stopped dead in his tracks, looking up at her with an annoyed expression. "Um, Kat, do you know how to get the hell out of here?"

She chuckled and nodded. "As a matter of fact, I believe I do."

She led him in the direction he had started to proceed initially, and within minutes they heard another approaching train. Halting their progress, she ushered him into one of the nearest wall niches and pressed his back to the wall. Stepping into the niche facing him, she placed her arms on either side of the concrete columns to hold their two bodies securely in place.

Caleb's right arm slipped around her waist to pull her closer into the niche with him. He stared up into her eyes, appreciating the closeness of her body, and closed his eyes again as the train's roar assailed his ears. A swift rush of air flowed over them as the train sped past. Afterwards, he opened his eyes, and both of them stepped from the small alcove to resume their journey up the tunnel.

"Geez, it's really creepy down here," he observed warily, only to glance up and see her smirking at him.

After a short time, they encountered a dimly lit passageway just wide enough for two people to walk abreast that detoured from the tunnel at a right angle. Caleb pulled on Katrina's hand to halt her, gently beckoning her forwards to continue their journey down the tunnel.

"Probably just another dead end," he offered. "I tried one further down the tunnel that was abandoned."

"Really?" she chided lightly, instead urging him to follow her with an abrupt tug on his hand.

They went down the narrow, dark corridor at a brisk pace, and he noted that a heavy-duty metal cage loomed ahead. The area appeared somewhat different from either the initial corridor he had exited into or the older one leading to the dead end. Katrina barely paused in her brisk stride as her right leg whipped up to kick the lock mechanism. The metal cage door made a crashing metallic sound as it swung open with a powerful reverberation that nearly took it from its hinges.

My God, she's powerful, Caleb noted with awe.

He wasn't often able to appreciate Katrina's abilities firsthand, but they amazed him on each occasion.

She led him by the hand to a metal door set into a concrete wall. Firmly grasping the metal handle, she effortlessly pulled it open with a single jerk of her arm, causing the door to yield with a loud pinging sound and a metallic groan of its rusty hinges.

Caleb found himself being half-pulled up the concrete stairs behind her, and within seconds they were standing in a deserted, well-lit maintenance access corridor. A sigh of relief emitted from him, and she turned to look into his eyes with a satisfied smile.

"Back to civilization, as promised," she remarked.

He elevated himself on his toes slightly as she bent her head down towards him, and he kissed her lips appreciatively.

"Thanks, Kat," he offered with a firm squeeze of her

hand.

She winked at him, paused for a moment to get her bearings, and led them down one of the lengths of hallway back to the main terminal area. She withdrew her cell phone and called Alton as they proceeded on their way down the corridor. Minutes later, they were on the Tube heading towards his location.

* * *

Alton stood between two vampires dressed in business suits and the Fullers as Katrina and Caleb exited from the train that had pulled up at the station near Alton's office complex.

The stately vampire was dressed in an immaculately tailored dark gray suit. Caleb's eyes widened slightly as he exited the train car amidst the other passengers and noted Alton's dour expression. However, Katrina looked like she had just won the lottery, if the broad smile on her face were any indication.

"I'm glad you found him so quickly," Alton complimented as he glanced at Caleb reprovingly. "And as for you, young man, I'm happy that you weren't harmed. Please allow me to reassure you that I won't be underestimated like this again. I intended for your stay in London to be memorable but for the appropriate reasons, naturally."

He nodded with an appreciative expression. "Thanks Alton."

"However, if there is a next time, perhaps follow the advice of your escorts," he suggested.

"I would have," Caleb countered innocently. "But another vampire was heading my direction."

"Another vampire?" Alton inquired with narrowed eyes. He glanced to the Fullers, but they each shrugged and shook their heads negatively.

"You didn't see him?" Caleb asked with a frown. *I'm sure*

he was a vampire, he considered. "He was coming down the second escalator, so I turned and ran down an alternate corridor. But then I got lost in the subway tunnels."

"We'll examine the substation's security camera footages," Alton said. "Our mysterious vampire should turn up on one."

"You have access to the Tube security systems?" Caleb asked.

"My dear boy," Alton replied, "we have access to a great number of things, some of which might actually surprise you."

"Let me guess," Caleb ventured wryly. "You own the Tube system, don't you?"

The edges of Alton's mouth upturned ever so slightly, and he reached out to place a hand on Caleb's shoulder. "Rubbish. Honestly," he retorted. "You're an absolute scamp. You know that, don't you?"

Caleb grinned back at the tall vampire as Lynne Fuller recalled, "Scamp, indeed. One minute he was running towards the escalators in my line of sight. As soon as I was down on the next level, I turned back to spot him again, but he had already disappeared into nowhere. You're fast, Caleb, almost like a vam—"

The blonde agent refrained from completing her sentence given their public surroundings, but her suggestion was obvious to everyone present, and her eyes fell upon Alton and Katrina in equal turn. Alton's eyes briefly darted to Katrina's, both of them exchanging a similar consideration of Lynne's observation. Alton turned to stare inquisitively at the woman.

"Not entirely as fast, obviously," Lynne amended. "But remarkably swift."

Katrina frowned as she considered how quickly Caleb seemed to be able to move for a human. She had noted that when she had first revealed herself to him in the park near her estate, and he had run away at a rapid pace.

Likely, he would be a very fast vampire, she mused.

"Our apologies, Caleb," Rob offered. "The matter is quite an embarrassment on our part, and we won't get caught off-guard again."

"Exactly," Alton agreed as he gestured for everyone to follow him from the terminal area. "Next time, we keep Caleb top-side in the light of day. And there will be additional resources available at a moment's notice, if needed."

"It sounds strange, but I'm not convinced they were actually looking for us," Caleb speculated.

"The timing is too convenient," Alton reflected. "Why else would they have been there, if not to intercept you?"

Katrina frowned as she followed directly behind Caleb and Alton. The two other vampires and the Fullers brought up the rear. Alton led them through a length of the terminal until he reached a non-descript, solid metal door. He punched a series of codes into a numeric keypad, and a metallic clicking emitted from inside the wall. They walked into a well-lit, carpeted hallway with pictures of London night scenes placed intermittently down the length of both walls.

"Please remind me, and I'll provide you with the codes to these access doors, Katrina," Alton suggested as they walked down the hall.

"Thank you," she replied, wondering how many such corridors existed.

Eventually, they entered an open, well-lit lobby area located deep beneath Alton's office building. The central portion of the room contained a carpeted floor decorated with professional reading chairs and couches, a mix of end tables, coffee tables, and some live potted plants.

A few men and women in business attire either milled around the nearby elevators and seating area or were gathered at the small coffee shop set off to one side of the elevators. While the area was obviously in a subterranean portion of the building, it appeared much like a traditional office lobby.

"Yet another professional gathering area for humans and vampires alike," Alton commented just loud enough for Caleb to hear him clearly. "It also tastefully bridges the office complex with the subway system."

Katrina scanned the area and complimented suspiciously, "Very impressive, Alton. This is all very elaborate, actually. But to what end, I wonder?"

He smirked with a gleam in his hazel eyes. "Why, Katrina, I would have thought that was readily apparent. I intend for London to be a major hub of interaction for our kind, and all alongside the common commerce of humanity. Certainly London is a multifaceted center: commercial, cultural, and social. How much more so for our own kind?"

She began to understand the implications at hand. Alton appeared to be establishing the complex to act as a sort of base of operations or centralized venue for vampires. However, what were missing from his explanation were the barriers to his success.

Namely, who would have an interest in seeing the venture fail? And more to the point, why?

However, rather than broach the subject with him in such a public setting, she merely nodded and looked at Caleb, who appeared somewhat tired or shell-shocked from his recent adventure. She reached out to grasp her young, sandy-haired mate by the hand and smiled at him. "You look tired," she observed with a supportive squeeze of his hand.

He offered a half-smile. "A little. But actually, I'm kind of thirsty and maybe a little hungry."

She rolled her eyes at him, always amazed at how robust his stomach seemed to be despite the accompaniment of stress or hardship.

"But of course," Alton neatly interjected. "I'm always hungry following a romp in the Tube tunnels," he teased.

She cast a withering glace at her former mentor, while the Fullers quietly smirked. But Alton's amused visage quickly turned serious, and he turned to address the Fullers.

"Thank you for your service today. I'd like to go over events with you again tomorrow morning, but I'll bid you a good evening for now," he instructed.

They both nodded and turned to Caleb.

"Again, my apologies for today's finale," Rob offered as he reached out to shake Caleb's hand. "I assure you a better showing of our abilities all around, if we're allowed the opportunity for a further tour of London."

"I'd like that very much, thanks," he replied with a grin. "I had a great time, and you've both been very kind."

Lynne extended her hand in kind and offered, "My apologies as well. But it's been a pleasure, Caleb. I enjoyed our time today, and as Rob said, I'd enjoy showing you around some more."

"Thank you," Caleb replied as he shook the former agent's hand. "I'd love that, in fact."

Each agent nodded deferentially to Katrina while silently shaking her hand and nodded to Alton before departing towards the nearby elevators. Alton turned to address the two sharply dressed vampires standing nearby.

"Activate the others," he instructed in a near whisper. "Search the immediate area where they were. I want to know who was down there and why. Most importantly, we need to know where they're operating out of."

Both vampires silently nodded and departed in the direction of a nondescript door with keypad panel inset in the wall located off to the left side of the nearby coffee shop. Alton turned back to Caleb and Katrina with an apologetic expression.

"I hope to have some answers by tomorrow," he offered. "Are you sure you're okay, Caleb?"

Caleb looked up at Katrina with a thankful expression and replied, "I am now, thanks."

"Good. I'm happy to hear it," Alton offered and looked at Katrina. "I'll call you in the morning, okay?"

She nodded, and he turned to depart.

"Alton?" Caleb called after him, to which the dark-haired vampire turned to look at him curiously. "Rob and Lynne were wonderful today," he said. "Don't be angry with them. I felt really safe and welcome around them, and I'm the one who ran in the wrong direction."

Alton nodded and walked towards the nearby elevator.Katrina wrapped her arm around Caleb's shoulders and led him towards the underground corridor across the room that connected to their hotel. He slipped his arm around her waist as they walked.

"Any chance we might stay in tonight?" he asked after a quiet moment.

She smiled, turned to kiss him on the lips, and replied, "I think I can arrange that."

However, as they walked, her thoughts returned to the events in the tunnels. She wondered who had attacked Caleb and the Fullers and why.

And Caleb mentioned a second vampire. Who could that have been?

CHAPTER 8

Forgotten Realms

Caleb slept in late the next morning. When he woke, his thoughts were immediately of the previous afternoon's exploits in the Tube substation, rather than the pleasant daylong sightseeing excursion with the Fullers. Entire spans of enjoyable, peaceful activities could be negated so easily by a single, brief, negative experience involving a vampire.

Let's face it, potentially lethal events tend to focus one's thoughts.

Katrina appeared by his bedside moments after he woke, and she bent down to kiss him. While her expression was tender, it seemed to him that there was tension simmering just beneath the surface of her outward demeanor.

She regarded him with a curious expression as he stretched his body, as if pondering how to say something. He suspected that it had to do with yesterday's Tube episode.

"Good morning," she offered pleasantly, though it seemed a little forced.

"Just waking up to you is a good morning," he offered with a grin.

She shook her head at him while running her fingertips across his forehead, tickling his skin. "I've been thinking about today's agenda," she began with a tentative, tight-lipped expression.

I bet she would prefer that I stay close today, he anticipated.

He understood that concern and didn't want to cause her further undue stress by challenging her on the matter. Instead, he offered her an easy out over the topic.

"Yeah, about that," he interjected quickly. "Would you mind if we stuck around the hotel for the most part? With all the power-touring the past day or so, I'd kind of like to just relax a little bit, if that's okay."

"Are you sure?" she asked in surprise.

"Sure," he reassured her, feigning a hesitant look. "I mean, unless you have other plans or something. I wouldn't want to disappoint you or anything."

She smirked, and he suspected that he'd just hit the nail on the head.

"No, that's fine, actually," she responded readily. "We'll just rest and maybe go out together later tonight. Sound okay?"

He nodded agreeably. "Yeah, great. I was thinking about getting brunch in the hotel restaurant. Care to join me?"

"Definitely," she concurred. "I wouldn't mind a hot cup of tea, actually."

As he shaved and dressed, he was inwardly satisfied with himself for deftly negotiating what could easily have become an argument.

I'm getting better at sensing her mood, I think, he congratulated himself with a grin.

In the hotel dining room, she watched him eat as they passed the time discussing London sites they still wanted to visit. As he finished eating, she sat back in the chair with her arms crossed before her and gazed at him with an appraising expression.

"What?" he asked somewhat self-consciously.

"So, now that you're giving me a pass on the whole 'stay around the hotel today' suggestion, what can we do to occupy your time?" she asked plainly.

His eyebrows rose slightly at her unexpected candor. It was apparent that he hadn't been fooling her at all. *How does she do that?*

"I do appreciate it, of course. And don't feel bad, my love," she offered with a smug expression. "I've come to know you rather well. That, and I have over five hundred years of human observation under my belt."

"Oh," he managed with a dazed expression.

Her cell phone rang, and she smoothly extracted the device before he could blink an eye. He glanced around them to see if anyone else noticed her speedy reaction, but there were few patrons lingering about the dining room.

"Sure, Alton," she replied while watching him with amusement. "No, as luck may have it, we don't have any specific plans for today."

Caleb rolled his eyes and glanced at their server, who had walked up to the table to check on them. Katrina smiled politely and subtly tapped the edge of her tea cup with her fingertip, to which the lady inclined her head in acknowledgement of the silent request.

Caleb merely smiled, shook his head, and offered, "Nothing more for me, thanks."

Their server departed to retrieve more tea for Katrina.

"That's fine. Until later this afternoon," Katrina replied and smoothly closed her cell phone as Caleb's eyebrows rose in silent query.

"Well, part of our schedule is set," she said. "Alton would like to meet with us this afternoon regarding your encounter yesterday."

Just great, he thought with a sigh, *more intrigue. Such a pleasant diversion while on vacation.*

She observed him curiously, but he merely glowered where he sat.

In the end, they lounged around the hotel suite for nearly half the day. She read a mystery novel, while he unsuccessfully tried to contact Paige via email, cell phone, and text messaging.

"Hey, what's with Paige lately?" he called from the dining room where he was using his laptop while looking out upon the city.

Katrina paused from her reading to consider his question.

She has been uncustomarily out of touch lately.

Paige's only communiqué had been a phone call to her saying that she hadn't been implicated in Gil's fatal "accident."

"She's not in trouble, after all, I hope," he said with a hint of worry in his voice.

"Gil's death was ruled an accident, Caleb. I'm sure she's fine," she tried to reassure him. *Paige is a resourceful alpha vampire, after all. Likely she's just preoccupied.*

"Too bad she lives in California," he muttered, clicking at pages on the Internet. "It'd be better if she lived closer."

Katrina stopped reading. "How much closer?"

He stopped clicking, but didn't look over at her. "Like, Atlanta, maybe?"

"Yeah, good luck with that," she quipped and returned to reading. *Not enough clubs and social diversions in the whole of Georgia for Paige Turner.*

"So, you wouldn't mind her moving to the Atlanta then?" he asked with upraised eyebrows. He knew that Kat and Paige were close friends, but wasn't sure how his mate liked the idea of her close proximity on a permanent basis.

She stopped reading again and stared at him, noting his tense body language. *He's not sure what I'd think about the idea, I bet.*

She immediately came to a decision, shrugged, and returned to her novel. "I'm okay with that," she conceded. "It would be more convenient."

He grinned, and then his phone beeped. He read the text message and noted irritably, "Finally, a reply from Paige. She says she's wrapped up in a project and can't 'chit-chat' right now. She hopes we're having a good time. Geez, glad I didn't really need anything."

Katrina frowned, but didn't press the matter with him. *Paige's strange behavior is something else I need to get to the bottom of, it seems.*

She glanced at her watch.

"Time to meet with Alton, my love," she offered with an almost relieved tone. She didn't want him spending time dwelling on the situation with Paige. It wasn't as if anyone could do anything about it for the time being.

Half an hour later, they sat in Alton's office before his expansive oak desk. As he recapped information acquired by his staff's investigations, Caleb absently reflected on just how big the vampire's desk was.

"You know, I've seen smaller aircraft carriers," Caleb teased. "I mean, just how much paperwork do you actually spread out on a daily basis?"

Alton cast a bland look at him as Katrina stifled a chuckle.

"So, did the Tube's security cameras catch a glimpse of the blond vampire I saw coming down the escalator?" Caleb quickly asked to change the subject.

Alton paused as he considered his question. "Actually, no. Unfortunately, the cameras in that particular substation mysteriously went offline just a few minutes before your encounter. They began operating again soon after the injured vampire departed."

Katrina stared at her former mentor in a penetrating manner.

"Sound familiar?" she asked pointedly. She and Aton had used an electronic jamming gadget that he had acquired from British Intelligence when they were hunting the vampire, Chimalma, last December. Perhaps a similar device had been used to suspend the security system's operation.

He anticipated where her thoughts were leading and replied, "Yes, I already considered it. There must be a number of those jamming devices running around the country by now. Technology rarely stays a secret for long these days."

A silent moment passed before anyone said anything.

"You know, I've been thinking. It seems unlikely that we

were intended as a target yesterday," Caleb ventured. "It didn't feel like an overt attack. It was more like we interrupted something."

The two vampires exchanged curious glances, and then studied him closely.

"Interesting theory," Alton finally replied. "A meeting of some kind?"

"Maybe," Caleb agreed. "Anyway, the idea occurred to me after you ordered your vampire agents to go looking around the terminal and nearby tunnels. What if the location is somehow meaningful?"

Katrina listened to her mate's statement with interest and interjected, "Your theory has merit, actually."

He smiled up at her with an appreciative expression. She returned the smile and reached over to trail her fingernails down the back of his neck. It caused the desired effect of sending a tickling sensation down his neck and into his shoulders, and he shivered slightly.

"Well, my staff haven't turned up anything yet," Alton said. "And frankly, I'm not sure what I expect them to find." His eyes darted to Katrina's. "Perhaps if we go over some of the information I collected over recent months regarding vampire operations in the area, it might reveal something that we've overlooked."

She nodded with an introspective expression. "Perhaps."

While the development was somewhat intriguing given their experience the previous day, Caleb didn't want his and Katrina's vacation to get detracted by something that might very well have just been a coincidence. He felt fidgety and wanted to stretch his legs a little.

Maybe this is a good time to take a break, he pondered.

"Um, I'm thinking about going down to the little coffee shop in the lobby for a snack," he explained as he rose from his seat. "Anybody want anything?"

Alton looked up and shook his head negatively, while Katrina winked at him and smiled. "Thanks. Nothing for me, my love."

He nodded and hastily exited the office. He walked down the hallway, made his way to the elevator, and pressed the call button. A glance up at the LCD display indicated that a car was on its way up.

He looked around the small alcove in the corner, and his eyes caught on a nondescript leather couch sitting there, which looked familiar for some reason.

The elevator doors opened, revealing a pale figure in a dark business suit. Caleb recognized him as the blond vampire he had seen on the escalator in the Tube station the day before.

The vampire immediately recognized him with a wide-eyed expression, and his hand darted out to grasp Caleb's upper bicep in a vice-like grip. Caleb started to shout, but the vampire's other hand shot to his mouth, and he quickly found himself twisted into an arm bar.

Caleb looked into the hallway to try to get someone's attention. However, the corridor was empty, and he was forcefully propelled towards the nearby stairwell.

He struggled and knew that in order for the door to open the vampire had to release either the arm bar or the coverage of his mouth. The vampire chose the latter, but banged Caleb's head into the metal door jamb, briefly stunning him. Then the vampire forced him into the stairwell.

A moment later, Caleb felt himself being half-carried, half-propelled down the stairs. At the foot of the first tier, he managed to kick his leg in front of the vampire, causing him to trip slightly.

"Help!" Caleb barked, but was slammed into the nearby wall, where the breath was knocked out of him.

The stairwell door opened at the top of the stairs, and Marla Kendrick's face peered through the opening. "Did someone cry out?" she asked tentatively. But her eyes immediately focused on Caleb, and she entered the stairwell.

"Davison! What the hell—" she demanded, only to have her words cut short by the impact of the vampire's zooming upstairs into her. He yanked her down the stairwell, throwing her head-first downstairs.

Her head impacted the floor tier with a dull pounding sound, and her body slammed against the stairs. She lay still, her eyes closed. Davison sped to her side and bent down to squeeze the woman's throat. Caleb managed to gather his faculties enough to grab a fire axe from the wall next to a fire hose box. He hefted the axe in his hands and swung with all the strength he could muster.

As Davison turned from Kendrick, the blade caught him in the upper left chest with a meaty thud. Initially, the impact propelled the vampire backwards, but he fell forwards onto the floor as his mouth opened to emit a raspy hiss.

Davison's body fell next to where Caleb stood and slumped motionlessly with his right hand grasping the axe hilt just below the blade.

Caleb immediately rushed to Marla's side and felt her neck for a pulse. A swift intake of breath surprised him, and her eyes suddenly shot open. They glowed with a washed-out green color, and her hand darted up to grab his wrist so quickly that he didn't have time to react.

"Friend!" he yelped before she tried to attack him.

She released his hand, muttering, "It's okay. I know."

He started to say something more, but her eyes suddenly went wide. Her arm managed to throw him aside before the whooshing sound of an axe blade went past him to clank against the stairs where his body had been a mere second prior.

A small shower of cement erupted from the stairs, and Caleb glanced back over his shoulder to see a profusely bleeding Davison with a contorted expression of rage on his face. His violet eyes blazed as he quickly swung the axe over his head for another strike.

Caleb barely registered multiple simultaneous events. As he viewed the axe blade's being raised with a horrified expression, he heard the stairwell access door erupt open, smashing into the wall with a metallic crash.

A feral-sounding scream assailed his ears, forcing his

hands to the side of his head, while Davison's face shone in momentary surprise as his eyes flickered up.

A blast of air whipped past Caleb, and suddenly Davison and the axe both disappeared. A blur of movement seemed all around Caleb, pausing briefly as Davison's body was smashed against the nearest concrete wall, then the ceiling, then the floor, and then disappeared as it was thrown further downstairs towards the next flight.

He thought he saw a flash of red trailing from the blur movement, and his eyes searched to follow it downstairs. At nearly the same moment, Alton placed a firm hand on Caleb's shoulder while kneeling next to Marla.

"Don't!" Davison yelled from downstairs, but his voice was cut short by the sound of a meaty thunk. Something heavy fell to the floor, followed by an eerie silence.

Caleb jerked free of Alton's grip and quickly crawled around the corner of the stairwell until he could peer downstairs. Katrina appeared menacing as she stood over Davison's prone body, the axe handle sticking up at an odd angle from the blade buried in his head.

"Stay dead," the red-haired vampire seethed in a cold, lethal-sounding voice.

She glanced upstairs towards Caleb, and her eyes were pulsating like miniature green suns. A shiver went down his spine as he stared at her in partial shock, partial horror. She turned and began a slow, progressive rise up the stairs towards him while his eyes were locked onto hers, unable to tear his gaze from her. She looked like a demon incarnate, beautiful and terrifying all at once.

Holy crap! was all he managed to silently process in his overwhelmed brain.

Katrina stared at him, trying to banish the rage and frustration of the previous moments. She almost wished that the vampire had struggled more, because she wanted so very much to pound on him further.

If I'd been a few seconds later, Caleb would be dead.

The realization was nearly unbearable as she towered

above Caleb, suddenly cognizant that his face was still awash with fear. A pang of guilt washed over her as she suspected that part of it may have been due to her, rather than solely Davison's actions.

"Be calm, Caleb. She's just angry," Alton encouraged from behind him as she squatted down beside her mate.

"He's knows he's safe with me," she admonished Alton with aggravation between clenched teeth.

Her soft hand went to the side of Caleb's face, and he finally managed to blink his eyes, breaking the spell he had been under. His hand shook as he reached out to touch the side of her face in response.

Her skin felt so soft, but her jaw was firmly set. They just stared at each other for a few seconds in silence. The corners of Katrina's mouth upturned ever so slightly, and her eyes were no longer pulsating, merely glowing brightly green.

"Are you okay?" she asked quietly.

He nodded and mumbled, "Angel Amber."

She pulled him into an embrace as she wrapped her free hand around the base of his head, gently cupping it. No words were needed between them as, in that moment, each sensed what the other was feeling. It was the universal communication of love, affection, and relief.

"So, Davison must have been the second vampire from the Tube station," Alton surmised while observing them from behind. "It would have been nice to know what he knew. Couldn't you have merely wounded him?" Alton asked Katrina carefully.

She sat back from Caleb, looked over at Alton with a determined expression and stated flatly, "No, not after what I saw from the top of the stairs."

Alton sighed heavily and turned his attentions back to Ms. Kendrick. "Marla, are you okay?"

"My body's healing, thanks," she said confidently. "Thanks to Caleb, that is. Davison would've finished me off if Caleb hadn't axed him in the chest."

Katrina's eyes glanced to him with stark surprise, and

even Alton seemed taken aback as all eyes fell upon the young human. Caleb swallowed and felt himself blush.

"Well, I mean, Marla distracted him, so I got in a lucky hit," he stammered.

Katrina arched an eyebrow. "I noticed the wound and thought Marla had caused it."

Alton nodded approvingly, supplementing, "As did I."

Katrina's eyes still showed surprise as she contemplated the revelation. *Caleb's come so far in his skills that I underestimated him. Perhaps he's no longer quite so helpless.*

She was utterly proud of her mate.

"Well, we're still somewhat in the dark," Alton lamented as Caleb, Katrina, and Marla followed him back upstairs to the fifteenth floor.

As they walked through the door, numerous vampire and human faces stared at them with curiosity. Caleb ignored everyone, instead glancing towards the elevator area where he had spied the leather-covered bench sitting next to a fake plastic tree. Something about the bench struck an odd chord in his memory.

Alton glanced at a nearby gray-suited vampire and ordered, "Davison's body is lying in the stairwell. Coordinate the sterilization of the scene, and see that our people dispose of the body."

The vampire nodded and proceeded into the stairwell.

"I'm inclined to believe that Caleb may be correct regarding there not being a prearranged attack against him and the Fullers. We had a spy in our ranks, after all," Alton surmised. "Perhaps a rendezvous of sorts got interrupted by their sudden arrival. But, if so, why there?"

"But what are the odds of Caleb's being present on scene at just the right time?" Katrina queried, her mind only partly focused on the topic after all that just transpired.

They fell silent for a moment and proceeded down the hall towards Alton's office. However, Caleb stopped abruptly in the hallway, staring back at the bench near the elevator. Katrina sensed her mate's lack of proximity and darted back to where he stood. She followed his gaze towards the elevators.

"What is it, my love?" she asked guardedly.

"Maybe we're not back at square one, after all," he mumbled, to which she arched an eyebrow in silent query.

"That bench," he said, pointing towards it with an outstretched arm. "I've seen another one just like it recently."

Alton stopped to see what was holding up the pair. He easily heard Caleb's statement, walked back to him, and explained, "Indeed, my boy. We have them throughout the building. They're so popular, in fact, that one was stolen from our lobby earlier this year."

"I know where you can find it. It's in the Tube tunnels," he stated resolutely as he stared at the dark-haired vampire with a vacant expression. "Next to the old door," he mumbled.

Katrina's eyes shot up with surprise, and she reached out to touch him lightly on the arm. "You mean, when you were lost in the tunnels? What old door?" she asked carefully.

His eyes found hers and he smiled from his odd impression when he had first encountered the door. "The one leading to Oz, or Alice's rabbit hole."

Alton and Katrina exchanged odd glances and looked back at him as if he had lost his mind. He frowned when he noted their expressions and reassured them, "It's real, and I'm pretty sure I can take you there."

Twenty minutes later, Alton's office buzzed with activity. Alton and Katrina strategized at the large oak desk regarding a plan and arrangements for raiding the Tube tunnels later that night.

Caleb rinsed a washcloth in Alton's wet bar sink and proceeded to daub the back of Marla's head with it. While the blonde vampire's wound healed quickly, there was still blood smeared through her hair. She smiled appreciatively at him for his ministrations as she sat on the office's leather couch. Caleb merely thought it was the most useful thing he could offer to do.

"You should be resting," she said appreciatively. "You were assaulted as much as me, you know. And you're not a vampire. I'm as good as new already, and you're likely very sore."

Katrina glanced up from her conversation with Alton upon hearing Marla's statements and observed Caleb's reaction closely.

"Well, I'm kind of—" he started to concede until he noticed Katrina's attention. Instead, he replied, "Fine, actually. I feel just fine."

Katrina frowned and shook her head at his cavalier response, but let the topic drop as she returned her attention to Alton. The English vampire grinned momentarily, but reverted to a more serious expression when he noticed Katrina's focus upon him. Caleb thought that he might actually have a subtle advocate in Alton.

The truth was that he felt both achy and sore after the altercation, and his neck was a little stiff. But he wasn't about to give Katrina any ammunition to use in her attempts to dissuade him from accompanying the vampires on the upcoming investigations.

Unlike his experience last fall with the vampire Chimalma, he refused to be left behind while Katrina ventured into dangerous waters on his behalf.

Then again, it isn't as if anybody is specifically targeting me this time, right?

"Well, I appreciate your assistance with my hair," Marla offered with a smirk. "Perhaps I can get you something to eat or drink?"

He grinned. "Sure, a Coke would be nice. Thanks."

"Coming right up," she said and quickly moved across the office to the wet bar.

After sipping his drink and leaning back into the couch's cushions, he found even the ingestion of caffeine wasn't enough to keep his eyes from drooping. He was dozing before long, and his head bobbed a number of times before he finally leaned against one side of the couch to get more comfortable. He dozed off in virtually no time at all.

"Caleb, my love?" Katrina's soft voice cooed as his mind regained consciousness.

He stretched and immediately moaned from his sore muscles before he had a chance to recall that he had been trying to hide his discomfort from his mate. His eyes snapped open to see Katrina's face watching him with a raised eyebrow and a knowing expression.

"Thought so," she said.

"I'm fine," he countered.

She merely shook her head at him. "It's time for you to show us where you saw the door. Alton has a map of the underground Tube tunnel system on his desk."

"No need," he insisted. "I'll show you myself."

"No, you won't," she countered with a note of finality.

He glanced around the room for the first time since waking and realized that they weren't alone. Alton stood just behind Katrina, while Marla Kendrick and three other men dressed in black combat fatigues sat around the conference table across the room.

Another moment of inspection suggested to him that two of the men were vampires based upon their pale skin and piercing eyes. A wave of embarrassment grew in him from the rather public exchange that he and Katrina were having.

However, Katrina paid no attention to the others in the room and remained solely focused on him. "Your recollections, if you please."

He bit the inside of his lip, looked away from her and quietly asserted, "I'm afraid it's not that easy. I'll need to show you in person."

Her gaze turned steely, and she grasped his chin in her hand to turn his face back towards hers. "No games, Caleb," she whispered, although he was well aware that every vampire in the room had clearly heard her.

"I'll have to retrace my steps," he stated flatly. "Besides, given the attack by Davison, wouldn't I be safer with you and Alton?"

She gave no visible reaction as she stared back at her mate, but her mind considered all the angles. *He's got a point. But I also know he's lying about not being able to recall his route.*

She briefly glanced back at Alton, and the stately vampire merely shrugged.

"Reasonable arguments either way, really," he replied in a non-committal tone, although he smirked slightly at Caleb once she looked away from him.

Caleb tried to hold back a smile, but her completely deadpan expression spoke volumes regarding her displeasure, and he quickly lost his inclination for humor. Instead, he swallowed and awaited her response with a straight face.

"Fine," she said and turned to look across the room at the men seated at the conference table. "Suit him up properly, gentlemen," she ordered.

"Thanks for—" Caleb began appreciatively, but she cut him off abruptly.

"Don't," she warned with a stern look. "I'm not happy with you right at the moment."

She stood, motioned to Alton, and stalked out of the office. Caleb watched her go and looked over at the others seated at the conference table. Each of them watched with mild amusement on their faces.

"Well," Marla began with a penetrating smirk. "You heard Ms. Rawlings. Let's prepare him."

Caleb wasn't sure he liked the way she said that.

Within an hour, Caleb's clothes had been replaced with black combat fatigues, black combat boots, and heavy-duty rubber pads secured to his elbows and knees. Only when a vampire approached him with a black flak vest of some kind did he realize there was yet more to come. He felt like he was being outfitted for a cricket match.

Katrina, Alton, and others busily prepared gear for the evening's activities. They were all dressed in similar black combat fatigues and equipment, though Caleb was the only one not sporting web gear of some kind.

The large room they were in was like a miniature armory

located on the floor below Alton's main offices. There was an array of combat weapons, including large standing vaults containing ammunition, explosives, and other equipment that he couldn't even begin to identify.

"Caleb, a word of advice. This time, please remember not to turn your back on a wounded vampire, young man," Alton advised with a mock-stern expression.

"Well, yeah, but...Hello?" Caleb retorted. "Axe to the chest!"

The corners of Alton's eyes wrinkled from a broad smile as he shook his head in satisfaction. Katrina smirked for the first time since their earlier exchange, watching her flustered mate squeeze into a black bullet-proof assault vest with the aid of one of the fatigue-garbed vampire agents.

Once the vest was over his head, Caleb caught the amused expression on Alton's face.

"Well, that's good advice, I suppose," he admitted.

Katrina walked over to the vampire helping Caleb, waved him off, and proceeded to adjust the straps on his vest herself. "Take a deep breath and hold it," she prompted before cinching the straps down with a tug. "Okay, you can let it out now."

He shifted in the vest and pulled at it as if trying to get more comfortable. "Man, this thing sure weighs a ton," he complained. "Crap! No wonder, there's a huge metal plate sewn in the front of it."

She smacked him on the chest with a firm whack from the flat of her hand, causing him to stumble backwards a couple of feet.

"Feel that?" she asked.

He nodded while walking back towards her awkwardly.

She arched an eyebrow. "Did it hurt?"

He shook his head. "Not at all."

"Exactly. That's why it needs to 'weigh a ton,'" she observed dryly as she turned to slip large combat knives into sheaths arrayed across her combat belt.

"Hey, don't I get one of those?" he asked. "Or maybe a

gun?"

She regarded him slyly. "No, in fact, you don't."

"But—"

"You have me," she interrupted. "And Alton, and a team of other vampires. But most importantly me."

He shook his head and rolled his eyes at her. She quickly reached out and mussed his hair.

"Hey!" he retorted, reaching up to smooth his hair back into place, although he was happy to see that her mood had lightened somewhat.

She handed him a Kevlar-lined steel helmet. "No harm anyway. You're about to have helmet hair."

"Aw, come on," he complained.

Her expression turned edgy as she narrowed her eyes at him, pointing to the helmet with her index finger. "Wear it, or else," she commanded.

He sighed, popped it on his head, and groaned. "Geez, this is lame. I feel like one of those rebel soldiers in Star Wars or something."

"And it might just save your life, so keep it on," she insisted.

"Fine," he said while trying to tighten the chin strap.

She smirked at him while he wasn't looking.

Alton announced, "The Tube tunnels will be shut down by the time we arrive at the substation. Let's move."

Vampires in black fatigues and body armor moved around grabbing equipment and firearms, but Caleb cast a wide-eyed expression at Alton. "You managed to shut down the entire London Tube system?"

He returned a slightly amused look and replied soberly, "Of course. Train operations will be temporarily suspended under the guise of structural inspections. I happen to have key vampire-supportive contacts in the Tube transit system, you realize."

"Yeah," Caleb said dryly. "Obviously."

This guy's unbelievable, he thought as Katrina ushered him towards the nearby elevators.

The Tube substation where Caleb had fled into the tunnels was completely deserted by the time they arrived. Six vampires and two humans wearing gear accompanied them into the substation. Caleb appreciated that at least he wasn't the only one in an armored vest, but noted that Katrina and Alton had forgone them. They proceeded into the lobby and down the first tier of escalators, and he immediately recognized the location.

"This was where I saw Davison," he stated quietly, although his voice seemed to echo somewhat in the large, open area.

Everyone looked at him, and Katrina prompted, "Okay. Where did you go from here?"

He led them to the same side corridor that he had run through, albeit at a normal walking pace this time. When he arrived at the metal door at the end of the hallway, Katrina abruptly stepped in front of him and pushed through the door first. Caleb followed her and glanced over his shoulder briefly to see Alton at his heels.

At the foot of the stairs, Katrina proceeded through another metal door and into the dimly lit corridor leading into the tunnel system. As Caleb and Alton stopped next to Katrina, Caleb recalled out loud, "The door locks as soon as you shut it."

One of the two humans, Mullins, grasped the door with one hand while extracting some black tape from a small pocket on his fatigues. Caleb watched the man tape up the striker plate so that the lock mechanism wouldn't engage.

"Clever," he commented absently.

"Ballistics tape," Alton explained. "Comes in handy for lots of things, actually."

Caleb nodded, but then noticed everyone staring at him expectantly. "Oh, yeah, waiting on me," he said and walked towards the end of the corridor.

Katrina and Alton moved ahead of him while the other eight individuals followed in two single-file lines of four. Caleb tried to focus his memory on his trek through the tunnels, which was hampered by having to look past Alton and Katrina in order to get his bearings. He hesitated twice and had them backtrack on one occasion.

Finally, after contemplating an upcoming intersection, he stopped abruptly in the middle of the darkened tunnel, causing the two lines of agents behind him to halt.

"Just stop," he announced irritably.

Alton and Katrina paused to glance back at him with frowns.

"What is it?" Alton asked.

He sighed. "I need to be in front of everybody. It's too hard doing this while trying to look past you all the time."

Katrina's eyes momentarily flashed, but then she gestured with her arm and invited in a calm voice, "After you."

His efforts at leading them were much easier, although he was constantly aware of Katrina's presence at his back. Still, it was fortunate. On one occasion, he tripped on a rail and fell forward barely two inches before she had grabbed the back of his vest to hold him in place while he reacquired his footing. Alton and a couple of the team members chuckled at that, causing him to blush furiously.

After what seemed like a nerve-wracking eternity, Caleb happened upon the section of tunnel wall where the older, dimly lit corridor led away into the darkness. He started to walk into it, but Katrina's hand firmly grasped the back of his combat vest and jerked him backwards.

"What the?" he complained.

"Sh!" she admonished in a whisper and inclined her head towards Alton.

Alton nodded in silent reply and used a series of hand gestures to the team members behind him. Mullins stepped aside and adopted a combat stance with his automatic rifle in the middle of the larger tunnel, and four vampires proceeded into the small darkened corridor, followed closely by Alton. Katrina reached behind her to grasp Caleb's hand and place it against her back. The two of them went into the corridor after a few seconds' delay. The remaining two vampires and one human followed behind Caleb.

Walking in near-total darkness was unnerving for Caleb, but he found the contact with Katrina's back both helpful and reassuring. His touch enabled him to stop as soon as Katrina did, though he was nervous standing in the dark. A light suddenly erupted in the room as the human agent produced a handheld lamp very bright for its size. The man nodded at Caleb, who gratefully smiled in return.

Caleb noted the couch sitting along the wall and the small alcove where the old metal door was located. He pointed to it from behind Katrina, although two vampires were already moving towards it. Suddenly, firearms were pointed towards the door by the remaining team members. Katrina stepped backwards while reaching behind her to press Caleb further away from the door, still keeping her body situated in front of him. Alton stood to one side with his arms folded before him.

One of the vampires closest to the door began pressing putty-like plastic explosives around the door frame, over the door lock, and around the hinges. Another vampire placed wires into the material, pulling additional wire a short distance from the door. Everyone moved away, and Katrina turned around to embrace Caleb in her arms. A second later, a muffled boom emitted in the room while a mild concussion wave passed through Caleb's body.

"Stay put!" she ordered as the metal door was pried out of place.

The room erupted with activity all at once, and Alton ordered, "Brown and Jenkins, stay with Caleb!"

Alton, Katrina, and the remaining team members all moved in a blur through the doorway. Caleb barely had time to react before Brown and Jenkins adopted a guard-like stance in the room. He was grateful that Brown, the human, had placed the box-lamp on the floor in the center of the room to provide light.

A series of shouts and gunfire erupted downstairs past

the open portal. Caleb's heartbeat pounded as he helplessly listened to the commotion, and he glanced up at the two team members standing near him with a wide-eyed expression. However, they seemed unaffected, although both had grim expressions on their faces.

After a few tense minutes of continued sporadic gunfire and other noises of combat, Brown turned his back to the open doorway to address Caleb. "Everything will be just fine."

A blur of motion exited the doorway behind Brown, and a tall figure with blazing hazel eyes reached up to snap Brown's neck with a sudden twist. The body fell to the floor, and Caleb barely had time to open his mouth before Jenkins slammed into the assailant's body. The two smashed into the nearby concrete wall amidst a flurry of loud impacts being exchanged between the two combatants.

"Katrina!" Alton's voice emanated through the dark doorway, followed by a woman's angst-ridden cry.

Caleb's mind raced. *Kat's in trouble!*

He ran towards the open portal, but stopped short to reach down and retrieve an automatic pistol from the dead agent's hip holster. He preferred the rifle, but it wasn't anywhere in the immediate vicinity. The two vampires behind him continued to slam each other against walls and pound on each other as he ran through the nearby entryway.

The portal opened into a poorly lit hallway ending with stairs leading into darkness. Heedless of his footing, Caleb sped down a flight of damp concrete steps until reaching the lower level.

He stepped into a dimly illuminated concrete corridor extending left and right from where he stood. He cocked his head to one side and paused only a moment to listen. Hearing a skirmish coming from his right, he immediately headed that way.

A tall figure with glowing yellow eyes appeared from a side doorway that Caleb hadn't noticed. The figure wore a leather trench coat and paused only long enough to identify

Caleb. In a split-second the figure raced towards him.

He raised his right arm and fired his pistol, but only managed a few shots before feeling a vice-like grip at his throat. His body was thrown against the wall, and his helmet-covered head slammed backwards with a loud clanking thud as it impacted the concrete.

Caleb instinctively raised the tip of his pistol and pulled the trigger rapidly. His ears hurt from the piercing sounds of gunfire as he began to choke under the vampire's grasp. A sharp, painful shock ran through his neck, and then abruptly ceased. The figure stepped back slightly, revealing blood running from his jaw as his eyes flared bright yellow.

Before he could react further, Caleb's body uncontrollably slid down against the wall, stopping only when his body hit the floor. The yellow-eyed figure started towards him again, but then disappeared from his view in the blink of an eye. He turned his head sideways to see Alton jam a combat knife underneath the vampire's chin and into his head.

Alton slammed the vampire to the ground as if casting a sack of flour to his feet.

Caleb heard a gasp to his right and immediately raised his arm to point his pistol down the hallway as he rotated his head that direction. His hand shook uncontrollably as he struggled to draw air into his lungs while trying to sight a target before him.

A second later, he recognized the oncoming figure as Katrina. Her eyes blazed brightly, and she stopped a few feet from him as her attention focused on the pistol in his hand.

He lowered his arm, and she was swiftly at his side. She reached out to take the weapon from his still-shaking hand, while using her free hand to swivel his head to the side so that she could see his neck.

Dammit, Caleb! Why didn't you stay put?!

"Are you okay?" she managed to ask in a strained voice, struggling to keep her emotions in check.

He nodded affirmatively while reaching up to his still-aching neck with one hand.

"What the hell were you thinking?!" she rasped.

"Get him topside," Alton commanded as he glanced down at Caleb. "It's not secure down here yet."

Caleb tried to rise, but his legs were only partially under his control, and he still had trouble catching his breath. Katrina frowned and reached down with one hand to grasp him by the combat vest just beneath his chin.

With one lurch, she stood upright, and Caleb felt himself floating above the floor. He glanced down, realizing that he was suspended before her.

She turned and began walking with him. As Caleb was facing her, he noticed Alton smirk at her and issue, "Have Brown come down here."

"Brown's dead," Caleb managed to utter in a broken, choked voice. His throat still ached badly.

Katrina's expression hardened, though she kept walking as Alton called, "Fine, then whoever's still alive up there!"

It was surreal to look upon Katrina's stony expression while also feeling himself floating before her as they ascended the stairs leading back to the open portal. He felt like a rag doll being carried in a child's hand.

"Show off," he mumbled in the same raspy voice. "This is embarrassing."

Her glowing eyes bore into his, but he thought that he saw the corners of her mouth upturn slightly. "You should've thought of that before you disobeyed me," she countered.

Moments later, she carried him into the main room where Brown's body lay on the floor. Jenkins looked up with a startled expression as she gently deposited Caleb on the leather couch against the nearby wall as easily as setting down a sack of groceries. The dead vampire combatant from earlier lay motionless on the floor not far from where Jenkins stood.

"Alton said to get downstairs on the double," she ordered flatly.

The vampire disappeared from view, and her attention returned to Caleb. *Thank God he's okay*, she rejoiced. *Now I should strangle him myself!*

The terror she had felt from seeing him crumpled on the floor downstairs had nearly been unbearable.

"Mad at me?" he asked in a less raspy-sounding voice.

She reached down to place the palm of her hand against the side of his face and used her free hand to unstrap his helmet and lift it from his head. She rotated the back of the helmet where he could see it, and he saw a large dented area where it had impacted the downstairs wall. His eyes widened in shock from the damage done.

"That could have been your head," she declared sternly. "You could be dead right now from that, if not strangled, or your neck snapped by that vampire downstairs. Although I noticed that you managed to get off a lucky shot to his jaw before anything fatal happened. So yeah, you could say I'm not happy right now."

He swallowed hard and managed to whisper, "But I heard a woman scream and thought you were in trouble. I had to help you somehow."

"So, you think I'm the only female vampire around here," she countered, but realized he had no way of knowing that. Her features softened somewhat, and she sat down next to him while maintaining eye contact.

He noticed that her eyes began to return to their normal hue.

"My love," she said gently, again touching his cheek with her palm. "My foolhardy, but brave, love."

Alton appeared at the top of the stairs and walked over to where they were seated. He glanced down at Caleb with a slightly raised eyebrow and touched Katrina on the shoulder lightly. "They managed to take one of two notebook computers that must have been their data collection systems. And at least one of them escaped through a metal grate leading into the city sewer system," he reported. "The area seems clear for now. Counting the one up here and the escaped one, there must have been six of them. It was pretty clear that none of them intended to be taken alive."

"Not surprising, given the way they fought," Katrina replied. "So, is this just the tip of the iceberg?"

"It would seem," Alton replied absently, as if already deep in thought.

"Hey Alton," Caleb offered. "I found your couch."

Alton looked up with a smirk while shaking his head. "Trouble-making scamp."

* * *

It was after midnight by the time Katrina and Caleb returned to the hotel. They stopped by Alton's office building to change back into their normal clothes before making their way back to their suite. Despite his pain-wracked body and exhaustion, Caleb insisted on a shower before collapsing into bed.

Katrina lay beside him, observing him sleeping soundly, and appreciated how peaceful and innocent he looked.

He shouldn't have accompanied us tonight.

She felt more comfortable having him close by, but detested his being in harm's way, even though he had been so insistent about it and complained so little once it was over.

Caleb's a real trooper that way.

She glanced at her wristwatch, noting it was after two o'clock, and stared out the window to the city beyond. While still overcast with thick dark clouds, the cold misting rain from earlier had stopped, leaving the city with a gloomy appearance.

Perfect vampire weather. Perhaps a walk?

After tying her hair into a neat pony-tail, she slipped into jeans, a sweater, and some leather boots and grabbed her leather jacket. It wasn't as if she needed it, but it was all about a proper public appearance and not attracting too much attention. It was at such times that she appreciated many of the qualities of her body's stamina, including the lack of impact from cold weather.

Following a final glance at Caleb, she slipped quietly

from the hotel room and proceeded downstairs. She went to the underground corridor connecting to Alton's office building and into the underground Tube station. From there, she walked to a nearby Tube system exit and onto the streets of London.

She wandered for an hour or so, appreciating the change of scenery from Atlanta. It had been many years since she last roamed the streets of London alone at night. Memories of another time flooded her thoughts, a time when such wandering was a requirement for stalking prey, a meal.

Sort of glad those days are long gone.

She loved to hunt as much as the next vampire, but it was tedious to have to hunt so frequently and an inefficient use of her spare time. But with the evolution of blood banks, refrigeration, and easy blood access came the boredom and the need for diversions that kept life interesting.

Now Caleb kept her life interesting. *He fulfills me in ways that I haven't enjoyed since being human.*

Memories of her late human husband, Samuel, came to mind. He had been a wonderful husband and a caring father to their children. Samuel was taken from her all too soon, and the children followed. After her turning, centuries of failed partners left her bitter and jaded. Finally, Caleb entered her life, first as a child helping her out of a dire circumstance, and later as a romantic partner, a true mate.

Not since Samuel had she found such an excellent pairing for her: a lover, a soul mate. Life felt complete again.

As the late-night walk continued, she tried to imagine life without Caleb. Just the thought of his absence sent a wave of sadness through her.

He's going to grow older and eventually die.

It was at that moment that she made the critical decision: *If it's his preference, I'll turn him. He'd like that, I bet. He'd be an amazing vampire.*

But she also realized that he wasn't quite ready yet.

Or rather, I'm not ready yet. I like him as a human for now, and he still has some maturing to do. Given a few more years, he'll be ready.

Like fruit on the tree, it needs time to ripen before it's plucked.

She reflected on how much he already seemed to have matured in the short time she had known him. Gone was the timid young man she had first met. He had gained self-confidence and a boldness of character. Yet he also needed to temper his enthusiasm with a better appreciation for the dangers facing him.

That's the maturity he needs to gain most of all. It will come in time with a little mentoring from me. Paige will be helpful, as well.

The thought of her friend and former pupil caused a pause in her musings regarding Caleb. The perky vampire had acted strangely as of late. Certainly, a reasonable period of time had been expected to pass for an investigation into the deaths of Gil Yeager and his friend to leave Paige in the clear. However, it had already been ruled an accident by the authorities. Just another senseless drug-related death, the L.A. Times had proclaimed. Marijuana had been found in both victims' systems, and the late-night conditions, coupled with the sharply curving seaside road, had provided an easy explanation for the men's deaths.

So, what's kept Paige from restoring contact with us the past four weeks? It's certainly bothered Caleb recently. Naturally, I'm going to have to deal with that soon, I think. She's important to us: a close friend and his surrogate vampire.

She sighed, glanced at her watch, and was surprised that she had been wandering the city streets for nearly three hours. She had enjoyed her walk through town, but daylight would be coming before long. Besides, she didn't want Caleb to wake and find her gone.

It's not like he couldn't call my cell phone. Her eyes widened as she felt inside her coat pockets and failed to feel a phone. I must have left it lying on the nightstand.

She walked quickly in the direction of the hotel, making sure not to move inhumanly fast for fear of being noticed or caught on one of the numerous public cameras casing the city. Vampires had to be more cognizant of such technological developments if they wanted to maintain their anonymity.

She finally decided to use the Tube for her journey back to the hotel and arrived within thirty minutes.

When she entered the suite, her keen hearing detected a rapid heartbeat, and her eyes immediately targeted Caleb as he stood in the dark living room before the large window looking out upon the city. She easily saw his concerned expression as he stood with his arms folded before him. She tossed her jacket onto the couch and moved in a blur to stand behind him, wrapping him in her arms.

He winced slightly as pain ran through his chest and shoulders as she hugged him. However, he clenched his jaw against the discomfort, not wanting to admit it to her. He didn't want her to exclude him from adventurous events in the future if they should arise.

However, she easily detected his body's reaction and noted his lack of verbal acknowledgement to it. *He's trying to hide it from me again.*

"What are you doing up?" she asked.

"I woke up about ten minutes ago and found you gone," he said in a tired voice. "And I worried you were out on an additional adventure with Alton or something."

She smiled, appreciating the warmth of his body, as well as his concern for her wellbeing. "I didn't mean to worry you, my love," she replied. "Just enjoying a walk."

He realized her opportunity to be outdoors began at sunset, and he tried to be supportive of that. Still, she seemed somewhat somber, and he frowned.

"Everything okay?" he asked tentatively as his arms reached behind him to embrace her awkwardly.

"More than okay," she assured him. "Everything's perfect."

He smiled at her tone and sighed happily. *I couldn't agree more.*

"Now, back to bed," she ordered mildly, though she anticipated no argument.

She removed her arms from around him, and he slowly

walked back into the bedroom. He turned off the lamp on the nightstand and sat gingerly on the edge of the bed while swallowing some ibuprofen and sipping from a nearby glass of water.

Meanwhile, she slipped out of her clothes, quickly slid beneath the covers, and held the sheet and blankets up for him to nestle underneath. Given that the room's temperature felt a little chill to him, he kept his sweatpants and t-shirt on and lay carefully back in bed.

She covered him up, gently nestled next to him, and kissed him affectionately on the back of the neck.

She lay next to him in the dark, listening to his strong heartbeat and regular breathing as he drifted back off to sleep. And despite not really needing the sleep, she dozed for a couple of hours herself.

* * *

By Thursday, Caleb was still quite sore, but made an effort to mask it from Katrina, deliberately telling her he felt just fine. However, she knew better and purposefully selected low-impact activities for them.

When he had toured the city with the Fullers, he located a few museums and tourist sites that could be accessed indoors via the Tube. She selected a couple of locations not far from the hotel, and they used the Tube to cover the distance to them.

Once there, she found frequent excuses to sit and "observe" paintings, sculptures, or other interests to allow him to rest. He was silently appreciative.

Halfway through the day at one such "observational stop," he put his arm around her and commented quietly, "You know it. And I know you know it. But thanks for not saying anything, just the same."

She smirked, having deciphered the nature of his comment, and kissed him lightly on the lips. *Anytime, my love.*

They returned to the hotel early, and Caleb took a long

nap before dinner. By evening, he was still quite sore, but felt much more rested. They went out to dinner at a locally owned restaurant specializing in Italian and had a wonderful, romantic time together.

They laughed, held hands across the table, and shared a bottle of dessert wine until late in the evening.

Another perfect day together, Katrina thought happily as she lay beside him in bed that night.

The brief remainder of the week went smoothly with no interruptions from wayward vampires, or assailants, or even any adventurous errands with Alton. Katrina and Caleb spent time together relaxing and enjoying each other's company. It felt like a real getaway, a true vacation. Thanks to the more sedate pace of activities, Caleb's body also recuperated, and by late Friday he felt more his usual self.

During the early part of the day, the Fullers returned to take him out on the town. However, they made sure to use a car and stay in the daylight, completely avoiding the Tube. It was very enjoyable, and Caleb was able to see sights located on the outer parts of the city, including a brief drive out to the country to see a more pastoral side of England.

Alton shared part of the early evening with them and took them out to dinner again at Shakespeare's. This time, Caleb tried the Shepherd's Pie and discovered that, much to his surprise, he found mutton somewhat tasty.

"I've really enjoyed seeing you again, Alton," he offered at dinner. "And thanks for saving my life the other night."

Alton observed him with an appraising expression. "No thanks are necessary, dear boy. And it's been wonderful seeing you again, to be brutally honest. Perhaps we'll see each other again this summer. There's a European conference on the horizon I've asked Katrina to attend, you see."

Caleb's eyes rose with speculative interest, while Katrina looked at Alton sharply, muttering, "Perhaps. We'll have to see."

Alton assumed a diplomatic expression and quietly sipped from a glass of rare vintage wine. "Our information systems staff have discovered that Davison was accessing reports of our surveillance activities in London," he informed them. "He was copying those reports and providing them to his contacts stationed in the Tube tunnels. It's likely that Caleb and the Fullers interrupted a 'data drop' that day at the station. And I suspect they took the leather couch as a bit of an inside joke, operating right under our noses, so to speak."

He paused for a moment to let that sink in before changing the subject. "I hope, despite a couple of speed bumps, you've enjoyed your holiday to England," he ventured.

Katrina glared at the dark-haired vampire from across the table and chastised, "Speed bumps? You have a gift for understatement, Alton."

"It's been very educational, actually," Caleb replied easily and added with a smirk: "I learned never to turn my back on a wounded vampire."

Katrina arched an eyebrow as she glanced at her mate, while Alton nodded.

"Well said, my boy. Now finish your wine. It's very old and expensive."

Katrina merely rolled her eyes while Caleb grinned. He once again marveled at the fact that he was sitting down to dinner with beings who had lived on Earth for five hundred years and more.

Vampires are absolutely amazing. Well, when they're not busy trying to terrify or kill you, that is.

Katrina caught his attention with a sparkle in her eyes, and he smiled warmly.

But most of all, when they love you, it's like being the center of their universe.

* * *

Early Friday evening, Katrina and Caleb paid a final, brief visit to Dr. Guilhelm. The three of them had a productive discussion regarding Caleb's progress in dealing with his new memories.

Later that evening, it was time for them to bid goodbye to Alton and the city of London. The stately vampire seemed quite sincere when voicing his regrets over the unplanned events that had overshadowed their stay. He promised a completely different experience if they were able to visit again. He even accompanied them in the limousine ride to the airport.

Katrina hugged her tall friend and former mentor, kissed him on the cheek affectionately, and whispered in a sincere tone, "Alton, you've been a consummate host for both Caleb and me. Thank you for everything. And come visit when you can. We'd both like that."

Alton nodded and kissed her on the cheek in return. "Count on it," he muttered with a disarming smile. Then he turned to Caleb and reached out to shake his hand.

But this time, it was Caleb who pulled Alton towards him and clasped him on the back briefly in a partial hug. The vampire chuckled and grinned with approval as they parted.

"Try to stay out of trouble, scamp," he teased.

"Keep an eye on your couches," Caleb replied.

Minutes later, Katrina and Caleb boarded the Sunset Air flight. Once they settled into their cabin, which was as elaborate and comfortable as the one in which they had traveled to England, Caleb felt his eyelids growing heavy. He had been on the go since early that morning. But the day's events had finally caught up with him, and he yawned dramatically.

Katrina smirked, settling down beside him. She rotated in her seat and kissed him warmly. "I love you," she offered after their lips parted.

He smiled. "Love you too."

Soon after takeoff, Caleb fell asleep, remaining that way for most of the return flight. Katrina frequently glanced at him fondly and read the mystery novel she had started back at the hotel.

CHAPTER 9

Reconciliation

Caleb and Katrina arrived back home in Atlanta on Saturday evening at the end of spring break. While Caleb had enjoyed his first venture outside of the country, at least the part not relating to being pursued or attacked by vampires, he was nevertheless happy to be safely back home.

It was evident by Katrina's lighter disposition that she felt the same. She called Alton and Devon Archibald to let them know they had returned home, while he called Paige.

Unfortunately, he had to leave voicemail for her since she didn't pick up. It was yet another unanswered call in a series since February, which bothered him a great deal.

I wonder what's up with her? Maybe it's the situation with Gil, he wondered.

It seemed reasonable to expect that such an event would have disturbed her, at any rate.

He spent the remainder of the weekend readjusting his body's internal clock to their home time zone. Naturally, Katrina seemed to be completely unaffected by the change, but she was both understanding and accommodating of his eating and sleeping adjustments.

Yet another enviable condition of being a vampire, he considered wistfully.

367

The next week was rather hard on him. Returning to the routine of teaching after such an international experience seemed surreal. In addition, Paige still hadn't returned his repeated calls and voicemails, a fact he mentioned to Katrina. Her response had been rather subdued, but it was evident to him that she was equally displeased.

Fortunately, Tanisha Browning was only too happy to listen to his overseas experiences, which were naturally devoid of any adventures involving vampires.

Still, he mentioned seeing Alton, whom he described as a close friend of Katrina's who operated an investment firm in downtown London.

By the second week following their return, Katrina received a request from Alton to fly to Richmond, Virginia to meet with prospective participants regarding the upcoming summer vampire convention. At least, that's how Caleb recalled the explanation.

In the end, it meant she had to leave town on a Tuesday evening with an expected return during the weekend.

By that time, he had stopped looking into dark corners or empty hallways expecting to see a rogue vampire jump out at him. His confidence was bolstered by the appearance of Devon Archibald in and around his office on the evenings that he taught. For once, he hadn't minded the hulking vampire's presence.

As a thoughtful gesture, Caleb gave Devon a leather-bound trilogy of plays by William Shakespeare he had purchased in London. The towering vampire had been pleased by the gift and even discussed some classic literature he'd been reading of late. Caleb found their interactions pleasantly unexpected and began to form a tentative appreciation for Devon's company.

By Wednesday evening, another of Caleb's failed attempts to contact Paige resulted in his throwing his phone across the room. It wasn't until Katrina called later that evening that he went to pick it up off the floor. The situation was starting to get to him, and an idea born of desperation formed in his mind.

If she refuses to return my contact attempts, then I'm just going to go hunt her down.

The only mitigation to his idea was Katrina; he definitely wanted her buy-in on the matter before proceeding. And he wanted to speak to her in person about it.

First, he reserved a late-night flight to Richmond using the exclusive credit card she had issued to him. Following his last class Thursday evening, he rushed home and packed a suitcase with a few days' worth of clothing.

He drove his car to the airport, parked in the extended parking area, and flew to Richmond.

Taking a taxi to the hotel where Katrina was staying, he acquired a key under the auspices of being her fiancé. The shared credit card account was particularly helpful for convincing the desk clerk, as well as a discreet cash gratuity, so he could surprise her.

When Katrina entered the hotel room, she nearly froze in place, seeing Caleb lying on the bed reading a novel he had brought with him.

"What are you doing here, my love?" she asked carefully.

"Hi, Kat," he offered, setting the book aside. "Just wanted to surprise you, that's all."

"I'm surprised," she conceded with raised eyebrows as she moved to sit on the edge of the bed beside him. She glanced at the novel he was reading and asked, "What're you reading?"

He grinned. "Oh, just *Twilight.* It's a vampire romance. It's actually pretty good. You should read it sometime. It's the first in a series."

She shook her head, smirked, and chastised mildly, "I'm sure. But isn't the reality of being with an actual vampire enough for you?"

He shrugged. "Well, truth is stranger than fiction. But what can I say? I'm a hopeless romantic, and maybe I can identify a little bit."

"I could use a little of that romance," she suggested.

He smirked. "Lucky I arrived when I did."

Following a passionate interlude, hot shower, and time holding her in his arms, Caleb broached the weighty subject on his mind. "I was hoping to ask you about something while I was here," he ventured carefully.

She heard his heartbeat increase anxiously and lifted her head from his chest to gaze into his eyes. "Oh?" she inquired.

"I'm concerned about Paige," he began, to which she frowned slightly.

"Oh, yeah, that," she noted.

"I feel like our friendship is on the line. And, well, I want to fly out to California and find out what's going on," he explained. "Of course, I'd like your blessing on the idea first."

Her eyes narrowed, and she regarded him for a few quiet moments. "And what if I said no?"

He seemed surprised by her question, but replied earnestly, "Well, I wouldn't go then."

"So, if I forbid it, then you won't go?" she pressed.

He looked directly into her eyes and touched the pendant around his neck. "I won't defy you, Kat. I'm your mate."

Her eyes flashed for a mere second, and her lips upturned ever so slightly.

He knew immediately that she liked his response.

That's exactly what I needed to hear, she thought with satisfaction.

She kissed him. "Fine, I approve."

She laid her head down on his chest, appreciating the strong sound of his heartbeat, which had calmed considerably after her issuance of approval.

"When are you leaving?" she quietly asked.

"Well, seeing as it's Thursday night, and I need to be back by Sunday night, I'd like to go—"

"Tomorrow morning. I understand," she interrupted. "I suppose you've already booked a flight from here?"

"Um, just in case you said yes," he replied sheepishly. He hadn't counted on her approval, but thought it best to be prepared just in case.

She chuckled. "You're unpredictable sometimes, my love. But then, I suppose it keeps life interesting, doesn't it?"

He merely smiled, not wanting to risk saying something stupid in response. Instead, he settled down to a few hours of sleep before he got up to prepare for his quick shuttle to the airport.

His flight to the west coast was aided by the upgrade of his tickets to first class, which Katrina had naturally insisted upon. He had initially resisted the suggestion, not wanting her to spend the additional funds, but she had merely smirked.

"The cost is of no consequence, you know," she told him. It was one of the few times she alluded to her financial state, which he knew was considerable after five hundred years or more of development. "Travel under my terms or not at all," she had insisted with an air of superiority. She could be quite imposing when she wanted to, and he felt the better part of valor was to acquiesce peaceably.

He had rolled his eyes and agreed, not wanting either to insult her persistent generosity or risk changing her mind about his trip altogether. Still, he felt that she spent too much money on him. It wasn't something he was used to in his life. He even felt uncomfortable carrying the exclusive credit card in his wallet. Still, it made his vacation purchases much easier to abide. His personal credit card wouldn't have lasted the trip.

European vacations sure are expensive, he had reflected on their flight home.

As he reclined in his first-class seat thinking back on events, he shook his head. His mate was one of the kindest, most loving women he could ever imagine.

How did I ever get so lucky? I certainly don't deserve her.

After a change of flights in Denver, the last leg of his journey went by quickly. He tried not to think about his upcoming meeting with Paige, though he was looking forward to seeing her. He hated confrontation and anticipated that she had been avoiding him for some reason that eluded him.

So he distracted himself with some in-flight music. He also tried reading more of Twilight. Given his current circumstances, he found the melodrama of the storyline a little too close to home, despite the expert quality of the author's writing.

If only vampire relationships could work out like in the romance novels, he thought darkly as he slipped the book back into his carry-on bag. *Still, sometimes relationships are just plain difficult, vampires or not.*

Finally, he watched part of an unremarkable film playing on the small monitor built into the back of the seat in front of him. After wiping down with a complementary hot towel and briefly napping, he sat quietly as the flight made its descent into Los Angeles.

It was early evening, and he was thankful for having gained a couple of additional daylight hours by coming west, though he'd miss those hours when he flew back Georgia.

After picking up his luggage and acquiring a taxi, he gave Paige's address to the driver and sat back in the seat to stare at the passing sites. It was remarkably warm for a March evening, and he marveled at seeming to have changed seasons as well as time zones by flying out to California.

It was his first visit to the west coast, and he momentarily wished that Katrina were there with him, partly because he loved traveling with her and partly because he dreaded his eventual meeting with Paige.

He took a moment to text Katrina to let her know he had arrived safely and was on his way to Paige's. He had just enough time to look up at the beautiful sky and waning sunset before her reply arrived.

Glad U R safely on ground. Call when U arrive @ Paige's condo.

Well, she's trying, he mused.

Another message arrived: *Luv U. Kat.*

He smiled as a warm feeling flowed through him. Then he leaned back against the seat with a sigh and tried to enjoy the ride. At least he didn't have to drive in an unfamiliar place, particularly at night. The traffic was fairly heavy, and he thought it would take the patience of Job to navigate through it on a daily basis.

Still, it was Los Angeles.

Darkness had fallen fully by the time the taxi finally delivered him to the address he'd given the driver. He almost thought there had been some mistake when Paige's two-story condominium proved to be one half of a duplex structure and appeared quite ordinary, though relatively new. It was a mix of reddish-brown brick and white vinyl siding. The surrounding neighborhood was a series of duplexes on both sides of three successive streets with medium-sized homes built on either side of the condominium neighborhood. Somehow, Caleb had envisioned something a little grander, or at least edgier, for Paige.

There wasn't a car in the driveway, but perhaps it was already inside the single-car garage. He shrugged, paid the driver his fee and a handsome tip, and took his luggage in hand. As the car pulled away, he silently appreciated the large quantity of cash that Katrina had forced upon him before heading out west. The amount of the cab fare had surprised him.

Score another one for Kat's generosity.

He sat his luggage on Paige's small front porch and rang the doorbell. Fortunately, the porch light was on, casting a comforting glow against the surrounding darkness. He paused and rang the doorbell again.

Vampires have excellent hearing and move as quickly as lightning, so Paige probably isn't home.

"Hm, sunset wasn't long ago, so I must have just missed her," he muttered under his breath. He honestly hadn't anticipated that possibility and pursed his lips as he considered his next action.

I probably should've called her when I landed.

Although he admitted he had been too reluctant to do so at the time.

Damn.

He pulled out his phone and called Paige. Her cell rang until rolling to voicemail.

"Crap," he muttered before redialing the number again. Once again it went to voicemail. So, he sent a text message to her: *Guess who? Big surprise for you!*

He sat on the worn wooden bench with wrought iron arms that sat next to Paige's front door and proceeded to call Katrina. Unlike Paige, his mate picked up on the second ring.

"Caleb? Are you at Paige's yet?" she asked in a concerned tone.

"Yep."

"And? Is she upset?"

He shrugged and replied irritably, "Don't know, Kat. She's not here; won't even answer my calls or return my text message. The sun already set by the time I arrived, so she's probably out doing...something."

There was a pause at Katrina's end of the phone for a few seconds, and he frowned. *Are you still there?*

"Maybe you should call a cab and check into a hotel, my love," she finally suggested.

A wave of annoyance flashed through his mind, and he clenched his teeth together tightly for a moment.

"Did you just grit your teeth?" she asked.

That startled him, and he blinked while abruptly relaxing his jaw. "Sorry," he apologized. "It wasn't you, naturally. I'm just annoyed, that's all."

She sighed wistfully, as if in a sympathetic manner.

He considered her advice and made an instant decision based more upon his temper than anything else. "No, I'm going to just sit here until she comes home," he insisted. "After all, she's bound to show up before morning."

"I don't like that idea," Katrina objected.

"I texted her," he countered. "She'll see my message and either call or text me back, and I can tell her I'm waiting at her condo."

"I'm not comfortable with that idea, Caleb," she insisted sternly.

There was no misunderstanding the tone of concern and displeasure in her voice, and he slumped dejectedly against the back of the bench. "Just give her an hour or so, and then I'll leave another detailed message," he negotiated. "How's that?"

She made a growling sound at the other end.

She just growled at me, he thought with wide eyes.

"One hour," Katrina stipulated. "Then call her again, and call me."

He paused for dramatic effect. "Okay, agreed."

"Okay," she concurred in a friendlier tone. "And please be careful."

"Will do," he promised and added: "Love you."

She made a purring sound. "I love you too."

The call ended, and he shook his head putting his phone away. He sighed and settled back to get comfortable.

It really seems like a peaceful neighborhood.

He watched an occasional car pass by and tried reading the vampire novel again. After twenty minutes, he sat it aside and closed his eyes to rest. As he relaxed, he failed to notice himself drifting off to sleep.

* * *

Katrina heated up a glass of blood in her hotel room microwave as she considered her conversation with Caleb. It annoyed her that Paige was acting so strange, and it frustrated her that she was disregarding Caleb's calls and text messages.

That's no way for a guardian to act, much less a close friend.

The more she thought about it, the more it upset her. She expected Paige to act more responsibly towards her and especially towards Caleb.

"Dammit!" she cursed and picked up her cell phone to speed dial Paige's number. The phone rang until going to voicemail, so she redialed again.

Failing that, Katrina sent a rapid text message to her: *CALL ME NOW! Red.*

Less than thirty seconds later, the phone rang. It was Paige.

"'Bout time!" Katrina barked into the receiver.

She heard the sound of loud rock music and voices trying to talk over it in the background as Paige answered, "What? I'm busy."

Out clubbing, I see, Katrina considered irritably.

"Sorry to bother you, but my mate is trying to get hold of you," she complained. "Maybe you could spare him the time of day?"

"Why? What's he done now?" Paige asked flatly.

Katrina's eyes flashed with anger, and she spat, "Wasting his time trying to see you, it seems. I should've told him no."

There was a pause at the other end, and Katrina thought she heard a slight intake of breath mixed with the sound of the rock music.

"What do you mean by 'trying to see you'?" Paige demanded in a quieter voice.

Katrina adopted a smug expression and replied, "As in, he's sitting on your front porch right now, and I'm half tempted to send a cab to get his butt to the airport. You're obviously too wrapped up in yourself for him to bother you."

"Crap," was all Paige muttered in a withering tone of voice. "Why did you let him do that?" she asked weakly.

Katrina inhaled a deep breath, let it out slowly, and answered patiently, "Because he flew all the way to where I'm at just to ask my permission. He misses you and doesn't understand why you've been avoiding him. As a matter of fact, neither do I."

"He flew to see you?" Paige asked blankly. "I thought you two just got back from England together. Where are you, anyway?"

"Oh, now you're curious?!" Katrina demanded.

"Okay, okay," Paige retorted defensively, "Geez, I made a mistake, all right? He's fine on my front porch; it's a nice neighborhood."

"*Not* all right and *not* the point," Katrina objected coldly.

Given all that had happened recently, she didn't like the idea of Caleb's being left alone in a strange place.

Paige emitted a heavy sigh, conceding, "Yes, I know, not the point. I'm on my way."

"Thank you," Katrina replied. "Bye, Paige."

She ended the call and casually tossed the cell phone onto the nearby bed. She removed the warm blood from the microwave and took a sip with a degree of satisfaction. She sat on the edge of the bed, slipped her feet from her high-heeled shoes, and stretched her toes out before her.

Paige is acting like a spoiled teenager.

* * *

Paige whipped her red BMW sports coupe into the driveway and immediately noticed Caleb sitting on the bench on her front porch.

Is he asleep? she wondered as she pulled her car into the garage and sped around the corner to where he sat.

Her frown turned into a smirk as she viewed him slumped against the back of the bench with his head cocked to one side and his mouth open as he slept.

He's so damn cute...Stop! That's exactly why you feel the way you do about him.

She cleared her throat audibly and perched her hands atop her hips as she waited for him to come around. After a moment, she stretched her leg out with the pointed heel of one of her stilettos, tapping him on the thigh as she cleared her throat again.

He stirred slightly and slowly opened his eyes as he yawned into a closed fist. His vision slowly focused on Paige as she stood before him. He took a moment to admire her in the tight-fitted black denim jeans and black leather halter top. He also took notice of the sexy, black high-heeled shoes. His eyes widened somewhat, and he adopted a playful grin as his pale blue eyes met her bright blue ones.

However, she merely glared at him. "I should bite you in

the neck for showing up here like this," she threatened.

That caught him off guard, and his smile immediately faded. *What's wrong with her? And just what've I done to make her so cross with me?*

"Well, you're here, so get up off the bench and come inside," she ordered with aggravation evident in her voice, leading the way back around the corner into the garage.

He blinked with confusion, picked up his luggage, and followed her into the dimly lit garage. He immediately noticed her sports car. "Wow! Your car's amazing!" he gaped, carefully sliding past it via the narrow space next to the wall.

"Yeah, well, don't scratch it, or I'll take it out of your hide," she challenged.

He frowned but didn't say anything as she led him into the house, pressing the garage door button on the wall as she entered. *She's not usually so mean to me.*

The garage door shut behind them, and she stepped aside in the small kitchen to let him pass before shutting the door leading into the garage.

Caleb appraised his surroundings as he sat his luggage in the small hallway leading to the front door just outside the kitchen. A small dining room combined with the kitchen and opened into a large living room with a high ceiling. To the left of the living room was a carpeted staircase leading up to the second level.

The living room was decorated in a surprisingly conservative manner with a white leather couch, glass coffee and end tables, and leather recliner. A plasma TV hung on the wall above a gas fireplace and white-painted wood mantle. He noticed that a small surround sound system had been installed in the ceiling, and a fully stocked media equipment rack was built into the wall next to the fireplace.

He turned to look at Paige with a hopeful smile. "Nice digs," he complimented.

She returned a flat expression and shrugged. "Thanks."

He bit his lower lip and sighed. *Damn, she's cold. What the hell?*

"Why are you here, Caleb?" she asked pointedly before he had a chance to consider the situation further.

He was taken aback by her query and noted she hadn't used any of the typical nicknames to address him since he arrived. Instead of playing games with further pointless banter, he simply looked her straight in the eyes with a hurt expression. "I had to see you. What have I done wrong? Why are you so pissed at me?"

She closed her eyes and sighed. *I can't be near you, that's all. I don't want to hurt you or Katrina.*

When she didn't answer, he reached out to grasp her hand in his own, and her eyes immediately snapped open. She jerked her hand from his and gestured towards the living room. "Don't do that," she snapped. "Just go sit in there or something. Do you want something to drink? I might have a soda in the fridge, I think."

He felt like she had physically slapped him, and he nearly winced. He shrugged and moved into the living room to sit on one end of the couch. "No, thanks," he replied glumly.

She immediately noticed how her actions and tone had bothered him, and a surge of both guilt and shame flowed through her all at once. She never meant to hurt him.

Dammit kiddo, why did you have to come out here looking for me?

She moved to stand on the other side of the coffee table, staring down at him with her arms crossed before her.

"You look really great," he offered. "Nice strappy shoes. I like them even better than the red ones you bought at the mall last Christmas."

She bit back a smirk as she fondly recalled the shopping trip he, Katrina, and she had gone on. He had helped her pick out some high-heeled shoes that evening, which were one of her favorite pairs to that day. But the memory only sent a fresh emotional pain through her. "Thanks," she replied politely, yet distantly.

He paused, uncertain how to proceed, completely taken aback by his reception. *Maybe coming was a mistake, he thought sourly. I wish Kat were here. She'd know what to say or do.*

Paige studied him and almost saw the wheels turning in his mind. Actually, his sensitive pale blue eyes spoke volumes to her.

Silent moments passed before either spoke.

"I'm sorry I came," Caleb finally said in a defeated tone of voice. "We're supposed to be best friends. But I think coming here was a mistake. I apologize for bothering you."

He wearily rose from the couch and moved towards his luggage as his mind raced with how to call for a cab. *Maybe I can call Katrina for a 1-800 number.*

"Where are you going?" she asked suddenly, stepping in front of him.

He looked up with confusion and started to speak but words failed him. "What?" was all he managed to get out.

"Red would kill me if I sent you out at this time of night," she explained.

"Well, I'm sure as hell not staying where I'm not wanted," he grumbled. "I'm already feeling like crap as it is." He turned to go around the other end of the coffee table, but she met him at the other end following a dart of movement. He had seen this before, of course, and realized that he wasn't getting past her unless she allowed it.

"Come on, just let me go," he said dejectedly as he looked over to his luggage across the room. "I won't bother you anymore." As soon as he said that, a wave of sadness washed over him so strongly that it nearly stopped him dead in his tracks. He swallowed hard and briefly looked into her eyes.

Why did it have to be this way?

She stared into his eyes, plainly seeing the pain she had generated in them. It hurt her worse than if he had punched her in the gut. Well, a lot worse, actually, because few humans could generate the kind of impact needed to cause that much pain to a vampire's body. She would have smirked at the realization had it not been for the look on his face.

Instead, she was left with only previously unfelt levels of self-loathing. Even killing Gil had caused less turbulent emotions than she was feeling at that moment.

Despite all of her attempts to shut him out, she merely felt the urge to reach out to him. She moved in a blur and wrapped her arms around him, pulling him to her in a firm embrace. It surprised her that her body had reacted almost before her mind registered what she had done, and she felt his body's muscles tighten in response.

"What?" he started to demand.

"Sh," she interrupted. "I'm sorry, kiddo. I can't do this to you anymore."

I just can't keep hurting him. And it's sure as hell not helping me!

He stood dumbfounded in her arms, remaining silent as his mind raced to process all that was happening. He felt completely out of his element at the moment. "I don't understand," he murmured.

She sighed and swiftly drew him onto the couch while still holding him in her arms. The velocity of her movement caught him by surprise, and he lost his breath for a moment as he bounced on the cushions.

She encircled him with one arm as she leaned back into the couch cushions next to him.

"Well, tiger, it looks like I'm damned if I do and damned if I don't," she muttered with resignation.

"Paige, what the hell are you talking about?" he demanded in a confused voice.

What's with the emotional rollercoaster? Do vampires get PMS?

She sighed. "I've been trying to avoid you and Katrina lately."

"Um, *duh!*" he retorted irritably. "Like we haven't noticed that."

She sensed his frustration in addition to his exhaustion. She took a deep breath and released her tight embrace, but still kept her arm draped lazily across his shoulder. "Okay, here we go," she began. "I'm a little scared by some recent feelings."

He frowned. "You? Scared?"

"Yeah. You see, I've never felt like this about a human

before, and it's unsettling."

"And by 'human' you mean…" he asked dimly.

"You, goofy," she chided.

"Me? But Gil—"

"No," she interrupted. "It's not like Gil at all. Gil was sex, and partying, and frustration."

"I can be frustrating," he observed.

She smirked. "On occasion, but not like Gil. He was unbearable."

He took a few seconds to digest everything she was telling him a rush of exhaustion wash over him. The traveling, dreading, worrying, and length of time he spent over it had finally caught up with him. But he was determined to get through it and try to understand everything and maybe salvage a friendship in the process.

"This is entirely new territory for me," she continued.

Another quiet moment passed. Me too, he thought.

"Well," he began uncertainly, "maybe if you try to describe it, that'll help. Just say the first things that pop into your mind when you think about your feelings. And me, I guess."

She nodded and considered him for a moment with an introspective expression. This was a whole new situation to her, and it made her feel insecure: yet another completely new feeling for her. Usually, she felt uniquely in control at all times, even when unpredictable things happened around her.

"Okay, thinking about you," she said. Her eyes narrowed slightly for a brief second, and she stared into his as she opened her mind completely to whatever entered it.

"Warmth, comfort, laughter, fun," she began, but paused for a few contemplative seconds. "Anxiety, maybe, obsession?"

"Obsession?" he asked with raised eyebrows.

She smiled wanly. "Yeah, I've been thinking a lot about you, kiddo. I miss you when you're not around, more than you might expect."

He was quite flattered and admitted, "I think about you a

lot too when you're not around."

"Teasing," she continued with a subtle smirk, to which he smiled. "Friendship, sincerity, caring, happiness, and protection."

"Protection?"

She nodded slowly. "I feel the need to protect you, keep you safe."

He nodded. *What Kat wanted from you.*

"Love," she finally said.

He smirked. "Well, I love you too."

She turned her face towards him with a serious expression and explained, "Yeah, but this is so strong. I've never felt this before. I mean, I love Katrina, but this feels a lot stronger."

He considered the revelation for a moment and admitted that he held very strong feelings for her. But it was nothing like what he felt for Katrina, and those feelings had only strengthened after the trip to England and the restoration of his childhood memories.

She watched the emotions playing across his face and arched one eyebrow. *What was he just thinking?*

Instead of asking, she continued with the exercise. "You mean so much to me. I've even saved your life with my own blood, no less. You're just so valuable to me. No, wait, that didn't sound right."

Something occurred to him that both she and Katrina had once said about vampire mates in the past. "So, do you feel possessive about me?" he asked with upraised eyebrows.

She stared into his eyes and considered that for a moment. "You know, no, not really. At least, not like Katrina seems to be towards you." She frowned. "That's interesting."

Vampire mates are usually possessive, especially about their human partners. It hadn't occurred to me to look at this from that angle before, she considered silently.

Sensing her distraction, he reached out to take her free hand in his and encouraged, "It's okay. Just keep talking it out."

She sighed and nodded. *He's being really great about this so far.*

"Caleb, I'm over a hundred years old already, and I've never felt about another person like this. Well, not a human anyway," she continued.

"Not a *human?*"

She smiled. "Yeah, well, there was this one vampire I met on a contract job in South America: Louis. He was something to behold, let me tell you. Well, it didn't work out with us, but for a while I saw him as a potential mate for me."

He nodded as he listened. But something she had just said about Louis struck him. "So, you're attracted to me, too?" he asked carefully.

She considered him for a moment and frowned. "What do you mean by that? I mean, you're an attractive man, after all."

He smirked. "Yeah, but are you wanting to, you know," he stammered. "I mean, sexually speaking..."

It dawned on her what he meant, and her eyes narrowed. *Do I want to have sex with you? She wasn't entirely opposed to the idea, but not at that moment.*

"Maybe sometimes," she replied with surprise. "But that's not at the top of my list right now."

He tried not to feel insulted by her response, instead realizing that he might have just dodged a bullet. "So, maybe love without sexual attraction then?" he asked.

A sly smile crossed her face. "Not that I'm not curious, however."

He smirked in response, silently conceding that he also found her attractive. "And blood?" he asked.

She grinned at him and nodded. "Oh yes. I definitely want your blood."

I've tasted you before, and now that I have, it's amazing.

Her response made him swallow hard, and he tensed. That was stupid.

"Wait," she reassured him, "I'm just saying, the desire for your blood is always there. But then, I guess that's a given. I'm a vampire, after all, first and foremost. But I would never just take it from you or anything. It's different with you in that way."

He nodded and relaxed a bit. Yep, that was a stupid question, he chided himself again. It had to be his fatigue hampering his ability to think more clearly. After a pause, something else occurred to him, something so important that he groaned to himself. *Idiot!*

"Crap! I was supposed to call Kat when you got here," he recalled and reached for his phone.

But she caught his wrist before he could speed dial Katrina. "Not a word about this, kiddo. We have to talk about this first," she instructed him carefully.

He nodded, and she released her grip on him. After pressing the button, he waited for Katrina to pick up. It took only one ring.

"Hey, Kat," he offered. "Paige made it home. We're sitting in her living room as I speak."

There was a pause at the other end before Katrina spoke. "Good, I'm glad she made it home," she said. "Is everything okay?"

"Okay?" he asked with as much innocence as he could muster. "Yeah, sure. We're just getting caught up, that's all."

"Hm," Katrina replied guardedly. "Okay, well, maybe give me a call in the morning, all right?"

"Sure, Kat. Will do," he assured her. "I'll talk to you in the morning."

"Sleep well, my love," she replied.

Paige quietly chewed the tip of one thumbnail as Caleb talked.

"Thanks. You too. And Kat," he added, "I love you."

Something in the way he said it made Paige suddenly look up into his eyes. *So much said in so few words.*

There was another pause, and Katrina replied, "I love you too."

He returned his phone to its holder. "Sorry about the interruption," he apologized.

She smirked and shook her head. "No, you needed to do that. She would've worried too much if you hadn't. Then again, she would've been angrier with me too."

He frowned slightly at her odd statement, but was too tired to connect the pieces in his mind. Instead, he merely rubbed at his eyes and stifled a yawn.

She reached out, squeezed his hand, and offered, "Hey, you look kind of tired, kiddo."

He shrugged, stifled another yawn, and admitted, "Well, yeah. I'm kind of beat, to tell you the truth."

"You're always supposed to tell me the truth," she noted with a smirk. She regarded him for a moment and suggested, "Why don't you go take a shower and turn in? I have a lot to consider and could use the quiet time to think. We can talk more in the morning."

"Sure," he conceded and considered it really was a good idea. In the morning he should be thinking more clearly and might avoid additional embarrassing questions. He leaned over to her and kissed her on the cheek lightly. "I missed you, Paige," he offered sincerely. "We're best friends, after all. And I'm not trying to make life more difficult for you."

She nodded and reached up to run her fingers lightly across his cheek. "I missed you, too, tiger," she replied with a grin.

He rose, and she darted from the couch in a blur. Before he could walk past the coffee table, his luggage disappeared from the floor, and a gust of wind whipped past him heading upstairs.

"You're in the bedroom at the top of the stairs and to the left," she called out. "And you have your own bathroom."

"Thanks," he replied, slowly making his way upstairs.

He took a shower, changed into a pair of sweatpants and t-shirt and was awake barely five minutes longer once his head hit the pillow.

An hour later, Paige quietly peered into the bedroom to gaze at him from the doorway. She fondly watched him soundly sleeping and quietly returned downstairs.

He's going to be hungry when he wakes up, she realized suddenly.

As with most vampires, she never kept much food in the house. There wasn't any need. Just some chocolate, which she had loved as a human, and some colas and alcohol. Her fridge was mostly filled with a variety of human blood packets.

She gathered her car keys, credit card, license, and some cash and went out to her car. Then she sighed, trying to recall any local all-night grocery stores in the area.

Moments later, she pulled out of the garage on her way across town. At least she had a mission to distract her thoughts for a short time.

An hour or so later, and with the stealth that only a vampire could manage, she tip-toed into the bedroom where Caleb still slept. She opened the blinds so she could glance outside at the night sky from across the room and lay down carefully on top of the bed next to him. Once settled, she propped herself up on one elbow, staring down at his peaceful features.

He's so adorable, she thought. It took her sheer willpower not to reach out and stroke his hair with her fingertips.

She lay on the bed just watching him for hours and considered her feelings, as well as the conversation they had earlier that evening.

It was nearly dawn when she heard a car pull up outside. She briefly cocked her head to one side and carefully moved off of the bed. Moving as a silent blur out of the room, she went downstairs and to the front door.

She swept open the door with a smooth motion and looked up into Katrina's eyes with a knowing smirk. "Hey, Red," she greeted with a sigh. "I wondered when you would get here."

"You know me so well, it seems," Katrina replied with a serious expression. "Let's talk, girlfriend."

Paige's eyebrows shot up, and she nodded with resignation, stepping aside for her to enter.

Later, Katrina sipped on a glass of warm blood as she

listened to Paige recount most of what was discussed with Caleb. Having grown concerned following the brief chat on the phone with her mate earlier that night, she knew immediately that she needed to get to California as soon as possible.

Somehow she guessed that both of them might need her; at least, she had hoped that was the case. She cocked her head slightly as Paige paused to reflect and heard the sound of Caleb's steady breathing upstairs. It was a comforting sound.

"You're not in love with him, you know," Katrina observed calmly. *At least, not right now.*

"What makes you so certain?" Paige asked with narrowed eyes. *It's not as if you know how strongly I'm feeling about him.*

The redheaded vampire responded smoothly, "You're not exhibiting any of the signs that would concern me."

"Such as?" Paige queried carefully. *Damn. I should have Googled for a checklist or something.*

"Well, you're not trying to initiate overt sexual advances on him," she began. "There's no secret communications going on between the two of you. You're not trying to exert any subversive emotional control over him. And you're conducting yourself honorably in other ways as well."

Paige raised both eyebrows curiously. "We're okay, so far. Go on."

Katrina shrugged. "You're not trying to lie to me once confronted about your recent strange behavior. There's no attempt to circumvent my relationship with Caleb. And you're not endeavoring to break any of my rules for him, much less convince him to break them."

"So, I get a pass then," Paige surmised. "And you're not worried about my feelings for him?"

One of Katrina's eyebrows arched imperiously. "I didn't say I wasn't concerned. But we've been best friends for a long time, and I trust your integrity."

Paige smiled supportively. "I appreciate that, Red."

"He's—" Katrina started to stipulate, but Paige cut her

off quickly and held up her hand.

"...yours. Yes, I know, and I have complete respect for you as his mate," Paige conceded earnestly. "That's why I've tried to stay away until I could sort out my emotions."

Katrina considered her friend with appreciation regarding her understanding of the situation.

But I'm not stupid, either, she silently acknowledged.

"You're smitten with him, Paige. And I would say that you love him," she continued. "That much is obvious. I'm okay with that, so long as it remains relatively harmless."

Paige nodded and sighed.

"But stop trying to hurt him like you have been," Katrina stipulated. "It's not helping either of you. And Caleb's been miserable over the development. It's not fair to *him*, okay?"

Paige seriously considered her friend's comments. She had no desire to hurt Caleb.

"Sorry about that," she apologized. "I really didn't know what else to do. Listen, I'm really not trying to cause trouble for you or him. But I do appreciate your advice and understanding. You're a good friend, Red. The best, in fact."

Katrina sighed with a wan smile. "Sure, Paige. It's just what friends do."

Both shared a quick embrace, and Katrina gently patted Paige on the back. Then she sat back and held up her empty glass. "A refill, perhaps?" she inquired with a hopeful grin. "I'm still thirsty after my flight, and I don't want Caleb to awaken two quarts lower."

Paige took her glass with a smirk and a slight shake of her head. She felt fortunate to have such a good friend in the tall, redheaded vampire, and she was relieved to have discussed everything so openly with Katrina.

But while she cherished her friend's advice and her understanding, she wondered if Katrina were truly as insightful as she had claimed to be.

* * *

Caleb awoke to the sunlight in his face and groaned as he rolled over in bed. He stretched his body and thought he heard voices talking downstairs. It took only a second before registering that it was Katrina and Paige. He smiled, surprised that his mate had made the journey out to California so quickly.

He rolled out of bed and took a moment to appreciate the sun shining in through the window. Quietly moving to the bedroom door, he slipped out into the hallway, closing the door behind him.

Try as he might, he still wasn't quiet enough to evade the acute hearing of the vampires downstairs, and their conversation stopped abruptly. He shook his head and sighed as he descended the stairs.

He stopped halfway downstairs to stare into Katrina's eyes while she sat on the edge of the couch next to Paige.

The childhood memories that seemed so recently acquired rushed through his mind, and he felt a warmth flow through him as he recalled the short-haired brunette who had saved him from the hands of his abusive father.

Angel Amber, he thought fleetingly.

Finally, his love for the redhead before him cascaded over those memories. *My Kat, my vampire.*

Katrina noted the emotions washing across his face in those few seconds and smiled at him warmly. *That's a look I would walk through hell for*, she realized.

Paige's eyes darted to Caleb, then to Katrina, and back to Caleb as she watched the brief, silent exchange between them.

I'd give anything to have someone look at me that way, she thought forlornly.

It was then she realized the difference between how she looked at Caleb and how her best friend did. She also understood in that instant just how devoted he was to Katrina.

A moment of clarity followed, and she mused, *Maybe Red's right. Maybe I'm not in love. But it's the closest I've come to it so far, and I do love him.*

"You two belong together," Paige muttered under her breath. It was a hard concession for her, but at that moment she believed it to be true.

Caleb and Katrina looked at Paige nearly simultaneously and back to each other with astonished expressions.

"Well? Don't just stand there, tiger," Paige insisted with a smirk. "Get down here and hug your old lady. And I mean the redhead, of course."

Katrina cast her friend a withering expression she rose from her seat, returning her attentions to Caleb, who walked into her opened arms. She placed a light kiss on his lips and embraced him.

"You got to California fast, Kat," he whispered in her ear. "How long have you been here?"

She parted from their embrace and pulled him down to the couch to sit next to her.

"Not long. A couple of hours ago, actually," she replied.

He glanced over to Paige to try to gauge her emotions. "It was the phone call, wasn't it?"

Katrina smirked knowingly as she placed her arm across his shoulders. "Face it. You're not much of a poker player, my love."

She reads me like a book, he considered with a roll of his eyes. Paige smirked back at him, but her expression quickly faded to a more sedate one.

"Is everything okay?" he asked tentatively.

"We're fine," Paige offered, but gazed at Katrina with a mildly curious expression.

Katrina looked at both of them and agreed, "Yeah, we're all okay now."

Relief washed through Caleb as he silently appreciated not having to continue the line of conversation from the previous night. He honestly had no idea of where to begin, and it was better that Kat and Paige talked it out.

After all, women understand each other better, right?

"So then, is Paige going to...?" He regrouped. "Did you

ask her about what we discussed in London?"

Paige frowned at him. "What is it you think I'm going to do, exactly?"

Katrina's eyes twinkled, and she gazed over at her friend with an expectant look, which immediately unnerved the youthful vampire.

Paige's gaze shifted from Katrina and back to Caleb.

"Well, you're moving out to Georgia, actually," he began. "Like somewhere in or around the Atlanta area, perhaps?"

Paige's eyes flashed with surprise. *Georgia? Where the hell did that come from?*

"Yeah, I'm not so sure about that," she objected.

He adopted a pleading expression and reached out to grasp Paige's hand in his own. She didn't pull her hand away, but her eyes went directly to Caleb's with a sharp look.

"We *need* you in Atlanta," he urged. "I mean, a true babysitter has to be close to the kids, right?" he asked with a smirk.

"But—" Paige began to protest.

He squeezed her hand and stated emphatically, "No, no buts. You. Atlanta. Soon."

Paige studied his face silently for a moment and read the urgency in his eyes. She looked over to Katrina. "Red?" she asked.

Katrina shrugged. "I already gave my blessing. And it would be a lot easier if you were closer. You are his surrogate vampire, after all."

"But Devon," Paige began.

"He's growing on me, I suppose. But he isn't you," Caleb interjected emphatically. "I need you. You're one of my best friends, remember?"

The sense of hopefulness that passed through Paige's mind was replaced by a moment's hesitation. *We just got through the emotions part of the problem, and now this?*

As if sensing the doubt in her mind, he added, "There's nothing in California for you now. Your family is in Georgia, which is where you need to be, too."

"Family?" Paige asked. "I thought you just said we were best friends."

Katrina's eyebrows rose. "Close friends are really just extended family, right?"

Caleb smiled at the tact Katrina took with the topic and sensed victory on the horizon.

"Well," Paige considered out loud, but in an uncommitted tone.

He squeezed her hand in his own and made a simple, final bid on the subject. "Please? For me?" he asked with an innocent, pleading look. His heartbeat raced a little bit, a fact not lost on either vampire.

Paige thoughtfully regarded him at length and shook her head. *You're quite the master manipulator, it seems.*

"Well, okay then. Atlanta it is," she conceded. Then another instant decision entered her mind, "But."

Caleb accepted her first statement, then frowned. "But what?" he asked guardedly.

"I've decided to accept a contract job offer for the early summer, so it won't be until after that's over."

He looked displeased. *Early summer? That's two months away still.*

"What kind of job?" he pressed.

Katrina seemed quite interested in her answer, as well.

"Never you mind," she said. "Just something that was offered to me recently, and I've decided that I could use the additional funds to replenish my savings."

"Anything dangerous?" he pressed.

Paige shrugged. "Dangerous? Nah, just a quick contract security job."

He considered the vague explanation and looked at Katrina with a silent question in his eyes.

She shrugged back at him and appeared unconcerned. "Paige is an accomplished alpha now," Katrina explained. "She can handle herself. But it's agreed, then? You'll move to Atlanta at the end of that job?"

Paige smiled smugly and nodded. "Yep, I'll move when I

return. No sense packing up and moving, only to leave a few weeks later."

Caleb considered the logic of that and conceded that it seemed sound. *It'll have to do, I suppose. At least she's moving by summer's end.*

"Okay, it's a deal," he agreed before changing the subject. "Now that that's all settled, I'm kind of hungry."

Katrina rolled her eyes, while Paige merely shook her head.

"Well, I made a quick trip out to the store before Katrina arrived," Paige offered. "There's frozen waffles in the freezer for breakfast."

"Great," he replied happily, rising from the couch with a lurch. "Where's your toaster?"

"Uh, toaster?" Paige asked with a frown. "Can't you just microwave them on a plate or something?"

He slapped his forehead with his palm and shook his head, while Katrina chuckled.

"Got a lot to learn about human food again, I see," the red-headed vampire observed. *Yeah, like I'm an expert already.*

"How about a ham sandwich?" Paige offered helpfully. "I bought mustard."

"For breakfast?" Caleb asked incredulously.

Katrina stifled a laugh and covered her mouth with her hand as Paige adopted a dark expression. The petite vampire crossed her arms in front of her and cast an irritated glance to the ceiling.

"Sorry. That's okay," he apologized after seeing her reaction. "I appreciate your buying food for me. That was very kind, actually."

Katrina smirked at the exchange and suggested, "Last night on my drive from the airport, I noticed a fast food restaurant that serves breakfast about a mile up the road from here."

He beamed with renewed optimism. "Great! Perhaps I could borrow Paige's car?" he asked with a hopeful expression.

"Ha!" Paige retorted. "Not likely, kiddo."

She envisioned her car being raced through the city streets by him, not to mention an expensive traffic citation. *He's a twenty-six-year-old male, after all.*

Katrina picked up a set of keys from the coffee table and passed them to him. "Here, take my rental car that's in the driveway. It's parked in front of the garage, anyway."

"Oh," he replied with a hint of disappointment. "Thanks."

Paige grinned victoriously, while Katrina suggested, "Now, go upstairs and get dressed. Paige and I still have some catching up to do regarding our trip to England. And please shutter the windows from the sunlight when you're done up there, too."

Caleb pattered halfway up the stairs, and then paused. He turned and looked back at Paige and Katrina with a satisfied smile.

And the ship pulls safely back into harbor from rough seas, he mused silently.

Paige's bright, blue eyes caught his, and she winked at him while flashing one of her classic mischievous grins.

ABOUT THE AUTHOR

Jaz Primo: Delving into flights of fancy and realms of imagination; eagerly sharing with you.

Jaz lives in the Great American Midwest where he writes paranormal romance, urban fantasy, and young adult literature. He's a history aficionado, Doctor Who fanatic, "pun-master", an all-around fan of vampires, and a caregiver to the world's most endearing cat.

You can easily find Jaz Primo online at the following locations:

Website: http://jazprimo.com

Twitter: @jazprimo

Sunrise at Sunset: Revamped
Sunset Vampire Series, Book 1
(Second Edition)
by Jaz Primo

The Sunset Vampire Series achieved Third Place in the Reviewer's Choice Award for Best Paranormal Series of 2012 (Paranormal Romance Guild).

This new, second edition of the original, has new never-seen-before material, *Revamped* includes a forward by Jaz explaining how this version improves over the original. Additional bonus material includes a new bonus chapter that bridges events between the first novel and the sequel, *A Bloody London Sunset.*

When is a bloodthirsty predator the best protection against a psychotic killer?
When the predator is both a vampire...and the woman you love.

Caleb is bravely overcoming a dark past while having no memory of the beautiful vampire that saved him.
Despite a promise to stay away, Katrina is compelled to return to him.
However, a vengeful rival from her past has dire plans for both of them.

Available in trade paperback and all major eBook formats!

Go to http://jazprimo.com/books for purchasing links!

Winner of the Paranormal Romance Guild's Reviewer's Choice Award for Best Young Adult Novel of 2012!

Gwen Reaper

A Young Adult Paranormal Romance
by Jaz Primo

Boy meets beautiful and mysterious, yet reclusive, girl who harbors a potentially-lethal secret.

"A thing of beauty is a joy forever: its loveliness increases; it will never pass into nothingness." John Keats, English romantic poet.

I never thought that my first exposure to real beauty would be tinged with the threat of oblivion...

~ ~ ~ ~ ~

When high school junior Scott Blackstone is forced to move from his childhood home in Springfield, Illinois to small-town Custer, South Dakota, he expects nothing less than to languish in complete disappointment. Instead, he discovers a beautiful and mysterious seventeen-year-old girl named Gwen, who captivates him from his initial, adrenaline-laced sight of her on the shores of Stockade Lake. Scott's pursuit of the elusive Gwen sweeps him into the midst of a potentially lethal family heritage that was birthed in hope, only to be passed into a legacy of guilt and death.

Scott engages in a journey of discovery, tinged with both angst and danger. Like many dire legends throughout history, he is unprepared for the untimely revelation that both love and despair are often two sides of the same coin.

A Bloody London Sunset
Sunset Vampire Series, Book 2
by Jaz Primo

In *A Bloody London Sunset*, a timid spirit rises to assert himself, a forbidden love sparks, and a forgotten past threatens to topple the power of love.

Katrina Rawlings is a vampire who has finally rediscovered happiness for the first time in centuries. But unwanted complications erupt with a vengeance. Decisions of necessity combined with dark memories from a forgotten past threaten her relationship with the love of her life. When a sacrifice must be made, can she endure her decision?
Caleb Taylor's life is finally back on track. He has rebounded from a near mortal injury, both physically and emotionally. Yet, his reality is shaken by the suggestion of a betrayal of trust from the woman he loves. Can the power of love overcome the power of a lie?
Paige Turner is a century old vampire who fearlessly revels in a simple existence pursuing blood, dancing, and sex. Simple needs, and all met in the same manner: hot, fast, and without regrets. But a spontaneous visit leads to heartfelt sacrifice, and unexpected complications strike fear to the core of her soul. Will she survive the revelations?
In the exciting second novel in the Sunset Vampire Series, a trust is betrayed, bonds of friendship are strained, relationships may end, and a tenuous neutrality among the world's vampire population is threatened. With stakes so high, some will not survive A Bloody London Sunset!

Go to http://jazprimo.com/books for purchasing links!

Summit at Sunset
Sunset Vampire Series, Book 3
by Jaz Primo

Does the fate of one innocent human soul outweigh the needs of the entire vampire race? The third, and most exciting, novel in the *Sunset Vampire Series* has finally arrived!

Powerful vampire Katrina Rawlings and her human mate, Caleb Taylor, are once more drawn into dangerous circumstances. Representatives of the most powerful and influential vampires from around the world converge upon a scenic mountain retreat located in Slovenia's Upper Bohinj Valley for a summit of historic proportion. Mystery leads to treachery, and events quickly spiral out of control. With the fates of both vampires and humans in jeopardy, Katrina desperately struggles to reconcile the balance of worldwide vampire power against honoring her commitment to the love of her life. Unwilling to be rendered helpless, Caleb initiates a desperate gamble that leads to a mortal decision. Meanwhile, the sexy and sassy vampire, Paige Turner, spearheads her own mission involving both surprising revelations of heart and grave circumstances for those around her.

In *Summit at Sunset*, unlikely alliances will be sought, eternal bonds of friendship will be tested, unrequited love will be unleashed, blood will be shed, and one pivotal person's fate will collide with destiny.

Available in trade paperback and all major eBook formats!

Go to http://jazprimo.com/books for purchasing links!

Wicked Sunset
Sunset Vampire Series, Book 4
by Jaz Primo

After exploring urban fantasy with Bringer of Fire, and young adult romance with the award-winning Gwen Reaper, author Jaz Primo returns to his beloved and extremely popular Sunset Vampire series with the eagerly-awaited fourth novel, Wicked Sunset.

Security, more than ever, is an illusion.

The world's vampires are on a terrifying course of destruction, putting everyone in mortal danger. Katrina has a confrontation with dire consequences. Caleb, surrounded by darkness, and facing challenges at every turn, makes a surprising decision- that has even more surprising results.

Even his relationship with Katrina, something he could always believe in, may be changed forever. But if Caleb can finally come into his own, he may be able to claim a legacy he never dared imagine.

Available in trade paperback and all major eBook formats!

Go to http://jazprimo.com/books for purchasing links!

Sunset Rising
Sunset Vampire Series, Book 5
by Jaz Primo

In *Sunset Rising*, the exciting fifth installment in Jaz Primo's Sunset Vampire series, life is the ultimate prize in a race against time.

Vowing retribution, Katrina tenaciously seeks out those behind the attack against Caleb, whose research to unravel a centuries old mystery attracts both unexpected competition and mortal danger.

Paige's conflicted feelings erupt, altering the lives of those she loves and leaving emotional disaster in her wake.

Battle lines are drawn as the vampire world's fiercest beings choose sides, rendering those undecided few as hotly contested spoils in a growing war.

In *Sunset Rising*, all bets are off!

Available in trade paperback and all major eBook formats!

Go to http://jazprimo.com/books for purchasing links!

Bringer of Fire
Logan Bringer Urban Fantasy Series, Book 1
by Jaz Primo

Spinning "a wonderful first book in his Logan Bringer series" (Paranormal Romance Guild), Jaz Primo has created a new urban fantasy hero in this story packed with explosive action, danger, and intrigue.

Logan Bringer is a cancer survivor and war hero who should have his hardest battles behind him. But when he develops the ability to move things with his mind, he's hunted by corporations, terrorists, and his own government.

Darkness and corruption are everywhere.

When even his family is threatened, he fights to control his new powers— and becomes more powerful than his enemies can possibly imagine.

Available in trade paperback and all major eBook formats!

Go to http://jazprimo.com/books for purchasing links!

www.ingramcontent.com/pod-product-compliance
Lightning Source LLC
Chambersburg PA
CBHW070350260626
47161CB00001B/87